UNRAVELING HIM

THE BAILEY BROTHERS BOOK THREE

CLAIRE KINGSLEY

Always Have LLC

ISBN: 9798676988074

Published by Always Have, LLC

Edited by Elayne Morgan

Cover design by Lori Jackson

Cover photography by Furious Fotog

Cover model: Chase Ketron

www.clairekingsleybooks.com

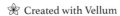 Created with Vellum

This book is dedicated to the Calm meditation app and the lovely people at the Hilton Homesuites. Without them, this book would never have been finished.

ABOUT THIS BOOK

She's the sunshine to his storm cloud

Stoic, growly Evan Bailey has enough on his plate. A growing business, a pack of brothers who drive him crazy, a gossip-loving small town, and a rivalry that runs deeper than any family feud. Love? That's a hard pass. He already learned the hard way that he's better off alone.

Fiona Gallagher has a problem. Or more like ten, but who's counting? The trouble with her car is just the cherry on top of the crap sundae, but she won't let that get her down.

Besides, she has a plan. Evan Bailey—that brooding custom car builder who happens to hate her father—is going to help her. He just doesn't know it yet.

The last thing Evan needs is the overly cheery Fiona crashing into his solitary life. But her offer is too compelling to ignore.

Fiona isn't there to pick through the wreckage of Evan's heart. If he has one, he won't let her anywhere near it. But the tension between them is hot enough to combust. And when she starts to see the cracks in his stony façade, she realizes she's getting more than she bargained for—a lot more—in that big surly man.

Author's Note: *A grouchy, broody loner meets an adorable badass (who talks to her houseplants). It's the grumpy one is soft for the sunshine one with some engine-revving twists. Have a fan ready —you're in for a Kindle-melting ride.*

The Bailey Brothers series is meant to be read in order. Start with book one, **Protecting You.**

PROLOGUE

EVAN

This prologue also appeared as the epilogue at the end of Fighting for Us: The Bailey Brothers Book Two.

The cold night air rushed past me as my bike raced down the empty highway. The scenery flew by, unseen, save for the patch of road illuminated by my head-light. I wasn't sure where I was going. Away, mostly. I was too restless to go sit at home. I needed to drive. To cut through the wind and lean into the turns. I needed speed.

The highway curved and I had to slow down when I got into Pinecrest. I could drive right through and keep on going. There wasn't much to do in this little town. But the Crooked Owl Tavern caught my eye. A beer didn't sound bad right about now. I'd been here before; it was a dive, but the beer was always ice cold.

I parked outside, took off my helmet, and went in.

The light was dim and classic rock played in the background. The rough-around-the-edges crowd hung out here. A few biker types—I'd seen their Harleys outside—and guys with thick beards and work boots. There was a group of twenty-somethings playing pool, a few girls who eyed me when I walked in, and a couple of grizzled old-timers at the bar.

I picked a stool away from everyone. I wasn't here to talk about the weather, or sports, or whatever the fuck passed for news in a shit hole town like this. I was just here to kill time and get a drink.

The bartender came by and I ordered a beer. True to form, it was ice cold. Had a nice bite to it. I hunched over my drink, bored. Restless. Dissatisfied. But that was how I felt most of the time, so it wasn't exactly new.

My phone buzzed in my pocket, so I checked my messages. It was from a client asking about the car I was restoring for him. I'd get back to him later. Taking another swig of my beer, I flicked through a few things. I'd been waiting to hear about a lead on a forties Dodge Power Wagon I was hoping to get my hands on. It didn't look like much, but if I could get it for the right price, I'd flip it and make a shit ton of money.

I accidentally hit the contacts icon and a name I didn't recognize flashed on the screen. Jill? Who the fuck was that? Why did I have the number of some girl I didn't know?

Oh, shit. She was pink cardigan girl, the one Luke Haven had been hitting on. That made me crack a smile. Fucking Luke Haven. As a Bailey, I was obligated to hate the Havens on principle. Truthfully, I didn't really give a shit about the feud, or the Havens as a whole. But Luke Haven? I'd keep that goddamn feud going just to feed my hatred for that piece of shit.

I selected Jill's contact info and hit delete. It wasn't like I was ever going to call her. She'd tasted sweet when I'd kissed her in front of Luke, and sweet was a hard no. A girl like her looked harmless, like a kitten. But kittens had sharp claws, and they were damn good at convincing you it was your fault when you got scratched.

My younger brothers hadn't learned that lesson yet.

Asher... he was another story. But he'd always been the exception to most rules. And Grace was no kitten.

I was happy for my brother. Glad he'd gotten his shit together enough to work things out with Grace. I didn't envy him the demons he'd had to battle, nor the time he'd done in prison. The whole thing still pissed me off. But there wasn't anything I could do about it. And he was home now.

But fuck, this meant there was going to be a wedding. I'd probably have to be in it. And if not, I'd certainly have to go.

I fucking hated weddings.

The beer wasn't putting me in a better mood. Neither was thinking about weddings. I'd left my brother's impromptu engagement party hoping to outrun the hollow ache I'd been feeling. It was irritating how it kept trying to follow me.

A beer wasn't going to cut it. I'd go home and drown it in whiskey.

Leaving my bottle half-full, I was about to get off my stool and cut out of here, when someone sidled up next to me.

A girl in a black leather miniskirt and a leopard-print top that barely contained her tits perched at the bar. "Hi."

My brow furrowed. "What?"

The corner of her mouth lifted. She was pretty, even though she wore a lot of makeup, and she had flower tattoos on her shoulder. "You look a little lonely over here all by yourself. I thought maybe you could use a friend."

My eyes swept up and down. She was about my age. The type of girl who knew exactly how hot she was. Definitely not sweet. By the way she watched me, I could tell what she wanted. Girls didn't openly stare at your dick like that when they were hoping you'd ask them out to dinner.

She wanted a night. Maybe a string of them.

"A friend?"

"Yeah, although who am I kidding? I could use a friend, too. I've had a shitty week."

I grunted and took a drink of my beer.

Her eyes flicked to my crotch again. I followed her gaze, making it obvious I could see what she was doing.

"I'll just cut to the chase. Do you want to get out of here?" she asked.

I raised an eyebrow. "Aren't you going to buy me a drink first?"

She licked her lips. "I was thinking of something better than just a drink."

I looked away, considering. Usually if I was going to grab a girl to take home with me—or more accurately, take to her place, because I never took girls to mine—I liked to be the one on the prowl.

But this girl was hot, no denying it. And she was right, I was fucking lonely. A little company didn't sound half bad.

Plus, it had been a hell of a long time since I'd indulged in this kind of thing.

"Look, I know I'm being really forward," she said. "But I'm the type of girl who isn't afraid to go after what she wants."

"I see that."

She lightly traced a finger down my arm. "A guy like you —tall, thick, rugged—is like crack to me. I can't resist. And I really did have a shitty week."

"So did I."

"See? This works out for both of us."

She had a point. There was no doubt this girl looked like trouble, but at least she was up front. I knew what I'd be getting into. And damn it, it really had been a long time. Why the fuck not?

I put my beer down. "You live nearby?"

"Yeah. Just up the road."

"Let's go."

We left, and I got on my bike. Followed her up the road to a little house tucked behind some apple trees.

She didn't turn on the lights when we went inside. Just led me straight back to her bedroom.

This aggressive thing wasn't bad. No forced small talk. No bullshitting. No games. She'd brought me home to fuck, so why waste time pretending we were going to get to know each other first? She hadn't even given me her name, and I didn't want to know. Didn't care. It was just sex. Just a release.

Just a way to feel a little less empty for a while.

AFTERWARD, she lay sprawled out on the bed, like I'd fucked her unconscious. I had no interest in staying, so I got up to deal with the condom and clean up.

She had a bathroom right off the bedroom. I shut the door and flicked on the light. Tied off the condom and tossed it in the trash. I caught sight of myself in the mirror and quickly looked away. I wasn't exactly a fan of what I saw there these days.

I washed my hands and splashed water on my face.

When I turned off the faucet, something on the counter caught my eye.

I stared at it, a sick feeling erupting in my gut. If that was what I thought it was—and it sure looked like it—there was no part of this that was okay.

Fuck.

1

EVAN

This was not how I meant for my night to go.

I didn't hear a sound through the closed bathroom door. The girl was still sprawled out on her bed in the other room in a post-fuck coma. Clearly not wrestling with her conscience, which was more than I could say for me.

My eyes flicked back to the counter. Damn.

She'd picked me up at a bar, and I should have known she was trouble. I didn't indulge in this sort of thing very often, but sometimes that itch was hard to ignore. Why not anonymously fuck some girl's brains out? We were both adults. We knew what this was. Why not take the edge off? Fill the emptiness for a little while.

It should have been fine.

I braced myself against the counter and dropped my head. It wasn't fine. Not if that was what I thought it was.

A lot of guys wouldn't have cared. They wouldn't have thought twice—been on their way without a twinge of guilt. Maybe even come back for more.

I wasn't one of those guys.

So why the fuck was I here?

I should have known better. There were reasons I stayed alone.

My random hookup's wedding ring sitting on the counter was one of them.

For a second, I tried to tell myself it could be something else. Her mother's ring. A ring she wore on her right hand. Maybe it wasn't even hers.

A quick peek into the medicine cabinet told me that was bullshit. Alongside nail polish, lotion, and makeup remover —typical girl stuff—I found men's deodorant, shaving cream, and aftershave.

A man obviously lived here. And I'd just fucked his wife.

That was a line I didn't cross. Ever. I didn't care what her excuse was. Maybe he was an asshole who treated her like shit. Maybe she'd already decided it was over. Maybe he was out cheating on her and she wanted revenge.

Didn't matter.

My principles were probably a little loose on a good day, but there were some things even an asshole like me wouldn't do. Sleeping with another man's wife was at the top of that list.

But it was too late now. I *had* slept with her, and it had been every bit as hollow as I'd known it would be.

I'd left my brother's impromptu engagement party tonight trying to outrun the emptiness inside me. Instead, I was drowning in it.

I opened the bathroom door. The girl—we hadn't bothered to exchange names—had an arm over her forehead, her eyes closed. I'd certainly given her what she wanted.

And I needed a goddamn shower.

I didn't care how hot she was, looking at her now made my skin crawl. I had to get the hell out of here. I grabbed my clothes off the floor and tugged my boxer briefs back on. I got my jeans halfway up before she even moved.

"Mm." She stretched, purring like a cat. "Come back to bed."

I didn't answer. Just pulled my jeans up and fastened them.

She opened her eyes and her lips twitched in a smile. "You have somewhere better to be?"

I grabbed my shirt off the floor and tugged it on.

Her smile faded. "So that's it? You're not going to say anything?"

"What do you want me to say?"

"I don't know. Thank you?"

I glanced away. A part of me didn't want to know for sure —wanted to be able to walk away thinking maybe I'd been wrong. But I couldn't leave without asking. "Are you married?"

She brushed a tendril of hair off her forehead. "What?"

"There's a ring on your bathroom counter."

Her eyes flicked to the door, then back to me. "It's nothing you need to worry about. He won't be home tonight."

He won't be home tonight? As if my only concern was getting caught. A low growl rumbled in my throat.

"Come on," she said, the corners of her lips curling upward. She patted the sheets next to her. "Come back to bed. I'll suck your dick to get you hard again."

"Jesus." I shoved one foot in my shoe, tasting bile on the back of my tongue.

"I told you he won't be home."

"I don't give a fuck." I bent over to grab my other shoe.

"I mean it. He's locked up."

Straightening, I stared at her. "What?"

"He's serving six months in the state pen." She got on her hands and knees and slowly crawled toward the edge of the bed. "So come back to bed, because after what you just did to me, I definitely need more of that monster cock."

"Your husband's in prison and you brought me here to fuck you in his bed?"

Her forehead creased. "It's my bed for now. And why do you care?"

"Because I do."

"You came home with me without even asking my name, but now you have an attack of conscience? It's six months; what am I supposed to do? I have needs. I'm just taking care of them. He never has to know."

"Un-fucking-believable," I muttered to myself.

Without giving her a chance to say anything else, I put on my other shoe and walked out.

The cold October air helped clear my head, but I still felt like shit. I got on my bike and revved the engine. The girl didn't follow me out, thank fuck. I tore out of her driveway and away from her house without looking back.

I hadn't been in that bar looking for a hookup. All I'd wanted was a fucking beer.

That's what I was telling myself, at least.

And it was partially true. I had stopped for a beer, not to find an easy lay.

But she hadn't needed to work very hard to talk me into it, either.

Like I'd told myself in the bar, it had been a long time. And after that shitshow, I wasn't doing it again any time soon. It meant going without sex, which sucked. I loved sex as much as the next guy. But getting any on the regular either meant dating—not an option—or random hookups like tonight, which had their own set of risks. Fucking a married woman was only one of them.

The truth was, I didn't particularly like banging some girl I didn't know just for the sake of getting off. There was a time when I wouldn't have even considered it. I wasn't like my brother Logan, happy to enjoy his flavors of the month —or week, or night—free of any strings or attachments.

But there was also a time when I'd been naïve enough to believe in the fantasy of love. That had blown up in my face. I was definitely not doing that again.

The girl tonight wasn't my problem. I didn't know who she was—and I didn't want to—and I'd avoid that bar for a while. There wasn't anything I could do about the twinge of guilt I felt for her husband. Poor bastard was in prison and his wife was cheating on him. It was too bad he hadn't married someone like Grace. She'd waited seven years for Asher, and they weren't even married yet. Now that was loyalty.

But Grace was a unicorn. There wasn't another woman in the world who would have done what she did. Asher was a very lucky man. To his credit, he knew it. And even though I hated weddings, I was glad he was finally going to marry her.

As for me, I needed to be content with what I had: my own business doing work I loved, a house on acreage with no neighbors, a loyal dog, a family I didn't hate. I'd been burned by people I'd thought I could trust—burned badly —so I had no interest in trying again. I'd leave that to Asher, and maybe my younger brothers. Me? No thanks. Tonight I'd been stupid enough to give in, but it had just been a reminder that I'd always be better off alone.

2

EVAN

Five months later

"Sasquatch, you've got nothing."

My ninety-pound German shepherd sat on the other side of the coffee table, his big ears sticking straight up. I'd brushed him earlier, so his tan and black coat was smooth and shiny, and the way he cocked his head when I spoke made it seem like he was trying to figure out what I was saying.

"Sorry, big guy, your cards are shit." I put down my hand. "I win again."

He lowered his chin onto the table.

"Tell you what, I'll slip you an extra card and let you have this one."

I pulled a queen out of the deck and set it in front of him.

Yeah, I was spending my Friday playing poker with my

fucking dog. So what? He was better company than most people.

My phone had buzzed a few times, but I was ignoring it. Usually Friday-night texts were from my brothers, and I wasn't in the mood. They were on the very short list of people I could actually stand, but only in small doses.

I took a sip of whiskey, feeling the bite as it slid down my throat, warming me from the inside. I was an edgy mix of tired and restless. It had been a long week. Productive, but long. I wanted to relax, but my mind kept snapping back to Eleanor out in my garage.

Eleanor wasn't a girl. I was done with women. I was going to die a grumpy old bachelor, probably alone out here in the woods, and that was fine with me. Eleanor was a car.

Not just *a* car. She was *the* car. A 1967 Mustang GT500.

I'd been dying to get my hands on one of those since I'd started my shop. She was in rough shape, but that was the only reason I'd been able to afford her. It was a dream build for a guy like me, still working to make a name for myself. And if I pulled it off, Eleanor had the potential to change everything.

Now that I was thinking about her, I couldn't stop. Sasquatch tilted his head, like he knew what I was about to say.

"What do you think? Make a little more progress tonight?"

He stood.

"Might as well." I swallowed the last of my whiskey and got up. "We don't have anything else going on."

Sasquatch followed me outside into the cold night air. It was dry—no sign of a spring snow—but chilly now that the sun had gone down. A cool silence hung over my land, the only sounds the pad of dog feet and crunch of my boots on the gravel walkway. A twig snapped in the distance, making Sasquatch pause, his ears swiveling toward the sound.

"Probably just a raccoon."

I lived in a small two-bedroom cabin that had already been on the land when I'd bought it. It had needed some work, so I'd fixed it up. It wasn't fancy, but it was livable, and a guy like me didn't need much.

I'd bought the land more for the space—I liked not having neighbors—and the shop. The building had been here, but like the cabin, it had needed work. I'd rebuilt the whole thing, and now I had a custom car garage with room for three project cars, plus an office and a bathroom.

Somehow I'd turned a hobby I'd picked up from my grandad into a business. Not bad for a college dropout.

I flipped on the shop lights and turned on a space heater and some music. I was working on two different projects right now. One to flip—a '69 Dodge Super Bee that I'd be able to sell for three times what I had put into it when it was done.

The other was Eleanor. My '67 Mustang GT500. She wasn't a flip car. I had something special planned for her. The Pacific Northwest Classic Car Show was coming up and she was going to turn heads. If she turned the right heads, it would mean big things for me and my shop.

I rolled up the sleeves on my flannel shirt and got to work while Sasquatch laid on his bed in the corner. Despite the fatigue in my body, it felt good to do something. The glass of whiskey had been just enough to take the edge off, and the work occupied my thoughts. It was better to stay busy. Less room to think that way.

There were too many things I didn't want to think about.

A car pulled up outside, the throaty rumble of the

engine carrying through the shop walls. I groaned. I knew that car. It was Logan.

What the hell did he want?

Sasquatch was already on his feet to investigate the noise. I opened the door and waited with my arms crossed. Sure enough, Logan's 1970 Chevelle was parked outside. He'd bought the car years ago and had been tinkering with it off and on ever since. Sometimes it even ran. Six weeks with her and I could have had her in mint condition, but it was his project. Plus, he was my brother; I couldn't have charged him, and the last thing I needed right now was to sink time into a freebie.

Logan wasn't alone. His identical twin, Levi, got out of the passenger side, and our youngest brother Gavin climbed from the back seat. No Asher, but unlike the rest of us, he actually had a life.

"Hey, bronut," Logan said, but his smile quickly faded.

Sasquatch stood in front of him, barring the way in.

He hesitated, shifting to his right, then his left. Sasquatch mirrored him. "Dude, can you call off your dog?"

I watched for a few more seconds, mildly amused. "Sasquatch, come."

My dog obeyed, moving over to sit next to me without taking his eyes off my brothers. Although he was well trained, he was also highly territorial. Made him a badass guard dog.

He knew my brothers, so he wouldn't actually do anything. But watching him scare them was entertaining.

"What are you guys doing here?" I asked.

"You weren't answering your phone," Logan said.

"So?"

"Are you still working?" Gavin asked. "It's Friday night."

"You need a hobby." Logan took a step closer, but Sasquatch growled.

Gavin swept past the others, patting me on the shoulder as he walked into the shop. Of course that crazy son of a bitch wasn't afraid of my dog. Gavin had been born without the gene for fear.

"Sasquatch, let them in," I said before he could bark. Stepping aside, I pushed the door open wider for Logan and Levi.

My brothers and I all looked a lot alike. We got our dark hair, brown eyes, and olive skin from Gram's side of the family. Logan and Levi's features were more angular, with sharper cheekbones. Although they were identical twins, it was easy to tell them apart by their mannerisms and facial expressions.

And clothes. Levi dressed like a normal person. Logan, not so much. Tonight he was wearing a t-shirt that said *This is my Halloween costume*—in March—with an open plaid flannel shirt, sweats he'd cut off at the knee, and a pair of tube socks pulled up to his shins.

Gavin was the spitting image of Dad, and it still freaked me out sometimes. I hadn't noticed it when we were growing up, but now that he was in his mid-twenties, there was no mistaking the resemblance. More than any of us, Gav looked like our father.

I wondered if he even remembered Dad. He was the youngest; he'd been pretty little when Mom and Dad had died.

"Holy shit, is this her?" Gavin asked, gaping at Eleanor.

I couldn't help the twitch of my lip, hinting at a smile. "That's her."

They all circled the car slowly, taking her in. Her paint was stripped, the interior was gone, and the hood was off.

But anyone could see the potential in her sleek lines and wide-set tires.

"This is going to be gorgeous," Levi said. "How'd you get your hands on something like this?"

"There's a guy just outside Seattle who sells a lot of project cars and rare parts. I ran into him at an auction and he told me about the car. Said he was looking for a buyer. He gave me a pretty good deal."

"It's rare, isn't it?" Levi traced the rear fender with his fingertips.

"Yep. Fully restored, these are worth six figures."

"No shit?" Logan asked.

"She's not even about the money, though." I hesitated, debating whether to tell them. I hadn't told anyone yet. "I'm taking her to the Pacific Northwest Classic Car Show. The curators from America's Car Museum in Tacoma are going to be there. They're looking for something new to add to their permanent collection and they'll be making their decision at the show."

"Holy shit," Gavin said.

Rubbing my chin, I gazed at the car. "Having a build with my name on it in that museum... it would be a big deal."

"That's an understatement," Levi said.

He was right. It was an understatement. That kind of accomplishment would be huge for me and my shop. Reputation was everything in this business, and there was no better way to solidify my place than the prestige of having a restoration of this caliber in one of the best car museums in the country.

"Is Haven doing a build too?" Gavin asked.

My back tensed at hearing that name. Luke Haven had been my nemesis for as long as I could remember. Our families had been feuding for generations, but there was more than that between me and Luke. We'd been fighting since we were kids, and the fact that we'd gone into the same business, in the same town, had ignited an all-out war between us.

"Yeah," I growled. "I don't know what he's restoring, but you can bet your ass he'll be there."

"There's no way he can compete with you," Logan said. "Not with this car."

"Keep your hands off her," I snapped at Gavin, and he jerked his hand away. "Don't get her fucking dirty. I already have a lot of time into her and she has to be perfect."

Gavin held up his hands. "Sorry."

"Let's go in the house before Gav gets his hand bitten off," Logan said.

"Cool, bro," Gavin said, heading for the door. "You got beer?"

"You're not going in my house."

They all ignored me, filing their way out the door, probably planning to raid my fridge.

"Hey, assholes," I barked. "Go home. I have work to do."

Gavin poked his head back through the door and grinned at me. I took a breath to yell at him, but he hit me with my one weakness. "I brought Gram's cobbler."

I paused, my mouth still open. "She gave you cobbler?"

He nodded, still grinning like an idiot. "We ate some at her house, but she sent me with leftovers for you."

"Fine," I grumbled and followed him next door.

I sent Sasquatch to lie down on his dog bed while my brothers pulled beer out of the fridge and I took the container of still-warm blackberry cobbler to the couch.

Fucking Gavin.

But god, it was good.

"I still say we go for a play on the forks-in-the-yard bit," Logan said and handed me a beer. "Only we hit all their houses on the same night."

"We're not fucking amateurs," Gavin said. "We can do better than forks in their yards."

"How many forks are we talking?" Levi asked.

"We could use flamingos," Gavin said. "I think that's been done before, but it's been years."

Logan glanced at me. "What do you think?"

"Hell if I know." We'd been pulling pranks on the Havens our entire lives—pranks were the lifeblood of the Bailey-Haven feud—but I was too busy for this shit.

"Super helpful, man, thanks," Logan said. "Hey, what if we plastic wrap their cars? That's a pain in the ass to get off but it doesn't do any damage."

"I like it," Gavin said. "If we spread out, we could get at least five or six cars. That'll piss them off."

"Wrap the plastic around a light post and it's even better," I muttered, not looking up from the cobbler.

"See?" Logan said. "This is why we came over. The grumpy one still has prank mojo."

"And beer," Gavin said, holding up his bottle.

I rolled my eyes.

Sasquatch got up, his attention on the front door.

"Is someone here?" Levi asked.

I put my cobbler and beer down. "Asher?"

"No, he and Grace had stuff to do tonight."

Sasquatch barked once and someone knocked. I sent him to his bed to wait while I answered the door.

Jack Cordero, Grace's stepdad and the chief deputy sheriff, stood on my doorstep. That was probably not a good thing, considering it was nine o'clock on a Friday night, and he was in uniform.

"Jack."

"Hey, Evan."

"Oh shit, what'd you do?" Gavin asked behind me. "Jack, if you have to cuff him, can I do it?"

Jack leaned to look past me. "Baileys."

"Something wrong?" I asked.

"Can I talk to you for a minute?" he asked, giving a subtle nod toward my shop.

"Sure." I glanced at my dog. "Sasquatch, stay."

"Dude, don't leave us alone with that thing," Logan said.

Ignoring my brother, I followed Jack outside, feeling the cold bite of the late March air. I had a bad feeling about this. What would bring Jack out here? I unlocked the shop door, flipped on the light, and led him inside.

"Sorry to barge in unannounced," Jack said. "But this can't wait."

"What's going on?"

"I got a call from someone in the FBI office in Seattle. They're investigating a car theft ring."

"And?"

His eyes flicked to my latest project car. *The* car. The one that was going to change everything. "That's a 1967 Mustang GT500?"

"Yeah."

"You have a title for that car? Bill of sale, all your paperwork?"

"Of course."

"Can I see it?"

My eye twitched. "Jack, are you suggesting I stole this car?"

"No. But whoever you bought it from might have."

"Hang on, I've got everything in my office."

Jack waited out in the shop while I went into my admittedly disorganized office to hunt down the paperwork for the GT. I found it in an envelope on my desk.

"Here," I said, holding the envelope out to Jack as I walked back toward him. "This is everything."

He pulled out the title and bill of sale. "Mind if I take these for a few minutes?"

I gestured toward the door. "Sure. I have nothing to hide."

It was true. But I didn't particularly like the look in Jack's eyes when he turned to take the paperwork out to his car.

Nervous energy thrummed through me while I waited. The car was legit... wasn't it? The guy I'd bought it from hadn't tried to pull any shady shit, like claiming he'd lost the title. Everything had been in order from the beginning.

It was only making me anxious because I had so much riding on this car. It had to be perfect. And if word got out that there was even a suspicion that this car had been stolen... Fuck. I didn't want to think about how long it would take me to recover from a hit to my reputation like that.

After what seemed like fucking forever, Jack came back into the shop. His face betrayed nothing and in the back of my head, I made a note to be more careful next time I sat at a poker table with him.

He didn't hand my paperwork back to me. "We have a problem."

"What kind of problem?"

"This is a stolen car."

White-hot anger burned like acid in my veins. But Jack was a cop, so I held it in check. "What?"

"I think the VIN number was cloned and the title faked to match. The VIN on the title is for a 1966 Mustang, registered in New Jersey. And this car is the same make and model as one reported stolen down in northern California that the feds have tied to this particular group."

"Are you kidding me?"

"You couldn't have known. It's a perfect forgery. These guys are sophisticated."

A sick feeling spread through my gut and I met Jack's eyes. Possession of a stolen car was a crime. "Do you have to arrest me?"

"No. There's a clear paper trail that proves you didn't steal it. I know the agent who's working this case, so I gave him a quick call—totally off the record. The guy you bought it from is the one listed on the bill of sale?"

"Yeah. Shane Gallagher."

Jack nodded. "He's probably a middleman. My friend says he has ties to someone named Felix Orman. Does that name ring a bell?"

I shook my head. "Never heard of him."

"Okay."

"What's going to happen to the car?"

The way he hesitated told me everything I needed to know. "They'll have to impound it."

I couldn't keep my cool any longer. Turning around, I slammed my foot into a stray piece of metal, sending it crashing across the floor. An overwhelming urge to trash the entire shop flooded through me. I wanted to rip everything off the shelves. Take a sledgehammer and smash the fucking car to pieces.

"Fuck," I roared at the wall.

Jack didn't say anything while I raged. I ground my teeth together and took ragged breaths. I was going to lose the car. All the time and money I'd already put into it, fucking wasted.

And now I didn't have *anything* to bring to the car show,

let alone a build good enough to show the curators from the museum.

"I'm really sorry about this," Jack said. "But I didn't want you to hear it from someone else."

I took a slow breath, still angry, but my temper was under control. "It's not your fault."

"The feds will be out here in the morning. I'll be here to make sure everything goes smoothly."

"Thanks, Jack."

He gave me a nod and left.

With my hands resting on my hips, I shook my head at Eleanor. So close. I'd been so fucking close.

And now I didn't know what I was going to do.

FIONA

*T*he best part of this trip was the view.

Mountain slopes rose around us, rocky and beautiful, covered in patches of snow. Forests of evergreen trees blanketed the deep valleys and crawled up the mountainsides. We'd passed a waterfall a few miles back, and I'd been momentarily transfixed, wondering if it had been frozen all winter. How long had it taken for the ice to break free and the water to begin flowing again?

Although even frozen, water was always moving. Always going somewhere. Unlike me.

My father was quiet as he navigated the winding highway through the Cascades. His auburn hair had a sprinkling of gray, mostly at the temples, and his beard concealed a scar on his chin. He'd rolled up the sleeves of his button-down shirt, revealing thick, hairy forearms.

A new song came on the radio. Almost without thinking, I started quietly singing along. I didn't know all the words, but I hummed the parts I didn't know.

"Do you have to do that?" he snapped.

Without looking at him, I shut my mouth, the lyrics dissolving in my throat. "Sorry."

We were driving out to a shop in some remote town in the mountains to look at a car. I didn't know if Dad wanted it for his personal collection or if he was going to resell it. He hadn't bothered to clue me in, despite the fact that I basically ran his business for him.

Not that he acknowledged that. I was just an admin assistant. Even though I kept the books, worked with clients, and did all the scheduling, not to mention hunting down deals and finding rare parts to finish our custom builds.

That was my dad for you.

"We're almost there," he said, breaking his long silence.

"Really?" I looked out the window for a sign of civilization, but it was mostly rock and tall pine trees. We'd driven through a little town a while back—the kind that you'd miss if you blinked—but since then, nothing.

"The guy lives out of the way. Pain in the ass."

"Then why go to him?"

Dad glanced at me. "He doesn't realize how good he is yet."

I wondered if that meant Dad thought he could low-ball him.

"What kind of car is it?" I asked.

"Sixty-nine Super Bee."

"That's a great car."

The normally hard line of his mouth twitched in a small smile. "It's a beauty. He hasn't finished it yet, but it'll go fast once it's done."

"And you want to make sure you get your hands on it first."

"Exactly."

If there was anything my dad loved in this world, it was

cars. He'd been raised in his father's garage and had grown it from a one-man repair shop to a much larger business. Now we did everything from custom builds and restorations to buying and selling project cars and rare parts.

And his personal car collection was his baby. He'd restored a few himself, but often he purchased finished or custom-built cars from other builders, especially when they had a make and model he loved. I got the feeling he enjoyed letting other people get their hands dirty before he waltzed in with a big wad of cash like a high roller.

I brushed my bangs out of my eyes. Unlike Dad, who wore his Irish ancestry in every one of his features, I had thick brown hair. I'd recently dyed it a deep chestnut brown. I'd gone inky black once, in my teens, but with my fair skin and hazel-green eyes, it had made me look like a corpse. Since then, I'd experimented with a number of shades, but this was my favorite. Especially since my hairstylist had added a few streaks of purple that came out in the sunlight.

Dad turned off the highway and followed a curving road that seemed to be taking us up to a higher elevation again. He slowed a few times, peering out his window into the trees. Finally, he apparently found what he'd been looking for. An unmarked dirt road that cut straight through the scrubby pines.

"Wow. You weren't kidding when you said he lives out of the way."

Dad grumbled something incoherent.

The road climbed a steep incline and I started to wonder if it actually went anywhere. Then the trees opened into a wide, flat clearing.

Dad stopped in front of a large building with three garage bays. One of the doors was open, revealing the familiar sight of a custom car garage. But there was no sign, no big logo painted on the side of the building. Just the simplicity of shelves full of parts, tall red toolboxes, and a man crouched next to the frame of an old car.

Further back, almost behind the shop, stood a small house. Probably where he lived.

Dad got out of the car, so I followed, jumping down from the tall SUV. It was cold out. The air felt dry against my face, like it might freeze all the moisture right out of my skin. I huddled in my thick winter coat, glad I'd thought to wear it even though it was probably too big for me. It hadn't been nearly this cold in Seattle when we'd left.

A large German shepherd appeared in the open garage bay and barked a warning.

Dad walked to the shop like there wasn't a huge dog barking at him.

Despite the temperature, the man crouching next to the frame of a half-finished Dodge Super Bee wore nothing but a t-shirt and jeans, revealing thick tattooed arms.

And his hands. Was it a trick of perspective, or were his hands *that* big?

He glanced at the dog. "Sasquatch, quiet."

The dog stopped barking, but didn't take his eyes off my father.

Dad stopped a short distance from the open garage bay —and the dog—and crossed his arms. "Bailey."

So this was Evan Bailey. I'd never met him in person, but I'd spoken to him on the phone. He sourced parts from us sometimes. He was known for being gruff and short with people, but he did good work.

Evan uncoiled to his full height—which was considerable—and leveled my dad with a hard glare. "Gallagher."

My heart skipped behind my ribs. Something was going on. The look of menace in Evan's eyes was unmistakable.

"Is there a problem?" Dad asked.

Evan's voice was a low growl. "Yeah, there's a fucking problem. You have a lot of nerve showing up here."

The shiver that ran up my spine had nothing to do with the cold. In fact, I was suddenly feeling uncomfortably warm.

Dad's shoulders were relaxed, although he kept his arms crossed. "I'm just here to look at the Super Bee."

"No."

My eyebrows winged up my forehead. No one talked to my dad that way. Ever.

"Excuse me?"

"You sold me a stolen car."

Dad's eyes flicked to me for half a second, then back to Evan. "What car?"

"The '67 Mustang. Let me guess, you had no idea."

"I didn't. I acquired that car from an associate and had every reason to believe it was a legitimate sale."

"An associate named Felix Orman?" he asked.

My heart sank straight to my toes. That name. I'd never wanted to hear the name Felix Orman again.

Dad, no. How could you?

"Look, this is obviously a misunderstanding," Dad said, his tone mollifying.

"Misunderstanding? Tell that to the feds."

"I'm sure we can come to an arrangement that—"

"No." Evan's sharp reply silenced my dad. "Maybe you didn't know the car was stolen, or maybe you knew and didn't think you'd get caught. I don't care either way. I'm not doing business with you. Ever. So stop wasting my time and get the fuck off my property."

I couldn't take my eyes off Evan. His thick muscles were tense, veins popping against the skin of his forearms. His sharp cheekbones and chiseled jaw could have been carved from marble, save for the careless stubble roughing up that olive skin.

But it wasn't his body that held me captive—impressive as it was. It was his eyes. Whiskey-brown pools glittering with unmasked anger.

He didn't appear to have noticed me, which was a good thing, considering I was gaping at him like a crazy person.

"Word travels fast in this business," Dad said. "It's never a good idea to make enemies."

"I'll take my chances."

For a second, no one moved. I forgot to breathe. Would Dad walk away? He turned his chin just enough to cast a glance at me.

"Sorry to have wasted your time," Dad said, his tone indicating he wasn't the least bit sorry.

Evan didn't answer. For the first time, his gaze flicked to me. Those eyes reached straight into my chest, filling me with a strange sense of warmth. Which was so odd, because his eyes were ice cold.

Without a word, Dad went back to his SUV, clearly expecting me to follow. My breath felt trapped in my throat and my feet stayed rooted to the ground. Evan Bailey's shop looked deceptively warm and inviting. A space heater hummed in the background and I could just smell the familiar scents of rubber and oil. He had a vintage Indian motorcycle parked off to the side.

Evan looked at me again, a groove forming between his eyebrows. He was probably wondering why the weird girl was standing in front of his shop, staring at him. That's what I'd be thinking if I were him. But I wasn't him, I was me, and *I* was thinking about the width of his chest and shoulders.

The way his forearms flexed. The size of his hands. God, they were enormous.

"Is that a '57?" I blurted out.

Evan's brow furrowed deeper. "What?"

I pointed to the motorcycle. "The bike. It's a '57 Indian Chief, isn't it?"

"Fifty-six."

"Oh, I was close. It's beautiful."

"Thanks?"

"Fiona!" Dad snapped behind me.

Brushing my bangs out of my face, I gave Evan an awkward smile, then scurried back to Dad's SUV and climbed in.

A sick feeling crawled through my stomach as Dad drove down the long bumpy road, away from Evan Bailey's property.

Stolen car. Felix Orman.

Dad was supposed to have left that all behind. He'd promised.

"Don't even ask."

"But Dad—"

"I said don't ask."

His tone stole the words from my mouth, silencing me. It was never a good idea to argue with my father, especially when he was angry. And there was no doubt he was mad. I could feel it charging the air, crackling and potent. Dad had never struck me, but he knew how to lash out. And considering I worked for him, he was impossible for me to avoid.

I didn't want him to make my life miserable for the next week, so I kept my mouth shut.

But... Felix Orman. Dad had worked with Felix back in his criminal days. When he'd used his shop as a front for moving stolen cars and car parts. After narrowly escaping prison, Dad had gone legit. He'd cut ties with Felix and all the others like him. Focused on running an honest business dealing in classic cars and rare car parts. I'd helped him build that business—helped make it successful so he'd never have to steal again.

He'd promised me.

"I didn't have anything to do with it," he said out of the blue as he pulled onto the mountain highway.

"You didn't know the car was stolen?"

"Of course not," he snapped. "How the hell would I know that?"

I kept my eyes on the passing scenery. "But... did you get it from Felix?"

Dad didn't answer right away. "Felix knows I don't do that anymore."

"I just don't understand why you'd do business with him at all. If he told you the car was legit, he obviously lied—"

"Jesus, Fiona, let me handle this, okay? It's not your problem."

I shut my mouth again.

Maybe Felix had lied to my dad—convinced him the car was clean. A '67 Mustang was valuable. Dad had probably made a good profit selling it to Evan Bailey. I could understand the temptation to believe him.

But why would he trust a man like Felix Orman?

Dad didn't think I knew what it had taken to extricate himself from the criminal world, but I did. He'd almost lost everything. He wouldn't take that risk again, would he?

I knew I was trying to rationalize why my father would go back to doing business with a known criminal. But the thought that he'd broken his promise and was getting involved in that world again made me sick to my stomach.

He couldn't be.

"Stop worrying," Dad said, his tone gentle. "This was nothing but a misunderstanding, and I'm going to clear it up. It's not what you think."

I took a deep breath and nodded. "Okay."

"I should have known not to come out here anyway. Evan Bailey's an asshole. He does good work, but he's a pain in the ass."

"Sounds like most of the guys in this business."

Dad cracked a smile.

Looking out at the passing scenery, I took another breath to relax the tension in my back and shoulders, and tried to think about something other than whether my dad was dipping his toes in the criminal world again.

It was surprisingly easy. Because suddenly, Evan Bailey flooded my mind. I couldn't stop thinking about the man who'd told my father no. About those menacing eyes that, for a heartbeat, had seemed to see straight through to my soul.

4

FIONA

*H*umming along to the music coming through the wall of my apartment—at least my neighbor had decent taste—I tipped my red plastic watering can, giving Myra a drink.

"You're looking a little forlorn today, Myra. Are you getting enough sun? Should I move you closer to the window? Maybe you can switch places with Blanche for a little while."

Yes, my houseplants had names, and yes, I knew how weird that was.

I moved Myra to the windowsill and put Blanche on the side table. "There. Blanche, you're a tough old bird, you'll be fine. Myra needs a little extra love right now."

"Why do you talk to them like that? It creeps me out."

I glanced back at the sleepy voice coming from the hallway. My best friend and roommate, Simone, blinked tired eyes at me. Her platinum blond hair was disheveled and she'd obviously slept in her makeup.

"You're a ray of sunshine this morning."

"I hate mornings. You know this about me."

"Are you just getting up? We're supposed to leave for work in five minutes."

She shrugged, like it didn't matter if she was late. As always, I ignored her casual disregard for her responsibilities. That was just Simone. I'd grown up with her so I was used to it. She worked with me at my father's shop, and I was convinced he'd given her the job—and let her keep it—because he felt responsible for her. He'd been friends with her dad before he'd passed away. I figured giving her a job was my dad's way of helping.

I sprinkled a little more water in Myra's pot. "Well, I'm not waiting for you. I'll just see you when you get in."

"I'll be late," she said flippantly as she turned to go back down the hall. "I have a thing."

Yes, she was a crappy employee—and she'd be the first to admit it—but we'd been friends since we were kids. And I didn't have many of those. I'd moved around a lot growing up, which hadn't given me many chances to form long-lasting friendships.

Plus Simone understood me in a way not a lot of people could. She knew about my father's past and didn't judge me for it. Her father had been involved. And we'd both lost our mothers, although for different reasons. She knew what it was like to be raised by a busy single father. Like me, she'd grown up in garages, among mechanics and gearheads. And, for a while, thieves. We had history.

Leaving Simone to get ready for her thing, whatever that was, I gathered my stuff and went downstairs to my car. A light mist blew through the air—not heavy enough to be called rain, but wet enough to cling to my hair and make my coat shiny with moisture. I got in and checked my makeup. It had smeared a little beneath my left eye. That was what I got for using liquid eyeliner on a wet day. I wiped it away with the tip of my finger and started the engine.

Traffic was surprisingly light this morning. I stopped at a drive-through espresso stand for a latte. When I pulled out onto the street again, my clutch slipped.

Uh-oh.

My car wasn't exactly what you'd call nice. Or reliable. In fact, it was basically a piece of crap. But I was trying to crawl out from under a mountain of student debt, and this was all I'd been able to afford without taking on an additional payment.

Plus, I knew cars. I'd known what I was getting when I bought her, and I knew how to fix her. I just hoped she'd keep running until I could afford the parts to replace the clutch. And whatever else she needed.

I made it into work—small wins!—and went into the front office. The familiar sound of power tools came through the walls and the faint scent of cheap coffee hung in the air. Dad's office was dark, and I had no idea if he'd come in today. He came and went, always chasing down deals or meeting contacts, and he worked in his home office a lot.

Truthfully, I was relieved he wasn't here this morning. No doubt he was still in a bad mood after the trip to Evan Bailey's shop yesterday. If he were here, he'd probably take it out on me. No thanks.

I put my things down at my desk and tried not to groan at the stack of work waiting for me. There were things I liked about my job. I liked most of the guys who worked for my dad. I liked the challenge of hunting down a rare hood ornament or finding an awesome deal on a great project car. But lately I'd been feeling more and more dissatisfied.

It would have helped if Dad wasn't such a cheapskate.

He claimed my low pay was so no one would accuse him of nepotism. I'd believed that for a long time, but I was beginning to feel like maybe he was just taking advantage of me.

Not a pleasant thought for a girl to have about her father, but here I was.

I glanced at Simone's empty seat, wishing she'd hurry up and get here. I needed to talk—process what had happened yesterday. She'd been out last night, and I'd gone to bed before she'd come home. I was hoping she'd be able to put my mind at ease about Dad. Maybe she could confirm Dad's explanation about the stolen Mustang, and I could stop worrying about it.

And then there was Evan Bailey.

I had no idea why I kept thinking about him. Actually, that wasn't true. I knew exactly why I kept thinking about him.

Those eyes. That jaw. Those hands.

That body.

He'd looked powerful and intimidating but I hadn't sensed cruelty. Although his dog had been alert and wary of the strangers in his territory, he'd seemed calm and well-behaved—a sign of a good owner.

And those hands.

They were very distracting.

I was definitely not going to Google him or his shop, nor was I going to spend time searching through his gallery of car photos, hoping there was one with him in it.

That was a big fat lie. I definitely did that.

The phone rang, jolting me back to reality, and I quickly closed the tab.

"Gallagher Auto, this is Fiona."

"There's my girl," a wheezy old voice answered.

I couldn't help but smile. "Hi, Mr. Browning. It's been a while. I was starting to worry about you."

"Oh, don't worry about me. I'm healthy as an ox."

"Good to hear. What can I do for you?"

"Well, I'm looking for a grill for a '66 Pontiac Catalina. You have anything like that lying around out there?"

"I don't think we do. I take it you haven't had luck locally?"

"There's a guy out here who has one, but it's rusted to shit. I can't use that. You know me, only the best. I have standards."

I wondered if Mr. Browning was actually working on his Catalina or just buying more parts. He was something of a hoarder. He lived in northern Arizona, but he had a thing for rare cars, which meant parts were particularly hard to find. Sometimes if he got stuck trying to find something specific, he'd call me. He knew I loved a challenge.

"Of course you have standards. We don't have one, but I can keep my eyes open and let you know."

"Thank you, sweetheart. Appreciate that."

"You bet. Hey, speaking of Pontiacs, is your GTO still tragically sitting in your barn?"

He chuckled. "Is your daddy going to come sniffing around again, trying to take it off my hands?"

"I don't know, Dad's got a lot on his plate right now. I'm just curious. It's a beautiful car. I'd love to see it running again."

"Ain't that the truth. I'm thinking about selling it, finally. Been sitting in my barn a long time."

Among Mr. Browning's extensive collection of moldering classic cars was a 1970 Pontiac GTO convertible, nicknamed the Judge. Years ago, my dad had tried to buy it from him, but he hadn't been willing to let it go. It was hard to blame him. The Judge was a rare find. There were only a dozen or so ever made. His was in terrible shape; whoever had owned it before him had left it out in the weather for years. It would be a daunting restoration for anyone, so I wasn't surprised Mr. Browning was finally thinking about letting it go. He had to be in his eighties; it was hard to imagine him being able to do all the work to restore it.

"Are you really?"

He sighed. "Yeah, it's probably time I let it go. I got a guy coming in a few days to take a look."

"Make sure you hold out for the right price."

"Oh, I will. I know what I've got."

"Good for you. I'll let you know if I come across a grill for your Catalina."

"Thank you, sweetheart. I'll talk to you later."

"Bye, Mr. Browning."

I hung up the phone and fought down the urge to search for Evan Bailey again.

Barely.

The morning got busier, especially since Simone still hadn't come in. I had some bookkeeping to catch up on, but Dad hadn't brought in all the receipts and expense reports. Again.

Nothing new there. I'd just swing by his house and pick them up—and water his plants while I was there. I was pretty sure I was the only one who watered them, so an excuse to stop by wasn't so bad.

He lived in a quiet neighborhood a few miles from the shop. I pretended my clutch wasn't slipping on the short drive over. I added *shuffle some things around on the shop schedule* to my mental to-do list so I could use space in the garage to work on it. If I let this go too long, I could be in trouble.

I knocked softly before using my key to go inside. He wasn't in his office. I'd probably just missed him. Humming quietly to myself, I rooted around his desk for the latest receipts, adding what I could find to a folder.

His laptop was open, as if he'd been working and something had interrupted him. My eyes flicked across the screen and I did a double take when I saw the name Felix Orman.

Oh no.

It was a brief email to my dad from Felix. It simply said, *I already took care of it.*

My heart sank. I wanted to believe my dad had legitimate reasons for corresponding with Felix. No girl wants to think the worst of her father. But what were the chances that Felix had gone legit and this was all a big misunderstanding? I was usually an unfailing optimist who saw the best in people, but even I knew that was a stretch.

If Dad was dealing in stolen goods again, he'd broken his promise.

This really sucked.

I left the folder of receipts on his desk and went to the kitchen to get the watering can I'd left here. I felt like crap, but that didn't mean his plants needed to go without water.

After filling it up, I went to his living room to give his plants a drink, but a noise from upstairs made me stop in my tracks. Maybe he *was* home.

Except.

Oh no.

Oh, please no.

Rhythmic banging. His bedroom was on this side of the house, right above me, and yep, that was a woman's voice.

"Spank me, Daddy. Yes."

Oh my god. Gross.

Unfortunately for me, this wasn't the first time I'd overheard my dad with a lady friend. Not even close. My mom had left when I was little, and my dad had been more or less single ever since. He'd dated several women, and I'd even met a few of them. But mostly he seemed to indulge in... whatever was going on upstairs that I didn't want to think about. I was aware of it, but did my best to ignore that part of his life.

Although, when I thought about it, he'd never tried very hard to hide it from me.

I quickly flitted around, watering the last plants. The noise stopped and I heard the shower turn on.

Time to go.

"There you go, pretty," I whispered to the last plant in his office. "Isn't that better? I know, but just ignore them. She'll be gone soon. You're looking awfully droopy, but who could blame you?"

I turned to take the watering can back to the kitchen and came face to face with a woman standing at the base of the stairs.

She squealed, startling me, and I dropped the watering can. It bounced on the hardwood floor, spraying water everywhere.

I blinked at her, confused. Her platinum blond hair was messy and a pair of heels dangled from her hand. Her eyes were wide with shock, her mouth open.

"Simone?" I asked. "What are you doing here?"

5

FIONA

Simone seemed to recover quickly, closing her mouth and straightening her shoulders. "Fiona, what are you doing here?"

"That's what I just asked you." I felt frozen, rooted to the spot while a pool of water from the overturned watering can spread around my feet. My eyes flicked up the stairs, then back to her. "Why are you here?"

"I didn't mean for you to find out like this."

"Find out about what?" It was a stupid question. I knew. I'd heard it with my own ears. But my brain suddenly felt cloudy, a shroud of disbelief settling over me. They couldn't have.

"About me and Shane."

"Shane? You're calling him *Shane* now?" I asked, keeping my voice low.

"What else would I call him?"

"Daddy, apparently."

She didn't even have the decency to blush. "Oh my god, it's not that big of a deal."

"Are you kidding me? He's my *father*. He's known you

since you were little. How could you possibly think this is okay?"

"You're seriously going to be a bitch about this, aren't you? After everything we've been through together, you can't be happy for me?"

I stared at her in disbelief. "Happy that you're sleeping with my dad? Are you nuts? How long has this been going on?"

She shrugged. "Five or six months, I guess. You know, off and on. I was going to tell you, but he wouldn't let me."

"Five or six *months*? I thought you were hooking up with your ex again."

"Yeah, I kind of let you think that. It was a good cover."

Nausea spread through my stomach and I tasted bile on the back of my tongue. "I think I'm going to be sick."

She scowled at me. "Really? I'm such trash you're going to puke at the thought of me being with your dad? Great, I'm glad you think so highly of me."

"That's not what I'm saying."

"No? I thought you'd be happy for us. I won't turn into a wicked stepmother, Fiona."

"What, like he's going to marry you?"

Her eyes narrowed. "And why not?"

"Do you know how many women he's kicked out the door over the years? So many. I got very good at pretending I didn't notice them. What on earth makes you think you're any different?"

"I should have known you'd be jealous."

"How am I jealous? It's my dad, Simone. It's gross. And you've been lying to me."

She rolled her eyes. "You made it easy, Fiona. You don't want to see the truth. Not everyone wants to be nice like you. It doesn't get you anywhere."

"What is that supposed to mean?"

"You know what, we'll talk about this later when you can be rational," she said, her voice so patronizing I wanted to smack her. "I have to go to work."

Without putting on her shoes, she walked out.

I blinked with disbelief. I hadn't seen her car outside, but maybe she'd parked on the street and I hadn't noticed.

Oh my god.

The shower upstairs turned off, making my heart jump. I did *not* want to be here when he came down. I quickly cleaned up the mess from the watering can and put it away. Then I darted back into his office, grabbed the folder, and left—hoping I hadn't missed anything. The last thing I wanted was to have to come back.

As if my car knew I needed a break, the clutch didn't slip on the drive home. I didn't go back to work. Simone would be there. Dad would come in eventually. I couldn't stand the thought of looking at either of them right now.

She'd been calling him *daddy*.

God, it was so gross, I still thought I might puke.

I got home and brought my stuff inside. I put my things down on the kitchen table and looked around numbly at the apartment Simone and I had shared for the last few years. When I'd moved here, I'd thought I was making progress toward building my own life. But I hadn't gone anywhere.

I sank down into a chair. "Is she right, Myra? Should I be happy for them?"

The deep sense of betrayal I felt was too acute to entertain that possibility. What had she been thinking? What had *he* been thinking?

Although a bigger question thrummed through my mind. What was I still doing here?

I'd thought about moving so many times. Finding a

different job. Making a life for myself that wasn't tied to my father. But talk was cheap. I was twenty-six years old and still living under his thumb. Still letting him call the shots. Deep down, I knew why.

I was afraid of what he'd do if he didn't have me around to keep him in check.

Dad had narrowly escaped going to prison once already. I'd made him promise he'd stay legit. And wrapped up in that promise had been the unspoken acknowledgment that I'd always be here to see that he kept it.

But he wasn't keeping it. I didn't know what he was into, or how deep it went. But the fact that he was sleeping with Simone and lying to me about it was only one more sticky layer in his web of deceit.

And I was done trying to hold everything together for him.

"Myra, Blanche, we're leaving."

I stood, my resolve giving me a rush of energy. It was like I'd flipped a switch and suddenly felt in control of my life. It was a heady sensation, making me light on my feet. Almost giddy.

I was getting out of here.

The beginnings of a plan formed in my mind as I packed some of my things. There was only one place I could think to go where Dad wouldn't follow.

Mom.

If my relationship with Dad was difficult, my relationship with Mom was a twisting labyrinth of complications. Which was why Dad wouldn't dream that I'd go there.

Sure, she was eighteen hundred miles away in Iowa, and my car probably wouldn't make it that far without a clutch replacement. My bank account was pathetic, I owed a ton of money in student loans, and walking out on my job meant no income for the foreseeable future.

It felt like the universe was staring me down, waiting to see what I was made of. Trying to tell me this wasn't possible.

You know what, universe? Hold my beer.

A COUPLE OF HOURS LATER, I was on the road, my car stuffed to the ceiling. Myra and Blanche sat happily—they really looked quite perky—on the passenger seat beside me.

I'd left Simone a note, telling her I'd moved out and wasn't coming back. Maybe I should have felt bad for sticking her with the apartment, but I couldn't find it in me to care. I'd covered for her for years, doing her job, ignoring how shitty she could be. She wasn't getting anything else from me.

As for Dad, I left him a message telling him, calmly, that I wasn't coming back to work.

That left me with the pressing issue of my car. Had there been no emotion involved, it probably would have been smarter to wait and fix the clutch first, *then* uproot my life and move to a new state. But that would have meant seeing Simone and my dad every day until I got it done. And I just couldn't.

However, now that I was on the road, I had to face the reality of the big, gaping hole in my escape plan. It wasn't safe for me to make the trip to Iowa. That meant a pit stop to fix my car.

But I had an idea about that, too. An idea that, to a person who wasn't high on the thrill of changing her life in one fell swoop, probably would have seemed crazy. Possibly even stupid.

But I *was* high on that thrill, and as I raced east on the freeway, leaving Seattle behind, I decided it was simply going to have to work. I wasn't going to accept anything else.

I was going to see Evan Bailey.

My plan was simple. Evan Bailey had recently lost a valuable project car. It stood to reason he needed another one. I needed a place to fix my car that wasn't my dad's garage.

Evan Bailey had a garage. I knew of another car—Mr. Browning's Pontiac GTO. That would be an even better find than the '67 Mustang.

Yes, my plan was slightly convoluted and hinged on the cooperation of a stranger—who hated my father—and my ability to convince Mr. Browning to sell his car to Evan Bailey. But I wasn't going to let a silly thing like doubt or a high probability of failure stop me now. I was going to make it work.

"It's not that crazy, is it, girls?" I glanced at Myra and Blanche. "I know there are a lot of ways this could go wrong, but for right now, this is what we've got. Our alternative is going back, and I'll live in my car before I do that."

Despite the uncertainty of my current situation, I couldn't remember the last time I'd felt so light. I couldn't stop smiling. I was free.

However, I didn't want to show up at Evan's shop unannounced. Maybe I was crazy, but I wasn't going to be rude.

Plus, that was what Dad had done. I wanted Evan to know that I wasn't my father.

I stopped for snacks at a little mini-mart about half an hour outside the city—because road trips required snacks—and looked up the number for Evan's shop. My heart fluttered at the memory of his intense brown eyes, but I took a fortifying breath, and called.

"Bailey Customs."

"Hi, is this Evan Bailey?"

"Yeah."

"Oh, good. Um, you answered so fast and now I'm kind of nervous."

"What?"

"Sorry. My name's Fiona and my car needs a new clutch."

"I don't do that kind of work."

"No, I know you don't. But—"

"Are you local?"

"I'm not, but I'll be in your area—"

"Then call Dusty's Auto in Tilikum. Do you need the number?"

"No, I—"

"Okay. Bye."

My phone beeped as the call disconnected. Had he just hung up on me?

Brushing my hair out of my eyes, I hit send again. Evan Bailey was going to help me. He just didn't realize it yet.

6

EVAN

*M*y phone rang again and a spike of annoyance made my shoulders tighten. Same number. What the fuck was wrong with her? I'd told her to call Dusty's in town. I didn't replace clutches on whatever piece of shit car she was driving. Why was she calling again?

"What?" I barked into the phone.

"Don't hang up," she said, spitting out the words quickly. "Just please, listen. I know you're not a regular mechanic and under normal circumstances I'd take it in to a repair shop. But I can't."

"Why?"

"I'll explain in person, I just want you to know I'm on my way."

"What?"

"I'm calling to let you know I'm on my way. I can help you get something you want, so you're going to want to talk to me."

"Why would you—"

"I know, it's weird, but trust me, you'll want to hear me

out," she said. Why the fuck was her voice so cheery? She sounded familiar, but I didn't know why. "I'm pretty sure I can find the place, but if I have trouble, I'll call you back."

"No, don't—"

"Thanks, Evan! I'll see you soon!"

She ended the call and I looked at my phone. What was she talking about? She could help me get something I wanted? And why did I recognize her voice?

I was about to put the phone down when it buzzed with a text. Seriously, who was this chick?

But it wasn't the same number. Great, who the hell was this?

Hey, you! I'm back in town. Want to get together?

My throat tightened at the thought that it might be *her*. But there was no way Carly would text me out of the blue like that. We hadn't spoken in years.

I texted back: *Who's this?*

It's Jill, silly. Did you get a new phone and lose your contacts?

Jill? Who the fuck was Jill?

I hadn't been with anyone since that stupid hookup last October. We hadn't exchanged names, let alone phone numbers, so it couldn't be her. And before that... it had been a long time since I'd been with anyone. It wasn't like I dated anymore, and I certainly didn't remember a woman named Jill.

Then it dawned on me. She was pink cardigan girl.

Why was pink cardigan girl texting me? I'd deleted her number months ago.

Whatever. I had work to do.

I got busy working on the Super Bee and completely forgot about the girl who'd called. Until Sasquatch got up and a second later, I heard a car outside. I wiped my hands on a rag and went out to see who was here.

The car that parked out front had seen better days. There were dings and dents all over the body, a crack in the windshield, and the front bumper was crooked. Bits of rust and badly done repairs made an already ugly car look even worse.

The shapeless form of a person buried in a too-large winter coat got out of the car. Her eyes were partially hidden behind dark bangs and beneath that, she wore a lot of makeup. Her nose was pierced, right in the center, and it was actually...

Well, it was hot, but what the fuck did that matter?

She looked vaguely familiar, but I couldn't place her.

I glanced at Sasquatch. His tongue lolled out of his mouth and he sat next to me.

Wait, why was he sitting?

"Do we know her?" I muttered to him.

The girl flashed a wide smile and waved. "Hi, I'm Fiona. I called a little while ago."

This was the girl on the phone? "You need a new clutch?"

"Yes, but—"

"That's not what I do."

"I know and I'm not here to get you to fix my car." She cupped her hands together and blew into them. "Wow, it's so cold out here. Aren't you cold?"

I glanced down at my open flannel shirt, t-shirt, and jeans. "No."

"Really? I'm freezing. Isn't it spring? Must be the elevation." She blew into her hands again. "Anyway, I have a proposition for you."

"Who are you?"

"Fiona." She sighed. "Fiona Gallagher."

That was why I recognized her. She'd been here with Shane Gallagher.

I crossed my arms. "Gallagher? You his daughter or his wife?"

She winced. "Daughter. I'd point out the obvious age difference, but after this morning, that's not as relevant as I would have thought."

"What?"

"Never mind. Like I said, I have a proposition for you. This is going to sound weird but hear me out."

She rubbed her hands together and I could practically hear Gram's voice in my ear. My eye twitched. I didn't want to invite her in. If I invited her inside, it would be harder to get rid of her.

"I'm not selling the Super Bee to your dad."

"Oh, I know. You shouldn't sell it to him. In fact, if you were thinking about changing your mind, I'd tell you not to. He was probably going to low-ball you anyway."

That was... not what I expected her to say. "So you're not here about the car."

"Not that one. And I'm not here for my father, either. In fact, I'm here because I'm trying to get away from my father."

Sasquatch looked up at me. I groaned. Girl in trouble, standing in the cold. Not that it was very cold out. But god, now she was fucking shivering.

Don't do it, Evan. Don't get involved.

But Gram's conditioning was too deeply ingrained. I was basically an asshole, but I had limits.

"Come inside." I glanced at Sasquatch, about to tell him to go lie down so he didn't try to defend his territory and keep her out, but he didn't get in her way.

"Thank you so much." She followed me inside. "Your dog is gorgeous. Sasquatch, right?"

"Yeah."

She crouched down and held out her hand. "Hi, Sasquatch. Who's a good boy? Yes, you are."

He trotted to her, his tail whipping back and forth. She rubbed the top of his head, still talking in that ridiculous high-pitched voice, telling him how good he was.

Yeah, real good dog, letting some weird ass girl sweet-talk him like that.

"Some guard dog," I muttered.

"What?" Fiona asked.

"Nothing. Why are you here?"

She gave Sasquatch one last scratch behind the ears, then stood. "Okay, here's the thing. This morning I found out... no, you don't need to know about all that. Although it does provide context. Maybe I should start at the beginning."

I rested my hands on my hips and raised my eyebrows. "Seriously?"

"I swear, this made so much sense when I was driving here. I had everything I was going to say all worked out, but you're very big and intimidating up close."

I had no idea what to say to that, so I just waited.

She took a deep breath. "Let me try this again. For various reasons, I walked out on my life today. I'm heading for my mom's in Iowa, but I think my clutch is going out. I know how to fix it, I just need a place to do it."

"What does any of that have to do with me?"

"Well..." She took another breath. "I'm hoping we can come to an arrangement. You let me use your shop and your tools so I can replace my clutch, and I help you get something you want."

"What do you think I want?"

"I was here when you told my dad about the Mustang. It was an Eleanor, wasn't it?"

I eyed her. "Yeah."

"So would it be accurate to say you need another restoration opportunity? Maybe one that's rare and valuable?"

It would be accurate to say that, but I wasn't sure where this was going. "What are you talking about?"

She licked her lips. "What if I told you I know someone who has a 1970 Pontiac GTO. Convertible."

I rolled my eyes. "Yeah, right."

"I'm serious."

"You know someone who has the Judge." I shook my head. There was no way. Only seventeen had been made, and five of them had disappeared entirely.

"His name is Walt Browning and he's a collector down in northern Arizona. He's been sitting on it for years, saying he's going to restore it himself. But he's like eighty years old and he has dozens of half-finished cars. I think he's finally starting to realize he needs to let some of them go."

I didn't want to admit she had my attention, but damn it, she did. If she really did know a guy with a 1970 Pontiac GTO convertible, and could actually get him to sell it to me... holy shit. "Will he sell it?"

"I talked to him on the phone this morning and he said he has a guy coming to look at it already. That tells me he's at least thinking about it."

"He's in Arizona?"

"Yes, and I know that's a long way, but I'm telling you, Mr. Browning loves me. I'm sure I can talk him into it."

"Call him."

She crouched down to pet Sasquatch again. "I will,

because obviously you'll want to verify my story. But he won't sell it over the phone. He only deals with people in person. He has a real emotional attachment to his cars."

"So you're saying you think I should drive to northern Arizona on the off chance some old guy you know might sell me his car?"

"Yes. You lost the Mustang. And I mean, a '67 Mustang is awesome, but a '70 Pontiac GTO convertible? We both know a shot at restoring the Judge would put this shop on the map."

She wasn't wrong.

"And in exchange, you want to use my shop to fix your clutch."

Smiling, she straightened. Sasquatch stayed next to her. "Yep. And you'll hardly know I'm around. I'll be in and out in no time."

"Why come here?"

"It's a long story. All I can say is that things happened, and I had to leave. This is the craziest thing I've ever done in my entire life, but from the moment I decided to go, I knew it was right."

Oddly, I kind of understood what that was like.

"And if the old guy won't sell me the car?"

She shrugged. "Then the deal is off. I'll get my car fixed another way. But he will."

"You could still just take it to Dusty's Auto in town. He's a good guy, he won't overcharge you."

"And it'll cost me five times as much as it would if I do the work myself. I have more time than money right now, so a few days on the road to get you this car is a lot easier for me to justify than paying someone else for something I know how to do."

There was a strange sort of logic there. But she could also be insane. Maybe even dangerous.

She idly reached down to scratch Sasquatch's head again. He let her.

This girl wasn't dangerous. Not just because Sasquatch was at ease with her, although that told me a lot. I'd been wrong about people before, but those were times when I'd been off my guard. Not willing to see the truth. Right now, my judgment wasn't clouded by emotion. She was weird, but probably harmless.

And a 1970 Pontiac GTO convertible... If this guy had any idea of what he had—and it sounded like he probably did—it would cost me a fortune. But once it was restored...

"Call the old guy. If your story checks out and he'll show me the car, I'll think about it."

Smiling, Fiona scrunched her shoulders and clasped her hands. "Oh my god, thank you. I know you didn't say yes, just that you'll think about it, but that's progress. Small wins, right?"

"Just call him."

"Okay, okay." She rooted around the pockets of her giant coat, finally pulling out a phone. "That's so weird, neither of them has tried to call me."

"What?"

"Nothing. Just... nothing." She tapped her screen a few times. "I'll put him on speaker."

It rang twice before a wheezy voice answered. "Hello?"

"Hi, Mr. Browning. It's Fiona Gallagher."

"Well hello, sweetheart. I get to hear your voice twice in one day. What a treat."

She met my eyes and her smile widened. "That's so sweet of you to say."

"What can I do for you, dear?"

"Well, I'm wondering about your 1970 Pontiac. The GTO?"

"Beautiful car."

"It really is. When we talked earlier, did you say you have someone coming to take a look at it?"

"Yes, a guy coming from out of state. Seems pretty interested."

"Did you already agree to sell it to him?"

"No, no, I can't let one of my babies go to just anyone. Needs to be the right fit. I have to look them in the eye, make sure they're worthy."

Fiona practically bounced with excitement. "I know, I totally agree. It's an amazing car and definitely needs the right buyer."

"I hear something in your voice, sweetheart. What do you have cooking?"

"You see right through me, Mr. Browning. Actually, I have what just might be the perfect buyer."

"Do you, now? Not your father."

She smiled at me again. "No, definitely not my dad. His name's Evan Bailey, and he's very talented. An up-and-comer. He's looking for a really special project, and I can totally vouch for him. What do you think?"

Mr. Browning took a deep breath. "Coming from you, that does mean something."

"So you'd consider it?"

"I need to look him in the eye, same as anyone. But he can come take a look."

"Naturally," she said, her voice bright. "Just promise me one thing, okay?"

"What's that, sweetheart?"

"Don't sell it before we get there."

He was quiet for a moment. "Hmm. How soon can you be here?"

"A couple of days, I think."

"All right."

"Thank you, Mr. Browning. I'll be in touch."

"Sounds good. Bye, sweetheart."

Fiona ended the call and triumphantly slid the phone back into a cavernous pocket. "See? It's the real deal. But we should really get on the road. He said he'd wait, but I don't think we should take any chances."

I crossed my arms. "We?"

"Yeah. Obviously I have to come with you."

I leveled her with a glare, my nostrils flaring. "No."

She laughed—fucking *laughed*. "No?"

"That's what I said."

"He won't sell you the car if I'm not there."

"He said he needs to look his buyer in the eyes. I'm the buyer."

Her gaze flicked up and down, like she was sizing me up. "Yeah, exactly. I need to be there."

"You don't think he'll sell it to me if you're not there?"

"I *know* he won't sell it to you if I'm not there. Trust me. I've known Mr. Browning for years. He's very eccentric. We're going to have to play this just right or no one's getting that car."

My brow furrowed. "Why are you willing to drive that kind of distance with me? I'm a stranger."

She put her hands on her hips. "No you're not."

"I don't think seeing me for five minutes yesterday counts."

"We've talked on the phone a bunch of times. You bought a set of fenders for a '68 Camaro from us last year."

"How do you remember that?"

"Look, I'm trying not to let it hurt my feelings that you don't remember me *at all*. Can we just move on? Besides, I carry pepper spray, and I'm almost positive you won't murder me."

"Of course I won't fucking murder you."

She smiled. "See?"

God, what the fuck. How was she talking me into this?

It wasn't her. It was the Pontiac. I could practically hear the throaty roar of its engine. Smell the tang of gasoline in the air. I really wanted that car. I hadn't even seen it, and I wanted it. As long as there was enough metal left to hold it together, it wouldn't matter what kind of condition it was in. A restoration like that, done right, would guarantee me a spot in the museum's permanent collection. Nothing Luke Haven could build could compete.

I'd crush him with this.

"Fine. Let's go."

7

EVAN

I tossed my duffel bag in the back seat of my Toyota Tacoma extended cab. I had the trailer hitched and ready to go. I'd either be bringing home the biggest build of my life, or a shit ton of regret. But sometimes big wins meant big risks.

Sasquatch, experienced road trip dog that he was, jumped up into the passenger seat.

"Get in the back, big guy," I said. "We have company."

"That's okay; if that's his seat, I won't take it." Fiona carried a backpack and had two houseplants tucked under her arms.

"What are those?"

"Myra and Blanche."

I blinked at her. "What?"

She smiled. "I know, I named them, it's so dorky. My dad never let me have pets growing up, and my roommate was allergic. So I have Myra and Blanche."

"You're bringing plants on a road trip?"

"They can't stay here. Who'll water them?"

"Are you fucking kidding me?"

She smiled again. Why did this girl smile so damn much? "They can just sit at my feet. And they're not toxic to dogs. I looked it up."

I looked at Sasquatch. "Is she serious?"

Sasquatch scrambled into the back seat.

"What a good boy," she said, cooing at my dog. "You're such a gentleman, Sasquatch. Thank you."

"Jesus."

Fiona spoke softly to her plants while she settled in the passenger seat. I talked to my dog all the time, but these were *plants*. Ignoring her—and the implications of trusting a woman who held conversations with plants that had old lady names—I went around and got in the driver's seat.

"Ready?" she asked.

I didn't know if she was talking to me or her plants, so I didn't answer. Just started the truck and eased it down the road. I had to be careful with the trailer on this hill.

"Since you're driving, I'll be the navigator and road trip coordinator." She pulled out her phone. "How far do you think we'll get today?"

"I don't know."

She pulled her legs up onto the seat and crossed them. "That's fine, I'll keep an eye on the map and find us a good place to stop for the night."

"Okay."

"Do you have any food allergies?"

"No."

"What about hotel preferences? Anything I should know?"

"No."

"Do you know how to give answers that are more than one word?"

I turned to look at her. "Yes."

She laughed. Because of course she did. Apparently everything was funny.

My phone rang and I glanced at the screen. Gavin. I answered through the truck's Bluetooth. "What do you want?"

"Come down to the gym. I need a sparring partner."

"No."

"Dude, don't be like that. No one's around and I need someone good to practice with. Plus I really want to tie you into a pretzel."

"No."

"Fine, I'll go easy on you. Actually, that's a lie, I won't. But it'll still be fun."

"Can't."

"Why not? You work for yourself. Take a break."

"I'm not home. I'm on the road."

"Where are you going?"

"Road trip to look at a car. I'll be back in a few days."

"Are you out of town yet? Can I come?"

Fiona glanced at me, amusement dancing in her eyes.

"No you can't fucking come. Jesus, Gav, leave me alone." I jammed my finger on the button to end the call.

"Who was that?"

"My brother."

"Is it just the two of you or do you have other siblings?"

"There's five of us."

"Do you have any sisters?"

"All boys."

"Wow. Your parents were brave."

"We were raised by—" I paused, gripping the steering wheel. Why was I telling her things? "By our grandparents after our parents died."

"Oh. I'm so sorry, I didn't realize."

I rolled my eyes. I didn't want to have to sit here and soothe her feelings. "It's fine."

"I'm an only child. Sort of. I didn't grow up with my other siblings, so I suppose it would more accurate to say I was raised as an only child."

"Are you going to talk the entire way there?"

Her lips twitched in a little smile. "No."

"Good."

"Are you always so charming?"

I glanced at her from the corner of my eye. "What you see is what you get, sweetheart."

"Good to know."

THREE HOURS LATER, I already had regrets.

Lots of regrets.

All the regrets.

She was, in fact, talking the entire drive. Not necessarily to me. She'd asked me a few more questions, but I'd shut her down with one-word answers. But did that stop her mouth from spewing an incessant stream of chatter? No, it did not.

She talked to her plants, telling them about the things she saw outside. Cows were very exciting, apparently. She talked to my dog, reaching back and spoiling him with attention while she praised him for being a good boy.

She would not shut up.

Finally, she settled down and was quiet for a while. My shoulders relaxed, the tension easing with the hum of the tires on pavement, the scenery flying by. Sasquatch liked music when we drove, so I flipped on the radio.

Big mistake.

She sang.

Not only that, she sang *wrong*.

Her voice wasn't terrible, and she wasn't loud. But she sang along as if she'd forgotten anyone else was around, and she obviously didn't know the words. She mumbled through the verses, sang the words to the chorus, then mumbled again.

This girl was driving me crazy.

Of course it was my own damn fault for agreeing to this stupid trip in the first place.

A new song came on and she hummed the tune, throwing in words here and there.

Okay, so I didn't actually hate her singing. It was sweet and sort of... calming.

Until she sang *into the beehive* instead of *follow the straight line*—seriously, how did she get that wrong?—and completely ruined it.

"You know you can look up lyrics online."

She just laughed. "Do you like road trip games?"

"No."

"What about twenty questions?"

"No."

"Alphabet game?"

"No."

She sighed. "You're really no fun, are you?"

"Nope."

"What's your favorite car?"

I side-eyed her.

"I probably shouldn't have asked that question because now I'll have to tell you mine, and you're definitely going to make fun of me for it."

Okay, she kind of had my attention. "What is it?"

"Nineteen sixty-five Plymouth Belvedere."

"Seriously?"

She laughed. "I know, it's kind of boxy and it doesn't look nearly as badass as a lot of muscle cars. But give it a hood scoop and put that chrome stripe down the side, and it's a hot car. Plus, you know, hemi. Those things can haul."

I glanced at her again. Sounded like she really knew her cars.

Interesting.

"It's hard to pick a favorite," I said. "But I own a '68 Camaro because it was the first car I fell in love with."

"That's a hot car."

My mouth twitched in a smile. She was a hot car.

We stopped at a diner for a late dinner—the food was pretty terrible, but Fiona didn't complain—and she found us rooms at a motel a couple of hours away. If I'd been alone, I would have driven farther, but getting a decent night's sleep wasn't a bad idea, so I didn't argue with her choice of rest stop.

It was after eleven when we pulled into the parking lot of a run-down motel. We got our keys from the office and found our rooms.

"Okay, well, goodnight." She had her backpack slung over one shoulder and carried her houseplants in her arms.

I watched her set one of her plants down while she unlocked her door, feeling oddly unsettled. Her room was only three doors down, but for some reason, it bothered me that there was more than one wall between us.

Sasquatch looked up at me with judgment burning in his brown eyes.

"What? This place isn't too bad. Her door locks."

He blinked.

She disappeared into her room, taking her plants with her.

"Do you want to go sleep in her room with her? I didn't think so." I cast another glance at the empty space where she'd been standing. "She'll be fine."

Of course she'd be fine. What was I worried about? She was a grownup. It wasn't like I was responsible for her.

Still, I resolved to make sure we had rooms closer together tomorrow night.

8

FIONA

I woke up with a smile on my face.

The bed was lumpy, the pillow flat, there was no way I was walking barefoot on the carpet, and I didn't want to think about what I'd heard the people doing in the room next door. But I'd never felt as good as I did waking up in a crappy roadside motel in the middle of nowhere. Because for the first time, I was living on my terms.

Today, I wouldn't have to cover for Simone or pick up the slack because she'd come in late again. I wouldn't have to feel the rush of anxiety as I went through my dad's books, worrying about what I might find.

"Good morning, girls," I said to Myra and Blanche. Despite all the travel, they were looking lush in their spot near the window. "Ready to get moving again?"

They were. I could tell.

I took a quick shower and put on some makeup before Evan texted to see if I was ready. I grabbed my things and met him in the parking lot.

It wasn't as cold here as it had been in the mountains, so

I'd stuffed my coat in my backpack. I had a comfy sweatshirt on, along with a pair of leggings, so I was warm enough.

Evan stood outside his truck looking crazy hot with damp hair and sunglasses, his well-muscled physique filling out his t-shirt and jeans like nobody's business. How was a guy like him still single? Assuming he was single, which I actually didn't know for sure. It seemed like he was. He hadn't mentioned a girl, or texted anyone, or—

I needed to stop worrying about whether he was single. Was he hot? Dear god, yes. He exuded a potent aura of masculinity that made strange things happen in my lower regions. But that wasn't why I was on this trip with him. Enjoy the view? Sure. Get tangled up with a man right now? Absolutely not.

Plus, he wasn't into me anyway.

"Hurry it up," he said. "We have a lot of ground to cover today."

"I'm coming." I set Myra and Blanche down so I could open the truck door while Evan went around to the other side to get in. Sasquatch was already in the back seat. "If you're in such a hurry, you could help me with all this."

"You're the one who brought plants on a road trip."

I sighed and finished loading them into the truck. "Yes, but—"

He turned on the truck. "I know, who would water them? You said that yesterday."

"So what should we do for breakfast?"

He made a low growly noise. I'd already learned that meant he was annoyed or frustrated.

"Aren't you hungry?" I asked. "I thought after last night's mediocre dinner you might be in the mood for a big breakfast to make up for it."

His jaw tightened, but I could tell he was thinking about it. "All right. If we see a place that looks good, we'll stop."

We hadn't gotten far when we spotted a truck stop. He agreed it looked decent, so he pulled off the highway and found a place to park.

He took Sasquatch to get a little more exercise while I went inside and sat in a window booth.

The waitress came and handed me a menu. She was probably about my age, with dark hair swept up in a high bun, a few tendrils falling around her face.

"Coffee?" she asked.

"Please. What do you recommend ordering? Do you have a favorite?"

"The pancakes are good," she said. "You can get them with blueberries if you want."

"Yum, I love blueberry pancakes. But my friend is still coming, so I'll wait to order."

"Okay, I'll come back."

"Thanks so much," I said with a smile.

The waitress left and I stirred cream into my coffee. I wondered if Evan liked cream or sugar. Or coffee. I had no idea. Although when I thought about it, he seemed an awful lot like a black-coffee guy to me.

A man in the next booth turned around. He had light brown hair and striking blue eyes. "Hey, sorry, I'm not trying to be a creeper, but your voice sounds really familiar."

"That's funny. Does it?"

"Yeah. Are you from around here, or...?"

"No, I'm from the Seattle area."

"Huh. I'm not from around here either. But I swear I've heard your voice somewhere."

"Hmm, I don't know. Where are you from?"

"Little town in Washington called Tilikum. You've probably never heard of it."

My eyes widened. "You're kidding."

"No."

"I was just there."

"Were you really?"

"Yeah, but not for very long before getting back on the road."

He shifted so his legs were in the aisle and his arm draped over the back of the booth. He was attractive in a rugged kind of way. Thick upper body. Strong jaw. "What's your name?"

"Fiona."

His mouth hooked in a slight grin. "I'm Luke."

"Wait." I searched my memory. Luke from Tilikum? "Luke as in Luke Haven?"

He blinked in surprise. "Yeah. How'd you know?"

"I'm Fiona Gallagher, from Gallagher Auto. We've talked on the phone tons of times."

He snapped his fingers and pointed at me. "That's why I recognize your voice. Fiona? This is crazy."

"This *is* crazy. What are you doing out here?"

"I'm going to check out a car."

I laughed. "That's so funny. So are we."

His eyebrows lifted. "We?"

"Yeah, you must know Evan Bailey."

His smile disappeared in an instant and a second later, his eyes caught something behind me.

Evan stopped next to the booth and leveled a glare at Luke. "What the fuck are you doing here?"

The malice in Luke's gaze matched Evan's. "Eating breakfast."

Uh-oh. I'd thought Evan had looked mad when he'd

stared down my dad. But the anger in his eyes then was nothing compared to the inferno that raged in his expression now.

"I take it you two know each other," I said, keeping my voice light in the hopes of cutting some of the tension. "What a fun coincidence."

Luke shifted his gaze back to me. "You're with him?"

"Yeah. I mean, I'm not *with him* with him. But we're together. No, not together, like that kind of together. We just met. Except, no, that's not what I mean. We're going to look at a car together because I know the guy selling it."

Luke's eyes moved back to Evan. "What car?"

I wasn't sure if he was asking me or Evan, but I answered anyway. "A Pontiac."

Evan didn't move, his thick body tense, those veins popping in his forearms again. His jaw hitched and his eyes blazed.

"A Pontiac GTO?" Luke asked, still staring at Evan.

"No fucking way," Evan growled.

I didn't know the specifics of what was happening, but two things were perfectly clear. Evan and Luke didn't like each other, and both men were after the same car.

"How do you know Mr. Browning?" I asked.

The friendliness in Luke's eyes had totally evaporated and his voice was flat. "He knows my dad."

"Don't talk to her like that," Evan said, his voice low.

"Evan, it's fine."

"Talk to her like what? I just answered her question."

"Go home, Luke," Evan said. "You're not getting that car."

Luke scoffed. "Fuck you."

"I'm serious. The car's mine."

"Like hell it is."

The waitress hesitated nearby, her expression drawn with concern, and the tension was palpable. Luke's nostrils flared and Evan's eye twitched. They were like two wild animals circling each other, waiting for the right moment to attack.

"Guys, maybe we should—"

"Stay out of it," Luke snapped.

Evan stepped forward. "Don't fucking talk to her."

Luke stood. "Kiss my ass, dick. Can't hide behind your brothers out here."

"Neither can you, asshole."

They were attracting the attention of everyone in the diner. Two guys with barrel chests and thick necks came out of the kitchen and headed toward our booth. This was a truck stop diner. It was probably not the first time they'd broken up a fight in their restaurant.

"Um, guys—"

Luke's eyes flicked to me. "Kitten, why don't you take your ass outside and let the men talk."

Evan grabbed Luke's shirt at the collar. "I said don't fucking talk to her."

Luke pushed Evan and they stumbled into the aisle. Some lady near the back screamed—which was ridiculous, it was just a little scuffle—and the two guys from the kitchen surged in. I scooted closer to the window to stay out of the way.

Evan landed a punch to Luke's jaw and Luke answered with a jab to Evan's ribs. A couple of blows later, the men from the kitchen were on them, hauling them apart.

"Let's go," one of them grumbled, forcing Luke toward the door.

Evan growled as the other one stood between him and Luke. "Don't even think about it, buddy."

He let the guy lead him out. It was clear from the look on Evan's face, and the way he stalked down the aisle between the booths, that he was walking out by choice.

I grabbed my purse, thinking I might need to make a quick exit. But Luke and Evan obviously weren't going to keep fighting outside. Luke went straight to a truck and got in.

The waitress came back to my table, casting preoccupied glances outside. "Do you still want to order anything?"

I looked out the window again. Evan was pacing outside his truck while Luke pulled out of the parking lot.

"Yeah, how about some sausage, bacon, and toast. Enough for two, and I'll take it to go." I didn't know what Evan liked, but I figured he'd be hungry. I sure was. I didn't want to leave without breakfast because of some silly tussle.

"Okay. I'll get that going for you."

One of the guys from the kitchen paused by my table on his way back inside. "You all right?"

"Oh yeah, I'm fine. I'm just waiting for my order, then I'll get out of your way. I'm really sorry about all that. I don't know what happened."

"It's all right. Not your fault." He eyed me for a second. "You need any help?"

"No, I'm really okay. But thank you for asking."

He nodded and went back to the kitchen.

I watched Evan out the window while I waited for our breakfasts. He took Sasquatch out of the truck and walked him over to a grassy patch again, then put him back inside. I sipped my coffee. I could tell he was angry—I could almost feel it from here. But it wasn't my fault he'd gotten kicked out.

The waitress came back with a bag and the check.

"I know it's none of my business, but was that your ex-boyfriend or something?" she asked.

"No, that didn't have anything to do with me."

She raised her eyebrows like she didn't believe me. "Huh. Well, your guy sure is protective of you. Must be nice."

"Oh, he's not my guy. We're not together. We're traveling together, but not because we're together."

She glanced out the window toward where Evan stood next to his truck, her eyes sparkling with interest. No, not interest. It was undisguised attraction. Lust, even. Her tongue darted across her lower lip and I had the sudden urge to start a scuffle of my own.

I cleared my throat. "I should get going."

She blinked her eyes back to me and set the bag and the check on the table. "Sure. Have a nice day."

I scooped up the bag, wondering what was wrong with me. Who cared if some waitress had just eye-fucked Evan Bailey through the window? We were leaving and he'd probably never see her again. And even if he did, what did that have to do with me? I barely knew him.

I left some money on the table to cover the check—and a good tip for their trouble—and went outside.

Evan scowled at me as I walked toward his truck. There was a little bit of blood on his lower lip, but otherwise, he looked okay.

"How's your face?" I asked.

He licked his lip but missed the spot. Without thinking about it, I reached up with my thumb and rubbed it away.

His body went completely still and for a second, all I could feel was the small space of skin on the pad of my thumb, pressing against the dip just beneath his lower lip.

He stepped back and wiped his mouth with the back of his hand. "What the fuck took you so long?"

I held up the bag. "I was getting our breakfast."

"Ours?"

"Yes, I ordered you something. I figured you'd be hungry."

He grumbled something incoherent and opened the driver's side door.

I went around to the other side and got in. "Are you going to tell me what that was all about, or do I have to make up my own version?"

"That was Luke Haven. We don't like each other."

"Really? You acted like best friends."

He glared at me.

"Come on. What happened?"

"His family and my family have hated each other for generations," he said.

"You're kidding."

"Nope."

"It's like some kind of feud or something?"

"It probably doesn't make much sense if you're not from Tilikum. But yes, it's a feud."

"What started it?"

"No idea."

"So you're telling me you got in a fight in a diner hundreds of miles from home because your families have been feuding for generations and no one knows why?"

He was quiet for a moment. "No."

"No? I'm so confused."

"The feud is a thing, but we mostly just prank each other. My issues with Luke are... personal."

"Why?"

"None of your goddamn business."

"It's because you guys are competitors, isn't it? His shop restores cars and builds customs just like you. It's a turf war."

He didn't answer.

"Or is there more to it? Is it about a girl or something?"

I chewed on the inside of my lip, immediately regretting the question. I really didn't want to hear him say he hated Luke Haven because of a girl. Why? I had no idea. An unrequited love story from Evan's past shouldn't have mattered to me any more than the eye-fucking waitress.

"No, it's not about a girl. Luke's a salesman more than anything. He gets off on chasing down a deal. And he loves trying to screw me over. He plays dirty."

"Do you play dirty too?"

He looked at me again and the fire in his gaze made my heart race and a very surprising sense of arousal bloom in my core. He turned back to the road without answering.

Wow, was the heat on in here?

It was time to change the subject. I pulled one of the to-go containers out of the bag. "Do you want your breakfast? I just got you a bunch of meat and toast so it would be easier to eat on the road."

The glance he gave me this time was softer, his eyes flicking from my face down to the food. "Yeah, sure. Thanks."

I smiled and passed the food over. "You're welcome. And don't worry about Luke Haven. This is why you have me."

He grunted and I decided to pretend it wasn't arousing.

It wasn't easy.

Because everything he did, from the way he gripped the steering wheel to the way he'd stood up for me to Luke, was stupidly hot.

9

EVAN

I opened and closed my hand a few times, feeling the dull ache leftover from hitting Luke yesterday. It fucking figured that he'd be hot on the trail of the same car as me. Ever since I'd opened my shop, he'd been there at every turn, ready to screw me over. We competed for clients. For parts. For deals. And now he thought the 1970 Pontiac GTO was his ticket into America's Car Museum.

It wasn't going to happen.

Although the fact that my success rested on a girl who wore too much black eyeliner and talked to her plants wasn't doing much for my confidence.

And where the fuck was she?

I'd gotten up early to take Sasquatch out for some exercise, then picked up breakfast from a fast food place down the road. We were about thirty minutes from the old guy, in a town that made mine look like a thriving metropolis. But it had a couple of restaurants and a not-too-disgusting motel, so as far as stops went, it wasn't terrible.

Fiona had called the old guy last night and he'd said we could come see the car this morning. I was anxious to get over there. The last thing I needed was to find out he'd already sold it to Luke because princess mascara had taken her fucking time getting ready this morning.

She came out of her room—finally—carrying her houseplants with that damn smile plastered on her face. I didn't know what she was so happy about all the time. Her life was in shambles but she acted like everything was sunshine and rainbows.

No huge winter coat today, but she was dressed in yet another oversize sweatshirt. To be fair, it was unnaturally chilly for northern Arizona. This one had a hood and a pocket in front. And I was not the least bit intrigued by the shape I could just make out underneath her clothes. It was hard to tell, but she might have been hiding some banging curves under all that fabric.

Not that I cared.

"Good morning, Mr. Scowlypants."

Sasquatch jumped down and trotted over to her, his tail wagging.

"There's a good boy. I'll pet you when my hands are free, buddy."

"What have you been doing in there? Dying your hair a darker shade of black?"

She laughed. "It's not black, it's chestnut brown with purple lowlights, and it's a semi-permanent, so it'll fade back to my natural color without giving me roots."

"I don't care. We need to get going."

"I know, I know, I'm sorry. I overslept a little."

"You overslept? Luke is probably down at the old guy's farm right now badmouthing me."

"His name is Mr. Browning. Walt Browning."

"What?"

"He's not *the old guy*, he's Mr. Browning. It would probably help your cause if you remember his name."

I groaned. "For fuck's sake, can we just go?"

She smirked at me—fucking *smirked*. "You're very lucky you have me, Prince Not-Charming."

"Yeah, it's worked out great for me so far."

She just laughed again and carried her stupid houseplants to the passenger side.

I hesitated for a second, hearing Gram in the back of my head again. It wasn't my fault Fiona's hands were full and she'd have a hard time opening the truck door. Who brought plants on a road trip?

Rolling my eyes, I went around and opened the door for her.

"Thank you," she said in that same cheerful tone.

I didn't know what she was so happy about. We hadn't even had breakfast yet.

We ate on the way over and the food in my stomach helped take the edge off. But I was still pretty amped. I'd driven a lot of miles for a shot at one of my top five dream cars. The fact that Luke Haven stood in my way made me even more determined to buy it. A bidding war could be dangerous—I wasn't exactly swimming in cash—but the upside on a build like this was almost limitless. Especially if it got me into the museum.

I had to get this car.

The GPS took us down a long two-lane road flanked by scrubby fields. Walt Browning's land came up on our left and as we got closer, I was hit with a pang of envy. Fiona had called him a car hoarder, and she hadn't been wrong.

At a glance, I could see a ton of cars and trucks I'd have loved to get my hands on. An early seventies Challenger. A fifties Bel Air. Mustangs, Camaros, Chargers. He had hundreds of cars in varying states of decay lined in neat rows. So much potential. For a guy like me, this was basically paradise.

We turned onto a dirt road that served as his driveway. His house was set back from the road and there were more outbuildings behind it. Several vehicles were parked out front, most of them probably his. Unfortunately, the one I didn't want to see was there. Luke had beat us here.

"See," I grumbled, gesturing toward his truck.

"It'll be fine," she said brightly. "You have me."

Although I didn't share her optimism, there wasn't much I could do about it now.

We got out and I clipped on Sasquatch's leash. My shoes crunched on the gravel. Fiona walked ahead, shoving her hands in her front pocket. The back of her sweatshirt pulled up, revealing two very round ass cheeks in those tight leggings, sloping up to a narrow waist.

For a second, I couldn't look at anything else, not even the row of cars we were passing. Just the sway of her hips and the curve of her heart-shaped ass. It was mesmerizing, the kind of ass a guy could sink his teeth into.

Jesus, what was I doing?

Forcing my gaze up, I shook my head a little to get rid of the very vivid image of Fiona bent over, my hands on those lush ass cheeks, spreading her open.

Two days in a truck with her had obviously messed with my head.

She waved while she kept walking. "Hi, Mr. Browning. I'm Fiona."

A grizzled old man with a bald head and a stoop to his shoulders turned with a smile at the sound of her voice.

And sure enough, Luke was with him.

Fiona glanced back at me over her shoulder. "Behave yourself."

I grunted in acquiescence.

"Hi there, sweetheart," Mr. Browning said. "Good timing. We were just heading out to see the car."

We stopped a few feet away. I put Sasquatch in a sit and met Luke's eyes.

"Bailey," he said with a slight tip of his head.

I returned the chin tip. "Haven."

"You know each other?" Mr. Browning asked.

"They're from the same town," Fiona interjected smoothly. "Isn't that funny? This is my friend, Evan Bailey."

"Call me Walt," the old man said. "I suppose I should show you boys what I've got. See if you're still interested."

"Lead the way," Luke said with a smile at Walt, then cast a glare in my direction.

I returned it.

Fucker.

Walt led us toward one of several outbuildings. Inside, he had a few cars covered with canvas.

He gestured to one and nodded. "Go ahead."

I handed the leash to Fiona. Then Luke took one side while I took the other and we peeled back the covering on one of the baddest cars ever made.

The Judge.

I drank her in, every line and curve. She needed work—a lot of work. The body was in rough shape and I had no idea whether she ran. Didn't matter. I'd bring her back to life and make her purr.

"It has a numbers-matching engine and transmission,"

Walt said. "Doesn't run, but I'm sure either one of you could get her going."

"Absolutely," Luke said.

I glared at him.

"How long have you had her?" Fiona asked.

"Probably twenty years," Walt said. "I always wanted to get working on her, but I never could seem to find the time."

"Totally understandable," Luke said. "You have quite the collection here."

I took slow steps, circling the car, only half listening. I could already see her finished. The way the light would glint off her sleek lines. The roar of that engine. She had the potential to be gorgeous—a true show piece.

I was fucking in love with this car.

Luke said something—I didn't catch what—and the fact that I wasn't following the conversation jolted me back to reality. Walt smiled at Luke, nodding along. Damn it. Was I going to have to schmooze this guy into selling it to me? I didn't want to have to sweet talk him, I wanted to make a goddamn offer.

"Your asking price is more than fair," Luke said.

I was about to tell Luke to shut the hell up when Fiona stepped smoothly in front of me. "So you said it has a numbers-matching engine and transmission, which is such a great find. There's a lot to be said for authenticity in a build like this. Evan, what do you think about the interior?"

"This will all need to be replaced," I gestured to the dash. "But I'd reuse the dials and replace the wood trim so it looks original."

Walt glanced between me and Luke, crossing his arms. "What about color?"

Luke shrugged. "You could go a lot of different directions with a car like this. Black is always classic. Or maybe red."

I kept gazing at the car, picturing the work she'd need. "No. Atoll blue, just like when she was new. Matching blue interior. Period-correct bucket seats won't be too hard to source, and I can reupholster them to get a color match if I have to."

"What else?" Fiona asked.

I was hardly aware that I had an audience. I kept doing the work in my head, seeing each step as it would unfold. "The engine just needs some love to get her humming again. This isn't a resto-mod; no modernizing her. She needs to be original from the suspension on up. Blue with the red pinstriping. I can get new side mirrors off a similar model. Put in a three-spoke Formula steering wheel."

"You're the one," Walt said, pointing at me. "You know what she's supposed to look like."

Fiona bounced up onto her tiptoes and clapped.

I stared at the car. Holy shit.

Walt turned to Luke. "Sorry, son. When I know, I know. But if you want, I can still try to make the trip worth your while, if there's something else you see that you like."

Luke's glare at me quickly melted into a smile for Walt. "Yeah, I actually saw a few cars I might be interested in."

"Feel free to take a look around," Walt said. "I have a '69 Mustang Boss in the building next door."

"That I definitely need to see."

"Fiona, sweetheart, I'll be right back. I'm just going to walk Luke over there, then we can come back and hammer out the details."

"Sounds great, Mr. Browning. Thank you so much."

Walt and Luke left us alone with the Judge. I caressed the back fender with my fingertips. This car was going to be fucking amazing when I was done with her.

Fiona beamed at me, flashing those bright white teeth,

and it hit me. She'd done it. She'd convinced the old guy—
or maybe *we'd* convinced the old guy—to sell me the Judge,
which meant I had to uphold my end of the deal. I had to let
her use my space to fix her car.

I wasn't getting rid of her when we got back to town.

And I had no idea how to feel about that.

10

EVAN

*F*iona pointed out the window. "It's up there on the right."

The sight of the motel sign was a relief. My eyelids had been getting increasingly heavy for about the last hour. It had been a long day on the road, but I'd wanted to cover as much ground as possible before we stopped. Pulling the weight of the car on the trailer slowed us down and I didn't want the drive back to take longer than necessary.

But I'd been driving for hours and I needed sleep.

I turned off the highway and found a spot with space for my truck and trailer. We left Sasquatch in the back seat and went to the office to get our room keys.

The front desk was illuminated by a broken light fixture on the ceiling. Dated wood paneling and thin carpet meant the rooms were probably shabby at best. But there wasn't another motel for miles.

A middle-aged woman who looked as tired as I felt gave us a small smile.

"Hi," Fiona said, approaching the desk. "I'm Fiona Gallagher. I called a few hours ago."

The desk clerk clicked her mouse and typed something on her keyboard. I stuck my credit card on the counter to cover my room.

"Let me get your keys," the woman said. She opened a drawer and pulled out two keys, each hanging from a large black keychain. "You're in one-twenty. Ground floor, down that way."

"Oh, um, we actually need two rooms," Fiona said.

I let out an annoyed breath. I'd been sitting right there when Fiona had called to see if they had any rooms available. She'd clearly asked for two.

"Sorry about that." The woman went back to her computer. "That's actually our last room. We're renovating, so half our rooms are under construction right now. I'm really sorry."

"Um..." Fiona brushed her bangs out of her eyes.

I swiped the keys off the counter and shoved one at Fiona. "It's fine. We just need a place to crash."

After paying for the room, we went out to the truck to get Sasquatch and our bags—thankfully she opted to leave her plants in the truck tonight—then headed to room one-twenty.

She went in first and paused just inside the door. "Oh boy."

I followed her in with Sasquatch at my heels, wondering what the fuck was wrong now. Everything looked fine. The room was dated and worn, but it seemed clean. Small TV, tiny fridge, thick curtains blocking out the light from the parking lot. The bed was—

The bed. The *only* bed. A queen-sized bed, at that.

Well, shit.

Sasquatch was already sniffing his way around, making sure there were no unexpected surprises lurking in the corners. For a second, I envied my dog. He could curl up anywhere and sleep like a baby. And it looked like I was going to be on the floor with him. Obviously, I couldn't make her do it.

"You can take the bed," I grumbled, dropping my duffel bag. "I'll sleep on the floor."

"No, you can't sleep on the floor."

"Looks like I have to."

She looked back and forth between me and the bed a few times, opening and closing her mouth like she wasn't sure what she wanted to say.

I kicked off my shoes. "Do you want the bathroom first?"

"Um, sure. But you really don't have to sleep on the floor."

"It's fine. I'm too big."

"Evan—"

"Just use the fucking bathroom so we can go to sleep."

She hiked her backpack up her shoulder and her lip twitched in a smile. "Okay, okay. I see he needs his beauty sleep."

I rolled my eyes, but she ignored me and went into the bathroom.

Sasquatch plopped down in a corner and looked up at me with his muzzle resting on his front paws.

"What?"

He blinked.

"I'm doing the gentlemanly thing and giving her the bed, even though I'm the one who needs sleep because I have to drive."

He got up, circled once, and laid back down.

"Yeah, buddy, you've got the right idea."

I found an extra blanket in the closet. It wasn't much, but it was better than the threadbare carpet. I spread it out next to the bed and grabbed one of the pillows. Not exactly comfortable, but better than sleeping in my truck.

I was tired enough that I started to drift off while Fiona did her thing. I heard the door open and I could see the glow of the bathroom light from behind my closed eyes.

"Evan," she whispered. "You can have the bathroom if you want."

Opening my eyes, I grunted a reply.

And almost choked on my tongue.

Fiona stood at the foot of the bed, folding her big sweatshirt. I'd only seen her wrapped up in too-large clothes. Her huge coat or baggy sweatshirts. Sure, I'd caught a glimpse of her ass being hugged by her leggings earlier, but that had done nothing to prepare me for what she actually looked like.

Fuck.

She was dressed in a blue tank top and a pair of blue plaid shorts. The whole getup looked like pajamas, but that wasn't what had my attention. As if I'd lost control of them, my eyes traveled from a set of tits a guy could get lost in, down to a narrow waist, wide hips, thick thighs. She was the definition of curves. Her body was a work of art—soft and feminine—adorned with floral tattoos on one shoulder and upper arm. I spied more ink on her thigh and when she turned—

Oh fuck. That ass. In leggings it had looked good, but barely concealed in plaid pajama shorts? Kill me.

The shock of sudden arousal made my head spin. What the fuck was wrong with me? So what if she was hot underneath her clothes? I'd seen hot women before.

But no one had made my dick react like this. She wasn't even looking at me and it was like she'd reached right into my pants and wrapped her hand around my cock.

That visual wasn't helping.

"Hey. Eyes up here, buddy."

Shit, she'd caught me staring at her ass. "I didn't know you had any ink." Not the best excuse, but she did have a tattoo on her thigh.

"Oh, yeah, I have several," she said brightly. She moved closer and turned so the side of her leg faced me, then pulled the hem of her shorts higher up her thigh. "This one kind of winds around back here too."

My heart pounded against my ribs as she slowly twisted, lifting her shorts across the smooth skin of one of those luscious ass cheeks. She was so close, all I'd have to do is sit up and I could haul her on top of me.

No, big guy. I sent my dick a mental reprimand. *Stand down. This is how we get in trouble.*

He didn't listen. I tried to ignore him. It wasn't easy.

Fiona, clearly oblivious to my struggle to maintain control of my own body, turned to face me again. She traced her finger along her shoulder and upper arm. "And this one, obviously."

"They're nice," I managed to grind out. "Are you done with the bathroom?"

"Yep. All yours."

"Took you long enough," I muttered and got up, keeping my gaze on anything but her.

I grabbed my bag and went into the bathroom, shutting the door behind me harder than necessary. My blood ran hot in my veins and the ache in my groin was annoying as fuck. How was I going to sleep a few feet away from... all that?

Easy. She was just some girl. A few days from now, she'd be gone and I wouldn't even remember her name, let alone the type of flower she had tattooed on her thigh.

Did she have any other tattoos?

Jesus, I didn't care about her tattoos. I just needed to get some sleep. The more ground we covered tomorrow, the sooner I'd be rid of her.

I needed to be on my own. I operated best that way. All this time spent in close quarters with her was fucking with my head.

Or rather, with my dick. My head knew what was best for me. The aching erection in my pants did not.

I decided a quick shower was in order. I'd wash off the road and take care of this biological overreaction so I could get some fucking rest.

The hot water felt good, calming my nerves and soothing my knotted muscles. I washed, half expecting my erection to go away on its own.

It didn't.

Fine. Bracing myself against the shower wall, I took my cock in my hand. Just pressure at first. A squeeze at the base. An answering pulse rippled through me. God, that felt good already. Apparently I needed this.

Closing my eyes, I took deep breaths as I started to stroke. The image that came to mind was only half real—I hadn't actually seen her like this—but was there any point in fighting it?

Not when I knew it was going to get me off fast.

I could practically feel my fingers digging into her ass. See her pussy on display for me. It wasn't her—didn't have to be her. It was just a fantasy. Just my imagination. Just some girl bent over in front of me, ready for me to fuck her dirty.

Stroking harder now, I kept that image in my mind. I needed to get this over with. Needed release. My cock was thick, throbbing in my fist, white-hot tension building fast.

I held the groans I wanted to unleash locked in my throat as I rubbed it out. That was it. Just a little more and I'd come all over that hot ass.

Fuck yes. My teeth ground together, my jaw tight, and the muscles in my back clenched. The tension in my groin skyrocketed as I raced to the edge, and I rolled with the fantasy in my head, picturing the come hitting her ass. Claiming her. Marking her as mine.

My dick pulsed hard and I barely contained a throaty growl. I started to come and, oh god, sweet relief. I stroked it out while my cock throbbed in my hand, over and over. Fuck, that felt good.

Pausing for a moment, I kept my eyes closed, basking in that brief moment of post-orgasm bliss. I was breathing hard but the aching tension in my groin was appeased.

There. Better. I was sated.

At least for now.

I finished cleaning up and got out of the shower. Now that my erection was gone, exhaustion swept through me. I dried off and tugged on some underwear and a t-shirt. Hopefully I'd be warm enough, although at this point, I didn't think it would matter. I was past the point of needing comfort to fall asleep. I'd be out as soon as my head hit the pillow.

Fiona was in bed when I came out, curled on her side beneath the covers. She hugged the edge of the bed, like she'd tried to leave room for me. Which was kind of sweet in a weird way. I'd told her I'd sleep on the floor.

Then again, maybe it wasn't sweet. Maybe she was trying to keep as much space between us as possible.

Didn't matter.

I got into my makeshift bed and closed my eyes. Clean,

relaxed. The hard floor underneath me wasn't so bad. Any second now, sleep would overtake me.

But it didn't.

I waited, trying to clear my mind and accept sleep. To slip into oblivion. But I still couldn't.

Then she moved.

Sheets whispered across her skin and my eyes flew open. I was thinking about her ass again. Was she wearing those pajamas to bed? I never thought I could be so preoccupied with blue plaid shorts, but here I was.

Not sleeping.

Fuck.

She moved again, and this time it sounded like she'd turned over. Maybe turned toward me. Was she having trouble sleeping?

An instinct I thought I'd suppressed flared to life. I had a sudden urge to ask her if she was okay. Maybe even climb up in that bed with her, hook an arm around her waist, and pull her next to me.

That was a good way to get punched in the throat, even if I'd wanted to do it.

Which I didn't.

I turned away from the bed and adjusted the pillow. This was fine. I just needed sleep.

Her soft voice tickled the back of my neck. "Evan?"

Don't answer. Pretend you're asleep. "Yeah?" *Damn it.*

"Are you sure you can sleep down there?"

"I'm fine."

"Because it's not a big deal if you want to sleep up here. I'll stay on my side of the bed so you have room."

There was something soothing about her quiet voice. I was tired, and I didn't particularly want her talking to me, but I didn't feel the urge to snap at her either.

And the bed would be more comfortable than the floor. "Okay."

I climbed onto the bed and slid beneath the covers, keeping my back to her. It was the oddest thing: She didn't move much, just shifted a little. But I could have sworn I felt her relax.

Stranger still, it made me relax.

I settled into the bed, my eyes heavy. In the back of my mind, I wondered why lying next to her made a difference.

It wasn't her; it was just the bed.

That was a lie. It was her.

But I was too tired to worry about what that meant.

*N*estling into the warmth of the bed, I decided not to open my eyes. It was probably morning, but my alarm hadn't gone off yet. I was so warm and comfortable, I didn't want to move until I absolutely had to.

Except, why was my pillow breathing?

That thought woke me up more, and as my awareness grew, I realized that maybe—just maybe—my head wasn't resting on my pillow. That it might be—

Oh god.

Keeping my eyes firmly closed for fear of what I'd discover if I opened them, I tried to make sense of what I felt. My cheek rested against something warm and firm, and I was lying at an angle that wasn't exactly flat. I was still in the bed, but I didn't feel the softness of a pillow or the mattress beneath me.

Risking a peek, I cracked one eye open and got a close-up view of a t-shirt stretched across a broad chest.

Evan took a deep breath, his lungs expanding beneath me. Oh my god, I was draped across his body, my face squished against his chest. Was the corner of my mouth wet?

Yep, I'd drooled on him.

This was how I was going to die, in a bed in a cheap motel with a guy I'd gone on the road with after knowing for ten minutes. Cause of death: abject humiliation.

I still hadn't moved, but I was afraid if I did, I'd wake him up. And I really, really didn't want Evan to wake up. Not like this.

Maybe there was a way I could slide off him and it would just feel like the covers moving. I could roll over and pretend I was still asleep.

It was the perfect plan.

Slowly, carefully, I lifted my head off his chest, trying to pretend there wasn't a drool spot right on his nipple. Maybe he wouldn't notice. Or it would dry before he woke up.

A girl could hope.

Still moving as slowly as I could, I started to roll to my side.

He moved, clamping his thick arm around me, and pulled me against him. My eyes squeezed shut and I froze, not even daring to breathe.

But his chest rose and fell in the same steady rhythm. He was still asleep.

Of course he was still asleep. He wouldn't have been holding me like this if he were aware of what he was doing.

Okay, new plan. Get enormous heavy arm off me, *then* roll over and pretend to be sleeping.

I moved a little, trying to wiggle his arm down without waking him. It moved off my waist, his open palm sliding across my body.

Almost there.

He stopped with his huge hand right on my ass.

My eyes widened.

His hand squeezed.

Suddenly I really wanted to know what he was dreaming about.

He squeezed again, kneading into my flesh in a way that made it very easy to guess what was going on behind his closed eyes.

I didn't know whether to be mortified or aroused. Truthfully, I was a lot of both.

The slow breath I took to calm my nerves didn't help. Dear god, he smelled good. He'd showered before bed and the result was a clean, manly smell, something no cologne could ever replicate. The weight of his arm and his hand on my ass gave me just a hint of his strength, and it was all too easy to imagine him manhandling me on a bed. Or a couch. Or in the back seat of a muscle car.

Focus, Fiona. You're using Evan as a pillow and he can never, ever know.

I waited for his grip on my ass cheek to ease a little, then carefully tried again.

His sharp intake of breath sent a rush of heat crawling across my cheeks. Oh no, was he awake? Reflexively, I lifted my head just enough to peek at his face.

His eyes were open.

Quick, Fiona, look away.

It was too late. We'd made eye contact. Horrible, horrible eye contact.

His eyebrows shot up, he let go of my ass, and I scrambled to get off him. The sheets tangled in my legs and I kicked wildly to get free, while Evan rolled over so fast he fell off the bed with a loud thump.

He groaned as he stood. I pulled at the sheets, still trying to disentangle myself.

"What the fuck," he muttered.

"Um..." These sheets were like a spiderweb.

Sasquatch appeared at his side, sniffing the edge of the bed, looking for the source of his daddy's distress.

Evan's gaze swung back to me, then his eyes widened and he quickly turned his head. "Uh, Fiona."

"What? I'm sorry. I don't know what happened." I kicked again, trying to get the spiderweb sheet off my foot.

"Your, um..."

My foot broke free. Finally. I looked up at Evan. Sure enough, he had a wet spot on his t-shirt. "I'm sorry I drooled on your man nipple."

He absently touched his chest, but kept his head turned, like he couldn't look at me. "No, that's not..."

"What?"

"Your shirt."

"My shirt?" My nipple tingled, hardening at the brush of air against skin. Not fabric against skin. Air.

Oh no.

I looked down to find my left boob hanging out of my tank top.

Instead of calmly moving my shirt so I was appropriately covered, like a normal person, I over-corrected. I yanked the fabric too hard, exposing my right boob to the air.

Fortunately, Evan wasn't looking. Or was he? I didn't lift my gaze to find out. I fixed my shirt so it covered both boobs and checked my shorts to make sure I hadn't undressed myself while I was sleeping. Why would I have done that? No idea, but I'd just woken up sprawled on top of Evan. Anything was possible.

"Well, after that I won't be needing coffee to wake up," I said, giving my tank top a final little tug. "I shouldn't be surprised that happened. My boobs are not small. I have the hardest time keeping them in my shirt when I wear a tank top to bed. I think the lesson here is, next time I'm sharing a bed with a guy I barely know, wear something with more fabric."

Evan cleared his throat. He still wasn't looking at me. "So much for not moving around when you sleep."

I winced. It was possible I'd exaggerated my lack of bed hog habits. But I hadn't slept in a bed with someone else in a while. Sure, my ex had complained that I always stole the blankets and could take up an entire king mattress, leaving him with no space. But I'd been comfortable with him. I'd been sure I'd stay away from Evan.

Except... wait...

I glanced around. Something still felt off.

"Didn't you start out over there?" I gestured to the other side of the bed.

"What? No."

"Yes, you did. Look, the blanket you had on the floor is over there. I woke up on top of you, but you were on my side of the bed."

His dark brow furrowed and he opened his mouth— probably to argue—but snapped it closed again.

"Note to self. Evan Bailey is a bigger bed hog than me, so make sure our next room has two beds."

"I'm not a bed hog."

I laughed. "You so are."

"I'm just big. I take up a lot of space."

I opened my mouth again, about to say something snarky about his size, when my eyes were inexplicably drawn to his groin.

Evan had morning wood.

A lot of morning wood.

Huge morning wood.

Stop staring at his dick, Fiona. Stop it.

But I couldn't. It was massive.

He was massive. His dick size shouldn't have been a surprise—kind of like my big boobs always falling out of tank tops while I slept. It was only logical.

But maybe it wasn't surprise that kept my eyes locked on his groin for more than long enough for him to see exactly what I was doing. Maybe it was awe.

Stare in wonder at the majesty of Evan Bailey's mighty dick.

"Sorry." I tore my eyes away. "Bathroom. I mean, do you need the bathroom? Sasquatch probably needs to pee. Are you going to take him, or do you want me to do it? So you can go use the bathroom. Or maybe you need to wait? I guess I don't really know how that works for guys in the morning. Guys like you, at least. With... all that. Never mind."

"You go first."

"Are you sure, because—"

"Fiona," he snapped.

"Fine, fine." I put my hands up. "I guess with all that bed-hogging you were doing last night, you didn't get enough sleep, grumpy-grump man."

"For fuck's sake," he muttered.

I laughed and scooted off the bed, careful to keep my boobs covered. "I know, hurry up, Fiona, we need to get on the road. I'll hurry."

"Good."

THE SCENERY FLEW by as Evan drove down the open high-way. We passed farmland, fences, horses and herds of cattle.

My eyes were heavy, my body lulled into relaxation by the hum of the tires on the road.

We'd left the motel early—true to my word, I'd hurried to get ready—and covered a lot of ground already. I shifted a little in my seat and my bladder reminded me that we hadn't stopped for a pee break yet. There wasn't much along this stretch of highway. I hoped we'd come to a town soon. Or at least a gas station.

A new song came on the radio and I idly sang along. I didn't actually know all the words to this song—or most songs—but I liked to sing anyway. Evan glanced at me out of the corner of his eye a few times, but didn't complain. So I didn't stop.

Not that I would have. I'd have just sassed him back until he grumbled under his breath.

Riling him up was fun.

We seemed to have recovered from the embarrassment of waking up on top of each other. Or, more accurately, me on top of him. The drool thing was pretty bad, and him seeing my boobs wasn't ideal. But we'd moved on. It felt like our fledgling friendship had been tested, and we'd passed.

It made me wonder if he thought of us as friends or if that was just me.

My phone rang and one glance at the screen had my stomach in a knot. It was my dad.

I thought about ignoring the call. But maybe I just needed to get it over with. Rip the bandage off, so to speak.

"Hi, Dad."

Evan's head whipped around to look at me.

"Where are you?" Dad asked.

"I'm on the road." Perfect. Not a lie, but I didn't have to tell him any details, either.

"You're supposed to be at work."

"I told you I'm not coming back to work."

"Fiona," he said, his tone maddeningly patronizing, "you can't just not show up to work."

"You can if you quit. That's actually the expectation."

He let out an exasperated breath. "Quit? Come on, don't you think you're taking things a little too far?"

"No.

"Fiona, you're an adult. Maybe it's time you learned to share your daddy."

The stream of words that tried to claw its way out of my throat was too thick and jumbled. My mouth opened, but nothing coherent would come out. "You think... but she's... that's not... oh my god."

"When you're done pouting, we'll talk. And hurry up. I'll let this go one more day, but I expect to see you at work in the morning."

He ended the call and I moved my phone away from my ear, staring at it like it might sprout wings and fly out the window. Anger pulsed through my veins, making me tremble.

I pulled my legs up onto the seat and hugged my knees to my chest. Evan didn't say anything, just kept his eyes on the road. Angry tears stung my eyes. I didn't want to cry, but sometimes I did when I was mad. I hated it. It made me angrier, which made the tears worse. A vicious cycle, especially when I had an audience.

Evan turned up the volume on the radio.

Really, Evan? Seeing a girl upset makes you so uncomfortable, you have to drown her out with music?

I opened my mouth to say just that, but before I could utter a single word, he started to sing.

His deep throaty voice was low but quiet, his lips barely moving as he mumbled the lyrics. The lump in my throat eased and the stinging in my eyes began to dissipate. Keeping my gaze on the passing landscape—I was afraid I'd break the spell if I looked at him directly—I took a cleansing breath.

Quietly, my own voice sounding timid in my ears, I started to sing along with him.

Without looking at each other, we sang softly. It wasn't an exuberant road trip melody, our voices ringing out in the cab of his pickup. Just subtle nods of our heads in time with the rhythm, murmured lyrics, and mellow voices. I hummed along when I didn't know the words, joining him again in the chorus.

A new song came on and Evan kept on singing. Although his baritone stayed quiet, I could practically feel the resonance thrumming through my body. His voice was rich and soothing and oh my god, so sexy. My insides went molten. It was a miracle I didn't melt into a puddle on the floor.

Sasquatch poked his head over my shoulder and I gave him a good scratch. And from the corner of my eye, I caught Evan glancing at me, the hint of a smile playing on his normally scowly face.

And a little voice in the back of my head said, *Uh-oh.*

12

EVAN

$\mathcal{T}$he trailer bounced along the road leading up to my place. Fiona was sound asleep, the lurching of the truck doing nothing to rouse her. Of course, it was almost three in the morning, and we'd been up early. It had been a long day.

I staunchly avoided thinking about our morning in the motel room, but the feel of her ass was imprinted on my hand. I couldn't get rid of it any more than I could unsee her naked boobs.

She had really great boobs.

Stop it, Evan.

The road flattened and my shop came into view. Fortunately, there was no need to unload the Pontiac tonight. I'd take care of it in the morning. Right now, all I wanted was my bed.

I glanced at Fiona again. She'd wadded up one of her sweatshirts as a makeshift pillow and curled her legs up onto the seat.

"Hey." I touched her arm. "Wake up. We're here."

Gasping, she sat up with a jolt. "Are we home?"

The way she'd phrased that almost made me chuckle. "Yeah. Come on, let's go get some sleep."

She rubbed her eyes and looked around. "Oh, okay. I figured you'd stop for the night somewhere, but here we are. Um, give me a second, my brain isn't working. I need my keys."

"Why do you need your keys?"

She was already digging through her purse. "I need to go find a place to stay. Is there a motel in town? I hope their office is open."

"No..." I paused and she blinked sleepy eyes at me. "Just come in. You can sleep here."

"That's okay, you don't have to do that."

"It's three in the morning. Come inside."

The corners of her mouth curved upward in a grateful smile. "Thanks."

I didn't like it when she looked at me like that. It poked at something deep inside my chest. Something I desperately needed to ignore.

While she gathered her things, I took Sasquatch to do his business, then met her at my front door. She was carrying her plants—because of course she was, the weirdo.

I unlocked the door and ushered her inside. "You can set those wherever."

"Thanks again. Really."

I shuffled down the short hallway and dropped my bag in my room. And there was Gram's voice in the back of my head again, scolding me about manners and being a gentleman. I didn't want to let Fiona have my room. After days on the road, I wanted to sleep in my own damn bed.

Fuck. Fine.

"Fi—" I stopped short. Where was she?

I found her already sprawled on the couch, an arm

draped over her forehead, her eyes closed. She was still dressed, although she'd taken off her shoes, and the blanket Gram had given me was pulled haphazardly over her.

Sasquatch looked up at me. He'd curled up right next to the couch, instead of on his bed, as if to keep watch over her.

"Really?"

He closed his eyes.

Whatever. She was fine. My traitor dog was fine. I was going to bed.

THE SMELL of food woke me. Light shone through the blinds but Sasquatch hadn't gotten me up yet. That was weird. And why did I smell food?

My sheets were a mess and apparently I'd kicked my comforter completely off the bed. What the hell was wrong with me? I was used to sleeping alone, and I was a big guy so I definitely took up the entire mattress. But this was ridiculous.

And what smelled so good? Was Fiona cooking out there?

My stomach rumbled and my mouth was already watering. After a steady diet of fast food and diner fare, a home-cooked meal sounded great.

I got up, but hesitated. What was she going to be wearing when I went out there? Those fucking blue pajamas again? She'd gone to sleep in her clothes, so probably not. But the thought of Fiona cooking breakfast in those shorts in my kitchen made my morning erection ache.

Not that I was attracted to her.

Okay, physically I clearly had an issue. But that's all it was. Just physical. I wasn't even sure if I liked her. She'd helped me get the Pontiac and I owed her big for that. But that was it.

I tugged on a pair of gray sweats, grabbed a t-shirt, sniffed it, and put it on. Then I ducked into the bathroom to take care of business—difficult, given the boner I was sporting. Which was only a case of morning wood and had nothing to do with the girl currently in my house.

Nothing at all.

Fiona was indeed in my kitchen, cooking breakfast. Something sizzled in a pan, and I smelled sausage and a hint of coffee in the air.

Thankfully she was back to her big sweatshirt and leggings. Her hair was up in a messy bun and her feet were bare. Sasquatch sat nearby, casually watching her cook. It was hard to tell if he was paying attention to her or the food. Probably both.

She glanced over her shoulder and smiled. "Morning, sunshine. I hope you don't mind me helping myself to your kitchen. And your food."

My mouth watered appreciatively. "It's fine."

"How'd you sleep?" she asked, turning back to the stove. "I slept surprisingly well, all things considered. Totally zonked out. I'm surprised I woke up as early as I did, but I guess I'd already been sleeping in the truck for a while before we got here."

I went to the cupboard for a mug. "I slept okay."

She smiled at me again while I poured my coffee. "Good. I'm sure you needed it."

I found myself oddly caught in her gaze. She looked different. With a quick flick of her fingertips, she brushed her bangs out of her eyes, and I realized she wasn't wearing makeup.

She probably hadn't been yesterday morning either, but

I hadn't noticed. To be fair, I'd been trying very hard to keep my eyes off her—for reasons I was not thinking about now. Her normally smoky eye shadow and thick eyeliner were gone, revealing naturally long lashes and eyes that existed somewhere on the spectrum between hazel and green.

"You okay?"

I tore my gaze away and set the coffee pot down. "Yeah. Fine."

God, she was distracting.

She finished cooking and we dished up in the kitchen. I had a small table with four chairs, so we each took a seat. Amazingly, she didn't talk much while we ate.

Sasquatch looked up, and a few seconds later I heard a car outside. That was weird. It was early, and I wasn't expecting anyone.

Which meant it was probably one of my brothers.

I groaned.

Fiona raised her eyebrows. "What's wrong?"

Great, now one of them was going to walk in—it's not like they ever knocked—and find me eating breakfast with her. Someone was about to get a hell of a lot of wrong ideas. I was never going to hear the end of this.

Before I could reply, someone knocked twice, then opened the door without waiting for an answer.

Gavin strolled in, his mouth already running. Sasquatch barked, but he knew him well enough so he let him in.

"Hey, you're back. I figured you were. So I was thinking —" He stopped mid-sentence with his mouth still open, his eyes landing on Fiona. "Oh shit. Sorry, I didn't know you had a lady guest."

"She's not a lady guest."

Gavin tilted his head, looking at her. "Well I don't think

she's a dude, and you just said *she*, so I'll take that as confirmation that she's a girl."

Fiona laughed and put her fork down. "You're correct about the girl part, but I'm not his lady guest. Which is to say, I wasn't here to sleep with him. I slept over, but not for that reason. I was on the couch. I'm just here to fix my car."

Instead of looking confused, Gavin grinned, like that all made perfect sense. He came to the table and plopped down in a chair. "Hey. I'm Gavin Bailey."

Something in his tone made my hackles rise.

"Fiona Gallagher," she said. "Very nice to meet you, Gavin. You must be one of Evan's brothers?"

"That I am. I'm the youngest. It took them five tries to achieve perfection, but they finally got it right with me."

She laughed again.

I made a fist under the table.

"Would you like some breakfast?" she asked. "I sort of overdid it, so there's plenty."

Gavin licked his lips. "I'd love to have breakfast with you."

I shot him a glare.

He ignored me.

"Don't get up," he said, rising from his seat. "You don't need to interrupt your meal on my account. In fact, is there anything I can get you?"

"What are you doing?" I asked.

"I'm just asking if she needs anything from the kitchen." He flicked his gaze back to her, his dimples puckering. "Anything you need, I'm happy to oblige."

She bit her lip, stifling a laugh. "No, I'm fine. But thank you."

He went into the kitchen and brought back a plate of

eggs and sausage. Before sitting down, he adjusted his chair, moving it closer to Fiona.

I growled at him.

He grinned at me.

"This looks delicious," he said, poking at his food with his fork. "I already ate, but who am I kidding, I'm always hungry."

"Why are you here?" I asked.

He took a bite of eggs and groaned as he slid the fork out of his mouth. "Oh my god. So good."

"Thank you," Fiona said, gracing him with another smile.

"I hope my brother was appropriately appreciative and made lots of yummy noises and said thank you."

"Yummy noises?" I asked.

She stifled another laugh. "There's definitely been a lack of yummy noises."

"He's kind of an animal, living out here all by himself, so there's no telling how he'll do when forced to relate to other humans."

"Shut up, Gavin."

"So, Fiona, tell me all about you."

She glanced at me, as if to say she wasn't quite sure what to make of my brother. "Well, you know my name. I used to work for my dad, but I quit, and now I'm on my way to stay with my mom in Iowa. I guess I'm looking for a fresh start."

"I love that," he said around a bite of sausage. "That's badass and brave."

Her cheeks flushed the slightest hint of pink. "Thanks. I don't feel very brave, though. I'm pretty scared."

"Bravery isn't the absence of fear," I said, surprising myself with my reply. "It's feeling fear and doing it anyway."

Fiona met my eyes and there was that sensation in my

chest again. A tightness—or maybe it was a fullness. Something pushing against the empty space where my heart used to live.

"I like that," she said. "Thanks."

"That's deep, bro," Gavin said and shoveled more food into his mouth.

I didn't want to admit it out loud, but I was curious if that was what Gavin felt. Whether he felt fear and faced it down, or simply didn't feel it at all.

"Why are you here?" I asked him again. "Other than to eat my food."

"The breakfast was an unexpected bonus, as was meeting you." He flashed Fiona another smile. "By the way, if you need a place to stay that doesn't remind you of a creepy cabin in a horror movie, you're more than welcome to come to our place. I promise none of us would try to see you naked or anything."

"That's very gentlemanly of you. And more than I can say of him." She winked at me.

"*Evan*," Gavin said, sounding an awful lot like Gram. "Why would you do such a thing to this sweet, beautiful girl?"

"For fuck's sake," I muttered. "I didn't try to look at her naked. Why am I even talking to you about this? Go home."

"Nah, home is boring. Peanut butter and jelly are both on duty today. That's why I came out here."

"Peanut butter and jelly?" Fiona asked. "Is that what you call your roommates?"

"Not where they can hear me."

I rolled my eyes. "He lives with two of our brothers. They're twins."

"Twins? That's cool."

"Yeah, they're identical, but total opposites, except they

have the same job," Gavin said. "Kind of fascinating when you think about it."

"If you're bored, why don't you bother Asher? He lives right next door to you."

"True, but I had a feeling I'd have more fun if I came out here. Which isn't usually the case, because let's be honest, you're a grumpy bastard." He grinned at Fiona again. "But it appears I made the right choice."

If he didn't quit flirting with her, I was going to—

Going to what? Why did I care if my brother flirted with her? Gavin flirted with everyone; it didn't mean anything. And even if it did... why should that matter to me?

It didn't.

"So, Fiona, do you have plans tonight?" he asked.

"Knock it off," I roared, standing so fast my chair fell backward.

"What?" he asked, feigning innocence. "I was just wondering."

I grabbed his plate and dropped it on top of mine. "No."

"No, what?" Gavin asked, putting up his hands.

Fiona did that lip-bite thing again, like she was trying not to smile. "I am pretty busy, actually. My car needs a new clutch and I want to get it done as quickly as possible so I can get out of your brother's way."

I took the plates and stalked into the kitchen, irritation knotting the muscles in my shoulders.

"That sucks," he said. "I have a better idea. Evan, you fix her clutch, and I'll show her around Tilikum."

The plates clanked when I set them on the counter. Any harder and I would have broken them.

"Thanks, but I've got it," she said before I could yell at him again. "He's nice enough to let me use his shop. That's all I need."

"Wow, he's doing something nice for a person? You must be magic."

Fiona laughed. "Not really. I helped him with something, so he's helping me in return."

"Huh," Gavin said. I turned and he was watching me with his arms crossed. "Interesting."

"What's interesting?" I asked.

"Fiona," he said without missing a beat. "Have you talked to her at all? She's fascinating."

"Don't you have something better to do?"

"No, this is really fun."

"Go away."

"Fine, but only because Fiona has work to do and I don't want to keep her." He stood. "Thank for breakfast. Bro, I'll see you tonight."

"Tonight?" I asked.

"It's Tuesday."

"Right. Dinner. Fine."

"Fiona, meeting you was definitely the best thing that's happened to me in a long time. Call me if you're bored, okay? He has my number."

"Okay," she said.

Gavin winked at her, smiled at me again, then turned and walked out.

"Well, that was entertaining," she said once the door clicked closed. "You didn't tell me your brother was so funny."

"He's not."

"Are your other brothers funny, too?"

"No."

She laughed softly as she picked up her plate and took it to the kitchen.

"I'm going to go—" I stopped. I was about to say go

shower, but I should probably offer it to her first. "Do you need the bathroom?"

"Go ahead. I can wait."

"I'm going to shower, then deal with the car. Do you need anything?"

"Yes, actually. I'm going to need to run to an auto parts store. Please tell me there's one nearby."

"There is."

"Good. I'll just do that first, then take the car apart."

"I'll drive you."

"You don't have to—"

"I can drive you into town," I said, cutting her off. "There's no reason to risk it with yours."

"Thanks, Evan."

I grunted a reply, then turned and started toward the bathroom. Hesitating, I stopped and looked over my shoulder. "Fiona?"

"Yeah?"

"Thanks for breakfast."

"You're welcome."

Her bright smile did uncomfortable things to my insides. Shoving the feeling away, I turned my back on her. I had work to do.

13

FIONA

*E*van Bailey was, hands down, the most fascinating creature I'd ever encountered.

He was so hard to read, everything buried deep beneath his scowls, dark brow furrows, and the occasional grouchy outburst. I'd wondered if his moodiness had been road-trip induced, but after spending most of a day with him in his home territory, I was convinced this was just Evan.

What was he hiding under all that bluster?

I'd probably never know.

He'd taken me into town this morning to get what I needed from the auto parts store. I had to give him credit, even though he had much more experience with cars than me, he didn't take over and try to mansplain everything. He just went in and got a few things that he needed while I did the same.

It was like he assumed I knew what I was doing.

No one close to me had ever treated me that way—particularly my dad. So it took me by surprise when Evan, a man I'd known for less than a week, did.

Of course, maybe he just didn't care. That was also a solid possibility.

My hands were greasy from working on my car, and I'd probably ruined my jeans. But there was a comfortable familiarity about getting under the hood again. I'd grown up in my dad's garage, learning from his crew. A few of them had been like cool uncles who'd been happy to teach me about cars.

I'd learned how to rebuild an engine from the ground up. It had been fun, and empowering to know I could fix something broken. It was why I'd bought a car that needed work instead of taking on more debt for something newer. If it broke, I could fix it. Of course, I hadn't counted on the timing of this clutch replacement, but that was another issue.

After our trip into town, Evan had spent the day working on the Pontiac. I'd helped him get it off the trailer and into the garage, and since then, he'd been in his own world over there. Music played in the background, and Sasquatch hung out with his daddy while he worked. Other than his dog, he existed in a bubble of solitude.

I stood and put my hands on my hips. My hair was up in a bun, some of the loose tendrils held back by a red bandanna I'd folded into a headband. The shop was warm, so I'd shed my sweatshirt, opting to work in a black tank top and jeans.

Evan was on the far side of the shop, stripping the Pontiac. He crouched next to the car, his back to me. His shirt stretched over his broad shoulders and back—all thick, bulging muscle—and his tattooed arms were nothing but trouble.

And those hands. God, they were huge. Wide palms and thick fingers.

He stood, his movements deceptively graceful. He was big, but not brutish, like he had perfect control over every inch of that body.

A body that also made a delightful pillow.

Tearing my gaze away from him before he caught me staring, I rolled my eyes. Evan Bailey was as unattainable as a man could be. He was so closed off, I was surprised he even had a dog, let alone any humans in his life.

Besides, that wasn't why I was here, and I certainly wasn't going to stay. At the rate I was going, I'd finish the clutch tonight and be on my way to Iowa sometime tomorrow.

Which meant I needed to call my mom.

Then again, I should probably be sure the car was ready for the trip before I gave her a heads-up. That way I could give her a more accurate arrival date. You never knew what could go wrong when you took out a transmission.

I was running into a little trouble with the flywheel, and I didn't want to bother Evan, but YouTube would have the answer. Everything that I hadn't learned from my dad's crew, I'd learned from YouTube.

My phone rang, so I pulled it out of my back pocket, a little spark of anxiety lighting like a match. But it wasn't Dad. I stifled a groan. It was Simone. That wasn't necessarily better. Against my better judgment, I answered. After all, we'd been best friends—even roommates—for years. Maybe she was reaching out to apologize.

"Hello?"

"Oh my god, I'm so glad you answered," she said, her voice thick with urgency.

My heart rate kicked up and my breath felt trapped in my throat. Had something happened to my dad? "What's wrong?"

"What's the code for the copy machine?"

I opened my mouth to answer, but for a second, nothing came out. The copy machine? Was she serious? "It's on a sticky note in the cupboard right above it."

"Is it really? Hey, you're right. Thanks, babe."

I scrunched my nose. Babe?

"Oh, wait, while I have you on the phone, we're almost out of staples."

"What?"

"Staples," she said. "You know, the pointy little silver things that hold paper together."

"I know what staples are. How do you not know how to order staples? Ordering office supplies wasn't even my job, it's yours."

"I know, but you're such a doll, you've always done it for me. You had the... I don't know what it's called, the thingy on your computer."

"I didn't have a thingy, I just had the website bookmarked."

"Huh. Okay, well, how do I order staples? You know what, I have a better idea. Why don't you just swing by this afternoon and you can do it really quick. Your desk is still here and everything."

"I'm not coming in to order staples."

"Why? It'll take you like five minutes. What else do you have going on?"

"Where do you think I am?"

"How would I know? I haven't seen you since you had your temper tantrum."

"I'm not coming into work and I'm not ordering your staples," I said. "I'm sure you can figure it out."

"But, Fi—"

I ended the call. I was not going to deal with her bullshit. Or her incompetence. She wasn't my problem anymore.

Evan was watching me from the other side of the shop, that deep furrow in his brow. It was positively stupid how sexy he was when he did that. And he made that face all the time.

All.

The.

Time.

For a second, I thought he might ask me if I was okay. A little piece of my heart yearned for his concern, hoped he'd offer me even the tiniest gesture of comfort. Which was silly, and I knew it. He didn't care about me. He just wanted to uphold his end of the deal so he didn't owe me anything.

Sure enough, he turned and went back to working on his car.

Which was fine. I didn't need anything from him.

Where was I? Right, flywheel.

Evan's office was at the back of the shop. He had a big bulletin board on one wall with printed-out ads for cars, Post-it notes, and strings connecting them, like a big conspiracy theory board. Some said *cash*, others said *trade*. Still others had Post-it notes with reminders like *call Jeff in January*, or *could trade up for project car*.

I sat at his desk and gently moved some paperwork so I had access to the mouse. It was kind of a mess in here. How did he find anything? I clicked around and found what looked like a good tutorial and turned up the volume.

Evan's phone rang. It sat carelessly near the edge of his desk, like he'd dropped it there without thinking.

He came in and grabbed the phone off the desk in one of those huge hands. "Bailey Customs."

I paused the video and watched him from the corner of

my eye, trying to pretend I wasn't. A cloud of irritation passed over his features.

"Yeah, I know." He moved around the small space as he talked. "It's not going to happen today. I lost half my morning to hauling a piece of shit transmission out of a piece of shit car."

I rolled my eyes. It hadn't even taken very long.

"You're just going to have to wait," he continued. "Sure, do you have the part number? Hang on, I need to write it down."

Leaning to my right, I tried to stay out of his way as he rooted around his desk.

"For fuck's sake," he muttered under his breath. "Hold on, Pete."

I could see a pen tucked beneath a receipt, so I grabbed it and held it up.

Evan took it out of my hand. "Okay, go ahead."

It was hard not to giggle. He was so big, the sort of man who took up all the space in a room without even trying. Maybe without wanting to. He paced around like a restless wild animal, and I wondered if he had any idea how often he growled at things. I found it very amusing.

And arousing. But I didn't want to dwell on that.

He wrote something down and kept talking. "Intake manifold? Yeah, I think so, but I need to check the invoice. Where the hell is it?" He shuffled through the paperwork scattered haphazardly across his desk. "No, it's fine, today's just a shit show."

Glancing at the paperwork on his desk again, the words *intake manifold* jumped out at me. I grabbed the invoice and smacked it against his chest.

Pausing for half a second, he met my eyes, then took the

invoice and checked it. "Yeah, it's on here. Okay, call you in a few days."

He hung up and tossed his phone on his desk.

"Have you ever thought about hiring someone?" I asked. "Maybe help with all the admin stuff?"

"I don't need business advice."

I put my hands up. "Sorry. You just seem really busy."

"I am really busy."

"That's what I'm saying."

He looked at me again with that damn brow furrow. I stared right back, meeting his intense gaze, hoping he couldn't tell what that look did to my panties.

They were not wet. Not at all.

That was a lie. They definitely were.

"I have to go into town," he said suddenly. "I'll be back later."

"Oh, okay. I'll just be here working."

He held my eyes for a long moment, like maybe there was more he wanted to say. I waited, the prolonged eye contact making my heart beat faster.

But he didn't say anything else. Just turned and walked out.

A slight trickle of disappointment flitted its way through my belly. But what did I have to be disappointed about? What was I expecting, that Evan was going to invite me to dinner?

He wasn't. And really, I didn't want him to. We were passing ships, nothing more. One day soon I'd remember him as a guy I met once. And he probably wouldn't remember me at all.

I had no idea why that thought made me so sad.

14

EVAN

*S*taunchly ignoring the pang of guilt I felt for leaving Fiona alone, I got on my bike. She would be fine. There was food in the fridge, and she obviously knew how to cook.

Although maybe I'd text her on my way back and see if she wanted me to pick something up for her. She'd been working on her car almost nonstop today. She had to be hungry.

But she could take care of herself.

I drove to Gram's and parked outside. I could tell by all the cars out front that everyone was here, and I was the last to arrive. I felt a pang of guilt at that too.

But they were used to it. I was busy. Owning your own business meant time spent not working was time spent not getting paid. I couldn't just finish my shift and go home.

Jack was outside his house next door, with his stepson Elijah. It looked like they were building something. They had a table saw and a stack of lumber. Jack lifted a hand in greeting. "Hey, Evan."

He said something to Elijah, then started toward me. I

walked over to meet him about halfway between the two houses.

"Hey, Jack. What are you guys building?"

"Some new bookshelves. Naomi wants more storage, and Elijah wanted to help. Listen, I'm sorry about the car."

Like Jack had said they would, the feds had impounded the Mustang. But since scoring the Pontiac, I'd practically forgotten about it. "It's okay. I found another project."

"Good. I figured you would. I haven't heard anything from the feds, but I don't really expect to. It's out of my jurisdiction. Whatever they're doing, they'll keep it to themselves."

"Yeah, of course."

"I'll let you get to dinner. Tell Gram and your brothers I said hi."

"I will. Thanks, Jack." I waved to Elijah. He took his hand out of his pocket and waved back.

I went over to Gram's house but paused on the front porch to check my phone. Not that I was thinking about Fiona or anything. Just in case.

I did have a text, but it wasn't from Fiona. It was from Jill. Jesus.

Jill: *Hey gorgeous! I haven't heard from you. Is everything okay?*

Why was this girl texting me? I'd ignored her last text but apparently she wasn't taking the hint. I didn't even know how she'd gotten my number.

I pocketed my phone without answering. She'd figure it out.

As soon as I walked inside, I was greeted by the familiar din of noise coming from the back of the house. Voices mostly, plus pots and pans, plates and silverware. The clink of metal, ceramic, and glass. Logan laughed at something.

Chances were, he was laughing at his own joke. He thought he was hilarious.

Hesitating near the front door, I took a deep breath, inhaling the scent of this place. There was something about this house. It smelled like home, but not in a way that made me feel at ease when I was here. It was hard to walk through that door and not feel loss.

It bothered me that I couldn't get rid of that feeling. I still had Gram. Still had my brothers, as much as they drove me crazy. And that was enough. I didn't need anything else. I didn't *want* to need anything else. I was fine.

The floors creaked beneath my feet—they always had—when I walked to the kitchen. Gavin was at the stove next to Gram plucking hot dinner rolls off a baking sheet and dropping them into a basket. Asher and Grace sat at the table, their chairs pulled close so Ash could drape his arm behind her. Levi and Logan sat across from each other and whatever Logan had just said had actually made Levi crack a smile.

"Hey," I said as I came in. I walked over to Gram and kissed the top of her head.

"There's the Lone Wolf." She turned and eyed me up and down, her forehead creasing. "Well?"

"Well, what?"

"Where is she?"

"Where's who?"

The kitchen quieted.

"The girl who's staying with you," she said.

"Fiona," Gavin offered.

I shot him a glare. "How do they know about that?"

He put his hands up in a gesture of surrender. "I don't know."

"Right."

"I didn't say a word. But seriously, where is she?"

"She's working on her car, where else would she be?"

"But it's dinnertime," Gram said.

"Wait, Evan, you really have a girl staying with you?" Grace asked. "I figured that was just a rumor."

Groaning, I briefly closed my eyes in frustration. "Rumors already? She's been here less than twenty-four hours."

"Do you remember where you live?" Grace asked. "Jessie Montgomery and Kaitlyn Peterson were talking about it in the café today. Kaitlyn said she heard you got a mail-order bride."

"What?" I asked, my voice flat.

"But Jessie insisted that wasn't true, that she's a hitch-hiker you picked up outside Ellensburg. They asked me to clear it up, but I had to tell them I didn't know anything. Except I was pretty sure you didn't get a mail-order bride."

"Pretty sure?" I asked.

Grace just shrugged while Asher stifled a laugh.

Gram folded her arms. "I don't care what the busybodies in town are saying. You still haven't answered my question."

"Gram, she's working."

"Why are you making that poor girl work through dinner?"

"No, that's not..." I paused, letting out a frustrated breath. "She's not working *for* me. She's on her way to her mom's in Iowa or something and needed a place to replace her clutch. I'm letting her use my shop."

"What does that have to do with why she's not here for dinner?" Gram asked.

"Why would I have brought her? She's just some girl who's passing through town."

Gram gave me the look—the one that, as a kid, would

have sent me running for cover. As a grown man, it still made me mildly uncomfortable.

"You might act like a wolf, but you weren't raised by one. I'll pack up her dinner and you can bring it to her."

"You don't have to—"

She cut me off with a swift arch of her eyebrow.

"Thanks, Gram."

"How was your road trip?" Gavin asked. "Was Fiona with you? Is that why you wouldn't let me come?"

"Whoa," Logan said. "Brofoot, you went on a road trip with her and now she's staying at your place, and we're supposed to believe this isn't a thing?"

"It's not a thing."

Logan turned to Levi. "Don't you think?"

Levi nodded. "Definitely."

"Definitely what?" I asked.

They just nodded to each other.

I hated it when they did that.

"There's no thing. She needed a place to replace her clutch, so she offered to help me get my hands on a rare project car. She had an in, since she knew the guy who owned it. But we had to go to northern Arizona to get it. So yes, I was on the road with her for a few days. She helped me get the car and now I'm letting her use my shop so she doesn't have to pay someone to replace her clutch."

"So she's like a lady mechanic?" Logan asked. "That's hot."

Fuck yeah, it was hot.

Damn it. No it wasn't. She wasn't. She was just some girl.

"What's the project car?" Asher asked.

Grateful for the subject change, I told them about the Pontiac.

It didn't take long before the conversation turned away

from cars, and random girls staying at my house, and me in general. Grace updated Gram on their wedding plans. After Asher had proposed last fall, they'd thought about getting married right away. But they'd decided they wanted an outdoor wedding and didn't mind waiting for summer so they had good weather.

I was quiet through dinner, half-listening while my mind drifted to the Pontiac. Now that I had a better idea of what it needed, I could start hunting down parts.

Was Fiona having any trouble with her car?

God, why was I thinking about her again?

The meal wound down and I helped clean up the kitchen. I knew that the rest of them would stay longer. An hour, maybe two. Gram would declare she was ready for bed and the last person out needed to turn off the lights and lock up. Then Asher and Grace would go home, and my younger brothers would go to their place, which happened to be next door to Asher.

It was the weirdest thing. Some small-town families scattered when children reached adulthood, the kids leaving in search of opportunities, or maybe love. Not us. Four out of the five of us lived on the same block, walking distance from where we'd grown up.

I only lived a couple of miles outside town, but like always, I was the odd man out.

But that was just who I was. Gram had called me Lone Wolf since I was a kid. And I lived up to the name. Always had.

They were my pack, but it had been years since I'd felt like I was truly a part of theirs.

Maybe I never really had.

Gram handed me one of her reusable shopping bags.

"Dinner for your friend and more for you. Don't you go eating all of it. There's plenty for two."

"Thanks, Gram."

Her eyes told me so much. I was cutting out early. Again. And she didn't like it. She wanted me to stay. To sit around with everyone. Talk and laugh and be a part of whatever it was they all had. Even Asher, who'd been gone for so long, seemed to have reconnected with the family in ways I couldn't.

But her eyes also told me she wasn't going to guilt me over it.

"I love you," I said quietly and kissed her on the head.

"I love you too, Wolf," she said, patting me on the arm.

I turned to go, but she touched my arm again.

"If something changes, and your friend is here next week, she's welcome."

I gave her a short nod. "Okay. Thanks."

Gram smiled, her eyes crinkling at the corners. "Goodnight, Wolf. Drive safe."

"I will."

Taking the leftovers Gram had packed, I went out to my bike. Fiona wouldn't be here next week. I was sure of that. She'd probably need some help getting the transmission back in her car, but that wouldn't take long. And then she'd be on her way to Iowa, or wherever the hell she was going. And that would be it.

Which was how it should be.

15

FIONA

"Myra, I'm positively delighted with your color. The mountain air is obviously good for you." I tipped the watering can and gave her just enough to moisten the soil. "Blanche, you're also looking very sprightly."

My plants were currently living on a small table near the front window in Evan's living room. A temporary situation, of course, but they were thriving.

"This place has much better juju. Not a single crappy so-called best friend in sight. Just a big grumpy man, but we don't mind him, do we?"

Evan was out in the shop. Although it was only my second day here, I'd already figured out Evan's favorite pastimes: working, growling at things that annoyed him, and talking to his dog.

The last one was awfully cute.

If he had any other hobbies, it was hard to tell. His house was spartan, like he hadn't bothered to get himself anything beyond the basics. Total bachelor pad. Not just a bachelor pad—a solitary, reclusive one. He didn't strike me as a man who had guy friends over for beers. And there wasn't even the barest hint of a woman's touch anywhere. If he'd ever shared this space with a girl, he'd purged every sign of her.

Although I had a feeling he'd always lived here alone.

My clutch replacement was taking longer than I'd hoped. I knew my way around a car, but I wasn't an expert. And despite the fact that I had an actual expert working just feet away from me, I didn't want to bother him. I was doing my best to stay out of his way.

And not stare at him too much.

That wasn't easy.

Everything Evan did was effortlessly sexy. The way he held his tools in those huge hands. The way he moved, his muscles rippling and flexing against his clothes. He'd casually adjusted himself when he thought I wasn't looking and the rush of tingles down my spine had made me shiver.

Even that perpetual brow furrow was hot. He always looked mad, but it was impossible not to picture him making that face for a very different reason—preferably accompanied by grunts and growls.

I didn't want to be attracted to him—it would only complicate things—but resisting his appeal was like trying to hold back the tide. Impossible.

Not that he was ever going to know about all the dirty fantasies I'd had about him while I watched him work. No way.

Those were my little secrets to keep.

And why not indulge in a little daydream here and there? It had been over a year since my ex and I had broken up, and I hadn't been on even a casual date since. Obviously now wasn't the time to jump back into dating. I needed to get to Iowa and get settled first. But enjoying the view while I was here? Didn't seem to be any harm in it.

I put my watering can back in the kitchen. It was one of the few things, other than my bag of clothes, that I'd brought in from my car. The rest was still in the trunk or stuffed in the back seat.

I'd slept another night on Evan's couch. When I'd mentioned finding a place to stay, he'd shot me a look that seemed to say, *do we really need to have this conversation*? I was grateful not to have to spend money on a motel room, so I was happy to take him up on it. And if all went well, I wouldn't be here much longer.

I felt gross from working all day, so I decided to take a quick shower while Evan was still in the shop. His bathroom was small and plain, but clean. I set my phone on the counter and turned on some music so I could sing along while I showered.

Singing in the shower, or while driving, was truly one of life's greatest joys.

When I finished, I dried off, then peeked out the door. It was so cramped in here, it was kind of a pain to get dressed. It looked like Evan was still in the shop, and his bedroom door was wide open. I figured he wouldn't mind if I ducked in there for a minute to put my clothes on.

Pausing just outside his room, I glanced at a closed door on the other side of the hall. I was pretty sure it was a second bedroom, but clearly he didn't use it as a guest room. Probably not an office, either, since he had one out in the shop. I was mildly curious as to what was inside, mostly because Evan himself was so intriguing. What did a guy like him keep in his second bedroom?

It was probably empty. His house and everything in it— from the steep bumpy road to get here, to the minimal furniture and kitchen supplies—seemed to be designed to discourage visitors.

I went into his room and set my clothes on the edge of his bed, still singing—which was to say, murmuring the lines I didn't know, then coming in strong for the chorus. I gathered my hair over one shoulder, pulled off the towel, and squeezed it along my still-wet hair.

A whisper of air brushed my skin, making the hair on the back of my neck stand on end. I froze in place, still gripping my hair with the towel, and slowly glanced over my shoulder.

Evan stood in the doorway, his eyes wide.

"I thought you were working," I said, fumbling with the towel.

"Why are you in my room?"

"Where else am I supposed to change?"

"The fucking bathroom."

I rolled my eyes and managed to wrap the towel around myself. Of course he'd walked in on me while I was naked. He'd already seen at least one of my boobs, probably both. Might as well add my ass to the list.

With the towel secure, I turned to face him. "Your bathroom is tiny and also, have you heard of knocking?"

"I didn't know you were in here. And it's *my* room."

He had a dark smudge on one cheek and I had the craziest urge to reach out and rub it away. See what would happen if I got close to him like this, wrapped in nothing but a towel. He was dirty from working, and I'd just showered, but really that seemed like a win-win.

His eyes smoldered, flicking up and down, like he was taking me in. A flush crept across my cheeks and the tension in the room skyrocketed. It was like a sauna in here, heat and pheromones permeating the air.

"I'm going to take a shower," he said, shattering the silence. He whipped around.

"I'll be out of your way before you get out," I said to his back.

He grunted something. It might have been a word, or maybe just an acknowledgment that he'd heard me. It was hard to tell.

I smacked my palm against my forehead. How many awkward encounters was I going to have with this guy?

But then, we were living and working in close quarters. Maybe it was inevitable.

I quickly got dressed and vacated his room.

Note to self, change in the bathroom even though it's a pain.

My cheeks were still warm, either from the shower or that tense moment with Evan, so I went outside for some fresh air.

The weather was pleasant, the spring air fresh. A light breeze blew through the pines surrounding Evan's house and shop, and I caught a hint of honeysuckle in the air. Sasquatch came out through the open door and sat down beside me.

"Hey, buddy. Why is your daddy so grumpy all the time?"

His fluffy tail beat against the ground.

"I bet he's told you all about it. You're a good boy for listening and making him feel better."

Sasquatch bolted to his feet and barked once.

"What's out there?" I didn't see anything. He barked again and I saw movement near the trees. "I think it's just a squirrel."

Sure enough, a little gray squirrel skittered out from behind a tree. It paused, sitting on its hind legs, its bushy tail swishing.

"Aw, look at the little guy. See, it's just a squirrel. You don't need to bark, he won't hurt you."

Sasquatch looked at me like he wasn't so sure.

"Come on, buddy."

I led Sasquatch back inside and went in search of something to tempt the squirrel closer. It was so cute, I wanted to see if it would get near the house. Evan had a can of mixed nuts in the cupboard, so I grabbed a handful and went back outside—alone this time, so Sasquatch wouldn't scare it off, the silly dog.

The squirrel was still sitting near the trees on the other side of the wide clearing. I crouched down and held my hand out, trying to show it that I had treats. Curiosity seemed to take hold, and it darted closer. It stopped and another squirrel appeared behind it.

"That's it, guys," I said softly. "Come a little closer."

I tossed the nuts a few feet in front of me, since I didn't want to actually hand-feed them.

"It's okay," I said. "The big scary dog is inside. Here's a peace offering. Come get it."

I stood and backed up toward the door. The second squirrel was bolder than the first, scampering past his friend and making straight for the nuts. The first one seemed to realize he was going to miss out, so he ran up to gather his share.

"I'm going to call you Peek and Boo."

They were so adorable, with their quick, jerky movements and bushy tails. When they'd grabbed all the nuts I'd scattered, they both turned and disappeared into the woods.

"Bye, Peek. Bye, Boo."

I was pretty sure we were friends now.

Brushing my hands off, I went back inside. Sasquatch looked skeptical, so I patted him on the head.

My hair was still wet, but Evan was in the shower, so I'd just wait to blow dry it. Or maybe I'd just put it up wet. It wasn't like I was going anywhere.

Contemplating my wet hair made me realize I'd left my towel in Evan's room. Oops. Glad I'd remembered before he got out, I went to his bedroom to get it.

As I walked by the bathroom, my eyes fixated on a sliver of light. The door wasn't latched. I'd noticed you had to pull on the doorknob to get it to close all the way—something Evan obviously hadn't done. The air displacement when I'd gone outside might have made the door open a little more.

I wouldn't look. Nope. Just keep walking right on by.

Okay, fine. I slowed down.

That's a big fat lie. I stopped.

I crept toward the little gap, ready to bolt like one of those squirrels outside as soon as he turned off the water. From this angle, I couldn't see the shower, but I could see the reflection of it in the mirror.

The glass shower. With a clear glass door.

I was only going to take a quick peek—he'd seen me naked ten minutes ago, so why not—but as soon as my eyes landed on that glorious specimen of a man, I couldn't tear myself away. He faced into the spray, water cascading down his huge, muscular frame.

He was sheer masculine perfection.

And oh dear god, he was hard.

Look away, Fiona. Don't be hypnotized by the majesty of Evan's cock.

Too late.

Every bit of Evan was big, and his cock was no exception. Huge and thick, standing up straight, swollen with need.

The things I could do with that bad boy.

I needed to stop staring. And I was going to. Until he

reached down, wrapped his hand around himself, and started to stroke.

My eyes widened and every muscle in my body froze. I couldn't move. An army of zombie squirrels could have been taking over the house, and I wouldn't have noticed a thing.

He braced himself with one hand against the shower wall and pumped his hard length with the other. This was so bad. I should not be watching. I needed to tear my gaze away from the hypnotic sight of Evan jerking off in the shower, but I couldn't make myself do it.

A jolt of heat hit me right between the legs. If I'd had the audacity to do it, I probably could have gotten myself off right there in the hallway. It would have been the fastest orgasm ever.

Instead, I watched, my clit pulsing with unrelieved pressure.

The mirror started to fog from the top down. I could still see his hand working that thick cock. His body stiffened, his hand moved faster, and heat swept through me as I watched him come.

Guilt slammed into me, like I'd been doused with a bucket of cold water. I shouldn't have stayed to watch. I shouldn't have peeked in the first place.

But as I walked away, I couldn't help imagining the impossible. Walking into that bathroom before he'd finished. Stripping off my clothes. Getting in the shower with him, pressing my front to his back. Reaching around to stroke him the way he'd stroked himself—only better. Finishing him while he growled with pleasure.

God, this was the worst. Maybe this was the harm in indulging in sex fantasies about a guy I'd never have. The inability to control myself and act like a decent human when presented with the tiniest bit of temptation.

Okay, a huge, thick, throbbing temptation.

Still.

I darted into his room and grabbed my towel off his bed. In his grumpy, standoffish way, Evan had been nothing but nice to me. He'd gone above and beyond, giving me not only a place to fix my car, but a place to stay. And I was so grateful for that. I needed to stop letting my mind go to that place—the place of the impossible, where Evan and I...

It wasn't going to happen. And that was okay. Like I'd told myself a million times, I was only passing through.

16

FIONA

I was starting to lose confidence in my plan.

Three days ago, I'd been riding high on success. I'd replaced the clutch—go, me!—and put my car back together. Once I'd double-checked to make sure every bolt was secure, I'd taken it out for a test drive.

First gear felt great. Good job, Fiona!

Second gear like a dream. I was such a badass!

It slid right into third. Hell yes, I did that by myself!

And fourth.

Fourth gear was where it all fell apart. Almost literally.

Slip. Grind. Slip. Grind. No fourth gear.

I'd driven back to Evan's shop and he'd confirmed the bad news. It wasn't just the old clutch causing the problem. The transmission was shot, too.

That had left me with no other choice but to stay a few more days so I could replace the entire transmission. And my bank account was not thanking me.

In fact, things were looking rather dire.

So here I sat, in the window booth in the Bigfoot Diner,

staring at a little group of squirrels on the sidewalk outside and questioning all my life choices.

I picked at the fries left on my plate. Evan had needed to come into town, so I'd asked if I could join him. I didn't want to be in his way more than necessary, but I'd also needed to get out of the shop and away from my car. It was almost finished, but it had cost more than I had to spare. So I needed some space to think.

What were my options? I could push on to Iowa. It was roughly a twenty-eight-hour drive from here, more with stops. I didn't think I could drive that far by myself without stopping somewhere to sleep, which meant another night in a motel. Which meant money. And I had to eat. I had enough cash left that I could make it, but I was one flat tire away from disaster. If anything else went wrong, I'd be screwed.

If I went home, I could go back to my job. Pick up where I left off and start getting a paycheck again, albeit a small one, considering my dad was a cheapskate. But it would mean an immediate source of income.

That didn't work either. I couldn't go back, not even temporarily. If I went home, I'd only wind up caught in Dad's web again. That wasn't going to happen.

Which left a third possible option. Stay in Tilikum. Get a temporary job. Save a little money. Then continue on to Iowa.

The squirrels outside scattered when a guy came down the sidewalk, distracting me from my thoughts. I recognized him, which was such a funny feeling, considering this wasn't my town.

It was Luke Haven.

He caught my eye through the window and I looked away quickly. Even without the feud between his family and

Evan's, I doubted Luke liked me very much. I'd taken the Pontiac right out from under him. It hadn't been personal, of course, but I had a feeling the fact that he'd lost out to Evan Bailey made it worse.

So I had no idea why he veered back to the diner entrance, walked right to my booth, and sat down.

"Hey." He cast a wary glance around the restaurant, like he wasn't sure if he should be seen here.

"Hi. Look, about the Pontiac—"

He held up a hand. "You don't have to explain. You knew how to work that deal better than I did and you won fair and square. The fact that it was for a Bailey..." He shrugged. "Shitty, but probably not your fault."

I let out a relieved breath. I knew Evan hated Luke, but he didn't seem so bad. "So your family is really feuding with the Baileys?"

"Yep. Have been for generations."

"That doesn't strike you as strange? To perpetuate a feud for no reason other than that's the way it's always been?"

One corner of his mouth hooked. "It's just who we are."

"But you don't hold a grudge against me? You probably should, you know. Evan wouldn't have known about the Pontiac if I hadn't told him."

"I guess Evan Bailey takes up my full capacity for grudge-holding. Besides, not many people manage to beat me at my own game. I respect that."

I had to admit, I preened a little at his comment. "Thanks."

"So what's your deal? Do you work for Evan?"

"Oh, no, I don't work for him." But wouldn't that have been a nice solution wrapped in a big, broody package? "I'm just passing through, really. Not sure how long I'll be here."

"Maybe someone needs to give you a reason to stay."

I couldn't tell if that was meant to be flirtatious or not. Did I want it to be flirtatious? Luke was a good-looking guy. Really good-looking, if I was being honest. And despite the fact that Evan hated him, he seemed nice.

"I don't know, maybe," I said. "I do think I'll need to stay longer than I'd planned, but I haven't figured out how to make everything work yet. That's sort of why I'm sitting here picking at my fries. You know, contemplating my future with greasy food."

"You seem like you have a lot weighing on you."

I couldn't disagree with him there. "Yeah, I do. But I'll figure it out."

"Would a job help?"

"A job?"

"Yeah. You obviously know cars. And I'd rather have you on my side next time, rather than working against me." He winked.

"Wow. This is really unexpected." That was an understatement. "What kind of a job?"

"Finding deals on project cars and parts. Helping me get the best price. Probably other things, depending on what you're good at."

I hesitated, not sure what to say. "I guess... I need a little time to think about it, if that's okay."

"Sure. No pressure. I threw this at you out of nowhere, so I don't expect you to give me an answer right this second. But think about it. Maybe we could—" Something out the window caught his eye and he stopped short. "Shit."

"What's wrong?"

"Here comes the feud."

Gavin and a man who had to be another Bailey came into the diner and sauntered down the aisle to my booth. Neither of them looked particularly hostile, although the one I didn't know stopped next to the table and shot Luke an annoyed glare. Gavin slid onto the bench seat next to me.

"Hey, Fiona," he said, draping his arm on the back of the seat behind me. "How's it going?"

"Fine. How are you?"

He grabbed a fry off my plate and popped it in his mouth. "I'm great, now. We missed you at dinner on Tuesday, didn't we, Logan?"

"We sure did," Logan said. Crossing his arms, he leaned against the edge of the booth on Luke's side. "Move on, Haven, you're in my seat."

Luke's mouth twitched in a grin. "I'm not finished talking to Fiona."

"And yet, you really are," Logan said.

Luke met my eyes, his lips pressed together, like he found the Bailey's intrusion more amusing than anything. He exuded confidence, despite being outnumbered by his rivals. "I'll talk to you again soon."

I smiled. "Okay. Bye, Luke."

He got up, but Logan didn't quite move out of his way. Luke had to slide past him to get by, but that didn't seem to faze him, either.

Logan dropped onto the other side of the booth and grabbed a fry off my plate. "Hey. I'm Logan. That was well played."

"What was well played?" I asked.

"Pretending to be nice to Luke."

"I wasn't pretending. Did you guys come in here just to hassle him?"

"Yeah, obviously," Logan said, like I'd asked a silly question.

"You know that's weird, right?"

Logan shrugged. "He and his brothers would have done

the same thing if one of us was in their diner. Plus, it's not just that he's a Haven. In case you aren't aware, you were just sitting at a table with Evan's mortal enemy."

"Oh, I know." He grabbed another fry, so I swiped it from him. "I watched them get in a fight in a diner, then helped Evan buy a rare Pontiac right out from under Luke's nose."

"We like her, don't we?" Logan asked with a half-smile.

"Fuck yes, we like her," Gavin said. "I like your nose ring, by the way. I don't think I told you that the first time we met."

"Um, thanks?"

"Where is the big guy, anyway?" Logan asked.

"He said he had to take care of a few things in town and he'd meet me here later."

"I'm just glad we saw you through the window," Gavin said. "Evan would have lost his shit if he came in and saw you sitting with Luke."

"It's not really Evan's business who I talk to, now is it?"

"Doesn't mean it wouldn't piss him off," Gavin said. "He's pretty territorial."

I was about to say, *I'm not anyone's territory*—which I really wasn't—but there was something archaically appealing about that. *Keep away, she's Evan Bailey's.*

Although I had a feeling a guy like Luke would be territorial, too.

"Anyway, what are you doing tonight?" Gavin asked, his tone full of suggestion. "We should totally go out."

"Gav, I wouldn't do that if I were you," Logan said.

"Why not? Evan doesn't get dibs just because he saw her first."

Logan's gaze swung to me. "Don't mind him, he's just messing with you because he has a death wish."

"That's not true."

"It doesn't matter, because a date with anyone is basically the last thing on my agenda right now," I said. "Sorry, Gavin."

He let out a sigh. "That's okay. My heart will heal. Someday."

Logan rolled his eyes. "Aren't you still dating what's-her-name?"

"Naw, we broke up."

"That's too bad," I said.

He took a fry off my plate and stuck it in his mouth. "Yeah, it kind of sucks, but whatever."

"Already?" Logan asked. "I swear, you spend more time chasing girls than you do actually dating them once you convince them to go out with you."

Gavin lifted his eyes, like he was thinking about that. "That's probably true."

Logan shook his head.

A girl with long blond hair, wearing a pink cardigan and cropped jeans, walked over to our table. She smiled, showing off perfect white teeth. "Hi, guys. Have you seen Evan?"

A flare of something that could not possibly be jealousy erupted in my chest. My cheeks warmed and I chewed the inside of my lip to keep my expression neutral. What the heck was wrong with me?

Logan glanced at Gavin, his forehead creasing. "Uh, no."

The girl's shoulders slumped and her lower lip protruded in a little pout. "Hmm. Well, if you see him, can you tell him to call Jill?"

"Sure," Logan said.

She smiled again. "Thanks. I'll see you guys later."

Logan swiveled in his seat, watching her leave, then whipped around again. "Do we know her?"

"Yeah, I've seen her around," Gavin said.

"Is Evan going out with her?"

Gavin shrugged. "I don't know, maybe. It's not like he tells us anything."

Was Evan dating her? We'd been on the road together for days, and he hadn't said a word about a girlfriend. I hadn't noticed him texting a lot and he certainly hadn't made very many phone calls. Maybe they'd been dating and broken up and she wanted to get him back. Or maybe they'd been out a few times but it hadn't developed beyond that yet, and she was hoping it would.

Either way, I did not like the idea of Evan dating her. Not one bit.

Why? No idea. She just looked so wrong for him. I didn't know why—who was I to judge what was right for him?—but I was sure of it. She was pretty in a sorority-girl kind of way, with a nice smile and gorgeous hair. But there was something about her.

As if on cue, Evan appeared on the sidewalk outside. Even with no one to glare at, his eyes were narrowed and he had that intense groove between his eyebrows. He was a storm cloud, dark and ominous, casting a broad shadow wherever he went.

Jill walked out the door just as Evan was about to come in. He rocked backward a half step, but his expression didn't change. Jill bounced onto her tiptoes a couple of times, all bouncy hair and flirty smiles.

Evan's brothers kept talking, but I wasn't paying attention. I was too busy trying to put words in Jill's mouth. What was she saying to him out there? Did he like her? It was impossible to tell anything by his face, but that was always the case. Evan might as well have been carved from stone. Broody, stormy, grumpy stone.

He said something, but I couldn't read his lips any better than I could read his expression. Was it *I'll call you*? Maybe *See you tonight*? Hopefully something more like *No thanks, I'm busy*. Whatever it was, it ended their conversation. Jill left in the opposite direction.

Evan came in and even if my eyes hadn't been trained on him, I would have known he was there. His presence was palpable, as if he displaced so much air that it pressed against me, gentle but insistent.

I bet his lips were gentle but insistent. That lower lip of his was very plump.

God, why was I thinking about Evan's lips? I had a busted transmission and a cash-flow crisis, and here I was staring at the man's mouth.

Logan looked up as Evan approached the booth. "Hey, brodozer."

He seemed to ignore Logan, fixing his stare on Gavin—who still had his arm draped on the back of the booth behind me.

"You're supposed to call *Jill*," Gavin said, emphasizing her name.

Evan's nostrils flared and I heard the hint of a growl coming from deep in his throat.

Logan watched his brothers, clearly amused.

"What are you guys doing here?" Evan asked.

"Keeping Fiona company," Gavin said. "We also rescued her from Luke. You're welcome."

Evan's eyes darted to me. "You saw Luke?"

"Yeah, but it was fine."

"Are you sure?" he asked.

Was I imagining things, or was Evan reacting with concern instead of anger? He couldn't be.

But there was no rage in those whiskey-brown eyes.

"Positive. He doesn't have any hard feelings about the Pontiac. He actually said he was impressed, not mad."

Evan's eye twitched and I wondered if he believed me. "Good. You ready?"

"Yeah, I'm done."

"I can take her," Gavin said. "What do you think, Fiona? We can go grab some dessert first."

"No," Evan said, his voice low.

"I'm pretty sure she can make her own decisions, bro," Gavin said.

"I know she can. I'm making your decision, and it's no."

"I'll save you the trouble of playing a game of who's the alpha brother," I said. "I need to get back to Evan's shop. I still have a lot of work to do."

"All right, that's fair." Gavin said, sliding out of the booth so I could get up. "But it's definitely me."

Logan laughed. "Yeah, right."

"It was nice meeting you, Logan," I said. "Bye, Gavin."

"Bye, Fiona," Gavin said. "Call me."

I just shook my head and left with Evan.

We drove back to his place, the roar of his motorcycle preventing conversation. I hadn't said anything about Luke offering me a job. But what was I supposed to say? I already knew he'd tell me not to take it. And a part of me felt like a traitor for even considering it.

But their weird family feud didn't have anything to do with me. Why did I have to choose a side?

I needed a job. Luke had seen something in me that had made him want to hire me, despite the fact that I'd helped his rival. Wasn't that worth something?

But if I took it, would Evan see it as a betrayal to our friendship? Was I willing to take that risk?

I was so confused.

Riding on the back of his motorcycle with my arms around his waist wasn't helping.

I liked Evan. But I had no idea if he liked me, or if he was just trying to discharge the debt he felt he owed me.

One thing I knew for sure: Whether I took Luke's offer or not, I was going to figure this out on my own. I'd helped Evan, and he'd helped me. The last thing I was going to do was ask him for anything more.

17

EVAN

*A*fter our trip to town, I left Fiona in the shop to finish up her car while I took Sasquatch out for a trail walk. I needed it as much as he did—needed space and fresh air to clear my head. I had too much bouncing around up there. It was distracting, keeping me from making good progress on the Pontiac.

Fiona's transmission had set her back a few days, but she was almost done. Which meant she'd be leaving soon. Probably tomorrow. Hell, maybe even today if she wanted to put some miles behind her.

I didn't know how to feel about that.

As much as I liked my space—I lived and worked alone for a reason—I was getting used to her. The way she hummed along to the music while she worked. The way she smiled when she caught me looking at her. Hell, even the way she talked to her plants, weird as it was.

Was I actually going to miss her when she was gone?

Of course not.

Except... maybe I was.

Fuck, this was confusing.

And what had Luke wanted? I trusted him about as much as old Harvey Johnston trusted Tilikum's squirrel gang—which was to say, not at all. He was up to something, and the thought that he might use Fiona to get back at me made me fucking furious.

But if she was leaving anyway, it probably wouldn't matter.

I hiked down the trail while Sasquatch veered into the brush and back again, following his nose. We stayed out about an hour, long enough that the temperature started to drop as the sun dipped lower in the sky.

When we got back, I went into the shop and found Fiona with her feet sticking out from underneath her car. Pausing, I watched her for a moment. I could just see her arms working; it looked like she was reattaching the exhaust. There was something undeniably sexy about a woman getting her hands dirty under a car.

Especially this woman.

She rolled out from under the car. "Oh, hey. How was your walk?"

I tossed her a rag so she could wipe off her hands. "It was good."

"Thanks." She got up and glanced over her shoulder at her car. "Almost finished, although I don't want to jinx it. I'm afraid if I say everything is fixed, the universe will come along and break something else."

"Yeah, no shit."

Out of nowhere, a thought popped in my head: *Ask her to dinner.*

It made sense. It was getting late and I was hungry. She was probably hungry, too. We'd eaten meals together plenty of times since she'd been here.

But if I asked ahead of time, would she think it was a date?

Did I want it to be a date?

Of course I didn't. I didn't date anymore.

And she was leaving anyway.

A goodbye dinner, then?

Still no.

"I'm going to reinstall the shifter, then take it out for another test drive," she said. "Shouldn't take me too long. Crossing my fingers everything works."

"It will. You've done a great job."

Her lips twitched in a smile. "Thanks."

"So, what did Luke want?" Jesus, why had I asked her that? It wasn't any of my business.

She blinked, like she was surprised by my question. "Luke? Why?"

"Because..." What was I supposed to say? *Because I don't trust him and I think he's up to something.* "It's just weird that he stopped to talk to you like that."

"I told you, he said no hard feelings about the Pontiac."

"That was it?"

She glanced away. "Mostly. Don't worry about it. I know he's your mortal enemy or whatever, but he was nice. We had a pleasant conversation and then your brothers showed up. Why are you so worried about it?"

Pleasant conversation? What the fuck was that supposed to mean? "Because I wouldn't put it past him to use you to try to get back at me."

"So you're saying you don't think he meant it when he said he was impressed with how I turned the deal in our favor? You think he's just trying to get in my good graces to somehow get back at you."

"I don't know."

"You do know." She crossed her arms. "You don't think he was being genuine."

Was he hitting on you? Did he ask you out? "I just think there's more to it than you're admitting."

"I don't see how it's any of your business."

You're right, it's not. But if he touches you, I'll rip his face off. "I'm just—"

"Since when do I have to tell you everything, anyway? It's not like you told me you were seeing someone."

"What are you talking about? I'm not seeing anyone."

"Even if you guys aren't serious yet, you should have mentioned it."

"Mentioned what?"

"Jill." She flung the name at me like an accusation.

"Fuck," I muttered. Hearing her name made my hackles rise. I was well aware that Jill was a problem I'd created—that my attempt to fuck with Luke by kissing her in front of him was coming back to bite me in the ass. But like hell was I going to admit it. "That isn't what you think."

"I know it's none of my business, but it sure would have been nice to know, especially considering we shared a motel room."

"I am *not* dating Jill."

"Whatever, it's fine if you are. You're allowed to date whoever you want, just like I'm allowed to talk to whoever I want, even if they're on the other side of some feud that makes no sense."

"I don't give a shit about the feud. Luke's an asshole who never misses an opportunity to fuck with my business." *And I'm afraid he's going to try to take you from me.*

Whoa. Where the fuck had that come from?

Thankfully, I hadn't said that last part out loud.

And what was I worried about, anyway? Fiona wasn't staying.

That thought didn't make me feel any better.

"Okay, fine," she said.

I didn't want to talk about this anymore. Not Jill or Luke or any of it. Every word out of her mouth twisted my insides. I didn't like it. "I have work to do."

She didn't say anything when I went to the other side of the shop. Sasquatch stayed with her, traitor dog that he was. He'd probably try to jump in her car when it was time for her to go.

Why did the thought of her leaving have me so knotted up? I'd known her for a little more than a week. That was almost nothing.

All these fucking feelings were precisely why I was alone.

Ignoring her, I tried to focus on the Pontiac. I had so much to do, I didn't need any more distractions. It would be better when she was gone. I could fucking work in peace.

So I was only vaguely aware of the sound of her working. I put it out of my mind when she lowered the jacks— she must have been done—got in, and started the engine. And I absolutely did not pay attention as she drove out of the garage.

She came back about twenty minutes later—not that I'd noted the time—and parked outside. Which probably meant the test drive had gone well. Her car was finished. She could finally go.

Good. It was for the best.

Sasquatch greeted her with a friendly sniff when she came back into the garage. She crouched down to pet him, murmuring something that I couldn't hear.

"Evan?"

I glanced at her, a knot sitting in the pit of my stomach. *Let's just get this goodbye over with. Then life can go back to normal.*

Her phone rang, interrupting whatever she'd been about to say. She slipped it out of her pocket, her forehead creasing when she looked at the screen.

"Hang on." She swiped to answer and put the phone to her ear. "Dad?"

A prickle crawled up my back and my muscles tensed. Without conscious thought, I found myself moving toward her, crossing the distance with slow steps.

She shifted so she was facing the open garage door. "I already told you, I quit."

"You can't quit," he said.

His voice was loud; I could hear him clearly. It wasn't my business, and I shouldn't have been listening. But I couldn't make myself walk away.

"Yes, I can," she said. "I can and I did."

"You've been gone for a goddamn week and things are chaos around here. Stop acting like a child and get your ass back to work."

"I'm not acting like a child. I'm doing what's right for me. I'm sorry you can't handle that."

"You're just like your damn mother."

Fiona stiffened. "Dad, that's not fair."

"Not fair is walking out on your family's business and leaving me high and dry. Jesus, Fiona, I have enough on my plate right now without this place falling apart."

"Why is it falling apart? You still have Simone. She was never busy anyway; she should have plenty of time to pick up the slack."

"You and I both know Simone isn't smart enough for... pretty much anything."

Her mouth dropped open. "God, Dad. Do you even hear yourself? Simone's your... She was... And you were..."

"Don't worry about Simone. She's not important. You don't understand the pressure I'm under right now. I need you back here."

She paused and a sickening thought rolled through my mind. What if she went back?

I ground my teeth together in frustration. Sure, I had my reasons for disliking—and more importantly, distrusting— her father. But that wasn't what was pissing me off. I didn't know the details of why she'd left, but she'd packed up and walked out on her entire life. This guy was at least part of the reason. And now he was trying to get her to go back.

None of this was okay.

"I'm sure you're under a great deal of pressure," Fiona said, her tone going icy cold. "Who's after you now? Cops? FBI?"

"Fiona," he snapped.

"I know you have some shady side hustle going on with Felix Orman again."

"You don't know what you're talking about."

"Don't lie to me, Dad. You got an email from him just before I left. I saw it."

"That's none of your goddamn business."

I clenched my hands into fists.

"You're right, it's not. Because I don't work for you anymore. So whatever you have going with Felix, you're just going to have to clean up the mess yourself."

"You want to see me go to prison?" he spat. "Is that it? After everything I've done for you?"

"Of course not. But if you do, it won't be my fault. I've been trying to keep you out of trouble for years." Her voice started to break. "I'm not doing it anymore."

She jammed her finger on the screen to end the call.

I stood there, staring at her, unable to move. I wanted to kick her dad in the teeth. Or gather her in my arms and hold her.

Maybe both.

She turned to look at me, her eyes filling with tears. She was on the verge of breaking, of falling apart right here in my shop.

I could have swooped in. Wrapped her in my arms and held her together.

But I didn't. Like an idiot, I hesitated, and a heartbeat later, the moment was gone.

Straightening her spine, she sniffed and wiped beneath her eyes. Without a word, she walked out.

Fuck.

A few minutes later, she came out of my house with her backpack hanging from one shoulder, her houseplants tucked under each arm. I watched, helplessly—stupidly—while she packed up her car.

Only half aware that I was moving, I went outside. She stood next to her open driver's side door.

"I'm finished, so I'll get out of your way," she said, her voice quavering slightly. "You've more than held up your end of the deal. So thank you."

I nodded. My mouth wouldn't move, my throat closed off. I needed to say something to her, but what? "Thanks for your help with the Pontiac."

That was it? *That's* what I was going to say?

Her bottom lip trembled. "Yeah. No problem."

My chest constricted. God, I was so fucking angry. At her father. At Luke. Hell, even at Jill.

But mostly I was angry at myself. Angry at the feelings that thrummed through me, twisting me up inside. I'd spent years avoiding attachments to anyone because this was always what I got for my trouble. Uncertainty and pain.

Let her go, Evan. Let her go, and this will all go away.

So I did.

She got in her car. And I went inside.

18

EVAN

The ache in my chest didn't go away.

Hours passed. I worked on the Pontiac, then closed up the shop for the night. Ate dinner by myself. Answered a text from Logan, if only to make sure he didn't decide to come out here and annoy me for not answering. Watched TV.

And I didn't miss her.

Except that was too big of a lie to convince myself it was true. I just didn't *want* to miss her.

Sasquatch wasn't helping. My traitor dog had spent the evening moping around like a lost puppy. Now he sat curled up in the opposite corner of the couch with his ears drooping.

"Really? You're just going to mope over there all night?"

He let out a whine.

I took a drink of my beer. "She was here for what, eight days? You got that attached to her?"

His ears drooped lower.

"Yeah, I know. I kind of did too."

It was the weirdest fucking thing. She'd crash-landed in

my life just over a week ago, and I was moping around as badly as my dog.

Pathetic.

But I deserved to feel like shit. She'd been upset, and I'd been too caught up in my own stupid feelings to do anything about it. What kind of man was I?

An idiot.

I let out a long breath. I was still confused. Why did this matter to me so much? She was upset, so what? Her shitty father wasn't my problem.

Except that despite the fact that I'd been kind of a dick to her, we'd become friends. I was reluctant to admit it, but it was true. Those hours we'd spent on the road had forged a fast friendship.

Which meant I cared about her.

Precisely what I'd been trying to avoid.

And yet, here I was.

"Fine." I put down my beer and grabbed my phone. "I'll text her and see if she's okay."

With my thumbs poised over the screen, I hesitated. What should I say?

I heard what your dad said on the phone, and—

No. Delete.

Fiona, I wish I had—

Nope. Delete again.

I'm sorry I didn't—

No again. Delete. What the fuck was wrong with me?

Just checking in to see if you're okay.

There. Good enough.

Her reply came through a couple of minutes later. *Yeah, I'm okay. Thanks.*

She was okay... which was good. Unless she wasn't and didn't want to tell me. And her reply gave me no useful information, like where she was or what she was doing. Whether she had a safe place to stay tonight. Had she left town? Was she already on her way to Iowa? Maybe I should have asked her something more specific.

Fuck.

I tossed my phone on the couch next to me. Now I was really being an idiot.

After finishing my beer, I watched TV until I felt sleep tugging at my eyelids. I went to bed, hoping I'd feel better—or just less—in the morning.

WITH SHARP INTAKE OF BREATH, I opened my eyes to the darkness of my bedroom.

Why was I awake?

I listened for a long moment. Silence. I didn't even hear Sasquatch walking around. Apparently whatever had woken me hadn't roused him.

I'd probably been dreaming.

My mouth was dry, so I got up and shuffled to the kitchen to get some water. Still no Sasquatch, which was weird. Normally if I got up in the night, he'd come investigate.

Chill air brushed my bare shoulders and chest. Why was it so cold in here? Had I left a window open or something?

I put the glass in the sink and went to the living room to check the windows. All closed, but I still felt a cold draft. And where was my dog?

"Sasquatch?"

Usually he alternated between sleeping in my room and on his dog bed in the living room, but I didn't see him anywhere.

With a growing sense of alarm, I checked the front door. Shut and locked. The spare bedroom was closed, as usual, so he wasn't in there.

A gust of cool air wafted across my skin and I heard the creak of hinges.

The back door was slightly ajar. He must have gotten out. How the fuck had that happened?

With a groan, I stepped out into the chill night air. "Sasquatch?"

I'd always wondered if he'd figure out how to work the latch on the back door. He was too damn smart.

"Sasquatch, come," I bellowed into the darkness.

He never ran off. Where the hell was he?

I was about to check the spare bedroom—I always kept the door closed, but just in case—when I heard a sharp bark coming from the tree line.

Sasquatch ran toward me, then did a U-turn and darted toward the trees. He circled back, running hard, his tongue hanging out of his mouth. He brushed past my legs and ran away from me again.

"What the hell are you doing?"

He repeated the pattern, like he wanted me to follow him.

"Who are you trying to be, fucking Lassie? Did someone fall down a well?"

He stopped near the trees again and looked at me.

Something had him all riled up. I'd never seen him behave like this before.

"Sasquatch, I'm not wearing any clothes."

That was apparently an unimportant detail. He ran to me, then toward the trees again.

"Fine. Hold on."

I ducked back inside to tug on a pair of sweats and a

flannel. I didn't bother with the buttons, just slipped it on, shoved my feet into a pair of shoes, and grabbed a flashlight.

Sasquatch was still waiting for me by the trees. My property extended pretty far up the mountainside, and my brothers and I had cleared a winding maze of dirt bike trails. Sasquatch darted though the woods until he met up with the trail, then turned downhill. He ran ahead, then circled back, as if to be certain I was still following him.

I was still half asleep, but starting to realize I was following my dog into the woods in the middle of the night with nothing on me but a flashlight. Not exactly my smartest move.

He ran ahead again and disappeared around a bend in the trail. The beam of light glinted off something just around the corner. It looked like a bumper.

What was a car doing out here?

Sasquatch sat next to it, as if to say we'd reached our destination. I crept closer until more of the car came into view. Was someone in it? Who the hell would have left a car on my property?

Wait. That was Fiona's car.

Fear jolted through me like lightning. Why was her car here? Was she in it? I ran, aiming the flashlight toward the back window, but her car was stuffed full. I couldn't see anything.

Imagining all the worst reasons her car would be out here, I hurried around to the driver's side and shined the light through the window.

Screaming, she sat up, raising her arm to shield her eyes against the beam of light.

"Fiona. It's me."

Blinking, she fumbled with the lock and opened the

door. "Evan? What are you doing? You scared the crap out of me."

"What am *I* doing? What are *you* doing?"

"I thought you were a murderer."

"I'm not a fucking murderer. Why are you out here? Are you sleeping in your car?"

She pulled the edges of a blanket tighter around her shoulders. "Maybe."

"Why? It's freezing out here."

Her teeth chattered together. "Yeah, I didn't count on it being this cold."

I stared at her, a primal instinct flaring to life from somewhere deep inside me.

Protect her. Keep her safe.

I had no idea where it had come from, or why the urge to protect was suddenly so strong I couldn't even fathom ignoring it. I'd have to deal with what it meant later. For now, she was cold and needed a safe place to sleep.

"For fuck's sake," I muttered. "Come on."

She adjusted her blanket and started to climb out. Before she could protest, I picked her up—one arm behind her back, the other behind her knees—and used her feet to push the car door shut.

"I can walk."

"No."

Thankfully, she didn't argue. Just draped her arm around my shoulders and clutched her blanket near her chin. She was shivering. It was spring, but spring in the mountains could still mean snow. And it certainly meant cold nights.

I carried her back to my house, Sasquatch trotting along beside me. How the hell had he known she was out there? Crazy dog.

The pine needles crunched under my feet as I walked. Fiona didn't say anything, just shivered in my arms.

We got to the house and I took her inside through the back door. I'd have to figure out how Sasquatch got out later. For now, I needed to get her warm.

Keep her safe.

I didn't even pretend I was going to dump her on the couch. Just took her straight to my bedroom and set her down on the bed. Sasquatch laid down nearby.

She clutched the blanket against her chest and her lower lip trembled. "Thank you."

I lowered myself onto the edge of the bed next to her and gently brushed her bangs out of her eyes. "Are you okay?"

"Yes. No." She glanced away. "Sleeping in my car is basically how my life is going, so there's that. But right now, I'm just cold and really tired."

"We can talk about it in the morning."

She nodded. "Okay."

I laid my hand over hers, feeling her cold skin. "Let's get you warm."

She let the blanket drop and scooted to get beneath my covers. I toed off my shoes and peeled off my flannel shirt, then slipped into bed with her. She curled up with her head on the pillow I usually used, but I let her have it.

I could tell she was still cold. There was one way to get her warmed up quickly. Me. My body pumped out heat like a furnace.

Memories of the last time we'd shared a bed raced through my mind. I'd woken up with her sprawled on top of me, my hand splayed over her ass cheek. If I touched her now, even just to help her warm up, what would I wake up to?

But she wasn't dressed in a tiny tank top and shorts. She was buried in a big sweatshirt and fleece pajama pants.

This would be fine.

"Come here," I said, reaching for her. "You'll warm up faster."

She didn't protest as I gently drew her against me. Just laid her head on my chest and let me wrap an arm around her. Within seconds, her body began to relax, the last of her shivers subsiding.

"Wow, you are warm," she whispered.

I took a deep breath, letting the scent of her in as I closed my eyes. "Yeah."

Her slow breath matched mine, and a strange thought pushed at the edge of my consciousness. I hadn't felt this good in a long time.

*M*y eyes were still heavy, but I blinked them open. For a second, I couldn't remember where I was.

Right, Evan's house. He'd found me sleeping in my car and brought me back to his place. I blinked again, wondering what I was looking at.

And why did it feel like I was lying on something other than a pillow? Again.

Taut skin against my cheek and the slight tickle of hair. And right in front of my face—

Oh my god.

I was lying with my cheek on Evan's abs, the spectacular bulge of his morning erection right in front of my eyes.

He was wearing sweats, thank god, but the covers were gone and that magnificent morning wood was mere inches from my face. From this angle, I was practically looking up at it. It was like standing at the base of a mountain, beholding pure majesty.

Also of note: Evan's abs made just as good a pillow as his chest.

Before we could have a replay of the awkwardness of the motel room—*please tell me I didn't drool on him again*—I sat up. The entire bed was a disaster. It looked like we'd spent the night having wild monkey sex, not sleeping fully—or in Evan's case, mostly—dressed. He was sprawled out diagonally across the bed, with his head in one corner, his feet in the other. I'd somehow managed to wind up perpendicular to him, using his abs as a pillow.

I swiped the corner of my mouth. Dry. Thank goodness.

My eyes lingered on his torso. He wasn't wearing a shirt, leaving his broad chest and defined abs on full display. His skin was golden brown, tight against all that hard muscle. A little trail of body hair led beneath his pants and I was so glad he wasn't waking up yet—it gave me a chance to drink in that delicious view without making a total fool of myself.

"Morning," he mumbled.

Never mind.

"Hi." I brushed my hair out of my face.

"Did we do it again?" he asked, a hint of amusement in his tone.

I glanced around the disheveled bed. "We did. And apparently you make a good pillow."

His mouth twitched in a sleepy smile and it was so cute I thought I might die right here.

I didn't want to ruin it, so I pretended like I wasn't melting inside. I jerked my thumb in the direction of the bathroom. "I'll just..."

"Yeah, you go first."

I got up and went to the bathroom. Catching sight of my reflection in the mirror, I winced. I'd slept in my makeup. Last night I'd used the restroom in a coffee shop in town before driving back out here to find a place to park so I could sleep. But I hadn't washed my face. Now I had dark smudges beneath my eyes that made me look like I'd been doing tequila shots at a stripper's bachelorette party.

Not a great look.

I washed my face, feeling entirely too naked without my war paint on. But my bag was in my car, which was out in the woods where I'd parked, hoping it would be a safe place to sleep for the night.

Evan was outside with Sasquatch when I came out. I wandered into the kitchen, put some coffee on, and rooted through his fridge for breakfast ingredients. It was pretty sparse. For a guy who seemed to like food a lot, he didn't keep much around. Just basics. At least he had eggs and cheese, so I got to work whipping up a quick meal.

I felt like I had to face the music today. Better to do it on a full stomach.

Evan came back inside, dressed in a t-shirt and sweats. He got Sasquatch his food, then poured us each a cup of coffee. I plated the eggs and brought them to the table.

"Thanks," he said.

I sat down across from him. "It's the least I can do."

He didn't say anything else as we dug into our breakfast. While I ate, I thought about what I was going to say. I wasn't exactly proud of the fact that I'd been reduced to sleeping in my car. Evan finding me out there was pretty embarrassing.

He finally broke the silence. "Are you going to tell me, or do I have to ask?"

"Why I was sleeping in my car?"

He nodded once.

I fiddled with my fork. "Where do I even start?"

"How about the beginning."

"The beginning. Okay." I put my fork down and tucked my hair behind my ear. "I pretty much grew up in my dad's garage. My mom left when I was little, so I spent a lot of time there. As a kid, I didn't know his shop was a front for criminal activity. He was part of a car-theft ring and used his garage as a chop shop."

"Shit," he said.

"Yeah. Then some people he'd been working with got busted. Somehow he avoided getting in trouble, but I told him he needed to stop. Actually, I begged him to stop. He was all I had; I don't have any other family, except my mom, but that's... complicated. Anyway, he agreed. In fact, he promised."

Evan stayed silent, watching me with those whiskey-brown eyes.

"I don't think I ever quite believed he'd keep his promise. In high school, he had me start working for him and I figured it would be a good way to keep an eye on things. I thought if I was around, he'd stay clean. Fast forward a couple of years, I graduated high school and wanted to go to college. He disagreed. He just wanted me to work for him forever, I guess, and claimed he couldn't help me pay for school. I still wanted to go, so I took on a mountain of student debt to pay for it. And I still worked for my dad. He wouldn't really let me quit.

"I thought about doing something else plenty of times, especially after I got my degree. I even got a different job once, but I ended up going back. And I put up with a lot. He was kind of crappy to me and he barely paid me anything. It was stupid of me to stay so long."

"It wasn't stupid," Evan said quietly.

I shrugged. "Anyway, this might not seem relevant, but I'm getting to the point. My friend Simone worked there, too. Our dads were friends when we were young, but her dad died when we were in high school. I think my dad felt like he needed to look out for her—or that's what I used to think. He gave her a job and I thought of her as my best friend, mostly because we'd known each other since we were little. Although now that I look back on it, she was never much of a friend to me.

"When my dad and I came here, and you said he'd sold you a stolen car, I suspected he'd broken his promise. He denied it, but then I saw he'd been emailing a guy named Felix Orman. Felix was from his criminal days. He's all kinds of bad news—really scary. There was no reason for my dad to have any contact with him, unless he was doing something illegal."

"Did you ask him about it?"

"Not right then. I didn't get the chance. Because that was when I found out my dad was sleeping with my supposed best friend, Simone."

His eyes widened. "What?"

"I know. It's as gross as it sounds. He's known her since she was little, and he still..." I shuddered. "I was at his house and I heard them... you know. I didn't know who he had up there. He's been through a lot of women over the years. But then Simone came downstairs."

"Jesus."

"That was the day I left—and that's why I came up with that ridiculous plan to help you buy the Pontiac from Walt Browning so I could use your shop to fix my car. I couldn't stay there another day. Simone was my roommate and I worked for my dad. I'd have to see them every day if I'd stayed."

"I would have left, too."

I met his eyes, grateful that he understood. "Thanks. I've second-guessed myself about a million times since I packed up my car and left. But at the same time, how could I have stayed?"

"You couldn't."

"No. So obviously you know what happened then. I somehow talked you into a crazy road trip. We got the Pontiac, came back here, and I found out my car needed not only a new clutch, but a new transmission. Which leads me to why I was sleeping in my car."

"And that's because…"

"I'm broke." I spread my hands, palms up. "I wasn't exactly swimming in money when I left. I've been trying to dig my way out from under my student debt, and my dad's a cheapskate who justified paying me almost nothing by saying he didn't want his other employees to be jealous or accuse him of nepotism. Really, I think he was just taking advantage of me."

Evan growled, sending a jolt of heat straight to my core. I shifted in my chair, trying to ignore it.

"So, that's where I am now. I barely have enough money to feed myself for the next few days, so I figured I'd just sleep in my car for a little while."

"Why didn't you ask me if you could stay here?"

I shrugged. "You've already put up with me using your shop for longer than we'd agreed to, and let me sleep on your couch. I didn't want to ask you for anything else."

"No more sleeping in your car."

I didn't even try to argue. "Yeah, that sucked, even for just half the night."

"You can stay here as long as you need to. I've got that extra room we could clean out. It's just full of shit now."

The little dip of disappointment in my stomach was so dumb. What did I think he was going to do, offer to let me mess up his bed with him every night? Obviously not.

"The couch is fine. It's comfortable." I picked up my fork

and pushed the last of my eggs around. "How did you know I was out there?"

"Sasquatch found you."

"Really?"

"Yeah, I got up to get some water and he'd managed to break out the back door. How he knew you were there is another question."

"He's such a good boy."

Evan's mouth twitched in that hint of a smile again.

"The good news is, I've had some time to think and I came up with a new plan."

"What's that?"

"I'll stay in Tilikum for a little while. I can get a temporary job, save some money, and when I'm in a better position that doesn't involve the need to sleep in my car, I'll go to my mom's in Iowa."

His brow furrowed and I wished I knew what he was thinking. "How long do you think you'll stay?"

"I'm not sure. A few months, maybe? I know this probably all sounds crazy, but I can't go back to my dad. And out here, I feel like I have at least a little bit of space from him."

"It doesn't sound crazy. What about your mom? Does she know you're not coming right away?"

I looked down at my plate. "I actually haven't called her yet."

"You haven't?"

"No. Things with my mom are... complicated. And I wanted to be able to tell her exactly when I'd arrive. Since I didn't know how long it would take to go get the Pontiac and then fix my car, I waited."

"But she'll be okay with you coming?"

"Yeah, of course," I said, ignoring the needle of doubt trying to poke tiny holes in my plan. "She's my mom."

He eyed me for a long moment, like he wasn't sure he believed me. "So now what you need is a job."

"Yes."

"I'll hire you."

My lips parted but nothing came out. I just stared at him for a long moment. "Wait, what did you just say?"

"I'll give you a job. If you want it. I'm sure you'll hate working for me, but if it's only temporary..."

"I thought you liked working alone."

"I do, but I guess I can make an exception. Plus I obviously need the help."

The humor in those whiskey eyes just about did me in. He smiled so rarely that when he did, it felt like basking in the summer sun.

"Okay. I accept. But there's something you need to know, and I totally understand if this makes you want to retract your offer."

"What?"

I nibbled on my bottom lip. "Luke Haven also offered me a job."

His jaw hitched, but to his credit, he didn't blow up. "He did?"

"That was the other thing he talked to me about at the diner yesterday. I wasn't expecting that, so I told him I'd think about it. And then your brothers showed up and he left. But I'll tell him no."

Taking a slow breath, he glanced away. "If it's a better job..."

"No. Even if it's better, I'd much rather be here with you."

Our eyes met and my heart fluttered behind my ribs. I didn't think I'd ever uttered a truer statement.

I'd rather be here with you.

20

FIONA

*W*ith a new plan made, a job secured, and a place to stay—for now, at least; I didn't want to overstay my welcome—things were finally looking up.

My bank account wasn't convinced yet, but it wouldn't take long before that started to change.

Evan and I trekked out to my car and drove it back to his place. Sasquatch ran around sniffing things while we brought my stuff inside, and I finally got a glimpse of the mysterious spare bedroom.

It was anti-climactic. Mostly just boxes. He used it for storage.

Although the way he side-eyed those boxes made me wonder what was in them.

Since everything about my temporary residency in Tilikum was more or less up in the air—how long I'd stay, when I'd find my own place—we stacked most of my stuff in the spare bedroom. He offered to clear it out and put a bed in there for me, but I assured him I was fine with the couch.

I certainly wasn't hoping he'd decide to let me sleep in his bed with him every night. That wouldn't make any sense.

Opposite sex roommates didn't just randomly share a bed for no reason.

Okay, I was hoping he might, but I also knew the chances were basically zero.

We spent the next few hours focusing on his business and my new, rather impromptu job. I told him more about what I'd done for my dad—everything, more or less—and we worked out the things he needed me to help with. That turned into a crash course in his barely decipherable organizational system and I decided his office needed an overhaul.

He left me to it and went out to the shop. I sorted through stacks of paperwork and a haphazard collection of office supplies, creating order out of chaos with the sound of Evan's tools and his heavy metal music in the background.

It was the best work day I'd had in... maybe ever.

I'd totally lost track of time when Evan appeared in the office doorway. His hands were dirty, his hair a little disheveled, and he filled out his t-shirt and jeans like they'd been invented for the sole purpose of making him look hot.

"It's getting late," he said. "Are you hungry?"

As if on cue, my stomach growled at me. "Starving."

"I was thinking of going into town and grabbing something. Do you want to come? It's on me."

I smiled at him. "That sounds great."

He nodded in the direction of the house. "I need a shower first."

Oh god. Evan in the shower.

I glanced away quickly, trying to erase the memory of—

Stop, Fiona. Don't even think it.

"Great," I said. "I'll just finish up with these and I'll be ready to go."

He nodded and left. I let out a long breath.

I needed to get my hormones under control. Had Evan

and I become friends? Yes, I'd say we definitely had. Had we shared a couple of comfortable and also awkward nights in a bed together? Yes, we'd done that too. But despite the way the mere sight of him could light me like a match, there was nothing sexual between us. Plus, I was working for him now. Sleeping in his house, yes. Sleeping *with him*, absolutely not. I needed to keep some boundaries in place, otherwise I was going to find myself in all kinds of trouble.

GETTING on a motorcycle behind a freshly showered Evan was not the best way to keep my resolve. My hormones danced and sang at his closeness, focusing my attention on how insanely hot he looked in his leather jacket and how good it felt to wrap my arms around his waist and hold on.

And really, what was the harm of enjoying the ride?

We rode into town and he parked outside a restaurant called the Caboose. Inside, we were greeted by a hum of noise and the alluring scent of bad-for-you food. The place was adorable, decorated with railroad signs and model trains.

Evan led the way to the bar area, but paused before we got to one of the open tables. "My brother's here."

I couldn't tell by his tone if that was a good thing or a bad thing. "Which brother?"

"Asher. Come on."

Once I knew he was here, I picked out Evan's brother Asher easily. He had similar dark features, although his expression was slightly softer. I had a feeling that had a lot to do with the pretty blond woman next to him. He had his arm around the back of her chair and he leaned close to smell her hair. She turned toward him and his gaze had such a mix of tenderness and desire, it made my chest ache.

Wow. Women of the world, get yourself a man who looks at you like Asher Bailey gazes at his girl.

Another woman sat at the table with them. She had gorgeous red hair and wore a black shirt with cropped jeans and cherry red heels. She idly stirred a drink with a small straw, her eyes wandering as if she were bored. Or maybe trying to ignore the happy couple across from her.

We stopped next to their table and all three of them seemed surprised to see Evan. Or maybe their surprise was for me. It was hard to tell.

"Hey, man," Asher said.

"This is Fiona," Evan said. He stopped there, as if my first name was the only thing they needed to know. "My brother Asher, his fiancée Grace, and that's Cara."

"So nice to meet you," Grace said. "Do you guys want to join us?"

Her offer gave me a little ping of happiness. I did want to join them. Asher's other brothers had been pretty cool to talk to, and the chance to meet more of his family sounded fun. I glanced up at Evan, but his expression gave nothing away.

Then again, maybe it did. He wasn't scowling. That was probably an affirmative.

"If you're sure you don't mind," I said.

"Not at all," Grace said.

Cara twisted around in her seat, as if to get a better view of me, and tapped her lips with a finger. "Definitely not a mail-order bride."

"What?" I asked.

"Could have been a hitchhiker, but that's not the vibe I'm getting either," Cara continued, scrutinizing me. "Lost in the woods never made any sense. I'd put my money on friend from college, even though that's boring, but I'm not ruling out live-in dog sitter."

I glanced at Evan as we took our seats, but he just shrugged, like he didn't know what she was talking about either.

"Did you really expect any of the rumors to be true?" Grace asked.

"You never know," Cara said. "Sometimes they're close."

"Rumors?" I asked.

"Sorry," Grace said. "People around here like to tell stories."

"And by that she means the entire town is full of professional gossips," Cara said. "Once you get used to it, it's actually quite entertaining."

"People think I'm Evan's mail-order bride?" I asked.

Evan groaned.

"I agree, too cliché," Cara said. "So what is your story?"

"Maybe let her get a drink first," Grace said.

"That's okay," I said. "The short version is that I made a crazy plan to escape a crappy family-slash-job situation, but things didn't quite go as planned. So here I am."

Cara's eyebrows lifted. "That's much more interesting than the rumors. What was so crappy that made crashing at the nightmare cabin with the broodiest Bailey a better option?"

I laughed. "It's not so bad. I worked for my father, which wasn't that great of a job in the first place, but he kind of made it hard to leave. Dad used to be into stuff that was... not legal. He almost got caught once and he promised he'd stay legit after that. But I found out he's been working with this creepy guy from his crime days again."

"That's not good," Grace said.

"No, it's really not good. And then I found out he was sleeping with my best friend."

"Wait," Cara said, holding up a hand. She put down her drink. "Your dad was banging your bestie?"

I scrunched my nose. "Yes. I even heard... never mind. It's gross."

Her mouth hung open like she couldn't believe what I was saying.

"Do you want to know what's really messed up?" I didn't know why I kept talking. I'd just met these people, but I couldn't seem to stop. "Neither of them seemed to think there was anything wrong with it. I guess they're both adults, but still. He's known her since she was little and he was friends with her dad. And it's not just that they were sleeping together; they'd been lying to me about it for months. She let me believe she was hooking up with her asshole ex because it made good cover."

"What's her name?" Cara asked, her voice monotone.

Grace reached across the table and put a hand over Cara's. "Easy, honey."

"Tell me who she is so I can burn down her fucking life."

I blinked at Cara in alarm. "That's okay, I don't need anyone to burn down her life."

"Simone something," Evan said, his voice casual. "I don't know her last name, but she works for Gallagher Auto. That should be enough to find her."

Cara gave Evan a smile tinged with malevolence. "Oh, I'll find her."

"Do I need to be concerned about this?"

Evan shrugged. "Probably."

"No," Grace said. "Because Cara's not going to do anything."

"Yes, I am."

Maybe I should have kept my mouth shut. "I don't actually want anything terrible to happen to her."

"Oh my god, Grace, she's so nice, it's adorable," Cara said. "Can't I ruin someone's life for her?"

"Maybe we should invite her to Stitch and Sip instead."

Cara took a sip of her drink. "Fine. We can gently fold her into Tilikum life with the Stitch and Bitch ladies. That's not nearly as fun, but maybe it's the healthier option."

"I think so," Grace said with a smile. "Stitch and Sip is our weekly crochet and knitting group. The sip part used to mean tea until our resident bartender joined."

"That's really nice of you, but I don't know how to knit or crochet."

"That's okay," Grace said. "Neither does Cara."

"I beg to differ, my vibrant tropical fish. You taught me how to crochet."

Grace tilted her head in acquiescence. "Let me rephrase. Cara can crochet, but she's terrible at it, and still a happy Stitch and Sip member."

Cara rolled her eyes. "I'd be offended, but you're not wrong."

"My point is, you can come anyway," Grace said. "It's a fun group. We'd love to have you."

My eyes filled with sudden tears and my throat closed up over my attempt to say thank you. Glancing away, I bit my lip, trying to get a hold of myself. I didn't understand where this sudden rush of emotion had come from.

"Sorry." I sniffed. "That's just so nice of you. I'd love to come."

"Good," Grace said brightly. "It's Monday nights at the Knotty Knitter. I can text you the details."

We ordered drinks and food and everything came out quickly. My cheeseburger was great and the onion rings were amazing. Evan and his brother chatted idly about cars, then moved on to a recent MMA fight they'd both watched.

"So, did Evan say you're Asher's fiancée?" I asked Grace.

She smiled and glanced at her ring. "Yep. The wedding is coming up soon."

"Congratulations."

"Thank you. I'm really excited."

"It's going to be the most beautiful wedding in the history of ever." Cara pulled out her phone. "I don't have pictures of Grace's dress, but this is what the bridesmaids are wearing."

Cara showed me a photo of a gorgeous pale blue dress. She also had pictures of the cake design, bouquets, and their ideas for the reception décor. The wedding was going to be at Grace's family's winery, and they showed me photos of that, too.

It was fun to talk weddings with a couple of girls. The only wedding I'd ever been to was a mechanic who'd worked for my dad. It had been in someone's backyard and they'd served barbecue and beer.

"Holy shit, Fiona, you actually got him out of his cave." Logan came up to our table, a beer in his hand. "Haven't you already been out in public this week, Evan? Are you feeling okay?"

"You're a dumbass," Evan said.

"That's an understatement," Cara said.

Logan glared at her and took the seat next to Asher. "Whatever, strawberry crazycake."

"Coming here was his idea," I said. "But I guess even the lone wolf has to come out once in a while."

"True. Did you meet Gram already?" Logan asked.

"Gram? Is that your grandma? No, I haven't."

"Huh." He took a swig of beer. "You said wolf, so I figured you got that from Gram."

Evan glanced at me with that brow furrow on full display. It made me all tingly inside and I had the strangest urge to slip my hand onto his thigh under the table.

"Do you want another beer?" he asked.

"What?" Had I been staring into his eyes? God, how embarrassing. "No, I think I'm good for now."

With a short nod, he got up and went to the bar.

I shifted in my seat, pretending that brief look hadn't hypnotized me in front of a table full of people. Under different circumstances, I probably would have had one more beer, but right now I needed to keep my faculties— and my inhibitions—intact.

Otherwise I was going to do something very stupid.

Grace and Cara shared a look. Glancing away, I brushed my bangs out of my eyes and tucked my hair behind my ear.

"She really is adorable, isn't she," Cara said to Grace. "Can we adopt her?"

"Hmm, how does one adopt an adult?" Grace asked, her tone suggesting it was a completely normal question.

"We'll just write up an adoption agreement. Do you have a pen?"

Grace pulled a pen out of her purse and handed it to Cara.

She slid a napkin in front of her and started writing. "Thank you, boo. Now, Fiona, you don't have to change your last name just because we're adopting you, especially since my idea for a joint last name for me and Grace is apparently off the table."

"Joint last name?" I asked.

"When Grace's marriage to Asher was still... let's say *up in the air*... I suggested we become platonic non-lesbian life partners with a sexless marriage, in which case I would have been delighted to take Grace's last name. Cara Miles sounds perfect. Unfortunately, my boo over there is marrying Asher —which, don't get me wrong, makes me happy because it makes her happy. But that puts me in a bit of a bind when it comes to my platonic non-lesbian life partner status, as well as what name I'll take when we make it official."

"Cara, she's marrying me," Asher said.

She waved her hand like that wasn't important. "Details. She's still mine in ways you'll never understand. But now she and I can't have the same last name because she's becoming a Bailey, and that's a hard no for me."

Logan choked on a drink of his beer.

"You okay?" Asher asked.

"Yeah." Logan wiped his mouth with the back of his hand. "I was just momentarily horrified at the thought of Cara becoming a Bailey."

"Not in your wildest dreams," she said.

Logan winced. "That would be my nightmare."

Cara lowered the pen, her eyes on Logan. "Where's Levi tonight? I bet he could use some company."

"You stay the fuck away from him."

"Why?" Cara asked, her voice sugary sweet. "I think Levi and I could be great together."

Logan's jaw hitched and his nostrils flared. He stood abruptly. "I need another beer."

I had no idea what was going on between the two of them, but they were as bad as Evan and Luke Haven. Cara blew a kiss at his back as he walked to the bar.

"Where was I?" Cara asked.

"Last names," Grace said.

"Right. Since Grace and I can't have the same last name, I'm thinking maybe I use her maiden name, Miles. It would be like a tribute to the Grace Miles I know and love. Or maybe hyphenate. Cara Goulding-Miles isn't bad. What do you think?"

"Why do you want to change your name at all?" I asked.

"It's symbolic."

"But maybe you'll wind up in a happy heterosexual marriage, with sex, and you'll take his name," Grace said. "Or hyphenate yours with his."

Cara laughed while she wrote something on the napkin. "You're so cute, but we both know I'm not wife material. Fiona, what's your current last name?"

"Gallagher."

She wrote something else, then slid the napkin over to Grace and handed her the pen. "Sign at the bottom."

Grace held the napkin in place with one hand and signed her name.

Cara took it and ceremoniously laid it in front of me. "Fiona Gallagher, Grace and I hereby adopt you to be our non-lesbian platonic life partner child."

I read the napkin. It reiterated what she'd said and had space at the bottom for me to sign.

"This is one of the nicest things anyone has ever done for me," I said, fighting back tears again. "I know you're just being silly, but I've never had a lot of friends. And the one I did have was banging my dad."

Cara put a hand on my arm and met my eyes, her expression completely serious. "I swear to you, I will never bang your dad. May my vagina wither up and die, never to be banged by a big dick again, should I ever betray you."

Evan stopped next to his chair, eying Cara like he was trying to decide whether to sit back down or grab me and run out the door.

I took the pen and signed my name at the bottom. "Done. Do you want to keep this, or should I?"

"You hang onto it," Cara said. "Just keep it safe."

"I will." And I meant it. Silly as it was, this really did mean a lot to me. I folded it gently and tucked it in my purse.

Had I just made two new girlfriends? Best day ever.

We hung out for a while longer, idly chatting, and I decided to have another beer. Instead of talking to his brother, Asher seemed to become increasingly preoccupied with Grace. He played with her hair and leaned in to gently kiss her neck. Eventually, they got up to leave and said good-bye. By the look in their eyes, I could tell exactly why they wanted to go home.

I was more than a little jealous.

Cara got up and dragged me to my feet so she could hug me. After making me promise I'd always wear a helmet when I rode with Evan on his motorcycle, she left.

"We can go if you're ready," I said.

Evan gestured to my half-empty beer bottle. "No hurry."

I sat back down. "Asher and Grace sure are a cute couple. How long have they been together?"

"They were best friends as kids. Started dating in college, I guess."

"They've been together since college? Why did they wait so long to get married?"

"It wasn't by choice. Asher spent seven years in prison."

"Oh my god. For what?"

"Manslaughter. A guy attacked Grace in a bar. Asher killed him."

"Are you serious? But why did he go to prison for that? Wouldn't that be considered self-defense or something?"

Evan looked away and I could tell this topic bothered

him. Surprisingly, he didn't shut down and change the subject. "It was bullshit. The state argued that Asher should have stopped before the guy died, especially because of his martial arts training. They charged him with murder, but he took a plea bargain for a lesser charge, so it didn't go to trial. He served seven years. Came home about a year ago."

"Wow. That must have been terrible for everyone."

He met my eyes and my breath caught at the hurt in his expression. "It was fucking awful."

This time, the temptation to reach out and touch him was too strong to ignore. I put my hand on his arm. "I'm sorry."

We stared at each other for a long moment and my heart fluttered.

He turned away and finished the last of his beer. "He's home now, so it's fine."

Realizing I was still touching him, I jerked my hand away, leaving me with the memory of his warm skin.

Warm and inviting.

Maybe I shouldn't have had that second beer after all.

But the moment—if there had even been one—had passed. He was back to being as closed-off as ever. Although for a second, I'd seen through his barriers. I didn't want to admit it, but every time that happened, I really liked what I saw.

21

EVAN

*M*y phone was ringing way too early for a Monday morning.

I was already up and working on the Pontiac, but I wasn't in the mood to talk to anyone. Granted, I'd talked to Fiona, but that was different. Why? I had no idea.

Didn't matter.

It was Levi, so I turned down the music and answered. "Yeah?"

"We have a problem."

It was hard to hear him through the background noise on his end. "What's going on?"

"The Havens hit the Caboose. Gav and Logan are on duty today, so we could use a hand getting this cleaned up."

I pinched the bridge of my nose. "Fuck. What'd they do now?"

"You won't believe me. Just get your ass down here. And bring your truck." He ended the call.

Fiona poked her head out of the office. She was wearing a t-shirt and a pair of leggings that made it very difficult to think about anything but her ass.

Her existence in my world made it difficult to think about anything but her ass. Apparently that was just my life now.

"Is everything okay?" she asked.

"Haven prank. They did something to the Caboose."

"You mean the feud thing?"

"Yeah. My brother Levi needs help cleaning it up."

"Cleaning it up? What did they do?"

I shrugged and slipped my phone in my back pocket. "He didn't say."

She rocked up onto her tiptoes, then back to her heels. And it wasn't one of the cutest things I'd ever seen when she did that. Not at all.

"Can I come with you?"

Yes, because it's impossible to say no to you when you look at me like that. "If you want."

She bounced on her toes again and clapped. "Yay."

Leaving Sasquatch at home, we got in the truck and headed into town.

"So, why did they pull a prank at the Caboose?" she asked. "Is the owner a Bailey?"

"Hank? No. But the Caboose is our territory—where we hang out a lot. It's not the first time."

"Do they have a place where they hang out? The Havens, I mean."

"Timberbeast Tavern."

"Have you guys pranked that place?"

"Yeah, a bunch of times."

She tilted her head. "Doesn't anyone get in trouble for this stuff?"

"Not usually. The cops ignore it as long as no one does any real damage."

"So it's not serious?"

I glanced at her. "No, it's serious. But there are unspoken rules. No injuries or property damage. And nothing too personal."

"What was the last prank you guys pulled on them?"

I shrugged. "I don't know. My brothers are usually the ones doing it."

We pulled into the parking lot of the Caboose to absolute chaos.

"What the fuck?" I muttered.

In front of the restaurant was a structure built of hay bales. Some of the hay had spilled out into a wide arc and at least a dozen goats meandered around, happily munching.

But that wasn't even the weirdest part.

Birds were everywhere. There had to be at least a hundred of them flying around, sitting on the roof of the restaurant, or dive bombing the goats. They circled, flitted around, and darted in, picking at something on the goats' backs, then flew up again, out of reach.

In the midst of the birds inexplicably trying to land on the goats were more squirrels than I'd ever seen in my life. They appeared to be in a battle with the birds for... the goats?

As if that weren't enough, people were trying to herd the goats—goats that clearly didn't want to be led away from their snack. All while tripping over squirrels and being dive-bombed by birds.

I had no idea what was happening.

"Shit." I started to open my door.

"Wait." Fiona put a hand on my chest. "What's going on out there?"

"Fuck if I know."

Levi ran up to the truck and I rolled down my window.

"What the hell did they do?" I asked.

"It's like the birdseed prank we pulled last year, only they went nuclear with it. Whatever they put in that hay is goat crack. We can't get the stupid goats away."

"Where's the birdseed?"

"On the goats. They smeared their backs with peanut butter and put birdseed on them. Then turned them loose."

Fiona gaped at the scene, her mouth open, eyes wide. "When you said pranks, I thought... I don't know what I thought, but it wasn't this."

Levi glanced at Fiona, then raised his eyebrows at me.

"This is Fiona," I said. "Fiona, my brother, Levi."

Smiling, she waved at him. "Hi. Oh, you must be the other twin. I met Logan already."

"So what's the plan?" I asked.

"Fuck if I know," Levi said. "Round up the goats and dump them in Josiah Haven's living room?"

"Where'd they come from?"

"They're Harry Montgomery's."

"Really?" I asked. "Does he know the Havens took his goats?"

"Yeah, but he's pretending to be pissed at us about it."

I shook my head. "Asshole."

"I'm so confused," Fiona said.

"The Montgomerys are another old Tilikum family," I said. "They act like they're Switzerland or something, but it's bullshit. They've helped both sides, they just won't admit it."

"Harry probably *accidentally* left his gate unlocked," Levi said, making air quotes.

"Maybe the Havens and Baileys should team up and prank the Montgomerys," Fiona said.

"Yeah right," I said. "Okay, we need to deal with these fucking goats. I'll back up to the hay bales and we'll see if we can herd them into the bed of the truck. Harry's place isn't far. I can just drive them over there."

Asher pulled up in Grandad's old truck, so we debriefed him, then each backed up at an angle to help pen the goats in. They happily munched hay, oblivious to the birds and squirrels coming after all the birdseed.

I got out and we moved a couple of hay bales behind the trucks to act as steps and scattered loose hay in the beds. I grabbed a handful and tried to coax the closest goat into following me. It looked past me with those creepy goat eyes, its jaw working a mouthful of hay.

"How the hell do you get them to move?" I asked.

"Come here, good boy. That's it. Come on." Fiona slowly walked backward, holding out a bundle of hay. A goat followed. "Up, up. That's it. Get up there."

I watched in awe as she convinced the goat to climb on the hay bale and into the back of my truck. The goat I'd been trying to move stood still, like its feet were cemented in place.

A squirrel ran past and a bird swooped so close to my face, I felt a brush of air from its wings. "Damn it."

Fiona was on her second goat. Asher was trying to herd another one onto Grandad's truck, but having about as much luck as I was.

Levi managed to coax one into my truck before a squirrel ran up his leg, clinging to his jeans with tiny claws.

"Jesus," he shouted, kicking the squirrel off.

"How much you want to bet they're recording this," Asher said.

"Undoubtedly," Levi said. "Assholes."

Another goat followed Fiona like she was the fucking goat pied piper.

"How is she doing that?" Levi asked.

I just shook my head. "No idea."

The goats in the truck started licking the peanut butter off each other. In the time it took me to get one stupid goat loaded up, Fiona got four more. She gave them compliments in that sweet, cheerful voice, telling them how good they were.

I was surprised she hadn't named them already.

Finally, we got all the goats loaded in the two trucks. Hank and a few other guys were busy moving the hay bales, so Fiona and I left with a truckload of bleating goats. Asher followed me out to Harry Montgomery's place and thankfully we had an easier time unloading our cargo. A bunch of the birds followed, but the goats clearly didn't give a shit. They wandered around, finding new things to chew on and licking each other, while the birds darted in and picked off the last of the birdseed.

"There goes my fucking morning," I said when I got back in the truck.

Fiona laughed. "That was the craziest thing I've ever seen. Are all the pranks like that?"

I shrugged. "It varies. Both sides like to put up fake signs around town and my brothers put a beard on Lola all the time."

"Lola?"

"The statue of the pinup girl outside the Dame and Dapper Barber Shop."

"Oh, I've seen her. Are you guys going to do something to get back at them for this?"

"My brothers will, yeah."

"Not you?"

I shrugged again. The pranks weren't really my thing. Although after this, I kind of wanted to get them back. I'd lost a lot of time because of their bullshit, and I had work to do.

We got back to my place and Fiona offered to take Sasquatch out for a trail walk so I could get to work. I thanked her and went straight out to the shop.

She'd only been gone about twenty minutes when Chief Stanley pulled up outside.

I went out to meet him, wondering what he was up to. He was dressed in street clothes—a flannel shirt and jeans. His dark hair had a sprinkling of gray and his eyes crinkled at the corners with his smile.

"Hey, Chief."

"Evan," he said with a slight nod. "Hope you don't mind me dropping in on you."

"No, come on in."

Chief Stanley had hovered around the periphery of my life since I was a kid. He'd been my dad's best friend, and after my parents died, he'd quietly stuck around. I was the only one of my brothers who hadn't wanted to follow in our dad's footsteps and become a firefighter, but Chief had been there for me just the same.

We went into the garage and he whistled at the Pontiac.

"That's going to be a great looking car when you're finished."

"I hope so. I already have a lot invested in her."

"She'll turn out. You do good work."

"Thanks."

"That's actually why I'm here. I wanted to talk to you about restoring a car for me. If you have time, of course."

"I'll make time. Do you have the car already?"

"Not yet. I have my eye on a few, but I wouldn't mind your help with that too."

"Of course. What are you looking for?"

"A '59 Cadillac series 62 convertible. Or a '60, they're similar."

I nodded my approval. "Good choice."

"I had one once, back when Skylar was little. I used to take her and her mom for long drives on sunny days. We'd stop for ice cream, enjoy the scenery, that kind of thing."

"Good memories."

"Exactly. I thought it might be fun to share with Skylar. Maybe a way to reconnect with her a little bit."

"I bet she'll love it. I'm honored you'd let me work on this for you."

"No one else I'd trust with this." He wandered around the Pontiac. "So tell me, what's new around here?"

I leaned against one of the work benches and crossed my arms. "What have you heard?"

"I think my favorite story is that you rescued her from a cult, but a close second is the theory that her parents thought the world had ended and she spent her whole life in an underground bunker that you didn't realize was on your property until she emerged and wandered over here."

I laughed. "Jesus. I thought the mail-order bride story was bad."

"I did wonder about that one for a minute or two."

I scowled at him.

"I'm kidding."

"She's *not* a mail-order bride. Fiona's a friend, I guess. Just someone who needed a hand."

"It's good of you to be the one to reach yours out to her."

"She made it hard not to. She's the reason I have that Pontiac."

"Like I said, beautiful car. And it's probably good for you to have some company."

I opened my mouth to argue, but realized I kind of

agreed with him. For years I'd been persistently telling myself I was better off alone. But Fiona was making me question that.

"Yeah, I guess so."

Chief's mouth twitched in a knowing smile. "Well, I won't keep you. I'm sure you're busy."

"I'll get to work looking for your car. Or, Fiona will. She's pretty good at that."

"Thanks, Evan. I'll be in touch."

Chief Stanley left and I went into the office to put a note on the bulletin board. *Fifty-nine Cadillac series 62 convertible.* Those looked amazing in glossy red with a red and white interior. I could add some custom touches, like the TFD emblem, to really personalize it for him. It was going to be a great car.

Half an hour later, while I was back at work on the Pontiac, Fiona came in with a happy-looking Sasquatch. My traitor dog loved spending time with her.

Not that I blamed him, really. I did too.

"I need to run into town," she said.

"Sure. Want me to drive you?"

"No, I think it's better if I go alone."

"Why?"

"I'm going to see your mortal enemy."

I put my wrench down. "What?"

"I need to go talk to Luke and let him know I took another job."

The corner of my mouth twitched in a smile. When I'd offered her a job, I'd been consumed with one thought: make her stay. The fact that I'd inadvertently stolen her out from under Luke was just a bonus.

Still, did she have to go see him? "Can't you just call?"

"I feel like I should talk to him in person. Unless you

think they'll take me prisoner or something. I don't want to become a POW in the Tilikum feud."

As much as I didn't like the idea of her going to Luke's shop, I didn't have a good reason to tell her not to. Luke was an asshole, but he wouldn't hurt her.

Although he very well could hit on her. Thinking about that made a coal of anger flare to life in my chest. But what could I say? Fiona was—what, my friend? My employee now? I didn't have a reason to be territorial over her. Not like that.

Hold on. Was I feeling territorial over her?

Fuck.

"Are you sure you don't want me to go with you?"

She brushed her hair off her face and smiled. "No, I think I'll avoid that kind of antagonism, but thank you. I'm a big girl. I can go talk to big scary Luke Haven by myself."

I grunted a reply. She was probably right. But I didn't have to like it.

She left and my eyes were glued to her ass when she walked out the door. I shook my head to clear the image of that ass naked in my bedroom.

Bent over my bed.

My hands all over her.

Sasquatch's eyes were on me, like he knew that I was fantasizing about her. Again.

"Stop judging me. You're neutered. You have no idea what this is like."

He went over to his bed to lie down.

I adjusted myself through my pants. Damn it. A two-minute completely non-sexual encounter with her had me all riled up, my blood running hot. Did she have any idea what she did to me, just by existing?

I hoped not.

But fuck, I was getting close to my breaking point. I had to figure out a way to be around her without imagining her ass.

Her tits.

All those fucking curves.

I was doing it again. Jesus, I was in big fucking trouble.

22

FIONA

*L*uke's shop could not possibly have been more different from Evan's.

Evan worked alone. Luke had a bustling garage with several mechanics and other employees. Evan's shop was secluded and difficult to find if you didn't know what you were looking for. Luke's was right in town with a big sign out front.

What they had in common were good reputations in the car world. Like Evan, Luke's shop was known for being up-front and honest, as well as doing good work. Evan had said Luke played dirty, and maybe he did when it came to their rivalry. But from what I knew, he ran an honest business.

After working for my dad for so long, I had to respect that.

I parked outside and went into the front office. No one was at the desk, so I did a slow circuit, wandering around the small room and looking at the photos on the walls. Most were cars they'd restored or customized. Some I recognized —I'd seen them at car shows over the years. A cherry red 1952 Corvette. A badass 1969 Charger. An old Ford Model-T.

Behind the desk were what looked like vintage car racing pictures. They were faded black and white, and from the look of the cars, taken in the early 1900s. One had a man sitting in what was probably a homemade race car, wearing a leather helmet and goggles pulled up onto his forehead.

A woman came out to the front. She looked around my age, give or take, with dark blond hair and blue eyes that reminded me of Luke. I wondered if they were related.

"Hi, can I help you?" she asked.

"I'm Fiona Gallagher, here to see Luke if he's in."

"Yeah, he's in the back. I'll go grab him for you."

"Thanks."

Luke came in from the garage, dressed in a t-shirt and jeans, with the woman right behind him. He smiled when he saw me—yet another contrast. Evan wasn't much of a smiler.

"Hey, Fiona. It's good to see you. This is my sister, Annika." He gestured to the woman.

"I wondered if you two might be related." I glanced around. "You have a nice shop. I like all the photos."

"Thanks." He gestured to the wall of cars. "Those are some of my favorites that we've done."

"I think I remember that Corvette. Didn't you bring it to a show last year?"

"Yeah, we did. Good memory."

"What about those?" I asked, gesturing to the vintage photos behind him.

He turned to look. "I inherited those when I took over the shop from my great-uncle. I think they're from the early 1900s. Those crazy bastards built their own race cars back then. Raced them on dirt tracks out in the hills."

"Early car racing was so dangerous. Look at the helmet

on the guy in that one." I pointed to a photo. "Would that even do anything if he crashed?"

"Probably not. I don't think they went very fast, but still. Plus, half the time the cars fell apart."

I laughed. "Can you imagine? Hugging the turn on a dirt track and a wheel goes flying."

"Yep. Like I said, they were crazy bastards. I think my great-aunt Alice told me who they were once, but I don't remember. Annika, do you know?"

"The only one I know for sure is him." Annika pointed to the man in the leather helmet and goggles. "His name was John Haven. He won a bunch of races in that car without it falling apart, which was a big deal at the time. He was kind of a local celebrity."

"That kind of family history is so interesting to me," I said. "I have no idea where my ancestors were in the early 1900s. I could probably figure it out on my dad's side, but not my mom's."

"Yeah, there've been Havens in Tilikum since it became a town," Luke said. "Anyway, should we head back to my office?"

"Sure, thanks. Nice to meet you, Annika."

She smiled. "You too."

He led me through his garage, full of the sound of power tools. I noticed he had a '69 Mustang Boss. That was a badass car. Apparently he'd recovered from losing out on the Pontiac.

His office was at the back, and he shut the door behind us, drowning out most of the noise.

"Have a seat." He gestured to a leather couch.

I sat in one corner and he took the other. He had a large desk with an open laptop sitting out, a file cabinet, and a two-year old car calendar hanging on the wall. He had more framed photos of cars on display, including several with him in the driver's seat.

"How have you been?" he asked. "Figuring things out?"

"Yes. To a point. I'll be staying in Tilikum for a while, although my long-term plan is to move to Iowa where my mom lives. But for now, here I am."

The corners of his mouth lifted in a smile. "I'm glad to hear that."

"It seems like a nice place. Can't be too bad, since your family's been here so long and never left."

"Most of us are still here, yeah." He crossed one leg over his knee. "Since you're staying, have you thought about my offer?"

"Yes. And I really appreciate it."

"But?"

"But I'm taking a job somewhere else."

"Damn," he said. "Mind if I ask where?"

I hesitated before answering. "Evan hired me."

Irritation clouded his features and he glanced away. "Of course he did. Any excuse."

"It didn't have anything to do with you offering me a job."

He rolled his eyes. "Yeah, it did."

It was frustrating the way both men seemed to assume the other only saw value in me as a pawn in their rivalry. "He didn't know you'd offered me a job. Believe it or not, Evan doesn't spend all his time trying to find ways to screw you over."

"Could have fooled me."

"Doesn't it go both ways? He thinks you take every opportunity to get at him. Are you sitting here plotting his demise, or do you actually have a business to run?"

He let out a breath. "Are you sure? What's he paying you? I guarantee I can beat it."

"Thanks, but I've really made up my mind. It's not personal, it's just what's best for me right now."

"Damn," he said again. "Not going to lie, I'm disappointed. I thought we'd work well together."

There was something in his voice, a hint of suggestion.

"Well, thanks again. I do appreciate the offer." I stood.

"Let me know if anything changes."

He got up and made for the door, but instead of opening it for me, he paused, his hand on the doorknob. "Have you ever wondered what would have happened if you'd met me first?"

"Luke, I get that you don't like losing out to Evan, but I'm telling you, the feud or whatever is going on between the two of you didn't have anything to do with his job offer."

"I'm not talking about the job."

"Then what are you talking about?"

He shifted closer. "You. I like you, Fiona. You're beautiful and you're kind of a badass. To be honest, when I saw you in the diner the other day, I couldn't decide whether to offer you a job or ask you out. I'm afraid I made the wrong call."

"No, you didn't. I'm really not looking for a relationship right now."

"I know you said you're not sure how long you're staying. But dinner wouldn't hurt, would it?"

I hesitated while his eyes dipped to my mouth. What was this really about? Did he actually like me, or was I just a toy he was trying to take away from another kid he didn't like?

And how did I feel about him?

It was impossible not to compare him to Evan. Broody

and quiet versus friendly. Luke was attractive, sure, but he didn't light a spark inside me the way Evan did.

But there was also no indication that Evan was interested in me. My little fantasies were fun, but silly and unrealistic.

Still.

I was taking too long to answer and the next thing I knew, Luke's lips were on mine.

Oh shit. Luke Haven was kissing me.

His kiss was restrained, like he didn't want to crowd me. But it also felt uncertain. Which made sense. He was going out on a limb here. Of course he'd be uncertain about my response.

Which, so far, was basically nothing. I wasn't kissing him back, but I wasn't stopping him either.

He pulled away and placed a knuckle beneath my chin, tilting my face up. "What do you say?"

"Luke, I'm sorry, but I just don't—"

"He doesn't own you."

"No one said he did."

"You want to work for him, fine. But that doesn't have to mean he gets all of you. Don't let him dictate your personal life."

I stepped back. "Do you see him standing here? Because I don't. Evan Bailey isn't dictating anything. And why do I feel like you're only doing this to try to take me away from him? So you can win."

"That's not what's going on."

"Really? He hires me, so what better way to stick it to him than try to date me."

"If you think he'd do anything differently, you're kidding yourself. Ask him about Jill."

"Look, you guys have issues, fine. But you can't use me to get back at him."

"Fiona, I—"

"No. I have to go."

He was still in front of the door, and for a second, I wondered if I'd have to ask him to move before he'd let me leave. But he opened the door and stepped aside.

I didn't know what else to say to him, so I walked out without looking back.

An uncomfortable mix of feelings swirled through me as I drove out of town. I'd come here expecting Luke to be disappointed in my answer. Maybe even mad at Evan.

I hadn't expected him to kiss me.

And I really hadn't expected to be kissed by an attractive man and feel... nothing.

What would have happened if I'd met Luke first? What if Luke Haven had been the name I'd thought of, and I'd called him instead of Evan? Would I have become friends with Luke? Maybe. Would I have taken a job in his shop? Quite possibly.

Would I have been attracted to him?

No. Even with a different build-up, that kiss still wouldn't have done anything for me.

Besides, I had no illusions that Luke actually liked me. Or if he did, his get-back-at-Evan motivations were just as strong as any attraction he felt for me. And I had no interest in being a game piece in their rivalry.

I turned onto Evan's private road, my car bouncing as I climbed the hill. The shop came into view and as if he'd heard me coming, he wandered out of the garage, that broody brow furrow on full display.

This was going to be interesting.

23

FIONA

J parked in front of the shop and got out, trying to pretend like I didn't have the memory of Luke's kiss on my lips. Seeing Luke, being near him, even being kissed by him hadn't made me feel much of anything. Not in any of the ways a man kissing a woman was supposed to make her feel. Mostly, I'd left feeling frustrated and a little bit used.

Evan stood just outside the door, drying his hands on a clean rag. Even here, in the open air, he took up so much space. His essence pressed against me, making my heart race and a blush heat my cheeks. Just seeing him made a knot of conflicting emotions clench inside me.

What would have happened if I'd met Luke first? I still would have been drawn to Evan, like a moth to a flame.

To my detriment. Evan was impossible to crack. He was all hard lines and rough edges, every bit of him jagged. And determined to be alone.

His eyes bored into me as I got out of my car. Was he angry that I'd gone? Worried that Luke had changed my mind?

Sasquatch ran over to greet me, then followed close at my heel while I walked to the shop.

"Everything okay?" Evan asked.

"Yeah, fine." I moved past him into the garage. "He wasn't happy, but I expected that."

"He give you any trouble?"

I hesitated. Was it any of his business that Luke had asked me out and kissed me? Despite the whirlwind of feelings he always managed to produce inside me, Evan and I weren't dating. Not even close. He was a friend, and now I worked for him, but nothing about that relationship meant I had to tell him everything.

Still. I felt like he needed to know.

"No, he didn't give me any trouble. He asked me out, though."

Evan's jaw hitched, but he didn't respond.

"And he kissed me."

Save for an almost imperceptible twitch of his eye, his face didn't change. He took a breath, his nostrils flaring, and when he spoke his voice was dangerously low. "He what?"

"I didn't ask him to. And I turned him down. The job, a date, the kiss, everything."

He didn't move, just stared at me. No growling or rolling his eyes. No stalking off and turning up the music, effectively ending the conversation. Just those whiskey-brown eyes looking right through me.

Without warning, he closed the distance between us. One second he was staring me down and the next his arm hooked around my waist, hauling me against him. His other hand gripped my hair and tilted my face up.

His mouth landed on mine like a storm breaking— strong and powerful. There was no hesitation, no holding back. He forcibly parted my lips with his tongue, delving into my mouth like he owned me.

My heart hammered in my chest and for a second, my mind went blank. Evan Bailey was kissing me. Kissing me hard and possessive, like no one had ever kissed me before. He lit my body on fire, sending heat through my veins, rushing to my core.

Except... wait.

Planting my palms on his chest, I pushed him away. A throb of need jolted through me at the loss of contact—my body wasn't happy. But my brain was catching up and I was not going to be the toy these two boys fought over on the playground.

"What the fuck?" I asked, breathing hard. "I tell you some guy kissed me and that's your response?"

He licked his lower lip and I almost dropped dead on the floor. Why did he have to be so freaking sexy? I was trying to protect my heart, here.

"You don't want me to?"

"I don't want to be the object of a game of *I licked it, so it's mine.* How do I know you didn't do that just because you'll fight Luke over anything?"

He stepped close again, crowding me with his size. "That kiss was because I'll fight Luke over anything. Especially you. But this one's because I fucking want you so bad I can't take it anymore."

His huge hands took control of me, one splaying across my lower back, the other fisting in my hair. He jerked my head back, and without conscious thought, my body submitted, going slack in his arms.

The slow sweep of his tongue through my mouth wasn't possessive this time. It was filthy. A promise of more, of things I didn't even know I wanted. He kissed me like he wanted to devour me whole. Like he'd never tasted anything better.

And he didn't stop. With his hand still wrapped around my hair, and his huge body pressed against me, he kissed the breath right out of my lungs.

The scratch of his stubble against my skin and warmth of his mouth tangling with mine stirred me into a frenzy. I clutched at his shirt, kissing him back with as much ferocity as he gave. I was frustrated, and confused, and so turned on I wanted to straddle one of his thighs and dry hump myself to orgasm right here.

He stopped just as abruptly as he'd begun, lifting his mouth from mine. His grip on my hair loosened, but he didn't let me go. Just focused all that dark intensity on my face, his gaze piercing through my soul.

"This isn't about him," he said, his voice husky. "You've been driving me insane. If you want me to stop, I'll stop. But I want you. I don't *want* to want anyone, but fuck it. I can't resist you anymore."

"Are you sure? Because if you're just reacting to what he did—"

"I wouldn't lie to you."

I swallowed hard. I knew I was about to douse us both with cold water, but I had to know. "Then tell me the truth about Jill."

"Jill? What about her?"

"I told Luke he was only asking me out to get back at you for giving me a job. He said you'd do the same thing, and he told me to ask you about Jill."

"Jesus," he muttered, dropping his arms. Taking a step back, he shook his head. "All right. Truth. Jill gave me her number in a bar once and I blew her off. Then I saw her in town and Luke was flirting with her. So I decided to cock-block him. I told her I'd lost her number and asked for it again. Then I kissed her in front of him. But in my defense, she kissed me first."

"That's a dick move, Evan."

"I know." He glanced away. "It was a stupid thing to do. Luke had just stolen a big client from me, and I was pissed. I saw an opportunity for revenge, and I took it."

"You know you should probably apologize to her."

"I did. That day at the diner. She came out and asked why I was avoiding her. I told her I was sorry for making her think I was interested."

"Well, that's good at least."

"Fiona," he said, his deep voice reverberating through me. He stepped closer and touched my face. "You're not another Jill. Me wanting you has nothing to do with him. I promise. I'm a man of my word. I wouldn't lie to you."

A lump rose in my throat. *I wouldn't lie to you.* I believed him. I believed he was a man of his word and after everything I'd been through, it meant more to me than I knew how to say.

"This wasn't supposed to happen," I whispered.

"You're telling me."

"What do we do now?"

He licked his bottom lip again and then he did something that truly blew me away. He smiled. The corners of his mouth lifted enough that I got a flash of teeth. "Let's stop talking about Luke and Jill."

Without waiting for me to reply, he kissed me again. The truth of what was happening slowly sank in as his lips worked their magic.

Evan wanted me.

Wanted me for what, and for how long, I didn't know. But in this moment, my body gloried in the feel of his mouth on mine. His hands roaming over my body. The hard planes of muscle pressing against me, his arms wrapped around me. He was warm and hard and rough and soft and I wanted every bit of him.

The ache between my legs grew as his velvety tongue made obscene promises in my mouth. My nipples hardened, tingling at the contact with his chest, even through layers of fabric. Just a kiss and he was unraveling me.

But this wasn't *just a kiss* any more than Niagara Falls was just a waterfall.

He grabbed my hair again and tilted my head to the side, exposing my neck. His lips traced a hot trail down my skin while he splayed his hand on my ass and pulled me tighter against him.

All these clothes were really getting in the way.

His mouth returned to mine and his hand trailed down, pausing to palm my breast. He squeezed gently as I softly moaned into his kiss.

"Do you know how long I've wanted to touch you?" he murmured near my ear.

"No. How long?"

"Since the motel." He kissed down my neck again.

I giggled softly. "It was me drooling on you, wasn't it?"

"Nope. It was your fucking pajamas."

His lips attacked mine again, so I couldn't answer. But I wasn't complaining. We could stand here and make out all day for all I cared.

"Do you want to know the truth?" he asked.

"Yeah."

He lapped his tongue just below my ear. "I had to get off in the shower before I could sleep that night."

My eyes rolled back and the pressure between my legs grew. "Really?"

"Really. I was thinking of you."

My breath came faster. His hands all over me, his body pressing against mine, and his low voice in my ear were driving me absolutely crazy. I couldn't stop thinking about the time I'd seen him in the shower. Had he been thinking of me then, too?

Oh dear god.

"Since we're being honest," I said, my voice breathy, "once you left the bathroom door open a little bit when you were taking a shower. I peeked."

A deep laugh rumbled in his throat and he kissed down my neck again. "Did you like what you saw?"

"Yeah... it was... well, you were..." Our mouths met again. I couldn't quite finish a sentence, but this was still the best conversation ever. "I know I shouldn't have, but I watched you make yourself come."

He pulled away again and gave me that smile. It was so subtle, barely there. But he was going to kill me with that thing. "You watched me?"

"Yeah. I'm sorry."

The corner of his mouth turned up a little more and his hand slid down to my hip. "Are you thinking about it now?"

"Little bit."

He kissed me again, deep and dirty. I'd never been kissed by someone who could do so many things with his tongue. He was leaving me off balance, my body thrumming with desire.

"Are you wet for me, Fiona?" he whispered close to my ear. "Can I find out?"

I was certain the answer to that was a resounding *yes*. All I could do was nod, my words swirling away in a whirlpool of lust. With one hand bracing me, he slipped his other into my pants. His fingers started to explore and I was glad he was so strong. The way my legs turned to jelly, I could barely hold myself up.

Evan's hands were a turn-on in and of themselves, but feeling his thick fingers sliding across the sensitive skin between my legs was unreal. He kept kissing me—my neck, my jaw, my lips—while he gently dipped one of those thick fingers into my opening.

My entire body trembled and he groaned against my throat. "You like that, don't you?"

I nodded again.

"You want more?"

"Yes."

This had escalated quickly, but knowing Evan had been thinking about me the way I'd been thinking about him, how could we have resisted any longer? My body cried out for more—more friction, more pressure. More Evan.

He slid his finger in deeper and his palm pressed against my clit. I rocked into his hand, my body taking over, greedy and wanting.

Evan's growly voice murmured his approval and he slid a second finger inside me. "That's it, baby."

He was playing me like an instrument, about to make me come undone. I'd never been so close to orgasm so fast. But this wasn't enough. I needed to feel him too.

With his mouth on mine and his fingers doing unbelievable things between my legs, I attacked his pants, ripping them open. I had one objective: get that magnificent cock in my hand.

He grunted hard as I plunged into his pants and wrapped my hand around his erection. He was stiff and swollen and oh my god, so thick.

"Fuck," he growled.

"You like that, don't you?" I asked, repeating his words.

"Fuck yes."

He pulled his hand out of my pants and rubbed my wetness onto his length. I watched, fascinated, as he touched himself, gliding a slick layer of moisture over his darkened cock.

I eagerly took him in my hand and squeezed. He grunted again, sounding so feral and raw. Leaning in to kiss me again, he slid his hand back into my panties and plunged two fingers inside me.

Oh god, yes. This was so happening.

With his tongue delving deep into my mouth and his fingers plunging in and out of me, I pumped my hand along his hard length. His fingers inside me felt amazing, but coupled with his cock in my hand, I could barely hold back. His muscles tensed and he jerked his hips into my hand.

I was determined to make him come, standing right here in his shop. The urgent craziness of it set my body on fire, my inner walls pulsing around his fingers. We were both racing toward the finish, inhibitions falling away. He pumped his fingers and rubbed my clit like a man on a mission. And I stroked that cock for all I was worth, every pulse and growl spurring me on.

"Fuck, that feels so good," he said, his voice strained.

The hint of vulnerability in his tone was as hot as the feel of his fingers inside me or the way his cock throbbed in my hand. I wanted to unravel him.

Because he was quickly unraveling me.

Our foreheads rested together and we watched as I stroked his thickness. Hot tension built between my legs, and I knew I was close.

"That's it," he said. Could he feel it too? "Fuck yes, Fiona. Give me what I want, dirty girl. Come for me."

The rhythm of his fingers abruptly changed and he

offered quicker strokes in just the right spot. My body tensed, the pressure almost at the breaking point. I whimpered as I kept rubbing his cock, desperate for release, and reveling in the feel of him losing control.

"Come with me," I said, almost breathless.

His entire body clenched and a low growl rumbled in his throat. My inner muscles tightened and released with a sudden spasm of pleasure, and I was coming, riding his hand, moaning with the sheer intensity of it.

With another deep groan, he jerked his hips hard and thick ropes of come burst from the tip. In a haze of erotic delirium, I watched it happen as if in slow motion. Every thrust of his hips into my hand, every pulse of hot come. Through it all, he rode out my climax with me, his fingers stroking inside me until he'd wrung out every last tremor.

Breathing hard, I let go, and he slid his hand out of my panties. I looked around, bewildered. What had just happened? I glanced down at my hand. We'd made a mess. "Oops."

"Here," he said, grabbing a clean shop towel. Looking almost sheepish—was that even possible?—he wiped the come off my hand. "Sorry about that."

"Wow, that was... I don't know what to... Did we just...?"

"Hey," he said with surprising gentleness. He drew me close and touched my face. "Was that too much? I didn't mean to—"

"No, no, it wasn't too much. That was amazing. I just wasn't expecting it."

"Me neither."

"Can I be really honest with you right now?"

"Always."

I nibbled my bottom lip. "I'm feeling a lot of things and I know you're probably not a cuddler, but after that I really need to cuddle. Could you maybe make an exception this one time?"

The corner of his mouth turned up again. He leaned in to place a soft kiss on my lips. "I actually love to cuddle. Let's go inside."

Grumpy, broody Evan Bailey loved to cuddle? Of all the surprises today, that had to be the biggest.

24

EVAN

I woke up lying sideways across the bed, face down. Fiona had her head on my lower back, as if I were her pillow. How we'd both moved around that much without waking each other was beyond me.

We clearly had issues.

The covers were a mess, but it was fitting. So was I.

I'd been determined to stay strong, hold out, keep myself from acting on any of my dirty fantasies about Fiona.

And I'd failed.

I'd kissed her. Fine, understandable. She'd told me Luke had kissed her—not that she'd kissed him, I'd noted—and that she'd turned him down. And yes, that first kiss had been all about erasing every trace of that asshole from her lips. I'd told her the truth, and if I had to do it over again, I would.

But that second kiss? All me.

I'd been fighting it so hard, and I hadn't been able to take it anymore.

She murmured something and turned onto her side, so I rolled over. After making each other come in the shop, it had seemed stupid to ask her to keep sleeping on the couch. But now a cloud of doubt cast a shadow over me.

We hadn't planned any of this. I'd only meant to give her a place to crash until she got back on her feet. And then yesterday had happened.

Did I suddenly have a live-in girlfriend?

I didn't know if I had room in my life for this. Could I trust her? Was I ready to trust anyone? I didn't know if I could open myself up to another person again—risk getting hurt.

And yet, here I was, waking up with her in my bed.

I got up and got dressed before she woke up. I needed some space. Sasquatch and I went for a walk in the woods, and the cool morning air helped relax me. When I came back, Fiona was drinking coffee in the kitchen, her hair wet from her shower.

I kissed her good morning—seemed like I should after yesterday—and told myself everything was fine.

Working on the Pontiac helped. Sure, Fiona was in and out of the shop while we both worked, and sometimes she sang along to my music. But I didn't mind her being there. I hadn't since we'd come back from the road trip. In fact, I could admit it was nice having someone around.

Especially her.

And then I remembered what day it was. Tuesday.

That meant dinner at Gram's.

Should I invite her?

She was standing in the office sorting through something on the desk. I watched her from across the shop. She wore a red headband in her hair and she'd put on a lot less makeup than usual. It made her hazel-green eyes stand out against her fair skin. She'd been cold earlier, so I'd given her my flannel shirt to wear. It was too big, looking more like a robe than a shirt, but it was cute with her tank top and jeans.

Jesus, I'd given her my shirt. Was a flannel the same as a hoodie? Was giving your girlfriend your hoodie still a thing, or had I aged out of that?

This was what I got for not dating anyone since college.

And now I was obsessing over what it meant that I let her wear my shirt. For fuck's sake, she got cold. She was always cold. I gave her my shirt; it wasn't like I'd given her a goddamn engagement ring.

But that didn't settle the question of dinner.

If I brought her with me, my family would be... my family. Gram would probably say something cryptic about the sky or the forest or something, and my brothers would be obnoxious. And they'd all assume me bringing her meant something.

All it meant was that I liked her and we'd made out like teenagers yesterday.

In reality, I already knew I was going to bring her, it was just taking me a while to talk myself into it. I hadn't brought a girl to dinner at Gram's... ever. My ex had never come to meet my family, which, in hindsight, should have been a huge red flag.

Sasquatch looked up at me.

"What? Your life is simple, you have no idea what I'm dealing with."

His head swiveled toward Fiona, then back to me.

"Yeah, I know. I like her, too. That's kind of the problem."

I took a deep breath and a jolt of nervousness hit me like a spark. What the hell was I nervous about? This didn't have to be a big deal. I was going to have dinner at Gram's. Why not bring her?

"Hey, Fiona?"

She looked up from whatever she'd been doing and a smile lit up her face. "What's up?"

God, she was beautiful. Not traditionally beautiful, like a model. She was badass beautiful. Dark hair, pale skin, nose ring, tattoos. She was no kitten hiding a set of razor-sharp claws. She was sweet beneath that rock chick exterior, but it was a different kind of sweet. It was honest.

I stopped in the office doorway and leaned against the frame. "My gram has dinner at her house every Tuesday for me and my brothers. Whoever's around just shows up."

"Family dinner every week? That's so awesome."

"Yeah. Anyway, today's Tuesday. Do you want to come?"

Her eyes widened a little and her mouth opened and closed a few times, like she wasn't sure what to say. "I'd love to."

The weird sense of nervousness faded. Had I actually been worried she'd say no?

Fuck, I was falling apart. I needed to get my shit together.

A COUPLE OF HOURS LATER, Fiona sat behind me on my bike, her arms wrapped around my waist. Riding with her was surprisingly enjoyable. I'd never asked her if she knew how to ride, but she seemed comfortable—not everyone was, even as a passenger. And I kind of liked the feel of her back there.

We drove to Gram's and for once, it looked like I wasn't the last one here. Asher's new truck was parked out front, but no sign of the other three. Unless they'd ridden in the bed of Asher's truck, which was a possibility. They basically all lived right on top of each other, and not that far away.

I parked and we got off. Fiona took her helmet off and glanced around.

"This is literally the cutest house I've ever seen in my entire life. Look at all these flowers."

I'd never really thought about it, but Gram's house was cute. It was an old farmhouse with a big porch and a yellow front door. Flowers were starting to bloom pretty much everywhere and the way the windows glowed with light as dusk fell, the whole place looked downright friendly.

"This is where you grew up?" she asked.

"Mostly, yeah. We came to live with Gram and Grandad after our parents died. We were all pretty young."

"I'm sorry."

I looked down at her, grateful for the sincerity behind her words. "Thanks. It obviously sucked, but we were lucky to have our grandparents."

"That's good at least. Oh my god, I'm suddenly so nervous. What if your gram doesn't like me?"

"She'll like you."

"But what if she doesn't?"

"I'm sure she'll like you."

I hesitated for a second. Should I hold her hand? Put my arm around her?

For a guy who'd had his hand in her panties yesterday, I was being awfully indecisive about casually touching her.

I grabbed her hand—it was so small in mine—and led her up the porch stairs to the front door. We went in and found Gram, Asher, and Grace in the kitchen at the back of the house.

Grace paused setting the table to give Fiona a friendly smile. "Hey, Fiona. It's good to see you."

Gram turned. She had a wooden spoon in her hand and she smiled warmly. "Well, hi there, Wolf."

"Hey, Gram. This is Fiona."

"Lovely to meet you, honey," Gram said, then lifted her eyes to mine. "Good boy."

"It's very nice to meet you too, Mrs. Bailey."

"None of that, now, Cricket. You can call me Gram."

Cricket? I glanced at Asher, but he just shrugged.

"Okay. Well, Gram, your home is so beautiful. I love all your flowers out front."

"Thank you. Gardening helps keep me young. So do my peckers."

Fiona gasped. "You have chickens? I love chickens. I love plants, too, but I haven't done a lot of outdoor gardening. I've never had the space for it. But I'd like to someday."

"If you're ever in the mood, you can come by. I'm always happy for some help."

"I'd love to. Thank you."

Gram caught my eye and smiled.

Half a second later, the front door flew open and the rest of my brothers barreled in.

"Dude, no," Logan said. "It would never work."

"I'm telling you, it would," Gavin said.

Levi snorted. "This from the guy who thought the snow blower idea was a good plan."

"It's still a good plan, you just don't—" Gavin stopped at the entrance to the kitchen and a wide grin spread across his face. "Hey, Fiona."

I put a possessive arm around her shoulders and drew her next to me.

"Hey, you guys," Fiona said.

Gavin patted me on the shoulder. "Thanks for bringing her, bro."

"I didn't bring her for you."

Gavin just smiled.

With all of us here, the kitchen descended into the chaos of multiple conversations. Somehow Gram peeled Fiona away from me and the two of them talked about chickens while they finished dinner. I took a seat at the table.

"Here, Cricket, would you mind opening this for me?" Gram handed Fiona a small carton of cream.

She set it on the counter and pinched the sides together to open the top. It seemed like it might be stuck, and I was just about to ask if she needed help, when it popped open, splashing cream all over.

"Oh no, I'm so sorry," she said.

The cream dripped off her hands and some was on her shirt. All I could think about was how much it looked like the mess we'd made in the shop yesterday.

We seemed to have the same thought at the same time. She met my eyes and her cheeks reddened.

My face got hot and I swallowed hard.

Gram handed her a kitchen towel. "Don't worry about it. These things happen. It's easy enough to clean up."

Fiona met my eyes again, pinching her lips together like she was trying not to laugh.

Gavin snickered. I whipped my face toward him. Logan was stifling a laugh behind his hand. Obviously the visual hadn't been lost on them.

Or maybe they were laughing at me. Was my face red?

Assholes.

Fiona got cleaned up and the rest of us helped get food on the table. People started taking their seats, saving Gram's usual place for her.

Gavin pulled out a chair. "Here, Fiona. There's a spot right next to me."

I growled at him.

He grinned again.

"Thanks, Gavin," she said.

I took the seat on the other side of her.

Dinner was delicious, as usual. Having Fiona here felt... different. Not like she didn't belong or I shouldn't have brought her. It was more like clicking a missing piece into place. She made easy conversation with everyone. Laughed, smiled, and enjoyed her food. Almost like this wasn't the first time she'd been here.

I liked it.

And the fact that I liked it freaked me out.

There'd been a time when I'd imagined the first family dinner with a different woman sitting next to me. That dinner had never happened, and as far as I was concerned, that woman might as well not exist anymore. I didn't miss her, and I didn't regret that we'd ended. But I'd also learned a hard lesson—a lesson Fiona was making me question.

I didn't know how to feel about that.

We finished dinner and for once, I didn't get up to leave at the first possible break in the conversation. Fiona was still chatting happily—mostly about gardening and chickens— and asking questions about Tilikum. And I didn't feel the urgent need to get out of here. So when Gram and Grace took Fiona out back to walk through the gardens, and Asher grabbed the rest of us beers from the fridge, I went with it.

I took my beer outside onto the porch, leaving my brothers arguing about some action flick in the kitchen. Asher came outside and stood next to me, leaning his forearms against the railing.

We stood in silence for a few minutes, just drinking our beers. It was good to have Asher back. Everything had felt so wrong without him here.

"You know, Gram's never given someone else a nickname," he said, interrupting the silence.

"What?"

"She called Fiona Cricket."

"Yeah, what's your point?"

"She doesn't give other people nicknames. Just us, and Grace."

I did know that. I'd been choosing to ignore it. "So?"

"Nothing." He took a sip of his beer. "Just an observation."

We stood in silence again, actual crickets chirping in the night. I had a lot of fucking feelings battering me from the inside, and I wasn't sure what to do with all of them. It had been a hell of a long time since I'd had an in-depth conversation with Asher—or any of my brothers. But a question crossed my mind, so I went ahead and asked.

"Ash, when you first got back together with Grace, did you have doubts?"

He turned toward me, clearly surprised by my question. "Yeah. Not about her. I had doubts about myself. Truthfully, I was scared shitless."

"Really?"

"Absolutely. I was afraid I'd screw it up and she'd wish I'd never come home."

"How did you deal with that?"

He took another drink. "Not very well. You were here, you saw my downward spiral. But mostly I just tried to break it down into pieces I could handle. At first, I couldn't cope with forever. That was too big. Felt like there were too many ways for me to fail her. So we decided to give it a summer. That felt manageable. It took the pressure off."

"So you didn't feel like you had to have all the answers right away."

"Yeah, exactly. The truth is, I knew it was forever with

her. A summer would never have been enough. But I still needed it to be that way so I could get my shit together."

I stared at my beer bottle. "Makes sense."

"You struggling with something, man?"

"No, I'm fine. Just wondering."

I *was* struggling with something, but I didn't want to talk about it. And what he was saying did make sense. I wasn't sure where things with Fiona were going, but maybe that was fine. Although it felt like we'd fast-tracked the getting to know each other part, I was probably putting unnecessary pressure on myself. I liked Fiona. She was here for now. Maybe it was that simple.

I needed it to be. I wasn't sure if I could handle anything else.

25

FIONA

I was in the best mood.

That dirty make-out session with Evan in his shop the other day—crazy? Yes. Unexpected? Completely. Mind-numbingly awesome? Why yes, yes it had been.

Going to dinner at Gram's and hanging out with his family last night? Scary for sure. But once I'd gotten comfortable—which had taken all of about ten seconds because Gram was the coolest human ever—it had been so much fun.

Gram had introduced me to her chickens and showed me around her garden. She'd kept calling me Cricket, which was the most adorable thing ever. I'd never had a nickname that I actually liked. Some people called me Fi, but that wasn't so much a nickname as a lazy way of not saying Fiona. The only other person who'd nicknamed me was Felix Orman, back when my dad had been working with him—in other words, at the height of his criminality. He'd called me Fifi, which was just the worst. Even as a little girl, I'd thought it was cringey.

But Gram calling me Cricket was sweet as the pie she'd fed us for dessert.

I'd been hoping for another dirty make-out session—or more—last night, but we'd come back late. And Evan had seemed a little distant. Or maybe he'd just been worn out. He seemed pretty introverted, so an entire evening with his family had probably been exhausting.

I'd gotten up early this morning, so I was already showered and dressed in a tank top and denim overalls. My hair was up and I'd tied my red bandanna like a headband. It was becoming my basic work attire.

I went into the kitchen and grabbed a handful of nuts. Evan was in the shower. I hesitated, wondering what he'd do if I went in there and surprised him.

But maybe we weren't quite ready for that.

I knew I was choosing to ignore the potential for complications with Evan. I was only in Tilikum temporarily and starting a relationship with someone here could wind up being a terrible idea. Maybe I was still riding the high of changing my life in one fell swoop. The thrill of walking away from the toxic people who'd been weighing me down was certainly strong. Or maybe it was just my optimistic nature. Things would work out somehow, right?

Regardless, I wasn't going to let a silly thing like practicality ruin my buzz. Not on this beautiful spring morning in the mountains.

Even Myra and Blanche were looking fantastic. I certainly didn't want to mess up their juju by getting anxious about the future or labels or what it all meant. We liked being here with Evan. And for now, that was enough.

I took a handful of nuts outside, making sure Sasquatch didn't follow. He'd only bark. I'd been teaching Peek and Boo to do a little squirrel obstacle course. It was amazing how trainable they were, given the right motivation. They particularly loved Oreo cookies, but I didn't want to feed them too much junk food.

One of them—I decided it was Boo, although I couldn't actually tell them apart—scampered down a tree trunk as soon as I came outside. He sat up on his hind legs, his tail swishing behind him.

"Hi, Boo. Come here, little guy. I have treats for you."

He didn't move.

"Maybe you're Peek? Sorry, it's hard to tell from far away. Or at all. No offense. Here, I have nuts."

I put the nuts in a little basket on top of a ramp I'd made out of a board and a log round.

"Come on, buddy. Show me how smart you are."

Peek—I decided he was definitely Peek—ran a little closer, then stopped. Boo scurried out of a tree and blew past his friend in pursuit of my tempting tidbits. He raced up the ramp and got his prize out of the basket.

"Yes! Success! You're so smart."

"What are you doing?" Evan asked behind me.

Peek and Boo ran off, disappearing up a tree.

I stood and turned, putting my hands on my hips. "I was trying to feed Peek and Boo, but you scared them off."

He made for an imposing figure, a man almost as wide as his big front door, his square jaw darkened by stubble. "Don't feed the squirrels."

Why did he sound so alarmed? "Why not? They're friendly."

"The squirrels around here aren't friendly. They're evil."

I laughed. "How can you say that? They're little animals, they're not evil. I taught them to climb the ramp. I'm going to see what else I can teach them to do."

"Trust me, Tilikum squirrels are evil. Don't teach them

anything. Next thing you know, they'll be breaking in the house and stealing our stuff."

"I'm sorry, are we still talking about *squirrels*?"

"Don't trust them."

I turned back around and tossed the rest of the nuts for them to find later. "There you go, Peek and Boo. I'll take the big scary man inside and you can come have your treats."

"Peek and Boo?" he asked as I walked past him into the house.

"What? You have a dog named after Bigfoot."

"And you have plants that sound like members of an old lady's bridge club."

I glanced at Myra and Blanche, still happily perched on a little table next to the front window. "Shh. Evan, they can hear you."

Shaking his head, he rolled his eyes.

He was only a couple of feet away and for a second, I thought he might reach for me. Maybe slip an arm around my waist and haul me roughly against him. Kiss me with that tongue that, the other day, had seemed intent on teasing out all my secrets.

"I need to get to work," he said. "I have a shit ton to do today."

I tried to ignore the little dip of disappointment. "Okay. I'll be over there in a few."

He nodded and headed for the door, then paused and glanced at Sasquatch. "Are you coming?"

The dog didn't move.

"Traitor dog," he muttered and left.

"You're not a traitor," I said, crouching down to scratch his chest. "You're the goodest good boy ever."

Sasquatch followed me over to the shop and took his place on his bed while I went into the office.

My office? Our office? Regardless, it was a far cry from my job working for my dad. There had been aspects of that job I'd enjoyed. I loved discovering hard to find cars or parts. It was fun to see an old rust bucket restored to its former glory, and the joy in the client's eyes when they saw their new ride.

I didn't miss the constant anxiety. The worry about what my dad was doing behind closed doors. Where he was going when he said he had a meeting. Obviously my fears had been justified. He'd been doing all sorts of things behind my back.

Working here was so much simpler.

I glanced around at the now-organized space. It was satisfying to have created a bit of order from chaos. There were so many things I could do to make Evan's business run more smoothly and the amazing thing was, he appreciated it. He'd actually thanked me.

A question danced in the back of my mind. A question I didn't particularly want to ponder, lest it ruin my good mood. Had my father ever appreciated me? Like, even once?

Letting out a long breath, I pushed that thought away. I knew I had some baggage to unpack when it came to my dad, but now wasn't the time.

I set my coffee down and glanced at the big bulletin board on the wall. There was a new note pinned in the top right corner. *Find '59 Cadillac series 62 convertible for Chief.* From what I'd learned about how Evan ran his business, some of his income came from cars he found and restored, then either sold or traded up for his next restoration. Others were client requests—cars people brought him to either customize or restore to their specifications. Those were usually quicker sources of cash, the kind of thing that kept a shop afloat during a project like the Pontiac he was working on now.

Tapping my finger against my lips, I searched my memory. Did I know someone who had a '59 Caddy convertible? There was a guy out in Arlington who might, and that was only a couple of hours away. Another guy I knew with a lot of project cars sitting around was just outside of Seattle. He'd be another one to call. Evan obviously had contacts, too, but I figured I could poke around and see if I could find one in decent shape—especially for a good price.

Evan also needed help tracking down a few hard-to-find parts for the Pontiac. And he still needed a buyer for the Super Bee.

I wondered if Luke had any of the parts he needed. He probably did. But Evan wouldn't bother asking. He'd rather drive hours out of his way than do business with a Haven—especially Luke. It seemed so silly to me, but their rivalry was deeply entrenched.

In any case, I had plenty to do, so I got to work.

PARTWAY THROUGH THE AFTERNOON, Evan poked his head in the office. "I have to go into town. Hardware store. Want to come?"

Getting out did sound nice. "Yeah, I'd love to."

He nodded and disappeared back into the shop.

Had I done something to spook him? Why was he so distant today?

Maybe he was trying to create a boundary around work. Or maybe he regretted making out with me and introducing me to his family. Or maybe there was something else going on in that broody head of his that had nothing to do with me.

It was so hard to tell with him.

I ran over to the house to change my shoes, then met Evan at his truck.

We drove into town and went straight to the hardware store. Like everything in Tilikum, it was quaint—a faded red building with a sign next to the front doors that read *your hometown hardware store*.

"I'm going to go look through the nursery while you do your thing," I said.

He shrugged, like it didn't really matter what I did. I narrowed my eyes at him as he walked away.

The indoor plants were in the opposite direction, so I let him go. I wasn't looking for anything in particular, just keeping my eyes open for a plant who might get along with Myra and Blanche. Or maybe something for the office in the shop. There weren't any windows in there, but if I could find something that thrived in low light, it would really perk things up.

A woman in a red Tilikum Hardware apron came down the aisle toward me. She looked to be in her forties, with blond hair in a careless ponytail and a friendly smile. Hopefully she was the garden specialist and could help me find some low-light varieties.

"Well hi there, Fiona," she said. "So nice to meet you. I'm Olive Hembree."

I blinked in surprise. How did she know my name? "Hi..."

"Looking for ways to make that dark old cabin more of a home?" she asked. "I don't blame you. I can't imagine it's very cheery out there. Although maybe you're used to that."

"Um, do you mean Evan Bailey's place?"

Still smiling, she nodded.

"It's actually fine. I just really like plants."

"Did you have a lot of plants where you were living before?"

That was a weird question. "I had a couple, yeah. Why?"

"I'm just so curious as to how that worked, being underground and all."

"Underground?"

"Mm-hmm. How much space did you have? Did you really survive on canned food for all those years?"

"I'm sorry, what? I used to live in an apartment and ate normal food."

"Oh," she said, raising her eyebrows. "So you didn't grow up in an underground bunker because your parents thought the world ended in 1985?"

I shook my head slowly. "No."

She rolled her eyes with a sigh. "I'm going to have to have a little chat with Mavis Doolittle. She had it all wrong. Don't tell me you really are a mail-order bride. I had the longest argument with Kaitlyn Peterson about that and I'd hate it if I was mistaken."

"No, I'm not a mail-order bride either."

"Pity. Evan Bailey could use a good woman in his life."

I laughed. "He probably could."

But was I actually up for that challenge?

"Is there anything I can help you find?"

"Yes, actually. I'm trying to find an indoor plant that can thrive in low light."

She nodded again, as if that confirmed something, then showed me several options. I chose a cute spider plant with narrow light green leaves, since they're both hardy and non-toxic to dogs.

I tucked the plant under my arm and looked around a

little more. They had the cutest polka-dot plant, with mottled green and pink leaves. I kept thinking about that spot near the window where Blanche and Myra lived.

"I think my ladies need a friend. You could be their friend, couldn't you? You're not very big."

It was a bit of a splurge, but I decided it would be worth it to make Evan's house a little cheerier.

I took my plants up front and paid, then waited for Evan outside. He came out a few minutes later and cast a suspicious glance at my purchases.

He was still acting distant on the drive back to his place. I was starting to wonder if I'd done something to make him mad. Had I said something wrong at Gram's last night? But why wouldn't he just tell me?

I wished I knew what was going on inside that head of his.

He parked in front of his house and took his purchases into the shop. I brought my new plant inside and set her next to Myra and Blanche. I'd need to come up with a name for her, but so far nothing was jumping out at me. Dorothy, maybe? Agnes? I wasn't sure.

"As for you, little pretty, let me show you your new home," I said to the spider plant.

I tucked her under my arm, contemplating names, and walked over to the shop. This one might be a Margaret. Or maybe a Zelda.

Evan glanced over his shoulder at me when I walked in. I took the plant into the office and started moving a few things around to make room. It fit perfectly on the corner of the desk. I stepped back, put my hands on my hips, and tilted my head to look at her.

"I know, you're an Edith."

"You have to put your plants in here, too?"

I turned. Evan was in the doorway giving me the full force of his broody glare.

"I thought it could use a little brightening up."

"It's in the way."

"It's not in the way at all." I gestured toward the desk. "She's just taking up one little corner."

"She?"

"Yes, Edith."

He rolled his eyes. "Of course it has a fucking name."

"So? I like naming my plants. Why are you in such a bad mood?"

"I'm not."

I crossed my arms. "Yeah, you are. You've barely spoken to me today and now you're giving me a hard time about a houseplant."

"Whatever, it's fine. Decorate with your damn plants."

He turned around and stalked out.

This was ridiculous. I followed him into the shop. "Why do you do that?"

He didn't look back at me. "Do what?"

"Act like a jerk. It's like you're doing it on purpose so people won't like you."

"Maybe I am."

"But why? Why are you being so defensive?"

He whirled on me. "Because I want to be left alone."

I put up my hands. "Fine. Be alone, then."

Without another word, I walked out.

26

EVAN

*F*iona walked out, and I let her go.

Fuck.

I felt shitty for being an asshole to her. She didn't deserve that. She was right, I was a dick to people on purpose. It was a good way to keep everyone out. To make sure people left me alone.

Because that was what I wanted. Wasn't it?

I'd certainly thought so.

I turned on some music and went back to work on the Pontiac. Busy hands gave me space to think. I'd spent the last couple of days completely off balance. I needed to get my head on straight.

This entire thing was my fault. I'd started it by kissing her. And in the moment, it had felt so damn good—and not just because we'd made each other come a few feet from where I was working. It had felt good to be touched. To have her hands on me, her mouth tangling with mine.

I'd wanted her, and I'd given in.

But I had to face facts. I liked Fiona. A lot. This wasn't just about wanting her body, although I craved her like a drug. I had feelings for her—feelings I'd sworn I'd never let myself have again. That was the part that was freaking me the fuck out. She wasn't a one-and-done, a fling I'd try to forget tomorrow.

Asher had said to break it down into something manageable. On the surface, that made sense. But I was an all-or-nothing guy. That was why I'd sworn off women. I'd dated and been in a long-term relationship. That hadn't worked out. I'd tried casual sex. That hadn't worked out, either.

So I'd decided I needed to be alone.

All or nothing.

And everything had been fine until Fiona had crashed into my fucking life.

Now I didn't know what to do. She was unraveling me. Everything was happening so fast. One day I was working out here by myself, and the next I was on the road with this crazy girl.

And now she was staying with me, sleeping in my bed, meeting my family, decorating with her fucking plants, driving me crazy.

I was supposed to be focusing on my business. This car had the potential to take my shop to the next level. I should have been busting my ass, working from dawn until dusk, as if nothing else mattered. The success of this project rested entirely on me. I wasn't like Luke; I didn't have a crew. I didn't have anyone else I could depend on.

Of course, I'd made sure of that.

I knew exactly why I was acting like a fucking lunatic. I was standing at the end of a dock, staring into the water. I had two choices. Jump in, or turn around and walk away.

As of right now, I could still choose the latter. It wouldn't be easy, and I wasn't stupid. I knew I'd hurt her if I walked away.

But would we wind up hurting each other more if I took that deep breath and jumped?

I didn't know.

For good or ill, I wasn't a guy who could do anything halfway. I'd worked my ass off in college—until I'd quit. Now I put everything into my business. No half measures.

I'd put my all into a relationship once, and it had been a giant fucking failure. Was I willing to risk it again?

Because, for me, a woman could be one of two things. A one-and-done, so I didn't have to commit anything to her. Or she could be mine. Those were my only options. I didn't know why I was that way. Maybe it was just how I was built. But there was no sense in denying it.

And there were so many reasons Fiona couldn't be mine. She wasn't even planning to stay. As soon as she saved enough money, she'd be on her way to her mom's in Iowa.

A traitorous voice in the back of my mind whispered that maybe she wouldn't leave if someone gave her a reason to stay.

Especially if that someone was me.

Fuck.

I worked for a while, trying to ignore all these damn feelings. Focused on the car. I had a long way to go before it would be ready for the show, and with all the distractions lately, I wasn't making enough progress.

And yes, I was avoiding Fiona. Obviously.

Eventually, I decided to quit being a jackass by hiding in my shop. I still didn't know what I was going to do about her. Maybe she was already sick of my shit and she'd be back on the couch tonight.

I turned off the music and closed up for the night. My traitor dog had gone with her—because of course he had— so I walked the short distance to my house alone.

Music spilled out when I opened the front door, and I stopped just inside. Fiona was in the kitchen using a wooden spoon as a microphone, belting out the chorus to the song. With a flip of her hair, she twirled in her socks. She obviously hadn't heard me come in.

The chorus ended, the next verse began, and she kept right on singing, even though she had no idea what the words were.

I stared at her, feeling like my heart might burst right out of my chest.

Why? Because she was singing the wrong words? That drove me nuts.

But I loved it.

And what was that smell?

She spun again, but her eyes landed on me and she stopped herself with her toe before she'd made a full rotation. She lowered the wooden spoon and turned down the music.

"I didn't hear you come in."

"Sorry. Didn't mean to scare you."

"It's okay." She glanced at the spoon like she wasn't sure why she was holding it, and tossed it into the sink. "You weren't supposed to come back yet."

"Why?"

"It's fine, I'll make it work. I have two surprises for you," she said. "The second one isn't quite ready and I wasn't going to tell you about the first one quite yet, but I don't think I can wait."

"What are you talking about?"

"You can probably smell the second one. I made black-berry cobbler. I've never actually made it before, and I'm sure it's not even close to as good as Gram's, but I thought I'd give it a try."

I stared at her. "Why did you make blackberry cobbler?"

"Gram told me it's your favorite."

This didn't make any sense. I'd yelled at her over something stupid. Why would she make cobbler? "I'm confused."

"Isn't it your favorite?"

"Yes, but—"

"I just thought it might make you feel better."

"Me?"

"Yeah, you, Mr. Grouchface Shoutypants. You were being all angry scowly man, so I thought some cobbler might cheer you up. Plus it gave me something to do instead of just being irritated with you. I feel better already and I haven't even eaten any yet."

The timer on the oven dinged.

"Hold that thought. I don't want it to burn." She whirled around and grabbed a pair of oven mitts, then took her cobbler out of the oven.

The scent wafted toward me and my mouth watered. Holy shit, that smelled good.

"That needs to cool, so let me tell you about the first surprise." She took off the oven mitts and picked up her phone. "I say first because it happened first, before I started baking. I seriously almost ran over to tell you as soon as I got off the phone, but I figured you needed some space."

That was true, I had needed some space. But what the hell was she talking about now?

The smell of the cobbler was very distracting.

"I found you a '59 Cadillac series 62 convertible." She held up her phone, showing me a picture. "Not only did I find you the car, this one has a numbers-matching engine and transmission, very little rust, and it has all the original dials in the dashboard. I'm seriously dying to see what you can do with this thing. Look at it."

I was looking. But I wasn't seeing the car.

"And you're not going to believe the price he's giving us. I'm telling you, all the time I spent chatting with these guys when I worked for my dad was so worth it. I don't want to sound braggy, but I'm positive he wouldn't have given anyone else that price. It's a freaking steal."

In that moment, with the smell of cobbler in the air and Fiona shoving her phone in my face, something clicked.

I didn't want to be alone anymore.

It wasn't just that she'd done something nice for me to make me feel better, although the fact that she'd baked blackberry cobbler made me momentarily consider proposing right here. It wasn't even that she'd gone out of her way to find the car for Chief Stanley without me asking.

It was all of it.

It was coming home feeling like shit and finding her singing in the kitchen with a wooden spoon as a microphone. It was her stupid plants with dumb names, and the stash of nuts she thought I didn't know about to feed the squirrels. It was the fact that my dog loved her more than he loved me and I didn't blame him one bit.

My house was lit up and warm and it smelled good, and this sexy tattooed badass fucking ray of sunshine had been twirling around my kitchen in her socks.

I wanted that. I wanted all of it.

I wanted to fucking keep her.

And suddenly I realized the truth. I'd already jumped.

"Of course, you might have come over here to tell me we made a huge mistake the other day and this whole thing isn't working out. I'm optimistic, but I'm not stupid. And the cobbler isn't to bribe you into letting me stay or anything. I just thought if we were both in a better mood, maybe we could talk."

I took the phone out of her hand and tossed it on the counter. She started to ask what I was doing, but I grabbed her and cut her off with a kiss.

"Or this works, too," she said.

"We didn't make a mistake, and I'm sorry for being a dick." I kissed her again. "I have an asshole habit that's hard to break."

She draped her arms around my neck. "Do you want some cobbler?"

"Later." I met her eyes. "Right now I just want you."

The desire in her eyes reflected mine. I was hard for her already, and at this point, I was done holding back. I grabbed her ass and pulled her in tight, letting her feel my erection.

"Please tell me you're going to give me some of that," she said, rubbing herself against me.

I groaned. "All of it, baby. Do you think you can take it?"

Her lips curled in a smile. "It's a lot, but you know me. I have a real can-do attitude."

Fuck, she was adorable. "Get over here."

I would have happily fucked her in the kitchen, but I needed a condom, so I grabbed her by the wrist and hauled her to my room.

Wasting no time, I pulled her shirt over her head. She tore at my clothes, like she was as desperate for this as I was. There was no slow exploration. No careful undressing, revealing new areas of skin. The other day in the shop had been nothing but a warmup, leaving us both frantic for more.

She let her bra drop and kicked off her panties while I shucked my pants. I had to pause, the sight of her naked body stunning me. I looked down at her, tracing my hands up and down her arms. She was all curves and softness. Her full tits tapered into a narrow waist. And those hips. That ass.

"Fuck, you're so sexy." I cupped her face and tasted her lips while I backed her up toward my bed. "I need to be inside you."

"Yes, please," she breathed.

She climbed on the bed while I got out a condom and put it on. She tipped her legs open and I growled my approval.

"Fucking look at you."

I crawled on top of her, feeling the glide of warm skin. She slid her hands up my chest and around the back of my neck, then brought my lips to hers. With my tongue invading her mouth, I pushed inside her slick opening.

There was nothing like that first thrust. She was hot and tight and so fucking perfect. I groaned into her mouth and held deep inside her.

"You good?" I asked, my voice sounding almost strangled. But she felt so fucking good I could barely contain myself.

"Oh my god, yes."

Bracing myself on top of her, I thrust in and out. Her tits rubbed against my chest and I couldn't stop kissing her—her mouth, her neck, her chest. I lapped my tongue against her nipple and she moaned in pleasure, sighing my name.

I pushed myself up to look at her and our gazes locked. Those hazel-green eyes held me captive, opening a space in my chest I'd long since closed off. My body was alive for her, my cock hard, the pressure almost unbearable. But this wasn't just sex. Not for me. I was feeling things that scared the shit out of me, but for once I didn't turn away.

I sank into them.

She pressed her hands into my lower back, inviting me

in deeper. Her cheeks flushed the sexiest shade of pink and her lips parted.

"You feel so good, I could explode inside you right now," I said, and it was true. My cock ached for release. "But I want to watch you come first."

She drew her knees up higher and, still holding her gaze, I fucked her hard. She clung to me, moaning with every thrust. Her pussy tightened around me, so hot I could hardly hold back.

"That's it. Come all over my cock, beautiful."

She gasped, her eyes fluttering closed, and dug her fingers into my back. Her pussy clenched, the pulses of her orgasm relentlessly squeezing my cock.

That was it. I came fucking undone.

With a loud grunt, I started coming, bursting inside her. My back clenched tight as I drove into her, the waves of ecstasy overtaking me.

Holy shit.

She wrapped her arms around me as I finished. Her breath was warm on my neck, her skin so soft. I stayed inside her and buried my face in her hair, breathing deeply.

So fucking good.

I lifted up to look at her and kissed her lips.

"That was amazing," she said, her voice quiet.

And I wondered if she knew how right she was.

27

FIONA

*R*eluctantly, I got up to use the bathroom, then Evan did the same. I waited in his room, wondering if I should get dressed or not. Was I hoping for too much by lying naked in his bed? Was he going to come in, throw on his clothes, and go back to being grumpy broody man?

God, I hoped not.

He came back and I got a little thrill when he immediately got back into bed. I nestled in against him as he drew me close, wrapping his thick arms around me.

Bliss.

I was so relaxed, I felt like I could melt right into him.

We lay together in silence for a while, just breathing. The sex had been incredible, but I felt like something more was happening. There was an intensity simmering between us. Something had changed. It made a zing of excitement ping through my body and nervous flutters stir in my belly.

"Thank you," he said, finally, breaking the silence with his low, rumbly voice.

"For what?"

Tracing little circles on my skin, he took a deep, slow breath. "For putting up with me, I guess."

I laughed softly. "You're definitely a handful."

"Sorry."

I lifted up and propped my head on my arm. "What's been going on in that head of yours? You're so hot and cold."

"Truth?"

"Yeah."

"I've been afraid."

That was probably the last thing I'd expected him to say. "Afraid of what?"

"Of how I feel about you."

A sense of warmth blossomed in my chest as I realized what was happening. Evan was opening up to me.

"Why would that scare you?"

He glanced away, pausing for another long moment. "I decided a long time ago that I wasn't going to get into a relationship with someone again. That I was better off alone."

"You got hurt, didn't you?" I asked quietly.

He nodded.

My heart was already breaking for him, and I didn't even know what had happened. "Does it have anything to do with the boxes in the spare room?"

"Yeah."

"Will you tell me what happened?"

He met my eyes again and the hurt nearly broke me. "I've never told anyone."

I placed my hand on his chest. "You can trust me."

He was quiet again for a long moment, and I thought he might say no. I hoped he'd start talking. I could sense that he needed to. He needed to get this out.

"I went away to college after high school and right away, I hated it. I struggled with my classes and I had this asshole roommate who spent most of his time getting drunk and smoking pot. It sucked and after just a few months, I was thinking about going home. Then I met Tucker Kosten. We had a class together and for whatever reason, just hit it off. He reminded me a lot of my brother Asher, I guess. We started hanging out and eventually got an apartment together off campus.

"We became pretty close. Honestly, he was my best friend. I would have trusted him with anything—with my life. He was like another brother to me. Anyway, sophomore year, I started dating this girl, Carly. Tucker had been dating a girl named Larissa, and the four of us hung out all the time."

He paused and placed his hand over mine.

"I fell hard for Carly. Really hard. I was infatuated with her. And everything was great. I thought I'd found my soulmate. Then Asher got arrested.

"I came home as soon as I found out what had happened. I hated being away from Carly, but my family needed me. The legal stuff happened pretty fast and all of a sudden, my brother was in fucking prison. That was it, there wasn't anything we could do."

"I can't even imagine how awful that must have been."

"It fucked me up a little bit. It fucked us all up, I think. Asher was... he was the oldest, you know? He wasn't perfect but we all looked up to him. And then all of a sudden, he was gone.

"After that, things got rough at home. I didn't go back to school for a while, but I talked to Carly all the time. I tried to convince her to come out here to see me, but she never did. Looking back, that should have tipped me off that something wasn't right, but at the time, that wasn't where my head was. After seeing things go down with Asher, I had this sense of urgency about Carly. Like she could be taken away from me in an instant, and I couldn't let that happen. So before I went back to school, I bought a ring."

I had a feeling I knew where this was going.

"I wanted to surprise her, so I didn't tell her I was coming back. I didn't tell Tucker, either. I went straight to Carly's, but as soon as I saw her face when she answered the door, I knew something was wrong. She went pale. I tried to hug her, we hadn't seen each other in months, but she crossed her arms and wouldn't look at me. She just kept saying she wasn't expecting me and I should have called first. And then Tucker walked out of her bedroom."

"Oh my god."

"They made a bunch of bullshit excuses about how they never meant for it to happen. But seriously, what the fuck? I thought I was going to marry her, I had her ring in my pocket, and he was my best friend. My brother had just gone to prison. And they knew. They knew what was happening at home, and they still started fucking each other behind my back."

"So you not only lost your girlfriend, you lost your best friend too. During what must have been one of the most difficult times of your life."

"Yeah."

I closed my eyes, letting out a long breath. Evan kept his hand over mine, holding it against his chest. I couldn't believe he'd been betrayed like that. It made my heart ache for him. For the man he must have been before they'd crushed him. No wonder he was so closed-off. He'd given his heart to someone and she'd stomped on it like it meant nothing to her.

Suddenly I really, really hated Carly.

"After that, I quit school. Packed up all my shit and

moved home. When I moved into this place, I brought it all with me, but I've never unpacked it."

"So that's what's in the spare bedroom? All your stuff from college?"

"Yeah. I don't know why I even keep it. I guess I keep thinking I should go through it at some point, but I never do."

"Evan, I'm so sorry that happened to you. And I hope they cheated on each other and gave each other chlamydia and herpes."

He laughed. "I don't know what happened to them. Carly tried to call me a bunch of times, but I never answered. I didn't have anything to say to her, and eventually she stopped trying."

"Did you ever hear from Tucker?"

"No."

"What an asshole," I said. "I don't even know them and I'm so mad. You know what, fuck them. I hope they got chlamydia, herpes, and some kind of rectal dysfunction that gives them chronic diarrhea for the rest of their lives."

"That's disgusting."

"They're disgusting. And they deserve it."

"You're very vindictive when you want to be."

"They hurt you." I said.

He squeezed my hand. "Yeah."

"So that's why you live out here by yourself and act like a jerk so everyone will leave you alone."

"That's depressingly accurate." He took another deep breath. "Or it was—before you showed up."

"And now you have this random girl sleeping here, and working next to you, when all you wanted was to live out the rest of your life in secluded loneliness."

"Yeah, so get the fuck out."

I laughed. "Really, though, I don't want to put a bunch of pressure on you, and under normal circumstances we could just... see where this goes. Like normal people would. But this isn't exactly a normal situation, is it?"

"No, it's not."

"So what happens now?"

His whiskey-brown eyes watched me for a long moment. No brow furrow. No frustration or anger. His expression was as smooth as I'd ever seen it.

"Now you're mine."

The possessiveness in his tone gave me tingles. "I'm yours? It's that simple?"

"It is for me."

I'd never had someone say those words to me before. But the thought of belonging to Evan Bailey? I liked it. I liked it a lot.

"So I can keep my new plants?"

One corner of his mouth hooked in a smile. "Beautiful, you can fill the house with plants if it makes you happy. Just leave some space for my dog."

"Done." I gasped. "Eugenia!"

"What?"

"Blanche and Myra's new friend. I couldn't think of a name, but I think it's Eugenia."

"Of course it is. And the one in the office?"

"Edith."

He looked at me like he was mystified. "Where the fuck did you come from?"

I shrugged one shoulder. "I just needed a place to fix my car."

"You got a little more than that, didn't you?"

I glanced at his dick. He wasn't hard anymore, but he

was still damned impressive. "I'd say I got a lot more. There's nothing little about it."

The corner of his mouth twitched in a smile. He rolled me onto my back, pinning his arms over my head, and kissed me.

You're mine.

This was a lot. It was big, just like the man caressing my lips with his. And for the moment, any doubts I might have had faded into the background.

If this was what it meant to be Evan Bailey's girl, sign me up.

28

FIONA

*T*he sun was warm and the air was filled with the scent of blooming flowers and rich soil. Gram had the most amazing gardens I'd ever seen. Flowers, vegetables, fruits, berries. I came over to work outside with her at least once a week. Sometimes we chatted as we pulled weeds and tended to her chickens. Other times, we puttered around in comfortable silence.

A month ago, Evan Bailey had declared that I was his. And he'd certainly meant it.

Not that he'd changed. He was still serious and broody with a perpetual brow furrow. He still growled at things when he was frustrated. He was still rough around the edges. Still Evan.

But somehow I was the lucky girl who got to see the Evan he kept hidden on the inside.

That man was affectionate and devoted. He kissed me tenderly, fucked me mercilessly, and never missed an opportunity for an ass grab.

What he hadn't said that day was that I wasn't just his. He was mine.

I knew how special that was. Evan Bailey didn't give his heart to just anyone. He guarded it fiercely, lest someone wound it again.

That someone was not going to be me.

I didn't necessarily know what the future held for us. My bank account was recovering, but I hadn't mentioned Iowa in weeks. The truth was, I already knew I wasn't going to leave. Not unless something changed. If things crashed and burned with Evan, I'd have to reevaluate, but for now, I couldn't imagine life without him.

So I didn't.

Gram came over to where I'd been pulling weeds for the last half hour. "Why don't we take a break? I made some iced tea."

"That sounds perfect."

I went inside to wash my hands, then joined Gram on the back porch. Her peckers clucked and scratched and the beautifully cultivated rows of her gardens stretched across the yard. Birds chirped and the creek trickled in the distance.

It was positively idyllic here.

"How's my Wolf doing?" Gram asked.

"He's busy. He's working on a car for Chief Stanley, plus the Pontiac of course." I nibbled on my lower lip. I spent more time with Gram than he did, and I wondered if that bothered her. "Maybe I should suggest that he stop by next time he comes into town."

"It's all right, Cricket. He'll come home in his own time."

"Come home?"

She slowly tipped back and forth in her rocking chair. "Have I told you the story of the lone wolf and the chief's daughter?"

"I don't think so." I settled in to my chair. I loved Gram's stories.

"When the world was still young, there was a great wolf pack. They roamed far and wide through their vast territory. One day, a young male wolf took a grievous injury. Not a mortal wound, but close. So he did what wolves do: He found a safe place to lick his wounds and heal. Except when he was up and walking again, he didn't return to his pack. He stayed in his cave and avoided them, as if they'd done the damage."

"He didn't trust his own pack anymore?"

"No, he didn't."

"That doesn't seem fair of him. Although I guess he was just a wolf."

"True. And fair doesn't hold much sway in the wild. Doesn't always hold sway with men, either."

"What happened to him?" I was afraid she was going to say he died alone in his cave.

Gram's mouth twitched in the hint of a smile. "One afternoon, the chief's daughter was out gathering berries when she came across the mouth of the lone wolf's cave. His yellow eyes glowed in the darkness and he growled a warning."

Involuntarily, I gasped.

"Her father, the chief, was friends with the wolf pack, so his daughter wasn't afraid, not even when the wolf bared his teeth to her. She knew the pack had traveled north in search of prey and this male must have been separated from his family. And as he paced back and forth in the entrance to the cave, she could see the signs of his injury."

"So she knew he'd been wounded and now he was alone."

"Yes. And she knew it wasn't good for the wolf to be alone. So she decided to help him."

"How?"

"She began leaving pieces of meat to coax him from the cave. At first she kept her distance, but gradually she moved closer. It wasn't long before he was eating right out of her hand."

"She wasn't afraid he'd attack her?"

"Oh, I imagine she had moments of fear. The lone wolf wasn't friendly to most people. He growled and bared his teeth to everyone else. But the chief's daughter became the exception."

"But what about his family? What about the wolf pack?"

Gram's lips turned up in a smile. "That's a very good question, Cricket. You see, the chief's daughter wasn't trying to tame the wolf. She was merely teaching him to trust her. Once he did, she started luring him farther from his cave, in the direction of the pack.

"One day, she led him close to where the pack was resting. The lone wolf sat at a distance and watched for a while, then went back to his cave. But the chief's daughter was determined. Each day, she led the wolf back to his pack, until he finally ran into their midst and made contact."

"Was the pack happy to see him?"

"Indeed they were. They circled and sniffed and did what wolves do. And the chief's daughter watched with a full heart as they accepted the lone wolf back into their pack. The story says the alpha wolf looked at the chief's daughter and dipped his head to acknowledge what she'd done."

A tingle raced down my spine. "That gives me chills. What a beautiful story. Do you mean I'm kind of like the chief's daughter, luring the lone wolf out of his cave?"

"A little bit," she said. "He's happier than I've seen him in a very long time. Soon I think he'll remember he can trust his pack. He'll be a part of it again."

I finished my iced tea with Gram and reluctantly said goodbye.

When I got home, Evan and Sasquatch were gone. His vehicles were all here, so he'd probably taken him for a trail walk. I threw in a load of laundry and glanced in the spare room. He'd thrown out most of the boxes he'd brought home from college without even looking in them.

There was a knock at the front door, so I went to answer it. I opened the door and almost choked on my own tongue. It was Simone.

Her platinum hair was down and she wore a flowy pink tank top, jeans, and bright red lipstick. She smiled and held her arms out.

"Oh my god, Fi, I missed you so much."

Before I could say a word, she grabbed me in a hug, pinning my arms to my sides. My back stiffened and I squirmed out of her grasp.

"What the hell are you doing here?" I stepped away from her. "Wait, how did you even find me?"

"I don't know, your dad talked to someone who said he talked to you a while ago about a car for some Bailey guy."

Oh my god. The Caddy for Chief Stanley. It wasn't like I'd been actively hiding, but I had liked the idea that my dad didn't know exactly where I was.

Damn.

She wandered into the front room, glancing around. "This place is kinda basic, but I guess it's cute. So you're shacking up with this guy? He must have a huge dick."

"What?"

"Well, it's obviously not because he has money."

I put my hands on my hips. "Seriously?"

"I'm just saying. Anyway, I know I should be all totally mad at you for abandoning me and everything. But I can't stay mad at you."

"*You're* mad at *me*?" I asked. "Did you forget the part where you were sleeping with my dad and lying to me about it?"

Rolling her eyes, she groaned. "Are we still on that topic? God, Fi, it's not that big of a deal."

"Are you still with him?"

She shrugged. "For now. He blew me off for a while, but he came crawling back. You know how men are."

That figured. It was typical of my dad. "Not all men are like that."

"Don't be naïve, Fi. Of course they are. I know exactly why he's with me." She gestured to her body. "And he knows exactly why I'm with him." Raising her eyebrows, she rubbed her thumb and fingertips together, signaling that it was because he had money—and spent it on her.

I stopped myself from asking whether she realized she'd just made herself sound like a prostitute.

"Simone, why are you here?"

She took a dramatic breath. "Because your dad needs to see you."

I gaped at her. He'd sent her to convince me to talk to him? Unbelievable. "I don't see how this is any of your business."

"I know you have this weird hang-up about me being with your dad, but we've been best friends our whole lives. Or close to it. Are you really going to let a man come between us?"

"When that man is my father and you both lied to me about sleeping together, yes. Yes, I am."

"God, Fiona, you're being so fucking unfair."

"Look, I don't care. Date my dad. Sleep with him. Move in with him if you want. It's fine. And I'll go see him eventually, but I'm just not ready for that right now. I need some space."

She crossed her arms. "Could you maybe stop being selfish for like five seconds? He's waiting in the car for you."

"He's here?"

"Yeah."

Letting out a frustrated breath, I glanced at the door. "Fine."

Simone gave me a self-satisfied smile. I wanted to smack her, but I settled for glaring at her back as I followed her outside.

Dad got out of his SUV dressed in a pale blue polo and dark slacks. He looked a little rough. There were circles under his eyes and his face was slightly puffy, like he was bloated.

He was stressed. He always ate too much salt when he was stressed.

"Fiona," he said, then glanced at Simone. "Wait in the car."

Her face twisted in a sneer. "But—"

"Just get in the damn car," he said.

Simone rolled her eyes, but got in the passenger side.

I crossed my arms. "Hi, Dad. Nice to see you too."

"Can we go inside?"

There was no way I was letting him into Evan's house. It was his den—his safe place. And right now, my dad felt more like an adversary than family. "I'd rather not."

His face darkened a single shade. "I didn't come out here to argue with you."

"Then why are you here?"

"To come clean."

I felt like a terrible person, but I was immediately suspicious of his motives. "Okay."

"You were right about me working with Felix Orman again. I got into some debt. The business wasn't making enough to pay it off. Felix came to me with an offer. Low-key stuff, not a lot of risk. I took him up on it because I needed some quick cash."

"What debt? I was doing your books and I didn't know the business was in debt."

"It was personal."

"So your solution was to join up with the guy who almost got you sent to prison once before?"

"Look, there are things you don't understand."

I rolled my eyes. *Of course, Dad, because I'm just a child.* "So you did know the Mustang was stolen."

He shrugged. "We were moving a lot of goods. Rare cars, parts. Other stuff. I found him a buyer, I didn't ask Felix for the car's history."

I raised my eyebrows. "You were moving other stuff? What other stuff?"

"It doesn't matter now. I'm getting out. Felix is into some heavy shit and even though the money's great, it's too much for me. Plus he's got the feds breathing down his neck. That wasn't what I signed up for."

"So you're out? Just like that? We both know it's not that easy."

"Yeah, I'm aware of that," he snapped. "I'm working on it."

"Well, I'm glad you're getting out. Believe it or not, I don't want anything bad to happen to you."

"Good. Then come home."

My shoulders slumped. So that was the catch. "Dad—"

He put a hand up. "Fiona, I know I broke my promise, and I'm sorry. I'll own up to that. But you have to come back. The shop is a mess without you."

My heart fluttered with sudden fear. I'd defied my father up until now. I'd left my home and my job, and I'd stayed away, even when he'd called, demanding I come back.

But standing here in front of him, looking him in the eyes, saying no was so much harder.

Because I'd done this once before. I'd told him no to his face.

And it hadn't ended well.

But what was my alternative? Leave with him? There was no way in hell I was going back.

I took a deep breath, wishing Evan were here. I'd have felt so much braver if I knew a six-foot-four wall of muscle was here to back me up.

"No." The word left my lips and the fear only intensified. "No, I'm not coming back."

He took a slow step closer and his voice was dangerously low. "Fiona, I want you to think very carefully about what you're saying to me right now. I'm your father. I raised you on my own because your mother was too selfish to stick around. I sacrificed for you and provided for you, even when I didn't have to anymore. And this is the thanks I get? You run off to live in some fucking cabin in the woods with a goddamn lumberjack?"

I was not taking the bait with that crack about Evan. This wasn't about him. "I had many reasons for leaving, and believe it or not, they weren't all about you. I'm an adult and I can make my own choices. And I chose to quit my job and find a new one. I found a new place to live. And I'm happy here. I'm sorry if that makes things hard on you, but you're not going to guilt me into coming back."

"That's not an acceptable answer."

My heart hammered in my chest and I clenched my fists, digging my fingernails into my palms. "It's the only answer you're going to get."

Just as Dad took another step closer, Sasquatch burst out of the trees. Barking loudly, he ran at us at full speed. Dad's eyes widened and he jerked away from me, stumbling back a few feet.

"Sasquatch, wait," I said, not entirely sure what he'd been trained to do.

The dog stopped. Growling, he positioned himself between me and my dad.

"What the hell?" Dad asked and backed closer to his SUV.

Evan appeared, coming toward us at a run. Sasquatch stayed in front of me, a ridge of fur standing straight up along his spine.

"You're going to regret this, Fiona," Dad said. "You should have come with me while you had the chance."

A sick feeling spread through my stomach as he got in his SUV, turned on the engine, and backed up to turn around.

Evan caught up, breathing hard. "What the fuck is he doing here?"

"Trying to get me to go home with him."

He put his arm around me. "Are you okay?"

"Yeah. No."

"Come on. Let's go inside."

Dad's SUV disappeared down the gravel road as Evan led me into the house with Sasquatch behind us.

"Did you send Sasquatch?"

"No. We were walking back and he just took off running. I figured something must be wrong."

"Just my dad being himself." I slumped onto the couch. Evan took off his flannel shirt and laid it over me like a blanket. "Thank you."

"He was trying to get you to leave?"

"Yeah, he wants me to come home and go back to work. He claims he's not working with Felix Orman anymore. And I don't know, maybe he isn't. Maybe he'll stay legit this time. It doesn't matter, I still can't go back. I don't want to go back."

"No, fuck that."

"Exactly." I tucked his shirt under my chin. It was soft and smelled like him. "Simone was with him. He sent her to the door first to coax me into talking to him."

"That's your friend who was..."

"Sleeping with my dad? Yeah. Apparently she still is. And she still has no clue why that bothers me."

He pulled me closer and I rested my cheek against his chest. The last thing Dad said kept echoing through my mind. *You're going to regret this, Fiona. You should have come with me when you had the chance.*

You're going to regret this.

Regret.

He'd said that to me once before. The last time I'd told him no.

The last time I'd tried to leave.

"Evan?"

"Yeah, baby?"

"I tried to leave once before. Two years ago, I walked out on my job. Told Dad I quit. I didn't move anywhere, I still lived with Simone. But I didn't want to work for my dad anymore. I got a job at a nursery. It was really small, just a few employees. I worked there for a few months and it was so great. I loved it. Then one night Dad came to my apartment. He said I needed to quit my job at the nursery and come back to work for him."

"What did you tell him?"

"I said no. And he said..." I paused and took a shaky breath. "He said I'd regret it and I should have come back while I had the chance. I thought he meant he was giving me one more chance to get my job back and after that he wouldn't hire me again."

"But he meant something else?"

"Maybe that was all he meant. I can't prove anything, but a couple of weeks later, there was a fire at the nursery. A big one. They weren't sure what caused it, but I always wondered if..."

"If your dad did it."

"I feel horrible for thinking that he could do something so awful. And yet, I still wonder if he had something to do with it." I swallowed hard. "He said the same thing just now. He said I'd regret it."

The motion of his chest as he took a deep breath was so soothing. He ran his fingers through my hair and kissed my head.

"You have nothing to worry about. I'll never let anything happen to you."

I nestled into the warmth of his chest and he squeezed me closer. But even the comfort of Evan's embrace wasn't enough to completely erase my fear. Because what if the fire at the nursery had been my father? And what if he did something to Evan to get back at me?

How could I live with myself?

"Trust me," Evan said, his voice soft and low.

Closing my eyes, I nodded against his chest. I did trust him. I'd never trusted anyone so completely and without question.

A warm sensation swept through me, sending pings of electricity across my skin and flutters in my tummy. In that moment, I realized that I was in love with Evan Bailey. Crazy, madly in love with him.

And I'd do anything to protect him from my father.

29

EVAN

I wondered if this was how Sasquatch felt when he sensed an intruder. Hyper-alert, senses alive. Twenty-four hours ago, Shane Gallagher had dared to show his face here, and I still hadn't calmed down.

That piece of shit. I hadn't liked him before, but after seeing how much he'd scared Fiona, now I fucking hated the bastard. It was one thing to screw me over. It was quite another to hurt my girl.

No one hurt my girl.

It made me want to stick to her like Velcro. Stand in between her and anyone who threatened her.

Not unlike my dog had done yesterday.

Could I still call him *my* dog? He'd bonded to Fiona almost from the beginning. He was already a lot more *our* dog than he was just mine.

But I was okay with it. I felt the same way. I liked her too.

Hell, I more than liked her. I was in love with her.

Admitting that to myself was getting easier, although I hadn't said it out loud yet.

I hadn't wanted to fall in love—with anyone, ever. But I

also knew from experience that life didn't always turn out the way you wanted it to. Sometimes that was for the worse. Other times a guy got lucky.

Speaking of, my lucky ran into the shop, an ecstatic smile lighting up her face.

I smiled back. I couldn't help it.

"Ask me how awesome I am," she said.

"I know how awesome you are."

"No, just play along. Ask me."

"Sorry. How awesome are you?"

"I'm so freaking awesome," she said, her voice laced with excitement. "You know how we couldn't find a bumper for the Caddy?"

"Yeah."

"I found one. It's perfect. A guy named Craig Shelton has one, and he isn't even that far away. And he'll totally take a trade instead of cash. You've got those old Chevy doors just lying around, but they're worth good money to the right person. So I found the right person, and I found the bumper you need."

I slipped my hand around her waist and hauled her roughly against me. "You're not just awesome. You're fucking amazing."

"Thank you."

Leaning down, I captured her mouth with mine. Slid my tongue along the seam of her lips, earning a little shiver. Not because I was glad she'd found a bumper for Chief Stanley's Cadillac. Because she was mine and I loved kissing her every chance I got.

But I appreciated the work she did, too. She was a badass.

"I should head over there and close out the deal before

he changes his mind or claims he forgot what we agreed to or something."

"*We* should head over," I said.

"Are you sure you have time?"

I kissed her again. "I'll make time."

WE PULLED up outside Craig Shelton's place. It was typical. A big field with rows of old cars in varying states of decay. Craig came out of the trailer he used as an office. He was a burly guy with dark hair everywhere—head, face, arms, peeking out above his shirt collar.

"Hi, Craig. I'm Fiona."

He tipped his chin to both of us. "Fiona. Evan. I've got the bumper out here if you want to take a look first."

"You show us yours, and we'll—" She stopped abruptly. "You know what, that was going to come out weird. How about we just follow you."

He led us around the side of the trailer. Sure enough, he had what we needed. Normally, I would have negotiated this myself, but since Fiona had done the work, I stayed back a few feet and let her take the lead.

"Looks good to me." She glanced at me. "What do you think?"

"Yeah, it's in good condition. We can use it."

"Great. So we talked about a trade. I'll show you what we brought."

Fiona kept chatting him up while we walked back to my truck. I let her do her thing. She knew her stuff, she didn't need me to butt in. She showed Craig the doors and gave him some details.

"This all looks good to me," Fiona said. "What about you?"

Craig rubbed his bearded chin. "I don't know. I'm thinking I'll take your trade plus a hundred."

"That's not what we agreed to," Fiona said.

I took two steps closer.

He shrugged. "Things got a little more expensive since we talked."

"We talked a few hours ago," she said. "Come on, Craig. We had a deal."

"And I'm saying maybe we need a new deal."

I took another step closer so I was right behind Fiona and leveled him with a glare. A low growl rumbled in my throat. Craig's eyes lifted to meet mine. I shook my head.

No one messed with my girl.

He cleared his throat. "Fine. We'll go with what we agreed to. A straight-across trade."

She glanced up at me, then back at him. "Thank you."

I unloaded the doors and put the bumper in the back of my truck. Fiona said goodbye to Craig—she was nicer to him than I would have been—and we left.

"Is that why Gram calls you Wolf?"

"What?"

"The way you growl at things. And people."

"I don't know. She's called me Wolf since I was a kid." I took a right onto the highway heading toward Tilikum. "Sorry for butting in. I didn't like the way he was talking to you."

She smiled. "That's okay. I liked knowing you had my back."

"Always, beautiful."

"You know, next time we should just go with it. Play good cop, bad cop. Obviously I'm the good cop and you're the growly loose cannon. I'll pretend I'm trying to hold you back and make you be reasonable, but if I let you at him, he's screwed."

Smiling, I shook my head. "It's probably a good plan."

"We make a great team."

She was right about that. I reached over and took her hand, bringing it to my mouth for a kiss.

"Oh, I just remembered, it's Stitch and Sip night, so that's good news."

I scowled. I wasn't crazy about her going anywhere by herself right now. Although the craft store with Grace and whoever else showed up for their girly craft night was probably safe enough.

"I'll drive you."

"You don't have to do that."

"I want to."

She glanced at me with a little smile. "Okay, Wolf. You can drive me."

By the time we got back and I unloaded the bumper into the shop, it was almost time for her to go. She changed into a clean shirt and jeans—they made me want to take them off her, but she squirmed out of my embrace with a giggle.

That was fine. I'd strip her out of them later.

We got on my bike and rode into town. She got off the bike and got out her little crochet bag. She was so fucking cute. I kissed her, then grabbed her and hauled her against me so I could kiss her again before letting her go.

I watched her go inside the Knotty Knitter, debating whether to just wait out here or find something to do. Sitting in the parking lot was probably overkill. She wasn't alone in there. Cara's car was out front, and that woman was enough to scare off just about anybody.

Still, I didn't want to go too far. I could head over to the

Caboose for a beer, but that sounded boring. I wondered if my brothers were home tonight. They lived close, I could swing by their place and pick up Fiona when she was done.

I drove over to the house three of my brothers shared. Asher and Grace lived right next door, in a house Grace had bought and started remodeling while Asher was in prison. It was pretty cool what she'd done. They'd talked about buying it before their lives had gone sideways, and Grace had done it on her own while he was away. They'd had an electrical fire last year that had set them back a bit, but we'd all pitched in to help fix it.

The symbolism wasn't lost on me. They'd brought the house back from the ashes, just like their life together.

Logan, Levi, and Gavin had moved in next door. I wondered how Asher was handling living so close to our three younger brothers. Levi was a lot like me, he tended to keep to himself. But Logan and Gavin were obnoxious, especially when they were together.

The location of my house—outside town—was not an accident.

Still, I found myself inexplicably in the mood for their company tonight.

And why not? They were my brothers. Just because I hadn't dropped by their house unannounced in a long time —or maybe ever—didn't mean it had to be a big deal.

All three worked for the fire department, so chances were at least one of them was on duty tonight. But there were three vehicles out front, so it looked like a full house.

I parked on the street and went up to the front door. Since they never knocked when they showed up at my house, I didn't bother either. Just walked right in.

And immediately wished I hadn't.

In the middle of the living room was a life-sized cardboard cutout of Asher. Angry Asher. It looked like one of them had caught him on camera getting out of the shower and he hadn't been happy about it. His face was twisted in a snarl, like he'd been yelling at whoever was taking the picture. He wasn't wearing any clothes, his hair was wet, and one hand held a towel over his crotch. The other made a fist at his side.

My other three brothers all stood around the cutout, dressed in nothing but white underwear.

White underwear with a picture of Asher's face—the same as on the cutout—right on the crotch.

They had one of their phones set up on a tripod, facing them.

"What the fuck?" I asked.

"Dude, awesome," Gavin said. "Do we have an extra pair?"

"Shit yeah, we got like ten," Logan said. "Hang on, I'll find the box."

"No," I said.

"Come on, your timing is perfect," Gavin said.

"I'm not putting those on."

"Never mind," Gavin said. "He's allergic to fun. Just take another one."

"Okay," Logan said. "On three. One, two, three."

They all posed around the cutout while Logan took a picture with a remote.

"Are we done?" Levi asked. "I have to get to work."

"Chillax, broseph. I gotta see if we got a good one." He took the phone off the tripod and started swiping through his photos.

Levi headed for the hallway. "I'm getting dressed. I can't wear Asher's face on my junk anymore."

Gavin looked down at himself, grinning. "These are so awesome."

"I probably don't want to know, but why are you guys wearing underwear with Asher's face on them?"

"For Grace," Gavin said, as if that explained it. "Where's Fiona?"

"Not here."

"That sucks."

I shot him a glare.

"Gavin got this picture of Asher coming out of the shower," Logan said. "So obviously we had to use it. Beer?"

"Sure. I'll get it. Want one?"

"Yeah, me and Gav are off until tomorrow."

I picked my way through their cluttered living room and went into the kitchen. It wasn't a total shithole—when they'd been younger, their place had been a health hazard—but it was still obvious a bunch of guys lived here. There were random dirty dishes sitting out, plus a few soda cans and beer bottles. I grabbed three beers out of the fridge and added to the pile of bottle caps on the counter.

Gavin hadn't bothered to get dressed. He lounged on the couch in his Asher-face underwear. Logan hadn't either—just wore his underwear and a pair of tube socks with a red stripe pulled up to his shins. I didn't bother commenting on it. For them, it wasn't really weird.

Levi came out in his Tilikum Fire Department shirt. "I'm heading out. I'll see you guys tomorrow."

"See ya, bromingo." Logan held his phone up so Gavin could see. "Check this out."

"That's the money shot," Gavin said.

I handed them each a beer and took a seat on their couch.

"So you're sending the picture to Grace?" I asked.

"We're going to get it framed for her. But first we're going to put the cardboard Asher in their window. Then we'll get cardboard cutouts of us wearing the Asher underwear and put those in their window. It's gonna be fucking hilarious."

"Just don't try to make one of me."

Gavin and Logan glanced at each other.

"Nah, why would we do that?" Logan asked.

"Do you have one already?"

Gavin put the back of his hand over his mouth, unsuccessfully stifling a laugh.

"No," Logan said and put his hands up when I glared at him. "I swear. We didn't make one of you."

It was the stupidest thing, but I was almost disappointed. Not that I wanted them to make a cardboard cutout of me. Or worse, underwear with my face on them. But the three of them had always been close—always in on something together. And now that Asher was home, he was right here too, although in this case, the prank was on him.

But me? I'd always lurked on the edges of their world.

"So what are you doing out here?" Logan asked. "Let me guess. Your woman is busy, so you're bored."

"I just wanted to stay close by while she's at the stitch thing the girls do. Her asshole father showed up in town yesterday."

"No shit?"

Gavin sat straight up. "Why are we just hearing about this now?"

"Was I supposed to call you immediately?"

"Yes," Gavin said, as if that should have been completely obvious. "Of course you should have called us immediately. What the hell, man? Also, what kind of asshole are we talking?"

"Her dad's a prick. Remember the Mustang the cops

impounded because it had been stolen? He sold it to me. Fiona used to work for him, but she left because she suspected he was getting into criminal shit after he'd promised her he wouldn't. Plus he was fucking her best friend and hiding it from her."

"That's messed up," Logan said.

"The friend thing is gross, yeah. But that's not what pisses me off. It's how much he scared Fiona. I didn't realize she was afraid of her dad until I saw her afterward. She was literally shaking."

"I'd be pissed too," Logan said.

"He was driving off by the time I got there, but I wanted to rip his fucking face off."

"Do you think he'll be back?" Logan asked.

"Maybe. I think she's worried he will. This is really fucked up, but she said a couple of years ago she quit her job working for him and he got pissed about it. Then there was a fire at the new place she was working. She said she can't prove it was her dad, but she's always wondered if he had something to do with it."

"He's that crazy?" Logan asked.

"He might be."

"Do you need any help looking out for Fiona?" Gavin asked. "Because I'd be happy to help."

I glared at him. "No."

"Don't worry, man, I'll take really good care of her."

Logan glanced at him. "What's with the death wish, Gav? You realize he's going to rearrange your face if you keep talking about his girl."

Gavin just grinned.

"Seriously, though," Logan said. "If you need us to keep an eye out or whatever, let us know."

I nodded and took a sip of my beer. "Thanks."

"Of course." Logan tossed me a video game controller. "Time for me to kick your ass."

I took the controller in my hands. I hadn't sat around playing video games with them in a long time. But why not? "You fucking wish."

He did kick my ass. But I didn't really mind.

Not that I told him that.

But hanging out playing video games and having a beer with my brothers wasn't a terrible way to fill my time.

I didn't tell them that either. But I was pretty sure they knew.

30

FIONA

*E*van dropped me off at the Knotty Knitter and I went inside, feeling a little buzz of anxiety. Dad's visit yesterday had thrown me off-kilter. I'd thought about staying home tonight—being with Evan undoubtedly made me feel better—but I also enjoyed Stitch and Sip nights.

And I wasn't going to let fear make my decisions for me. Not anymore. So here I was.

Like everything in Tilikum, the little craft store was adorable. It smelled of crisp paper with a hint of something floral in the air. The aisles were stuffed with crafting and sewing supplies. Someone had spilled glitter near the scrapbooking section and tracked it across the floor.

I stepped around the glitter and headed for the back of the shop. There was a shabby couch and mismatched armchairs surrounding a large coffee table. Gram was here tonight, as were Grace and Cara. Rounding out this week's group were Tillie Bailey-Linfield, a woman who looked to be in her late sixties and wore bright pink lipstick, Violet Luscier, who had taken some convincing that I wasn't a mail-order bride, and Lacey Hanson, a math teacher at Tilikum High School.

I said hello to everyone and got settled in one of the empty chairs. Cara and Grace had given me a Stitch and Sip tote bag my first time, along with a crochet starter kit they'd put together for me. I wasn't very good yet, but it was still fun.

"There's our happy little tulip," Cara said. She actually had a crochet project in her lap, although it was hard to tell what she was trying to make. "You look adorable. What's different?"

I tucked my bangs—which were growing out too much to be called bangs anymore—behind my ear. "I'm not sure."

"I think it's your makeup," Cara said. "Your punk rock look was super cute, but I like this more natural thing you're doing. Your eyes are freaking gorgeous."

"Thanks." I felt my cheeks warm a little. I had started wearing less makeup. There had been a time when I wouldn't have been seen by anyone without eyeliner and plenty of mascara. Not even Simone. But lately I hadn't felt like I needed it the way I used to.

I felt like I could be myself here.

"You do look amazing," Grace said. "I think Tilikum agrees with you."

"Something sure does." Cara winked. "But I don't think it's the town. Unless by Tilikum you actually mean Evan's dick."

Tillie choked on her drink. "Cara, for heaven's sake."

"Oh Tillie, don't pretend you don't love a good dicking. We all do."

Tillie pinched her lips as if she disapproved, but she had a glimmer of amusement in her eyes. Lacey laughed and shook her head.

"Cara, read the room a little," Grace said, giving a subtle head nod toward Gram.

Gram didn't look up from her knitting. "Don't hold back on my account. I'm well aware my boys grew up into men who do all the things men do. Besides, you don't have to tell me there are benefits to being with a Bailey man. I was married to one for many happy years."

Cara whistled. "Gram, this is one of the many reasons you will forever be my hero."

Gram glanced up and winked at me.

"Speaking of the boys, what are they doing tonight?" Violet asked.

"Asher took some of his students to a tournament," Grace said. "It was a couple of hours away, but they're on their way home now. Eli took first in his weight class."

"Good for him," Gram said. "He worked hard for it."

"That's so great," I said. "I'm not sure what Evan is up to. I'm a little bit surprised he isn't sitting out in the parking lot after yesterday."

"What happened yesterday?" Grace asked.

"My dad and Simone showed up at his place."

Cara sat bolt upright in her chair. "Oh hell no. Why didn't you call me?"

I shrugged, trying to act nonchalant. "It wasn't that big of a deal."

"Who's Simone?" Lacey asked. "Evil stepmother?"

"No, so much worse," I said. "She was my best friend until I found out she was sleeping with my dad behind my back."

Violet and Tillie shared a shocked glance. "You're kidding."

"I wish I was. It's part of why I moved out here." Fresh

anger bubbled up and I dropped my crochet hook in my lap. "You know what really pisses me off?"

"Let it out, baby girl," Cara said.

"He sent Simone in first to try to coax me into talking to him. Why would he think that would work? Do neither of them realize how much their betrayal hurt me? I haven't even talked to Simone in weeks and she walked in and hugged me like we were still best friends."

"She touched you? I'll claw her face off," Cara said, and Grace put a soothing hand on her arm.

"I just don't understand how they can be so clueless."

"Selfishness breeds blindness," Gram said. "I'm sorry that happened, Cricket."

"Thanks."

"What did they want?" Grace asked.

"Dad wants me to come home and go back to work. I told him no, but he wasn't happy about it."

"Was he always so controlling?" Cara asked.

"Pretty much. He doesn't like it when he doesn't get his way."

"Good for you for standing up for yourself," Cara said.

Lacey nodded. "Absolutely. That's not easy."

"Thanks. It was nerve wracking, but thankfully Sasquatch came running out of the woods and cut our little reunion short."

"I swear, you're the only other person that dog likes," Grace said.

Gram's needles clicked. "She's part of his pack, now."

I smiled. I was, wasn't I?

"Grace, I keep meaning to bring this up," Tillie said. "Did you ever discover anything more about that mirror you found?"

"Not much," she said. "Cara and I hit a dead end and

then I started planning a wedding. I haven't thought much about it."

"What mirror?" I asked.

"Someone hid a box with an old mirror and a stack of anonymous love notes beneath the floorboards in my house," she said. "The mirror was engraved with the name Eliza Bailey, but I've had a hard time finding out anything about her."

"Thanks to me, or at least thanks to me hiring Libby Stewart, we did find out that Eliza went missing," Cara said. "And it's possible a Haven had something to do with it."

"Is that how the feud started?" I asked.

"We don't know," Grace said. "Everyone in town has a theory about why the families started feuding. But people in town also say you're in witness protection because you're the daughter of a motorcycle gang leader, so…"

"People say that?" I asked. "What people?"

"Oh, I started that rumor," Cara said, her tone nonchalant.

I laughed. "Why would you start a rumor about me?"

"I just like to see how outrageous I can make them and still get them to spread," she said. "I also started the rumor that Asher escaped from prison."

Grace sipped her drink. "Mrs. Darby still believes that, you know. She gives him the side eye every time she sees him."

"And she probably thinks Fiona is in witness protection."

"Anyway, my point is, you can't believe town lore," Grace said. "And it's hard to find any reliable information from before the 1920s. There was a fire that burned down half the town and a lot of records were lost. All I know about Eliza is that she was receiving anonymous love letters, and then she went missing. There was a notice in the newspaper offering a reward for information on her whereabouts, and it had what looked like a list of people wanted for questioning. One was a Haven—John Haven. But we don't know if he was actually involved, or how, or whether the families were already feuding then or not."

"They could have been secret lovers torn apart by the feud," Cara said. "Or maybe he murdered her."

"Or maybe they died together tragically," Grace said with a sigh.

"Did you say John Haven? Why does that name sound familiar?" I searched my memory. The only Haven I really knew was Luke. Except— "I know! I saw a picture of a John Haven. It was a really old photo—black and white and very faded."

Grace let her crochet hook drop in her lap. "You're kidding. Where?"

"In Luke Haven's shop. He has some vintage auto-racing photos behind the front desk. I'm almost positive he said one of them was John Haven."

"Do you know how old the photo was?" Grace asked.

"I don't know the exact year, but early 1900s."

"Wow," Grace said. "That matches up with the style of the mirror. I bet that's the John Haven mentioned in the newspaper notice."

Cara arched an eyebrow at me. "You were at Luke Haven's shop?"

All eyes swung to me.

"Yeah. It was a month or so ago."

Her lips curled in a devious smile. "Why?"

Violet clicked her tongue. "I smell gossip."

"No, there's no gossip," I said quickly. "When I first came

to town, Luke offered me a job. I went to his shop to tell him thanks but no thanks."

"He what?" Grace asked. "I can't believe Luke offered you a job. What was he thinking?"

"I'd love to believe he simply thought I'd be a good fit, but I'm sure it was to get back at Evan more than anything."

"Could have been a bit of both," Gram said. "I have a feeling the boy liked you quite a lot."

"How do you know that?" Grace asked.

Gram shrugged. "A hunch."

"Well, he did kind of ask me out. And he kissed me."

Everyone in the circle gasped—except Gram.

"No, no, no. You're getting the wrong idea. I told you, this was a while ago. Before Evan and I were... anything."

"Was he a good kisser?" Cara asked. "I bet he was. Luke is completely fuckable."

Grace whirled on her. "Cara. You can't say that. He's a Haven."

"Oh come on, we all know the Havens are a bunch of fuck-hot mountain men. I bet they smell like pine trees, flannel, and bad decisions. Don't look at me like that, I put them all on my no-touchy list a long time ago. But that's entirely out of loyalty to you, and under protest."

Grace glanced at Gram, probably wondering if Gram was going to scold Cara for her language. I'd heard her tell her grandsons to watch their language plenty of times, but her no swearing rule seemed to be limited to her house. Or maybe just her grandsons.

Cara turned back to me. "So? How was he?"

"He was fine, but honestly, I didn't feel much of anything. I was surprised when he did it, but not the good kind of melty surprise when you really want to be kissed. It was very meh."

Cara's shoulders slumped. "Well that's disappointing. I guess you'd already been hooked by whatever makes some women," she said, gesturing toward Grace, "fall for those Bailey boys."

"There's three left," Grace said, her tone full of mock innocence.

"Do you even know me?" Cara asked.

Grace laughed. "Anyway, it's a good thing you didn't take that job with Luke. That would have been a disaster."

"Would it have been that bad?" I asked. "I know, I know, the feud is real, and Luke and Evan hate each other anyway."

"Most everyone chooses a side eventually," Violet said. "Or they default to one."

"But sometimes Baileys and Havens are friends. Marlene Haven comes to Stitch and Sip. She was here last week."

"Stitch and Sip is different," Tillie said. "The Knotty Knitter is sacred ground. The feud is neutralized here."

"Well, if it can be neutralized here, maybe it can be neutralized everywhere. Especially if you could figure out how it started in the first place."

Gram met my eyes and the corner of her mouth twitched in a hint of a smile.

"I don't know," Grace said. "It's so deeply ingrained in people here."

"I have to agree with my little tootsie roll," Cara said. "Tilikum is the feud."

Maybe they were right. But what if someone did figure out how the feud had started? Would discovering the origin make a difference?

I didn't know if anything could bring the feud to an end. But finding out how it had begun would have to do something. Maybe it would be the first step in finally burying the hatchet.

Not that there was anything I could do about it. I couldn't exactly go ask Luke questions about the photo in his shop. Whatever good rapport I'd had with him was certainly gone now. I hadn't seen him since the day I'd turned him down. I doubted he had any interest in being friendly with me, let alone helping me solve a century old mystery.

But I still had to wonder if someday, someone would bring the feud to an end.

31

EVAN

I sat on my bike outside the Knotty Knitter, waiting for Fiona. A few women had already come out. My great-aunt Tillie patted my cheek and inexplicably said, "Good job." For what, I had no idea, so I just said thanks.

Gram walked out with a bag hanging from her arm. Our eyes met and she veered toward me. I dismounted so I could see if she needed help with anything.

"Hi there, Wolf. Isn't this a nice surprise."

"Hi, Gram." I kissed her forehead. "Can I carry that for you?"

"No, I'm fine. And Cricket should be along soon. She's still chatting with Grace and Cara."

"Should I be worried about that?"

"Maybe."

I cracked a smile. "You love to make people wonder, don't you?"

"I make myself quite clear. It's not my fault if people don't always understand me right away."

"Fair enough. Speaking of, where'd you get the name Cricket?"

"From the night air."

"This is you being clear?" I asked. "The night air told you to name a woman you'd just met after an insect?"

She tilted her head and smiled at me, like I was a child who didn't understand a basic concept. "Cricket is who she is. She's the evening song that soothes the spirit of the restless wolf."

I gaped at her as she patted my arm, then turned and walked to her car.

The evening song that soothes the spirit of the restless wolf. Holy shit. That's exactly what she was.

How had Gram known?

"Hey, you."

I whipped around at Fiona's voice.

"Sorry," she said with a laugh. "I didn't mean to startle you."

I ran my thumb across her chin. "It's okay. Did you have fun?"

"Yeah, I'm glad I went."

"Good." Tilting her face up, I leaned in and pressed my lips against hers, then tasted her with the tip of my tongue.

I'd missed her. It had only been a couple of hours, but my hands itched to touch her skin and my mouth thirsted for hers.

"Ready?"

She nodded, her eyes glittering with the same desire that burned inside me. Suddenly I couldn't get her home fast enough.

The cool air did nothing to dampen the lust simmering between us as we raced down the dark road. I'd always enjoyed the feel of riding a bike—the speed, the control. But riding with Fiona holding on behind me was even better. I liked feeling her close, the way her arms tightened around me as we hugged the turns.

We got home and as much as I wanted to drag her inside and rip her clothes off, Sasquatch needed some attention. I took him outside and when I brought him back in, Fiona was in the bathroom.

I sat on the couch to wait for her, and when she came out, she was wearing those fucking blue plaid pajamas.

My eyes were glued to her, like I was a kid gaping at my first set of naked tits. Her hair was loose, her bangs tucked behind an ear, no longer hiding her eyes. With her shoulders bare and those tiny shorts, I could see her ink. The flowers on her shoulder and arm. The vine on her upper thigh.

So fucking sexy. I wanted to lick her. Everywhere. My mouth watered at the thought.

"What?" she asked, a hint of shyness in her tone.

I was watching her like a predator, my body tensing, ready to strike.

"Get over here."

The wicked smile on her lips told me she was thinking the same thing I was.

Good.

She slipped onto my lap, straddling my right leg. I grabbed her ass and pulled her closer, earning a soft moan.

"Did you wear this on purpose?" I asked, sliding my hands up her shorts to cup her ass cheeks.

"Maybe."

I kissed her, lapping my tongue into her mouth. She tasted like mint and sugar. "I love this on you. Although I love it even more when it's on the floor."

"You'll have to help me with that."

I smiled and kissed her again. "My pleasure."

Her hand skimmed down my torso while our mouths tangled, like she wasn't afraid to go right for what she wanted. She reached my pants and I grunted when she slid her hand over my erection and squeezed.

She smiled against my mouth. "You like that?"

I nipped at her bottom lip. "Fuck yes, beautiful."

Kissing her way along my jaw to my neck, she pulled my cock out of my pants. I rested my head against the couch cushion and groaned as she wrapped her hand around me.

I was helpless. She owned me.

She rolled her hips, rubbing herself against my thigh while she stroked my hard length. Her mouth was hot on my throat, her lips soft as her tongue danced across my skin.

So. Damn. Good.

But I wanted more of her.

I grabbed her wrists and she pulled away slightly, raising her eyebrows. I licked along the seam of her lips. "I want to taste you."

A little whimper escaped her throat.

"I'm going to fuck you, beautiful. I'm going to sink my cock inside you and make you scream. But first I want to lick you until you beg me to stop." Leaning closer, I put my mouth next to her ear. "I am the wolf, Fiona. And I'm going to eat you."

I nudged her off my lap and stood. Instead of taking her hand and leading her to the bedroom, I picked her up and hoisted her over my shoulder. She squealed and I lightly smacked her ass cheek.

Sasquatch looked up at me.

"She's fine. Stay."

I hauled her into the bedroom, kicked the door closed

behind me, and tossed her on the bed. I quickly stripped my shirt and dropped it, then crawled on top of her.

Wasting no time, I tore her clothes off. I wasn't soft or gentle. I was aggressive. I wanted her naked, and I wanted it right fucking now.

With her clothes gone, I took a moment to appreciate her. All that smooth skin. Her full tits, narrow waist, wide hips. Bracing myself over her, I kissed and licked my way down her gorgeous body, savoring every inch. I wanted to worship her. Revel in the tantalizing feel of her skin sliding against mine, my mouth all over her.

When I got to her belly button, I climbed off the bed and hauled her close to the edge. Kneeling in front of her, I pushed her thighs open.

Slow and careful wasn't my style. I went all in. My tongue lapped against her, attacking her clit with swift flicks. I already knew all her weaknesses. I held her legs open while her body trembled. She was so wet already, her arousal delicious on my tongue.

Fuck, she tasted good. Luscious and addictive.

Finding a rhythm she liked, I licked her relentlessly. I lifted my gaze to watch as she writhed against the sheets, moaning. God, she was beautiful. My cock ached to be inside her.

I slid one hand up her thigh and teased her opening. She whimpered as I stroked her delicate skin, dipping my finger inside her, then out again. The urge to possess her was so strong. To fill every bit of her. And that ass. Fuck, her ass was so tempting.

Without stopping the assault on her clit, I traced my finger lower. It was nice and wet, so I swirled it around with just a hint of pressure.

"Oh my god," she said.

Since she seemed to like it, I tried a little more. I gently pushed my finger against her ass, that forbidden little spot that was so fucking tantalizing. She moaned again, her hips jerking. I pushed in a little more. Another moan.

Fuck, this was hot. With my mouth all over her, my tongue relentless, I flicked her clit and played with her ass. It was tight around my finger, and as I went just a little deeper, she cried out, her voice breathless.

"Fuck. Evan."

I'd never been so turned on—my cock desperate. I didn't want to stop, but I couldn't take it anymore. Reaching down with my other hand, I fisted my cock and started to stroke.

"Yes. Oh god, yes."

I growled into her pussy as I licked her. Her cries were fevered, her control gone. She clutched at the sheets, her head thrown back. Stroking my steel-hard erection, I kept licking her. I wanted to fuck her—I'd promised her I would —but I wasn't sure if I'd make it. With the taste of her in my mouth and the feel of her tight ass, I was ready to fire off like a rocket.

Her silky inner muscles began to pulse and spasm. I moved my tongue with her, slowing down to match her rhythm, still rubbing my aching cock. She cried out as she came, rolling her hips against me.

A few more seconds and I might have come, but she slowed. I placed gentle kisses on her inner thighs and gently slid my finger out.

She lifted her head and blinked slowly. "Oh my god, Evan, what did you just do to me?"

With my cock still in my hand, I stood and licked my lips, savoring her taste. Her eyes traced down my body, landing on my throbbing erection.

"I couldn't fucking wait."

"Don't stop," she whispered.

I kept stroking, letting her watch. My hand glided over my cock, from root to tip, but it wasn't enough to alleviate the maddening ache.

"Get on your knees," I growled.

With a smile, she rolled over and put her ass in the air. I quickly grabbed a condom out of the nightstand and rolled it in, feeling like I was going to explode every second I wasn't inside her.

I needed her. Now.

Positioning myself behind her, I grabbed her hips, aligned the tip of my cock with her opening, and drove it home.

Oh. My. Fucking. God.

My eyes rolled back, the heat and pressure of her pussy overwhelming me. I had no control left. No will to hold back. I slammed into her, sliding through her wetness, fucking her relentlessly.

Palming her ass cheeks, I drove into her, my hips jerking hard. The bed knocked into the wall, and Fiona braced herself against the mattress, rocking back into me with every thrust.

I looked down, watching my thick cock disappearing inside her. There was that ass again—so fucking tempting. I slid my finger in, just the tip, and the pressure almost made me explode.

"Fuck, Evan. Yes."

That was it. I was a goner.

My muscles clenched, my abs tightening, and the intensity in my groin reached the breaking point. I thrust harder, over and over, letting the mind-numbing pleasure sweep through me. My cock throbbed inside her, pulsing as I unleashed. My hips slammed into her ass, my hands digging into her flesh. I growled like a fucking animal, coming so hard it made my head swim.

When I finally finished, I pulled out and Fiona collapsed onto the bed, breathing hard. I paused to catch my breath, then stumbled to the bathroom to take care of the condom.

I came back to the bedroom and Fiona hadn't moved. She was sprawled out on her stomach, one leg bent and the other straight, her cheek resting on the mattress. She blinked her eyes open and the corner of her mouth hooked in a smile.

"Can't move."

I crawled into bed and hauled her against me. Buried my face in her neck and breathed her in.

So fucking good.

This woman was mine. And no one was ever going to take her from me.

32

EVAN

*I*t was the moment of truth. Or one of them, anyway.

Fiona squirted gas into the carburetor while I sat in the driver's seat. It was time to see if the Pontiac's engine would turn over after all the work I'd done.

"Go ahead," she said.

Holding my breath, I turned the key and pressed the gas. The engine rumbled, so close to turning over. I gave it a little more.

"Come on, baby," I said under my breath. "Give me what I want. That's it."

Finally, it roared to life, the throaty growl echoing in the open shop. Fiona threw her hands in the air and did a victory dance.

I gently patted the steering wheel. Fuck, yes.

"It sounds great," she said, raising her voice so I could hear her over the noise.

I turned it off and leaned out the open door. "Yeah, that was a big win. Thank fuck it works."

She came around to the driver's side. "Of course it works. You're an expert at making an engine purr."

I was about to pull her into my lap—and was thinking about all the dirty things I could do to her in this car—when Gavin sauntered into the shop, a shit-eating grin plastered on his face.

Fucking Gavin.

"Hey, Fiona."

With a soft laugh, she straightened. "Hey, Gav."

"You're looking especially beautiful," he said. "You busy tonight?"

"Gavin, stop trying to hit on my girlfriend."

"Who's hitting on her?" He put his hands up. "I just asked if she was busy tonight."

I got out of the car and leveled him with a glare. As usual, he just smiled at me.

Logan came in behind him. "Hey, brotato chip. Levi's not here yet? I thought he'd beat us."

"Why is Levi coming? And why are you guys here?"

"We're riding today," he said.

"Since when?"

"Since we are," Logan said, his forehead creasing like I'd asked a stupid question. "We talked about it the other day."

"If you guys want to go, I can stay and keep Fiona company," Gavin said. "I don't mind."

I growled at him.

He grinned back.

"Riding what?" Fiona asked.

"Dirt bikes," Logan said. "We've got miles of trails out there."

"Are you serious?" she asked. "I love riding dirt bikes."

"You know how to ride?" I asked.

She put her hands on her hips. "Are you kidding? I grew

up around gearheads. They took me dirt bike riding all the time when I was a kid."

"Fucking awesome," Logan said. "She can ride Grace's bike."

"Grace rides?" she asked.

I shrugged. "Yeah, sometimes. We fixed up a bike for her when Asher was gone so she could come riding with us."

"So what do you think, Fiona?" Gavin asked. "Want to come?"

Her eyebrows lifted and she looked at me.

I needed to work, and no matter what Logan said, I hadn't planned on riding today. But the way Fiona's face lit up, I couldn't tell her no. Obviously we were going riding.

"Okay. Let's go."

She bounced up onto her tiptoes and clapped.

It took some time to get the bikes out and running, since we hadn't ridden since last year. Levi showed up while we were working, followed closely by Asher.

"You assholes," Asher said as soon as he got out of his truck.

"I have no idea what you're talking about right now," Logan said.

"Bullshit. That cardboard cutout scared the shit out of me."

Gavin laughed. "I knew it would."

Asher glared at him. "You're wearing the underwear right now, aren't you?"

"Am I?" Gavin unfastened his jeans and looked down his pants. "Oh yeah, I am."

"What does Grace think of the new family photo for the mantle?" Logan asked.

Asher rolled his eyes. "She won't let me take it down."

Gavin burst out in a fit of laughter. "Grace is the best."

"What's in the photo?" Fiona asked.

"They took a picture of Asher getting out of the shower and made it into one of those life-size cardboard cutouts," I said. "They also got underwear made with his face on them, and those three jack monkeys wore them and posed for a picture with the cutout."

"See?" Gavin started pulling down his pants.

"Keep your fucking pants on," I snapped.

"You're in the picture too," Asher said.

"Me?" I asked. "No I'm not."

"Yeah, you are. It's on my mantle and I assure you, you're in it."

"What the fuck are you talking about? I wasn't in the picture." My gaze swung to Logan. "What did you do?"

"It's called Photoshop. You could have posed with us, but you wouldn't, so what else was I supposed to do?"

"You Photoshopped that?" Asher asked. "Dude, it's very convincing. Although I did wonder why he seemed shorter."

"Son of a bitch, Logan," I said.

He just laughed, the dick.

Once we got all the bikes running, we geared up and headed out toward the trail.

Fiona looked hot in literally everything. T-shirt and jeans. Tank top and overalls. Tiny plaid pajama shorts. She'd even looked hot in her big sweatshirts and leggings when I'd first met her.

But Fiona on a dirt bike in full gear was somehow one of the hottest things I'd ever seen.

Maybe because she was such a badass. She handled the bike like a boss, hugging corners and kicking up dirt. She caught a little air on a drop, making my heart lurch, and landed it perfectly.

I didn't need to ride behind her—she could obviously

handle herself—but this view of her ass was too fucking much. I enjoyed that more than the ride itself.

Gavin took the lead, racing ahead like usual. We'd made these trails ourselves over the years—every twist, turn, drop, and curve. They followed the natural terrain in and out of the pine trees. One branch met up with the road that led into town and the other ended near a ravine on the far end of my property.

We hung out for a while in an open area where we'd built a big jump. Fiona decided the jump was a little too high for her, so she took a break off to the side. I joined her and we sat on a flat rock, watching my brothers do tricks.

"I can't believe you had dirt bikes this whole time," she said. "Why were you holding out on me?"

I smiled at her. "You never told me you could ride."

"You never asked."

"Did your dad teach you?"

She glanced away. "No. Dad was always busy working. After Mom left, he used to leave me with a couple of the guys in his crew a lot. They're the ones who taught me about cars. They used to take me to the racetrack, dirt bike riding, all kinds of stuff. And I'd help them in the garage. I had no idea that half the time we were stripping stolen cars. But considering they were basically criminals, they were good guys."

"What happened to your mom?"

"She had a drug problem," she said. "Pain pills. She hurt her back when I was three or four and got hooked on painkillers. That's why Dad got custody of me in the divorce."

"Shit. That's brutal."

"Yeah, it sucks. She got clean, though, so that's good."

"And now she lives in Iowa?"

She nodded. "Yep. She got married again and had two more kids. It's weird though, because I've never met them. They're a lot younger than me. I haven't actually seen my mom since she left."

"Are you serious?"

"Yeah. Dad didn't want me to have contact with her, but I tracked her down when I was in high school. I talk to her every once in a while on the phone, but that's it."

"Shit."

She took a deep breath. "It sounds bad, but I kind of understand. I don't think her addiction was just because she hurt her back. She knew everything my dad was doing—all the criminal stuff. Plus he's not an easy guy to get along with. I'm sure being married to him basically sucked. I think she used drugs to deal with all the stress. And after she left, she needed to stay away."

Something about Fiona's story hit a tender place in my chest. I looked out at my brothers. Levi and Logan had stopped and taken their helmets off. Asher circled around while Gavin hit the jump, soaring over some old tires we'd dragged out here a couple of years ago.

I knew what it was like to have a less than perfect family situation. Our parents had died, leaving five little boys behind.

But we'd never been alone. We'd always had our grandparents, and each other.

Who had Fiona had? A couple of car thieves who she thought were mechanics? I was glad she'd had a few people in her life to be there for her—or at least do cool stuff with her when she was a kid. But who did she have in her life that she could really rely on? That she could trust no matter what?

Regardless of how much my brothers drove me crazy,

they were my pack. I trusted them wholeheartedly. It would have sucked to have to grow up without that.

Without them.

I slipped an arm around Fiona and pulled her against me. She had us now.

"Um, Evan?"

"Yeah?"

"Who's that?" She pointed at something to our right.

A man in a tattered cowboy hat crested the hill. He was dressed in a leather vest over an old flannel shirt, and a pickax hung from a loop on his belt.

"That's Harvey Johnston," I said. "You haven't met Harvey?"

"No. Who is he?"

How could I explain Harvey Johnston? "He lives just outside town—wanders around a lot and doesn't always make sense. He's a little weird, but he's harmless. I wonder what he's doing out here?"

I stood and helped Fiona to her feet. I held my hand up in greeting as we approached. The noise of my brothers on their dirt bikes hummed in the background.

"Hey, Harvey."

Harvey took his hat off, scratched his head, then put it back on. "Evan Bailey?"

"Yeah, it's me. What are you up to out here? Are you lost?"

"No," he said, his voice full of conviction. "I know right where I am."

"How'd you get here? Did you walk?"

He looked down at his boots. "It ain't that far."

"Fair enough. Do you need a ride back to town?"

"No, no, not going to town. I went to town yesterday." He pulled his pickax off his belt loop and held it up. "Today is for digging. You want to come help? You can come, too, young lady."

"I'm Fiona. What are you digging for?"

He smiled a wide, toothy grin and his eyes lit up. "Treasure."

"Well, that was silly of me," she said. "What else would you be digging for out here? Do you have a map?"

"That's the problem. There is no map. He didn't leave one."

"Who?"

"Ernest Montgomery," he said. "He left the treasure for someone to find, but no map. Nope, none at all."

"That does make it more of a challenge."

"I won't give up, though. I know it's out there somewhere." He lowered his voice to a gravelly whisper. "People say I'm crazy, but don't you be listening to them, Miss Fiona. I'm right as rain up here in my noggin."

"Of course you are," she said with a smile. "Maybe we'll join your treasure hunt another time."

"Good." Still holding the pickax, he patted his vest with his free hand, as if he were looking for something. "Now where did it go…"

I tapped the top of the pickax with one finger. "Looking for this?"

He held it out, his eyes widening with surprise. "There it is. Good thing. For a second, I thought the squirrels got it."

Fiona opened her mouth, probably to ask why the squirrels would take his pickax, but I caught her eye and shook my head. No need to get Harvey started on a rant about the Tilikum squirrels.

"Okay, Harvey, be careful out there," I said. "Stop by my place if you need anything, all right?"

"Don't worry, if I find the treasure on your land, I'll be

sure to split it with you."

"Sounds fair."

He tipped his hat to us, took a wobbly turn, and started off in the other direction.

"Is he going to be okay?" Fiona asked.

"Yeah, he'll be fine. He's been wandering around Tilikum for decades."

"What do you think he's looking for? Does he mean a chest of gold or something?"

"Who knows. There's an old story that claims one of town's founders hid part of his fortune. But you know how it is with Tilikum stories."

"This town does love its tall tales. Did you know I ran away from home to be a trapeze artist in the circus until I developed a fear of heights?"

"I have no idea where they come up with this shit."

"The treasure story is kind of cool, though."

"Yeah, I guess so. Back in the 1920s, a journalist came out here and did a story on the Montgomery treasure. A bunch of people came to look for it, but of course no one found anything. Gram said excitement used to flare up once in a while and a bunch of new treasure hunters would show up. But it's been a long time since that happened. Now it's just Harvey."

"It does seem like someone would have found it, if there was anything to find."

"Exactly. Try telling that to him, though. He loves trea-sure hunting even more than he loves waging war against the squirrels."

"What does everyone have against the squirrels?" she asked. "Peek and Boo are the sweetest little things. Although I have a feeling Boo might have gotten into the shop and taken my torque wrench. Or maybe it was Peek."

"I told you not to feed the squirrels."

Smiling, she playfully smacked my arm.

We walked back to where we'd left our bikes and met up with my brothers. They were dirty, sweaty, and tired. Even Gavin looked like he'd burned off most of his energy.

"Summer project," he said. "We build a jump to cross the ravine."

"No," Levi and Logan said in unison.

"Why not?"

"Because you'll kill yourself trying to jump it, dork," Logan said.

Pouting, Gavin got back on his bike.

We all mounted up and rode back to my place. The sun was starting to set, the light fading to dusk, when we came out of the trees near my house.

The hair on the back of my neck stood on end. Something was wrong. I didn't know how I knew, but I was sure of it.

We stopped outside the house and as soon as the engines were off, I heard Sasquatch barking inside. He might have been barking at us, but the prickly feeling on the back of my neck didn't let up.

I dismounted and took off my helmet. My house looked fine, but the sense of danger grew as I jogged to the front door to let my dog out. As soon as the door was open, he ran past me, beelining for the shop.

"Stay here."

I followed Sasquatch and as soon as I came in sight of the first garage bay door, a flood of adrenaline hit my system. The windows were broken and the shop door was wide open.

Oh fuck. The Pontiac.

33

FIONA

*S*asquatch tore out of the house and ran toward the shop. Evan told the rest of us to stay and followed his dog.

"What's going on?" I asked.

The air felt like it was charged with electricity. My heart beat faster and a tingle ran down my spine. Something was wrong.

Despite the fact that Evan had told everyone to stay here, his brothers took off their helmets and went after him. So did I.

I didn't see anything unusual as I approached the shop. His brothers' vehicles were parked out front, but no other cars. I scanned the trees, but everything was still. Not even a squirrel.

But when I got around to the front, my heart skipped.

All three garage bay doors had deep dents and broken windows, like someone had attacked them with a baseball bat. I ran inside behind his brothers.

Chaos.

Someone had trashed Evan's shop. The floor was littered

with tools and parts, broken glass everywhere. The windshield on the Caddy had been smashed and there were dents in the hood.

Evan stood next to the Pontiac, his hand covering his mouth. I couldn't even look.

"Sasquatch, come," I called. He trotted over to me and I took him outside. "Good boy. Now, stay. I don't want you cutting your paws on the glass."

With my heart in my throat, I went back inside.

Evan stood next to the Pontiac while his brothers looked around. I crept closer, picking my footing carefully among the debris on the floor. The car had taken some serious damage—broken windshield, lots of dents in the body. One of the side mirrors lay broken on the floor.

"Jack's on his way," Asher said, pocketing his phone.

Evan didn't answer.

A sick feeling spread through my stomach as I took in the extent of the damage. The Cadillac had been hit, but only once or twice. They'd whaled on the Pontiac. It was like they'd known which car was more valuable—which car was more important.

"Who the fuck would do this?" Logan asked.

"If it was the Havens, they're all going down," Gavin said. "Fuck this."

"It wasn't the Havens," Levi said.

"You sure about that?" Gavin asked. "Luke's always had it out for Evan. Maybe he finally snapped."

"I don't think Luke would do this," I said.

Evan whirled on me, his eyes blazing. "How would you know?"

"This isn't a prank, it's a crime. And when was the last time you even saw him? Would he come up here out of the blue, totally unprovoked, and smash up your shop?"

"She's right," Asher said. "I don't think this was the Havens. If it was Luke, he's lost it. The rest of them wouldn't let him get away with something like this."

Evan ran his hands through his hair. "Fuck."

I could feel Evan's rage, the heat of it beating at me. He was a powder keg ready to explode.

My first instinct was to slink away. Be silent. Stay out of the way. Let him handle it.

But Evan wasn't my father. And I wasn't going to let him face this alone.

I slipped my hand in his and squeezed. He turned, looking down at me with a furrowed brow. A heartbeat later, his arms were around me, crushing me against him. He held me for a long moment, breathing into my neck, and the fact that he let me comfort him here, in front of the car that represented all his hopes for his business, made my eyes fill with tears.

Because I had a feeling I knew who'd done this. And if I was right, it was my fault.

"We should probably wait outside until the police get here," I said softly.

He let go and cast another glance at the destruction. "Yeah. Let's go."

We went outside and waited in front of the shop. A few minutes later, a police car pulled up and a man in his late fifties got out. He had salt-and-pepper hair and a thick chest. Asher and Evan walked over to meet him.

"That's Jack Cordero," Levi said. "He's Grace's stepdad."

"He's a good guy," Logan said. "He'll help get this figured out."

I decided to take Sasquatch back to the house while Evan and his brothers talked to Jack. I got him settled, then went back outside.

Evan and his brothers talked to Jack and showed him the damage. They disappeared inside the shop for a while. I didn't want to get in the way, so I waited out front. I couldn't decide if I felt like bursting into tears or throwing up. Maybe both.

Did I know who'd done this?

And if I did, could I turn him in?

I knew my dad was far from perfect. He was an awful combination of dismissive and controlling. He lied, cheated, and stole.

But did that mean he was capable of this?

I'd always felt so guilty for suspecting he'd been involved with the fire at the nursery where I'd worked. The cause had been inconclusive; they hadn't even officially ruled it an arson. But still, I'd wondered.

And this time he'd said the same thing—told me I'd regret not coming back.

Was this my fault?

Jack and Evan came out and I took a deep breath. I knew what I had to do. Yes, he was my father. But that didn't mean he deserved blind loyalty. Or any loyalty, really.

I walked over to Evan and Jack. "Excuse me, Officer Cordero. I'm sorry to interrupt, but I might have information that's important."

Evan's brow furrowed. "What are you talking about?"

I swallowed hard. "I think my father might have done this. Or had someone do it."

"What makes you think that?" Jack asked.

"He came here recently, trying to get me to come home. I used to work for him and he's not happy that I quit. Before he left, he said I'd regret it. And I know that makes it sound like I'm jumping to conclusions, but my dad is... he's been into some bad stuff. Criminal stuff. He was really angry, and I wouldn't put it past him to retaliate."

I made myself glance up at Evan. It was hard to meet his eyes.

But he didn't look angry. His expression was soft with concern. I wanted to melt in his arms.

"Tell you what," Jack said. "I'll finish up here and then you two come down to the station. We'll get the information we need and go from there."

"Thanks, Jack," Evan said.

Jack glanced at the shop, shaking his head. "I'm sorry about this, man. We'll do everything we can."

Evan put his arm around me and led me back toward the house.

My eyes stung with tears. "Evan, I'm so sorry."

"Hey." He stopped to pull me close and put his knuckle under my chin to tilt my face up. "This isn't your fault."

"If my dad—"

"Still not your fault. You didn't make him do this."

"But if I hadn't stayed, this wouldn't have happened to you. The car show is coming up and what if you can't fix it in time?"

He cupped my cheeks. "Listen to me. If you hadn't stayed, I wouldn't have you. Fuck the car, I can fix it. It's not important. You're what's important."

His lips met mine and I sank into his kiss. I hated that I'd brought this on him. Hated that my father kept poisoning my life.

I had to face the hard truth. I hadn't gone far enough. There wasn't enough distance between me and my dad. It was too easy for him to reach me here.

And I didn't know what I was going to do about that.

34

EVAN

*T*he incident at the shop had rattled Fiona. Since we'd come back from the sheriff's office, she hadn't said a word to her plants. I'd turned on some music, but that hadn't seemed to help. No singing. Even when I'd started to softly sing along, she hadn't joined in.

I didn't blame her for being upset. I was fucking furious. I had no idea how I was going to recover from this— whether I could fix the Pontiac in time. Or at all.

But glass could be replaced. Dents pounded back into shape. I'd figure it out.

The damage to my shop, even to the Pontiac, wasn't why I was mad. It was the broken look in Fiona's eyes when she'd told Jack she thought her dad was responsible.

Fiona loved her father. Not that he deserved it, but she was a good person, so of course she loved her dad. The piece of shit had let her down so many times, in so many ways. I hated him for it. Not for attacking me. For hurting her.

No one hurt my girl.

But for now, there wasn't much I could do about Shane

Gallagher. I had to leave it to the authorities. Right now, I just wanted to help my girl.

So when Asher texted to ask if we wanted to meet them for a drink at the Caboose, I didn't immediately say no.

Fiona perked up when I suggested we go out. She changed into my favorite pair of jeans—they made her ass look fantastic—and a black and gold top.

My badass little ray of sunshine.

The weather was decent, so we took my bike into town. There was still some hay around the edges of the parking lot in front of the Caboose. It made me wonder what my brothers were planning to do to get the Havens back. It had been a while; they had to be up to something.

We went inside and the place was awash with sound. The murmur of voices. The click of balls on the pool tables. Music in the background. The smell of fried food made my mouth water.

Asher and Grace were at a table in the bar. I kept my hand on the small of Fiona's back as we walked through the restaurant. A gentle but possessive touch. I saw the way guys looked at her. The way eyes traced her curves. I shot a few well-placed glares and they turned away.

She was mine.

Grace stood when we got to their table and hugged Fiona. "Asher told me what happened. Are you okay?"

"Yeah, I'm fine. It's just been one hell of a day."

We took a seat and ordered drinks and food. The girls chatted and I asked Asher how things were going at his gym. He'd been coaching martial arts classes for a while now and it was good to see him in a groove. His felony conviction had ruined his chance of being a firefighter, but he'd found a new path.

I was pretty fucking proud of him.

Cara swept up to the table out of nowhere, set down her drink, and grabbed Fiona's hands. "Oh my god, our precious little starfish. I heard what happened. Are you okay? Who do I need to murder?"

"I'm okay. Really. Besides, it's Evan's shop that got trashed."

She waved her hand. "He looks fine. You didn't get hurt, did you?"

"No, nobody was there when we got back."

"Well, that's something at least."

She eyed the table for a second, as if something about it bothered her. Finally, she grabbed a chair from a neighboring table and dragged it to the end of ours, putting her between Fiona and Grace. I glanced at the empty chairs next to me and Asher and shrugged. Cara did what she wanted.

Fiona tucked her hair behind her ear. "Let's talk about something else. I think I need to get my mind off everything. The wedding is soon. That's exciting."

Grace smiled, her whole face lighting up, and Asher slipped an arm around her shoulders.

"I know," Grace said. "So close. Everything is pretty much done. Between my sisters-in-law and Cara, I've barely had to do anything."

Weddings were not my favorite thing. As kids, Gram had dragged us to every wedding in our extended family, stuffing us into suits and ties that we'd shed at the earliest opportunity.

But ever since Carly, I hadn't just disliked weddings because of the monkey suits. I'd hated weddings. I'd never let myself admit it, but they made me jealous. Because the lucky bastard at the altar had what I'd thought I'd found. Which had turned out to be nothing but a big fucking heartbreak.

Listening to the girls talk about Grace and Asher's upcoming wedding, I realized something. I was looking forward to it. Mostly because I was happy for my brother. He'd waited a long time to marry Grace.

But Carly hadn't been my only chance. I'd known for a long time that marrying her would have been a huge mistake. In a way, she'd done me a favor by cheating on me with my best friend. She hadn't left any room for doubt. But I'd always assumed that she'd been it. She'd fucked me up badly enough that I wasn't going to try again. I wasn't ever going to be the guy at the altar. And it pissed me off, because deep down, that was what I'd always wanted.

To find my other half. Like Gram and Grandad. Like my parents.

I'd been built for it. I think we all were; Asher was just the first of us to figure it out.

I gazed at Fiona and fingered a strand of her hair while she smiled and talked. I wasn't dreading my brother's wedding, and it was because of her. Because she was mine. My other half. I'd found her. And sure, we weren't ready to walk down the aisle yet. But we would be someday. And just knowing that made everything else—the car, the shop, the feud, all of it—fade into the background.

So this was what happy felt like.

I took a sip of my beer and when I looked up, a pair of blue eyes were staring at me from across the bar.

Was that Jill? Why was she looking at me like that?

She was with two other girls I didn't know. One leaned close and said something. Jill nodded. Her eyes never leaving me, she marched over to our table and stopped with her hands on her hips.

"So this is how it ends," Jill said.

I glanced at Fiona in confusion, then back at Jill, not

sure what to say to that. What was she talking about? "This is how what ends?"

She shook her head slowly. "I've given you too many chances. I'm sorry, Evan, but it's over."

"What's over?"

"Us."

I stared at her. "There's no us. We've never dated."

"I warned you. I told you that you were going to lose me someday. And now you have." With a flip of her hair, she turned and walked away.

"What the fuck was that?" I asked no one in particular.

"You never went out with her?" Asher asked.

"Not even once."

Asher took a sip of his beer. "Sometimes you reap what you sow."

I put an arm around Fiona. "Sometimes you dodge a fucking bullet."

Fiona leaned into me. "I feel kind of bad for her. I think she's been dating you in her imagination this whole time."

"I guess it's good she broke up with me, then," I said. "I've been fake cheating on her for a while."

Fiona laughed.

Cara glanced toward the front and scowled. "Fiona, if you stay with Evan, you're really going to have to consider the ramifications of becoming a Bailey. Namely being related to *that*."

I glanced over my shoulder. Logan came in with a girl I didn't know on his arm. She wore a low-cut top and tight jeans. Dark hair loose around her shoulders. Lots of makeup. Pretty enough, but she had nothing on my girl.

"Oh my god, is that Dani?" Grace asked.

Cara's mouth dropped open. "It is. What's she doing here? And why is she with prince dickhead?"

"I have no idea."

Grace waved and Logan brought his date—Dani, apparently—to our table.

"Hey, Dani," Grace said. "I haven't seen you in forever."

Dani squealed and ran over to hug Grace and Cara. "You guys! I didn't know you still lived here."

Logan gaped at his date. "You know them?"

"Yeah, I did a semester at Tilikum College."

"Look at you, hottie," Cara said. "I love this top."

"Thanks. I was feeling sassy."

"What are you doing in Tilikum?" Grace asked.

"My aunt owns a little cabin by the river so I came out to recharge. Me time, you know? My boss has been a huge dick lately, so I needed a break."

Cara touched Grace on the arm. "Boo, why don't you scoot over so Dani can sit."

"Good idea." Grace nudged Asher so he'd move to the empty chair on his other side.

Dani took a seat across from Fiona. Logan's face fell.

"Might as well sit," Asher said, and I kicked out the chair next to me.

Logan slumped into the chair and narrowed his eyes at Cara.

Her lips twitched in the hint of a smile.

Grace was busy introducing Dani to Fiona.

"How do you know Logan?" Grace asked.

"Oh, we met at the Zany Zebra earlier. He struck up a conversation and asked me out tonight. I figured, why not?"

"Well, we won't keep you," Grace said. "I'm just so surprised to see you."

"What do you want to drink?" Cara asked. "It's on me."

"Thanks, sweetie. I'd love a margarita, but I'll come with you. Hey, remember shooting pool together in this place?"

"There's a table open," Cara said. "We should totally play."

"That would be so fun," Dani said, then turned to Logan. "You don't mind, do you?"

Logan faked a smile. "No, go ahead."

Grace gave Asher a quick kiss. "We'll be back. Fiona, want to join us?"

I moved my arm off Fiona's chair and winked at her. "Have fun."

Fiona and Grace went to one of the pool tables while Cara and Dani headed for the bar.

Logan looked like he was ready to blow a gasket. His jaw hitched and his nostrils flared. "Is she fucking kidding me?"

"Looks like you lost your date," Asher said. "Although, was she really a *date* or just your hookup for the night?"

"I was going to buy her a drink. That's a date."

I shook my head. "I'll get you a beer."

We spent the rest of our night having a few drinks and watching the girls play pool. It only took Logan about five minutes to stop pouting. We had a good time. Despite the shit show waiting for me back at home, it was nice to relax with my brothers for a while.

Watching Fiona's ass when she bent over the pool table wasn't bad either. In fact, it was the best part of my night.

35

FIONA

*A*fter the police finished gathering evidence in the shop and around Evan's property, he doubled down on the Pontiac, working hard to get it finished in time. It had been badly damaged, but it was nothing a guy like Evan couldn't fix, given the right parts and enough time.

Unfortunately, he didn't have either of those things.

I thought a lot about calling my dad to confront him. Demand he tell me the truth and admit he'd had someone trash Evan's shop.

But Jack had asked me not to contact him yet—to let the police do their job first.

And what did I expect my father to do? Be honest? Apologize? I had a feeling I'd only be setting myself up for disappointment.

I did, however, want to find a way to make it up to Evan.

When we took a close look at all the damage, the biggest problem was the convertible carriage. It was too broken to repair. He needed a replacement, but that wasn't as simple as running down to the auto parts store and buying one. Or even wandering through someone's wrecking yard. This was an extremely rare car, and for this type of restoration, it needed to be as authentic as possible.

So I made it my mission to find a replacement.

And for the next week, I hit nothing but dead ends.

A guy I knew outside of Tacoma had the body of a '72, but it wasn't a convertible. He referred me to someone he swore would have what we needed. Turned out he had several convertible carriages, but none of them were from a Pontiac. Another place had the convertible body of a '69, but no carriage. I made phone call after phone call, tracking down every lead—no luck.

But I was nothing if not determined.

I shut the office door to drown out the noise of Evan working. Next on my list was Craig Shelton. If he had one, he'd probably price-gouge the hell out of me, but at this point, I was getting desperate.

"This is Craig," he answered.

"Hey, this is Fiona Gallagher with Bailey Customs."

"What can I do for you?"

"I'm on the hunt for something pretty rare. The convertible carriage for a 1970 Pontiac GTO."

"Bailey really did get his hands on the Judge?"

"He did, and it's gorgeous. But the convertible carriage has too much damage to restore, and as I'm sure you can imagine, tracking down a replacement isn't easy. Do you have something similar out there?"

"I hate to tell you this. I used to, but I sold it a while back."

"Oh my god, are you serious?"

"Yep. I had a '70 convertible body. Guts and interior were all gone and most of the body wasn't really salvageable. But it had enough to be a donor car for a better project, even the Judge. Pretty sure that's what the guy bought it for."

"Who'd you sell it to?" I asked, although I had a feeling I already knew the answer.

"Guy by the name of Luke Haven."

Closing my eyes, I let out a breath. "Okay. Thanks anyway."

"Good luck."

I ended the call and dropped the phone on the desk. Of course Luke Haven would be the best lead I had left.

Was there any chance he'd actually sell it to Evan? Would Evan buy it if Luke agreed?

How deep did this feud really go?

The problem was, I'd looked everywhere. No one within a day's drive had what he needed. And he couldn't finish the car without it.

I thought about the Stitch and Sip ladies. Marlene Haven sat there right alongside several Bailey women. They'd told me Stitch and Sip was feud-neutral because sometimes the women of this town had to go around the men when the feud was making them get in their own way.

Maybe this was one of those times.

I wasn't going to lie to Evan. I'd never do that. But if I told him what I was trying to do before I did it, he'd try to talk me out of it. I'd tell him once I'd secured the deal—and then I'd talk him into using it despite where it had come from.

Assuming Luke still had it, and would sell it to Evan. Heck, I didn't know if Luke would even talk to me.

But I had an idea.

"What do you think, Edith?" I asked my office plant. "Can I pull this off?"

I wasn't sure. But I had to try.

∽

I PARKED outside Luke's shop, feeling a pang of guilt. What right did I have to ask him to do me a favor? I'd helped Evan buy a rare and valuable car out from under him. Then I'd turned down his job offer and said no to a date. I'd rejected this guy pretty hard, not to mention the fact that I was now living with—and sleeping with—his sworn enemy.

But I wasn't going to ask him to give me something for nothing. That wasn't how this business worked. And if I could talk grumpy Evan Bailey into going on a road trip with me to try to buy a rare Pontiac, maybe I could convince Luke Haven that we could help each other.

With my heart beating hard and my stomach swirling with nerves, I went into the front office.

Annika was at the front desk again. She smiled when she saw me. At least there was one friendly face in Haven territory.

"Hi, I don't know if you remember me, but I'm Fiona Gallagher."

"I do." She narrowed her eyes. "What brings you in here?"

"I know, it's weird because of the Bailey-Haven thing. But I need to talk to Luke. I'm hoping I can go around the feud. I have a good reason and I'll make it worth his while."

She shrugged. "You can sure try. I'll go get him."

"Thanks."

Minutes ticked by and I wandered around the room, eying the photos again. I took a quick picture of the racing photos, including one of John Haven. I figured Grace and Cara might like to see it.

Was Luke busy? Or was Annika having a hard time convincing him to see me?

Finally, he came out and by his expression, it had probably been the latter. Annika elbowed him on her way past.

"Come on back," he said.

I followed him through the garage to his office. He shut the door behind me. This time, he sat at his desk, rather than on the couch.

Keeping it professional.

That was good.

I sat in a chair on the other side of his desk.

"I didn't hit Evan's shop," he said.

My mouth popped open in surprise. "No, I know you didn't. That's not why I came."

"Oh. I figured he sent you in to get a confession out of me."

"No, not at all. In fact, he doesn't know I'm here."

His forehead creased. "Then why are you here?"

I took a deep breath. "Whoever did hit Evan's shop did a lot of damage to the Pontiac."

His eyes tightened with a pained expression. Any car guy would mourn the loss of a rare specimen like the Judge.

"He can fix most of it, although I don't know if he can finish in time for the show. He's going to try, but it'll be tight. Anyway, the biggest problem now is the convertible carriage. It's too badly damaged to fix and I've looked every-where for a suitable replacement. I can't find one anywhere."

"And you heard I have one."

I nodded.

He pitched his fingers together. "Well, isn't this interest-ing. Evan Bailey buys the car I want out from under me and now I have the part he needs to finish it."

"Look, I get it, you guys hate each other, and this is prob-ably a dream scenario for you. What better way to stick it to your sworn enemy than sit on the part he needs."

"Pretty much."

My heart sank. "Would it kill you to put aside your animosity for him this one time?"

"Do you really think he would if the tables were turned?"

"Yes."

He gave me a doubtful scowl.

"I really think he would. He's a good man, and I think you are too. You're both just so used to hating each other, you expect the worst. How did this even start? Is it really just because you're competitors?"

Luke shook his head. "Evan and I have been fighting over shit since we were kids."

I groaned. "You guys are ridiculous. Your families are feuding because reasons and you hate Evan because you always have."

"It's hardly one-sided."

"Oh, I'm well aware of that." I took another deep breath. I was not giving up yet. There was too much at stake. "I know you're going to think I'm crazy, considering the circumstances, but hear me out for a second. And I swear to you this isn't a prank. You have something Evan needs. You don't want to sell it to him because he's Evan Bailey."

He nodded.

"But what if I can help you get something you need in exchange for selling him the convertible carriage?"

"Like what?"

I bit the inside of my lip. This was a long shot, but I had to try. "Are you still working on the Mustang that I saw last time I was here? The '69 Boss?"

"Yeah."

"Do you have the original gauges for it?"

He narrowed his eyes again. "Not the originals, no."

A spark of hope flared to life inside me. "What if I could

help you get the originals? Those are hard to find and it would go a long way toward making your build more authentic."

"You'll get me a set of gauges for the Mustang if I'll sell Evan the convertible carriage?"

"Yes."

"What's the catch?"

"Other than you have to sell a rare part to Evan Bailey? The gauges aren't for sale. But I think I can talk the guy who has them into parting with them."

Luke rubbed his chin, eying me like he was trying to find the hole in my plan. Or maybe deciding how best to dash all my hopes.

I waited, crossing my toes inside my shoes. *Come on, Luke. Please.*

"I might regret this, but fine."

Relief made me bounce in my seat. "Thank you."

"But if you can't get me the gauges—"

"You'll maybe still sell him the convertible carriage because I tried?"

He groaned. "Maybe."

"I'll take that for now."

I called the guy I knew—Denny Horace—right then and there and asked if we could come see his set of '69 Mustang Boss gauges. I wanted to get this deal done before Luke had time to change his mind. Denny agreed, although he didn't say he'd sell them.

One thing at a time.

"Do you want to just ride with me?" Luke asked. "Or would it be too disloyal to be in a truck with a Haven, since you're basically a Bailey now."

Basically a Bailey now. I loved the sound of that. "I can ride with you. It's not that big of a deal."

We went out the back and got in Luke's truck. He drove a Toyota Tacoma extended cab, almost exactly like Evan's. They were like two sides of the same coin. I wondered if they'd grown up differently—without a feud—if they'd have been friends instead of enemies.

Then again, their competitiveness seemed pretty personal.

"Who's this guy we're going to see?" Luke asked. "Is he a car guy? I've never heard of him."

"Sort of. He's a collector. Not just cars. He used to be one of those barn hunters. He'd travel around and go through people's junk. He had a knack for finding rare collectibles that people thought were trash. He'd buy and then restore old artifacts. He has a lot of cool stuff."

"Does he actually sell any of it?"

"Sometimes. That used to be his business before he retired. One time my dad's shop was doing a custom Corvette Stingray and for the life of me, I couldn't find an authentic speedometer. I don't even remember how I found Denny, but he had one. Once in a while he has just the right thing to finish a build."

"How did you know he has the gauges for a Mustang?"

"I've seen them. I can't guarantee he'll sell them, but I know he has them."

"Well I've seen you in action. I have a feeling you'll convince him."

"That's the plan." I fiddled with my hands in my lap. "Can I say something?"

"Sure."

"I really am sorry about... you know."

"Turning me down?"

"Yeah. That."

"It's okay." He was quiet for a moment, his hands on the

steering wheel. "Obviously I was pissed that you picked Evan over me. But did you notice that when I kissed you... nothing happened?"

"Yes. Oh my god, you felt that too? Or didn't feel it, I guess?"

He laughed. "Yeah, it was pretty clear. It doesn't even make sense. You're beautiful and I have every reason to like you. Or I did before you went Bailey on me. But it just wasn't there. I could tell you felt it too. So, as much as it pains me to admit it, you probably made the right call."

"It's very big of you to admit that, Luke."

"Don't tell him I said that."

I laughed. "Don't worry, I won't. So can I ask if you're dating someone, or is that too weird?"

He shrugged. "I'm not, but there's a girl I'm thinking about asking out."

"Really? Who?"

"Her name's Jill."

"Wait. Do you mean blond-haired blue-eyed cute Jill? The one who Evan kissed in front of you?"

He glanced at me. "He told you about that?"

"Yes. He told me you were flirting with her and he totally cockblocked you. And then he blew her off, by the way. He never called her."

"Prick."

"I know, I'm not exactly on his side on that one. But are you sure about her?"

"Why?"

"First of all, didn't she give Evan her number right in front of you? That's kind of crappy."

"Yeah, she did."

"And this might make me sound like I'm being a jealous girlfriend, but I think she's a little..."

"What?"

How could I explain this? "You know that 'overly attached girlfriend' meme?"

"Yeah."

"That's Jill."

He eyed me like he wasn't sure if I was kidding. "What are you talking about?"

"It's just that she seemed to think she was dating Evan, but they never went out. She *broke up* with him," I said, making air quotes, "rather dramatically at the Caboose the other night. Walked right up to our table and said she'd given him enough chances, but now he was losing her. He had no idea what she was talking about. His brothers didn't either."

"Hmm. Okay, thanks for the heads up."

We were quiet for a few moments while the scenery raced by.

"Can I ask you something else that's probably even more random?"

"Why not."

"You know the old racing photos in your shop? Do you know anything else about them?"

"Not really. Why?"

"Just something Asher's fiancée Grace has been trying to figure out. She found some stuff that belonged to a woman named Eliza Bailey. It's old, early 1900s. She did a little digging and discovered Eliza went missing. There was a notice in the newspaper offering a reward for information, and someone named John Haven was listed as maybe being involved. She doesn't know if he was, or how. But I keep wondering if maybe that has something to do with the feud, you know? A Bailey woman goes missing and they want to question a Haven about it? And then you have a photo of John Haven in your shop. It sparks curiosity."

"Wow, yeah."

"Does your family know how the feud started?"

He shook his head. "I don't think anyone does. But Grace thinks this might be it? Something between John Haven and Eliza Bailey?"

"Maybe. Or maybe the feud had already started, or maybe none of it's related. That's the thing, we don't know."

"I don't know anything about him, other than he raced cars. Did Grace ask my mom? They know each other, right?"

"Yeah, but she didn't know much about him. Your mom's nice, by the way. I see her at Stitch and Sip, which seems weird but not. Anyway, I knew it was a long shot, but I thought maybe you'd heard a racing story about him or something."

"Sorry. I don't know."

"That's okay. It was worth a try."

We made good time getting to Denny's place. His house looked like a museum, even from the outside. Vintage gas pumps flanked his front door and he had old signs and artwork everywhere.

As predicted, Denny was skeptical about parting with his set of Mustang gauges. About halfway through negotiations, I'd wished I'd brought cookies to sweeten the deal—literally. But in the end, I talked him into it. Luke gave him a fair price, and we left. Mission accomplished.

Mostly.

"Well, you held up your end of the deal," Luke said as we headed down the highway back to Tilikum. "I'll sell Evan the carriage. But what if you can't convince him to buy it from me?"

I shrugged. "Then consider the gauges a goodwill gesture. But I'm on a roll, now. I'll convince him."

He shook his head. "I probably shouldn't doubt you."

I smiled at him. He shouldn't doubt me, because I knew Evan Bailey's weakness.

Blackberry cobbler.

36

FIONA

*E*van was working when I got back. Although I was excited to tell him I'd found a convertible carriage, this was delicate. I needed to handle it carefully or he'd just get mad.

Step one: blackberry cobbler.

Step two would undoubtedly involve getting naked. Was I a terrible person for planning to use sex to butter up my boyfriend? Maybe. But honestly, what other recourse did I have? Evan Bailey was the most stubborn man I'd ever met. A full stomach and empty balls would at least make him pliable.

Besides, he was going to thank me for all of it.

I flitted around the kitchen, getting out ingredients and humming along to the music I had playing. I'd stopped at the grocery store on my way home to get fresh blackberries. It was getting late, and it would take about an hour once I got it in the oven, but that was fine. I popped a blackberry in my mouth, savoring the burst of tart sweetness on my tongue. Oh yeah. This was going to be good.

The front door flew open and I whirled around, my

heart suddenly racing. Evan stood in the open doorway, huge and imposing. He had a groove between his dark eyebrows and his chiseled jaw was tight. Eyes fixed on me.

A predator who'd just spotted his prey.

Me.

He kicked the door shut behind him and stalked straight into the kitchen, his eyes never once leaving mine. I skittered backward a few steps, helpless as a baby gazelle. All my plans dissolved to nothing, evaporating from my mind like a puff of water vapor, replaced by the scorching need in Evan's eyes.

For half a second, I wondered if he was mad. Did he know what I'd been up to?

Wordlessly, he caged me in against the counter, crowding me with his huge frame. He smelled faintly of rubber and oil, the scents of his shop layered over the intoxicating smell of his body. He was so ruggedly male, so big and powerful. His closeness made my heart flutter and sparks dance across my skin.

Leaning in, he slid his nose along my neck and inhaled deeply. "I missed you today."

That tiny brush of contact sent a shiver down my spine. Nope, not mad. "I missed you, too. Where's Sasquatch?"

"In the shop with a bone." He inhaled again, then pressed his lips to my neck, just below my ear, leaving a hot brand on my skin. His low growl reverberated through me. "I thought you'd come find me when you got home."

"Oh, I..." I'd been about to do something, here in the kitchen. What was it? He palmed my breast, his thumb sliding over my nipple through my clothes. My eyelids fluttered and a soft sigh escaped my lips.

"I was thinking about fucking you over the hood of the car." His thumb traced circles over my stiff nipple, that little movement and his low voice in my ear making me squirm with need. "But the kitchen works, too."

Fuck me in the shop? On the kitchen counter? Any of it. All of it. Yes, please.

His big hand kept kneading my breast while his mouth found mine. He kissed me deep, with slow thrusts of his velvety tongue. I slid my hands along the hard ridges of his abs and fisted his shirt when he pushed his erection against me.

Why weren't we naked yet?

I went for his pants, but he grabbed my hair at the base of my neck and jerked my head back. Dove into my mouth with his tongue, leaving me breathless and trembling.

He wanted control. I happily gave it to him.

His mouth left mine long enough to pull my shirt over my head. He kissed me again, then ripped his shirt off and let it drop to the floor.

God, he was massive. His broad chest and thick arms rippled with muscle. Smooth olive skin. Tattoos down his arm. He was absolutely gorgeous.

And that was with his pants *on*.

Those huge hands picked me up and set me on the counter. I spread my legs wide while he yanked my bra straps off my shoulders and pulled both breasts out of their cups. With a groan, he held my tits in his hands and hungrily licked my hard peaks. My head dropped back as sparks raced to my core.

The throbbing pressure between my legs grew with every lap of his tongue. He licked and sucked and teased, making me ache for him, flooding me with warmth.

Finally, he headed south, but not because he was ready to take mercy on me and fuck me senseless. I braced myself against the counter while he took off my pants, but his remained frustratingly on.

"Evan—"

He silenced me with a look, his whiskey-brown eyes molten with lust.

Licking his lips, he leaned down to kiss my inner thigh. His stubble grazed my skin and he put his mouth everywhere but where I needed him most.

He was doing this on purpose.

Driving me crazy.

I loved it.

The tender flesh between my legs cried out for his touch, so sensitive the mere whisper of his breath sent a tremor through me. His tongue flicked out over my slit as he crossed from one thigh to another.

Fucking tease.

I hoped he'd do it again.

"You taste so good."

He nibbled and kissed, giving me quick brushes of his tongue, making me shiver and moan. My nipples puckered in the air, still glistening from his mouth, and if he didn't make me come soon, I was going to—

Without warning, he slid two thick fingers inside me. I cried out at the sudden pressure—glorious, glorious pressure. It wasn't his dick—and I really loved his dick—but it was so, so good.

Evan's hands were literal magic.

He licked my clit and pumped his fingers, finally giving me what I desperately needed. I held onto the edge of the counter for dear life, my breath coming in shallow gasps, pleasure consuming me.

His eyes lifted and I watched with erotic fascination as he sucked on my clit. Was there anything hotter than the sight of Evan Bailey's face between my legs? I couldn't think of anything.

Then again, I couldn't think at all.

Like the wolf he was, he growled against me, sending shock waves of vibration through my body. His fingers inside me and his tongue on my clit were a wicked combination.

And then he slid a finger from his other hand lower. A little lower. Pressed the tip against my ass.

"Oh god," I cried out, throwing my head back.

He played with my ass, swirling his finger around, applying gentle pressure. The new sensation made my head spin and my body teeter on the edge of climax.

A part of me wanted to wait and come on his cock, but Evan was having none of that. He curled his fingers and flicked my clit until I was panting for breath, my inner walls quaking. A ripple passed through me, making him growl.

I was hot and wet and so fucking ready.

Another lap of his tongue was all it took. Closing my eyes, I cried out while I shattered to pieces. My pussy spasmed around his fingers in a quick rhythm while he stroked and sucked, coaxing out every last bit of pleasure my body had to give.

He slid his fingers out while I tried to catch my breath. I was still braced on the counter, and he still had his pants on.

Not for long.

His eyes locked with mine and he slowly, methodically unfastened his jeans. Dear god, he'd gone commando. That thick cock appeared in all its unbelievable glory as soon as he popped the button. It was so big, I didn't know how he'd kept it inside his pants at all.

He lowered the zipper so his pants hung loose at his hips, then fisted his cock. His eyes tracked up and down, taking me in. I had to look a mess—sitting on the counter with my legs spread open, my bra half on, and I had no idea what was happening to my hair. But whatever he saw, he liked it.

The way he bit his lower lip and stroked his cock a few times told me that much.

A feeling bloomed in my chest. So much more than the happy brain chemicals and hormones rushing through me after an admittedly fantastic orgasm. The way Evan looked at me was lustful, yes. He wanted me. And I loved that—loved being wanted.

But it was more.

There was something else in his eyes and it was both beautiful and terrifying.

It was something that looked an awful lot like love.

Did Evan love me?

Before I had a chance to get lost in pondering the look in his eyes, he grabbed me off the counter and took me to the couch.

Not complaining.

I bounced on the cushions and giggled. He pulled a condom out of his pocket—he really had been planning to fuck me in the shop—then kicked off his pants.

"Ready for more, beautiful?" He rolled the condom onto that magnificent erection.

My core tingled with anticipation and I took a second to pop my bra the rest of the way off. "Yes. Yes, please."

He knelt on the couch in front of me, holding my legs open, and tilted his head. "Such a pretty pussy. She needs my cock, doesn't she?"

"Oh my god, so much."

His lips curled in a smile. "I'm going to fuck you hard and deep. Does that sound good?"

"Yes," I whimpered.

He moved closer, his swollen cock jutting out in front of him. His body was a masterpiece of masculinity—every bit of him thick and hard. He was rough around the edges, but in those whiskey eyes, I could see his melty center.

And I almost said it. I almost uttered the words.

I love you, Evan.

In my heartbeat of hesitation, he thrust inside me.

If I'd been any less wet and ready, I'd have struggled to accommodate him. He stretched me open, filling me to my breaking point.

His abs flexed as he thrust his hips, driving his cock into me. That groove between his eyebrows was so deliciously sexy. I loved the way he looked mean when he fucked me.

But he wasn't. He was tender, even when he was aggressive. Taking his pleasure, but always making sure I had mine.

Holding my legs open, he pounded me into the couch, grunting hard. Sweat glistened on his chest and his eyes didn't leave mine.

One orgasm was just a warm-up when you were Evan Bailey's girl, and in minutes I was racing to the edge yet again. He reached down and rubbed his thumb over my clit, making my eyes roll back and my inner walls clench tight.

"Fuck, your pussy feels good. I could do this forever."

A whimper was all I could get out. He thrust harder while he rubbed my clit. A flush raced across my cheeks and my nipples tightened.

His cock demanded another orgasm and my body happily complied.

Pulses of hot pleasure rolled through me like slow waves, the sensation deeper than before. My eyes fluttered closed as sensation washed over me. Evan's thick erection, thrusting, stretching me. His hands, his body, his skin against mine.

By the time it was over, my body was trembling. And Evan had yet to unleash.

He licked his lips. "You're so fucking beautiful when you come."

I let out a breath, feeling like I could sink right into the couch. How much more could I take?

"Knees." His voice was low and demanding.

I turned over, arching my back for him. I could take it all —everything he had to give.

He palmed my backside and traced his thumbs along my very wet slit. "So pretty. So wet. And fuck, this ass. I fucking love this ass."

Giggling softly, I arched harder.

Groaning, he slid his finger into my ass. Just the tip. It was wet, but I felt my muscles tighten around him.

"Is this okay?" he asked, his voice surprisingly soft.

"Yes," I whispered back.

He pushed in again, further this time, and his throaty growl was the sexiest sound I'd ever heard. While he gently massaged my ass, he slid his cock into my wetness. Thrusted and pushed his finger in deeper.

"Still okay?"

"Yes."

He thrust again, groaning, his finger working me. Evan was the only man who'd ever touched me there, but I liked it. I wanted him inside me, everywhere.

I wanted him to own me. Mark me. Claim me as his.

"You want it?" I asked, pushing my hips back. "Take it."

He grunted, his cock pulsing inside me.

"Fuck my ass, Evan."

His answering shudder made me feel strong and powerful. He was putty for me. He was mine.

"Holy fuck," he muttered, his voice strained. "Are you sure?"

"Yes. Do it. Come in my ass. I know you want it. Take it."

With a long, low growl, he slid his cock out. "Don't move."

I waited while he got up and a second later, I heard a cupboard in the kitchen. He came back with a jar of coconut oil.

His breath was ragged, but he didn't rush. Didn't force himself inside. He massaged me with his fingers, gently pulling, stretching—getting me ready.

I had no idea how he had so much control. I'd come twice already and I was dying for him again.

With his hands palming me, he positioned his cock and pushed in. Slow. Agonizingly slow. His body shuddered and he groaned again as the tip slid into my tight hole.

"Fuck," he muttered. "This is so hot."

The pain was nothing, the pressure more than worth the reverent awe in his voice. The way his body trembled behind me. He loved this, and I loved giving it to him.

"Do it. Fuck me. I want to feel you come in my ass."

He grunted, moving his hips so he thrust in a little deeper. I bit my lip and exhaled. It wasn't bad. He settled into a rhythm, his hands gripping my hips, his cock sliding in and out.

"Fuck, Fiona, I can't." He was almost breathless now. "You're so fucking hot. Oh my god."

His hips jerked harder and he growled like an animal. My muscles tightened around him as he started to come, the pulses of his orgasm rippling through me. My heart raced with the intensity of it and my eyes rolled back. It was a different sensation, new and delightfully dirty.

He made me feel bad in all the best ways.

His grip on my hips loosened and he carefully pulled out, breathing hard. "Holy shit. That was fucking unbelievable."

Still on my knees, I glanced back at him. The lazy grin on his face made me want to collapse into a melty ball of happiness.

He gently massaged my hips and ass and leaned in to pepper me with soft kisses. "Are you okay?"

"I'm great."

I held there while he babied me for a minute until my legs started to give out. He got up while I crumpled onto the couch.

"Don't move," he said. "I'll be right back."

My eyes drifted closed—my word, I felt good—and a few moments later, strong arms were turning me over. Lifting me up. He carried me into the bedroom and laid me down on the bed.

"Do you need anything?"

His voice was so tender. So sweet. Who would have thought that grumpy, broody man had this inside of him?

"Just cuddles."

"Anything you want, beautiful."

He got in bed with me and proved once again that Evan Bailey was the best cuddler in the history of snuggles.

Feeling blissfully warm and pleasantly sore, I relaxed in his arms. There was something in the back of my mind. Something I'd meant to do. And for some reason, it seemed like maybe now would have been a good time to do it.

But I didn't want to think. I shifted a little so more of my skin was touching his, and he hugged me closer.

I was so crazy in love with this man. I just wanted to drift for a while and enjoy this feeling.

37

EVAN

I woke up before Fiona, so I got out of our disheveled bed carefully so she could sleep. She was sprawled across the mattress, one arm hanging down, the sheets tangled around her waist.

Adorable.

She made me breakfast all the time, so I decided to return the favor. I wasn't a great cook, but Gram had raised me right. I could make a decent stack of pancakes.

There was a mixing bowl and a container of blackberries on the counter. Had she been about to make me cobbler last night? God, she was the best. I put the blackberries away for later and got to work. Pretty soon, the kitchen smelled like coffee and breakfast.

Fiona's sleepy voice came from the hallway while I was flipping the last pancake. "Morning."

"Hey."

Sasquatch trotted over to her and she petted his head. "Are you cooking breakfast?"

"Yeah. Thought you might be hungry."

She smiled. Her hair was messy and she'd thrown on a t-shirt, shorts, and a pair of pink slippers. "Starving. It smells delicious."

"Thanks."

She went to the coffee maker to pour herself a cup and I couldn't help but glance at her to make sure she was walking normally. Had I hurt her last night?

I put the last pancake on the plate and set the spatula on the counter. "Are you okay?"

"Yeah, I'm fine. Just waking up."

I gently slipped a hand around her waist. "Are you sure?"

"Positive. Why?"

"Last night was just..."

"It was what?"

Fucking mind blowing. "I just want to make sure you're okay."

Slipping her arms around my neck, she smiled. "Last night was fantastic. What are you worried about?"

"I didn't hurt you?"

"No. Okay, I'm a little sore, but not in a bad way. I liked it. I wasn't sure if I would, but it was fun. It felt naughty. I like being naughty with you."

I growled, low in my throat. "Beautiful, I love being naughty with you."

"So you liked it?"

"That's a fucking understatement. I can't remember the last time I came so hard."

Giggling softly, she nibbled her bottom lip. I leaned down to kiss her—I wanted to nibble on that lip too—but someone knocked on the door.

I groaned. "Who the hell could that be?"

"I don't know."

Reluctantly, I let her go and answered the door. I was surprised to see Jack Cordero, dressed in uniform.

"Morning," he said. "Sorry to bother you first thing, but I was wondering if Fiona has heard from her father."

"No, not at all," she said, gathering her hair into a messy bun and tying it with a hair tie.

Jack's lips pressed together, like he was considering what that meant. "We haven't had any luck tracking him down. No answer at his house and it's unclear whether he's been to work recently."

Fiona came closer to the door. "Have you asked Simone Stevens? She's his... girlfriend, I guess? She also works there."

"We did talk with Simone. One of your dad's mechanics pointed us in her direction, although she doesn't work for your dad anymore. I don't think she's his girlfriend, either."

"Really?"

"She's living with someone named Rodney Burke. It was clear that they were in a relationship."

"Rodney?" Fiona asked, scrunching her nose. "Gross. He's her jerk of an ex. Although she's probably a bigger jerk than he is, so I guess they deserve each other. She's living with him?"

Jack nodded. "And she had some rather colorful things to say about your father and why she left him, none of which were pertinent to our case or his whereabouts."

"Drama," Fiona muttered. "Wait, are you saying my dad's missing?"

"Successfully avoiding the police, yes. Missing, possibly. The only people who would see him on a regular basis are his employees, and the answers we got out of them are... inconsistent."

"They're trying to cover for him."

"That's what we think. Listen, I don't want to alarm you unnecessarily, but we do have reason to believe he might be here, in Tilikum. You're sure you haven't seen him?"

"No. I'd tell you," she said. "I really would."

"All right." He put his sunglasses back on. "Be careful. Both of you. And if you hear from him, let me know."

"I will."

"Thanks, Jack," I said.

He turned to go back to his car, and I shut the door.

"I cannot believe him," Fiona said. "He did this before, when I was in high school. The cops came sniffing around and he freaking disappeared for weeks."

"He didn't take you with him?"

"No. When he finally came back, he said he figured I was old enough to look out for myself."

"Jesus."

She let out a breath. "He makes me so mad."

"Yeah, I'd love five minutes alone with him." I grabbed her by the waist and pulled her close. "I want you to be careful, okay? Don't go anywhere alone."

"I'll be fine."

"Fiona, someone took a baseball bat to my shop. Stuff can be replaced, but you..." I couldn't even think it.

"He won't hurt me. Not like that."

Leaning down, I kissed her. I wasn't so sure about that.

My phone rang and I pulled it out of my pocket. Gavin. "Great, what does he want?" I swiped to answer. "Yeah."

"Bro, I'm pretty sure I can build a jump that will clear the ravine."

"No."

"Come on, I'll be the first to test it. It'll be fucking amazing."

"You're a jackass. Is that seriously why you called me?"

"Yeah. Also to chew you out for not letting us in on your prank on Luke."

"What prank on Luke?"

Fiona's eyes widened.

"Whatever Fiona pulled on him yesterday. I saw her car parked at his shop. What'd she do and why didn't you tell us?"

"There was no prank, Gav."

"What? Of course there was. You don't have to cover for her. Why else would she have been at Luke's shop?"

I stared at her, watching her face go pale. "I don't know."

Gavin was quiet for a second. "Oh. Maybe it wasn't her car then."

"Maybe not. Gotta go, Gav."

"See ya, bro."

Without taking my eyes off her, I ended the call.

My heart knocked against my ribs and my pulse throbbed in my temples. I had a hair trigger when it came to that name, and when I spoke, my voice was louder than I intended. "Were you at Luke's shop yesterday?"

"Yes, but—"

"What the fuck, Fiona?"

"Could you maybe not yell at me? I was going to talk to you about it."

"Were you? This was yesterday and I hear about it from my brother?"

"Yes, I was." She crossed her arms. "I went there to talk to him. Why is that such a big deal?"

"Because he's fucking Luke Haven," I roared. "You know what that means."

"I don't know why you have to make your childhood rivalry everyone else's problem," she said, her voice rising with every word. "Your families want to pull pranks on each other, fine. I get it, it's kind of funny. But this thing between you and Luke is out of control. One of your brothers sees my car there, and suddenly you're yelling at me about it?"

"Why didn't you tell me?"

"Because I haven't had the chance. I was going to last night but you attacked me in the kitchen—which, for the record, I'm not complaining about. But do I have to tell you everything, now? If I run into Luke on the street and wave, should I call you? I probably should in case the freaking Bailey patrol reports me."

"He wasn't reporting you. He assumed you were pulling a prank, because why the fuck else would you be there?"

"Why would you assume I was doing something bad? Don't you trust me?"

I was so fucking angry. Too angry too fast, and a voice in the back of my head tried to tell me to shut up. To stop yelling and listen to her.

But, like the asshole I was, I didn't.

"I thought I could trust you, but you're hanging around with Luke fucking Haven, so now I don't know."

Her mouth dropped open and her eyes blazed with fire.

Fuck. I'd gone too far. But I was too pissed and defensive to take it back.

"Fine." The word cracked like a whip. "If you don't trust me, I don't know what I'm even doing here." She stomped to the bedroom and came out with her purse and a sweatshirt slung over her arm. "Do not follow me."

"Fiona—"

"Don't." Without another word, she stormed out the door and slammed it behind her.

"Fuck." I raked my hands through my hair. I wanted to kick something, but there was nothing close. Which was probably a good thing. "Goddammit."

Sasquatch stood nearby, the fur along his spine standing up. I'd agitated him. He didn't know what to do when his humans were arguing.

"Sorry, big guy." I went over to the couch and sank down. Rubbed my hands over my face. "Why the fuck would she go to Luke's shop and not tell me?"

He came over and climbed onto the couch next to me so I could pet his head.

"Yeah, I'm sure she had a good reason. Maybe she's right. Maybe this thing with me and Luke is out of control. What do you think I should do? Go after her?"

I paused for a moment, scratching behind his ears.

"We probably both need a little time to cool off. She left her plants, so we know she'll be back."

Letting out a long breath, I leaned my head back. Damn it. I shouldn't have yelled at her. She didn't deserve that.

And maybe I didn't deserve her.

In that moment, a hard truth hit me. All this time I'd been keeping people out to avoid getting hurt. But I hadn't thought about how easily I could be the one doing the hurting.

38

FIONA

*F*uming with anger, I flew out of the house. What the hell did he think I'd been doing with Luke? Fucking him in his office? He hadn't even given me a chance to explain. Just started shouting at me.

I got in my car and left, heading toward town. I wasn't even dressed in regular clothes. Thankfully I'd put on a bra when I got up, but I was wearing a faded t-shirt, pajama shorts, and slippers. My hair was in a messy bun I'd done without looking.

Damn it.

Maybe I'd just drive around a little bit so I could calm down and cool off.

I'd known Evan would get mad when he found out I'd been to see Luke. What else had I expected? Other than to be feeding him blackberry cobbler—possibly while naked —when I told him so he wouldn't get so worked up. That would have changed the outcome significantly.

But why couldn't we just have a normal conversation where the name Luke Haven came up? Why did I have to go out of my way to coddle him over it?

And to say he doesn't think he can trust me? I was trying to fix his biggest problem. I did fix it. But all he was going to hear was *Fiona went to see Luke Haven.*

Cue shouty, angry Evan.

I got into town and slowed. It wasn't just Evan that had me worked up, and I knew it. Hearing that the cops hadn't been able to locate my dad had gotten my adrenaline pumping. I'd tried to act nonchalant so Evan wouldn't worry, but that unwelcome tidbit of news had put me on edge.

So maybe I'd overreacted a little bit, too.

My stomach rumbled. I wasn't dressed, but I was hungry, so I stopped at the Bigfoot Diner. I couldn't be the first girl to come in with messy hair and slippers.

I went in and choose a booth—the same booth I'd sat in when I'd been contemplating my life after realizing I was too broke to continue on to Iowa. Where Luke had offered me a job. Seemed fitting.

The waitress brought me coffee and I put in an order for eggs and toast. I thought about pancakes, but for no reason that made any sense, it felt like eating diner pancakes when Evan had made them at home would be disloyal. As if he'd care what I ate for breakfast while we were cooling off from an argument.

Still.

Naming my plants and talking to them like pets didn't make much sense either, and I did it anyway. It was just who I was. It made sense to me, so no pancakes.

A man at the counter swiveled around on his seat and grinned at me. It was Gavin.

"Hey, Fiona. Where's the big guy?"

"Just me this morning."

"Want some company?"

I shrugged. "Sure. Why not?"

He grabbed his plate and moved it to my booth, sliding onto the bench seat across from me. "Did I get you in trouble?"

"It's not your fault."

"Sorry. I just assumed you guys were up to something and I didn't know why he hadn't told us. I probably should have known. Evan hasn't pulled a prank in forever."

"Really? I thought with how much he hates Luke, he'd be all over that."

"No, he's pretty serious about the grumpy recluse thing he does." He met my eyes. "Or he was before you."

I took a sip of my coffee. "I don't understand why he can't let it go. Don't those two realize they don't have to hate each other? They could make peace and coexist."

"We're expert grudge holders out here." He took a bite of his hash browns.

"You're telling me. Do you have a rivalry with one particular Haven?"

"No, I like to fuck with all Havens equally."

The waitress brought my breakfast and I picked at my eggs. Gavin was being unnaturally subdued this morning. Normally he low-key flirted with me. But we were having a fairly normal conversation.

Of course, he didn't have an audience.

"So, have you thrown in the towel and decided to stop asking me out?"

He looked up from his food and grinned. "Definitely not. But, you know, Evan isn't here, so why waste a good line."

"You love to get him riled up, don't you?"

"So much. When he's really mad, he clenches his fists and makes those veins in his forearms pop. I like to see if I can get him there without him trying to tackle me."

I shook my head. All five Baileys were such boys.

"Gram must have had her hands full with all of you. How did she survive your childhood?"

"That's an excellent question," he said around a mouthful of food. "I'm sure we didn't make it easy on her."

"Which one of you was the most difficult?"

His brow furrowed as he wiped his hands on a napkin and swallowed his bite. "I don't know. Asher got in fights. Levi too sometimes. Logan was the class clown—got in trouble a lot for being disruptive. Evan would lose his temper and disappear in the woods."

"What about you?"

He smiled again, his dimples puckering. "I'm surprised I didn't give Gram a heart attack."

"I can only imagine." I paused to eat another bite of eggs. "I wasn't doing anything bad at Luke's yesterday."

"Oh, I know. He knows it, too, even if he said something stupid and that's why you're here."

"Kind of."

Gavin put his fork down on his empty plate, his expression serious. "He loves you. You know that, right?"

I glanced down. "I hope so."

"He does. Guarantee it. And you know what the good news is?"

"What?"

"You get to go home and have make-up sex." He wiggled his eyebrows.

I laughed.

But he wasn't wrong.

"Thanks, Gav."

"Anytime." He flagged down the waitress and paid for both our breakfasts. "Normally I'd take a selfie with you and text it to Evan, but even I know when to back off. But this was a great first date. I hope I get another one."

Smiling, I shook my head. "Thanks for breakfast."

"Sure. I gotta get to work. We're just running some training exercises today, so I'll be off in a few hours if you want to hang out. Maybe have date number two?"

"You can't resist, can you?"

"Nope."

"Bye, Gavin."

He left and the waitress came back to refill my coffee. I stared into the dark liquid. I didn't like fighting with Evan. It left me feeling like my insides were all twisted.

But the specter of my father loomed over me like the shadow of a storm cloud.

I hadn't given Dad what he wanted—hadn't gone home. And now the cops couldn't find him, and he might be here in town.

What was he going to do?

I'd told Evan he wouldn't hurt me, and I believed that. But would he hurt Evan? How far would he go to get to me?

Scattered memories flitted through my head. Dad with bruised knuckles. Bits of conversation I wasn't supposed to hear. Angry threats. Fear simmering in my belly. I'd seen things as a child that I hadn't understood.

As much as I hated admitting it, the truth was I didn't know what he was capable of.

Maybe I did need to go to Iowa. Not to start over. That plan had gone out the window a long time ago. Mad as I was, I loved Evan Bailey. I was never going to leave him. But he'd be safer if I wasn't here. That would give the cops time to find my dad. And I doubted my dad would suspect I'd gone to my mom's. That was why I'd planned to go there in the first place. It was almost like hiding in plain sight.

I knew it wouldn't end there. Someday, Dad could still

hurt Evan to try to get to me. Maybe by then I could find a way to make peace with him.

In the meantime, I needed to get Evan out of harm's way.

He wasn't going to like it, but he had a car to finish. That Pontiac at that car show with the museum there to see it? It was going to change his life. He had to be there.

More things to explain that Evan wouldn't want to hear.

It also meant I needed to suck it up and finally call my mom.

I went out to my car and brought up her number. My stomach fluttered with nerves. It had been a while since I'd talked to her. That last conversation had gone fine. Short—she was always busy—but there hadn't been too much tension.

Here goes nothing. I hit send.

"Hello? Fiona?"

"Hi, Mom. Do you have a minute?"

"Um..." She hesitated. "Sure, I guess so."

"If you're busy—"

"It's fine. What do you need?"

I took a deep breath. "I quit my job working for Dad."

"That's good."

"Yeah, but you know how he is. He's not making it easy."

"Of course not. But Fiona, you know I don't like talking about your father."

"Right, sorry. It's just that things are a little crazy out here. I think it would be best if I got out of town for a little while."

"Well, then do that."

"I was hoping I might be able to come there." I kept talking before she could interrupt. "He won't know. He doesn't know I talk to you at all. I told you I wouldn't tell him, and I never have."

"Oh, Fiona. I can't. We don't have any extra room. And it would be too disruptive for Matt and Chelsea. We're so busy with all their activities."

I stared at the dashboard, not really seeing anything. "It wouldn't be for very long. And I'm used to not taking up much space. You'll hardly know I'm there."

Her voice got quiet, like she was trying to keep anyone from hearing. "Why are you making this difficult?"

"Mom, I'm just asking for a place to stay until things calm down here. My boyfriend's shop got trashed and I'm worried about what's happening with Dad."

"That's why you can't come here," she hissed. "I can't get involved with him again. I can't risk my children."

Tears stung my eyes and a lump rose in my throat. Wasn't I her child too?

Apparently not. She'd left me behind and hadn't looked back.

"Sorry I bothered you," I managed to choke out and ended the call.

I dropped my phone in my purse and took a shaky breath. I'd thought—

It didn't matter what I'd thought. I'd been wrong.

Trying to pull myself together, I swiped beneath my eyes and turned on my car. I didn't care about our stupid argument. I needed Evan. I needed his arms around me, holding me tight. His lips on my skin, his deep voice in my ear.

I drove out toward his place. Toward home.

Home.

I couldn't leave, not even temporarily. Whatever happened, we'd face it together. That was how it needed to be. The only way it could be.

Not far outside town, a car pulled up behind me, driving

fast. Too fast. I figured they were going to pass me, so I nudged over to the right, hugging the shoulder.

The car got closer, looming in my rear-view mirror. Too late, I realized they weren't going to pass. They were going to—

They clipped my back bumper. My heart lurched as everything spun. I clung to the steering wheel but I was spinning, spinning, spinning out of control. My tires tore through dirt and rock. Chaos. I couldn't see where I was going.

I came to an abrupt stop, my head smacking against the window. Hard. But it didn't hurt.

Why didn't it hurt?

A face appeared next to the car as my vision faded into a tunnel of black.

39

EVAN

I wandered out to the shop, looking for a distraction. I owed Fiona an apology—a big one —but she'd told me not to follow her. I wanted to respect that—give her some space if that was what she needed.

I didn't like it, but it seemed like the right thing to do.

Usually it was easy to get lost in my work. Turn on some music, focus on the car. But I was too restless. Too edgy.

My phone buzzed with a text. I whipped it out of my pocket, hoping it was Fiona. But it wasn't.

Gavin: *Had breakfast with your girl earlier. She seemed sad. You better kiss and make up, dumbass, or she's fair game.*

Me: *Mind your own business.*

I glanced at his text again, the word *earlier* catching my eye. She'd been gone for a couple of hours, and he'd been with her earlier. Where was she now?

She could be anywhere. Maybe with Grace or Cara. She liked to hang out with Gram, maybe she'd gone there.

An unsettled feeling pricked at me. I really wanted to know where she was.

I texted her, just to make sure she was okay.

A minute went by. Then another. Then five. Why wasn't she answering me? Even if she was mad, she'd answer to tell me she was fine, wouldn't she?

A few more minutes went by and she still didn't reply, so I called.

One ring. Two. Three. Then four.

Voicemail.

What the fuck?

I hit end. Was she ignoring me? Maybe. I decided to text Grace.

Me: *Have you seen Fiona today?*

Grace: *No. Is everything okay?*

Me: *I'm an idiot. We had an argument. She had breakfast in town with Gav, but she hasn't come back and she's not answering me.*

Grace: *I'm off today so I don't know if she went to the coffee shop. But she didn't come here.*

Me: *Can you text Cara? I don't have her number.*

Grace: *Of course. Hang on.*

I waited, pacing around the shop, growing increasingly agitated.

Grace: *Cara hasn't seen her. She wants to know if we need to form a search party.*

Me: *Not yet. I'm sure she's fine. I just feel shitty.*

Grace: *Arguments will do that. If I see her, I'll tell her you're ready to grovel.*

Me: *Thanks.*

I brought up Gram's number and hit send. She answered on the third ring.

"Hi, Wolf. Everything all right?"

"Sort of. Is Fiona there?"

"No, she's not here."

"Have you seen her at all today?"

"I haven't. Should I be worried?"

I took a breath. I didn't want to freak her out. "Probably not. We argued and she left. Gavin saw her a little bit ago. I'm just…"

"Worried about her and feeling rotten?"

"Yeah."

"I'm sorry, Wolf. If she comes here, I'll make sure she calls you. And if you see her first, let me know."

"I will. Thanks, Gram."

I ended the call. Fiona still hadn't answered my text.

What the hell? Where was she?

Sasquatch brushed past me, heading for the door. Either my mood was working him up, or his instincts were flaring as badly as mine.

She wasn't just mad at me. Something was wrong. I didn't know how I knew, but I did.

"Let's go find her."

I went over to the house to grab the keys to my Camaro. I couldn't take Sasquatch on the bike, and I wanted to bring him.

A car pulled up outside. I almost breathed out a sigh of relief, but my dog started barking.

He didn't bark at Fiona. He never had.

"Stay," I commanded so he wouldn't rush out, and went to the front door.

A black sedan was parked out front. It wasn't Fiona's car. And it wasn't Fiona.

It was her fucking father.

A hit of anger flared through my veins and I clenched my teeth. I checked the passenger seat, but he didn't have her. She wasn't in the back, either.

Shane Gallagher flew out of the car and slammed the door shut. "Where is she?"

"What? That's what I was about to ask you."

He looked rough. Disheveled clothes. Circles under his eyes. "She's not here?"

"No, what the fuck are you talking about?"

"Shit." He stopped several feet away from me. "When was the last time you saw her?"

A wave of fear ripped through me. Something was definitely wrong. "This morning."

"Fuck. I was hoping they were lying."

"Who?"

"They took her. They took her to get to me."

I reached for my phone.

"Don't," he shouted, holding up a hand. "No cops. They'll kill her."

I froze, every muscle in my body tightening. "Gallagher, you need to level with me right now. What the fuck is going on?"

"It's not my fault. I needed money and I got in over my head."

"Got in over your head with who?"

He looked away for a moment and let out a breath. "There's a guy I used to work with back in the day, Felix Orman. Stealing cars, parting them out. No one got hurt. Cops broke it up, but he and I avoided charges. After that, I went legit. But last year I got into some debt and not with a bank, if you know what I mean."

"Loan sharks."

"These guys were serious, I needed to pay them off quick. So I called Felix. He set me up with some jobs, I helped him move some merchandise, no big deal."

"What the fuck does this have to do with Fiona?"

"Felix is into more than stealing cars. A lot more. I didn't want to know about his other shit. I didn't want anything to do with it. I just wanted to pay off those assholes before they came after me and broke my kneecaps." He rubbed his jaw. "But once you're in with these guys, it's hard to get out. I did what he wanted, but it wasn't enough. I know too much. And now he fucking wants me dead."

I took a step closer. "This Felix guy has her? How do you know?"

"He called. I've been hiding out nearby. I didn't think he knew where I was."

"You led them right to her, didn't you? Jesus, Gallagher, what the fuck? Was it you who trashed my shop, or was that them too?"

"That wasn't me," he said. "It was them, trying to send a message. Scare me by going after my daughter. He doesn't give a shit about her. He just wants to get to me. Wants to make an example out of me."

I was a breath away from losing my temper. From pinning this fucker to the ground and beating his face to a pulp.

But that wouldn't get Fiona back. If he was telling the truth, and someone had her, I had to stay calm.

The red tinge receded from my vision and my head cleared. "'He wants to make an example'—what does that mean? What does he want you to do?"

"Meet him. Exchange me for her. Don't get your hopes up. He won't let her go."

I narrowed my eyes. Was he saying that so I wouldn't make him do it? Or because he knew? "Where are they?"

"I don't know. He gave me a number. I'm supposed to text him back before three. Then he'll tell me where to meet him. And he said no cops. They get a whiff of a uniform, they'll kill her."

My mind raced with questions. Obstacles. I was way out of my depth here and Fiona's life was on the line.

But she was my woman. I wasn't going to let them hurt her.

I leveled Gallagher with a hard stare and my voice was ice cold. "This is your fault. I don't care if I have to tie you up, gag you, and drop you off on this piece of shit's front porch, I'm going to get Fiona back. And if they hurt her, if they so much as touch her, you're going to pay for it." I stepped closer and he flinched back. "Now you're going to cooperate with me or the first thing I'll do is unleash my dog on you. And that won't be the worst thing that happens to you today. Understood?"

Wordlessly, he nodded.

"Good. Now get in the fucking car."

"Where are we going?"

I didn't answer. Just glared at him again until he went to the passenger side.

We were going to get help. I didn't like relying on anyone, but Fiona was too important—she was everything. I couldn't do this alone.

40

FIONA

*M*y head throbbed, the pain yanking me back to consciousness. Nausea roiled through my stomach and I tasted bile on the back of my tongue. It was hard to think. What had happened?

I'd been driving. My car spun off the road. Why? Someone had hit me from behind.

A face. There'd been a face in the window.

Oh my god, where was I?

Carefully, I cracked an eye open and awareness began to return to the rest of my body. I was lying on my side, on the ground. Dirt, not a floor. It was dark and cold. As if my brain had just registered the temperature, I started to shiver. My feet were bare and my hands... tied up?

My heart raced, fear almost consuming me. Something bound my wrists and ankles. I was afraid to move, afraid to make a sound.

Squeezing my eyes shut, I took slow breaths, trying to stay calm. Panicking would only make things worse.

There was a noise behind me, a scrape of something against dirt. A shoe? Whatever it was, I had to assume I wasn't alone. Which made sense. If someone had gone to all the trouble to run me off the road, kidnap me, tie me up, and put me... wherever this was, they wouldn't leave me alone. Someone would be standing guard.

Who had done this? It couldn't be my dad, could it? Was he that crazy?

I didn't think so. My father was many things—few of them good—but I didn't think he was a man who'd kidnap his own daughter.

Then again, who else would have?

Who and why aside, I needed to get out of here. Of course, I was bound hand and foot, probably guarded, and I had no idea where I was or how long I'd been unconscious. I could be anywhere.

This wasn't exactly looking good. Even my eternal optimism was having a hard time finding the silver lining here.

Breathe, Fiona. Just breathe. And think.

I opened my eyes again and waited for them to adjust to the dim light. I was definitely on the ground, but it didn't look like open air. It smelled dusty, like a gravel road on a windy day, and there was a light source behind me, illuminating rough walls. Stone and dirt? Was this a cave? Trying not to move my head too much, I looked up. There was a dark ceiling above me, supported by thick timbers. So not a cave—not a natural one, at least.

A horrifying thought hit me, freezing my breath in my lungs. Had they gotten to Evan?

The pain of my pounding head was nothing compared to the anguish that tore through me. What if they'd hurt him? What if they'd done worse?

Would I ever see him again?

Did he know that I loved him?

No, this was not how we ended. We'd only just found

each other. We'd barely begun. I refused to believe our last moments together were tainted with anger. I was going to get out of here and he was going to be fine.

There was my trusty optimism, right when I needed it.

I decided I had to risk moving a little more to see what I was dealing with. Slowly, I rolled onto my back and turned my head.

Yep. I was being guarded.

And he had a gun.

Because of course he did.

This was nothing like the movies. I wasn't a badass secret agent or a plucky journalist ready to sass and ass-kick her way out of danger. I was just a girl, tied up on the ground, looking at a scary man with a gun. My heart raced, my body shivered, and all I really wanted to do was curl up in a ball, cover my head, and cry.

I swallowed hard and bit the inside of my lip.

Evan, please be okay. Please let it just be me.

And please let someone find me.

Was there any chance of that? Did anyone know I was gone?

My guard had a shaved head, rough stubble, and merciless eyes. He looked at me without a shred of concern or urgency. I was totally helpless. He had nothing to worry about.

He turned his head. "She's awake."

"I have to pee," I blurted out.

He looked at me again, his brow furrowing in confusion. "What?"

It was true, I did have to pee, but I had no idea why I'd just said it out loud. "There's probably no bathroom around here, is there?"

"No."

"Okay. I guess I'll wait."

His eyes flicked up and down, from my head to my bound ankles, like I'd just said the weirdest thing he'd ever heard.

Maybe I had. 'I have to pee'? Who randomly tells their captor they have to pee? It wasn't even like I had an escape plan that hinged on him letting me get up to use the bathroom.

What was wrong with me?

Oh, right. I'd hit my head. Maybe that was it.

Footsteps approached and a fresh wave of fear made me shiver harder. My back tightened uncomfortably and my head throbbed again. At this point, I hoped I'd get through the next few minutes without puking. Or being shot, but puking felt more imminent.

A man in a button-down shirt and dark slacks came around a corner. He had more silver in his hair and beard than I remembered, but I knew that face. I'd met him many times as a child. I'd once thought he was simply a colleague or a business associate of my dad's.

Felix Orman.

Tilting his head, he looked down at me like someone might regard a plant or a pattern in a brick path. No emotion, good or bad. There was nothing in his eyes—no malice or anger. No guilt or regret. He looked at me with cold calculation, like he hadn't been to my tenth birthday party or professed to be a loyal friend to my dad.

I was nothing to him. Just collateral.

Icy terror chilled me from the inside. I was too cold to even shiver anymore.

"Well hi there, Fifi. Lovely to see you again."

"No it's not."

His lips twitched in a smile and he pulled his phone

out of his pocket. "I know the accommodations aren't exactly comfortable, but the show serves a purpose. Look at me." He held up the phone and took a picture. "Good girl."

"What are you doing?"

"Making sure your daddy cooperates. He seems to think I'm bluffing."

"My dad?"

"He thinks he can disappear on me. I can't have that. Makes me look weak. Like I can't take care of business. So I'm offering him a little incentive. That would be you."

A mix of emotions swirled with the fear that thrummed through me. Relief that my dad didn't have me kidnapped. Anger that he'd gotten tangled up with this awful man again. Frustration that I had to pay the price for his bad decisions.

"What are you going to do to me?"

"Depends on your father. If he does what I tell him, nothing."

"You'll let me go?"

"Of course."

I looked into those calculating eyes and I knew he was lying. He wasn't going to let me go.

"And if he doesn't?"

"Don't worry your pretty little head about that. He will." He turned to the guard. "Keep an eye on her. He has an hour."

Felix left, his footsteps echoing as he walked away. The guard sat down with his back against the wall and took out his phone.

I looked up at the rough, rocky ceiling. This really wasn't like the movies. If it was, I'd have had a tiny knife tucked in my shoe or a pin in my hair I could use to get out of my bonds. I didn't even have my slippers anymore, and the only thing in my hair was a plain hair tie.

And I really did have to pee. This was going to get uncomfortable.

I didn't have a plan. No idea of how I was going to get myself out of this. There was nothing to negotiate. I didn't have anything to offer Felix, or this guard. I couldn't sweet talk them into letting me go like they were car collectors reluctant to sell a rare part. I didn't know what I was going to do.

The only thing I knew was that I couldn't give up. Felix Orman might have been planning to kill me and my dad. But that didn't mean he'd succeed.

Closing my eyes, I drew on the only thing I had left. It was silly and probably naïve, but I imagined Evan working in his shop. I held that picture of him, making it as sharp and clear as I possibly could. And I loved him. I sent out all the love I had, sent it out into the universe, hoping for the impossible. That somehow he'd feel it. That if all else failed and this was really how it ended, at the very least, he'd feel it and he'd know.

He'd know how much I loved him.

But maybe, just maybe, he'd use it to find me.

41

EVAN

I almost didn't believe Fiona's father. Held on to a shred of hope that he was delusional and we'd find her in town. Maybe feeding the squirrels in Lumberjack Park, her phone battery dead so she hadn't gotten my calls.

Until we saw her car, wrecked on the side of the road.

It was far enough in the trees that I nearly missed it. I swerved across the other lane and slammed the brakes. Flew out of the car, my heart in my throat.

She wasn't there.

Her purse had fallen, the contents spilled out onto the floor. Her phone was there, my messages unread. Sasquatch sniffed around, but trained as he was, he wasn't a search and rescue dog. He undoubtedly smelled her, but he wouldn't know how to find her.

"I told you they took her," Shane said. "Probably ran her off the road."

I ignored him, desperately looking for any sign that she was alive. There wasn't any blood. Hopefully that meant she'd survived the crash.

She had to have survived. I wasn't going to entertain any other option.

If her car was here, she'd been on her way home. On her way back to me. That thought made my chest ache.

"Let's go."

I'd group-texted my brothers before leaving my house—told them I had an emergency and I was on my way. My phone dinged with replies, but I didn't answer. We were only minutes away and it would be easier to explain in person.

I pulled up in front of the Bailey bachelor pad. Asher and Grace were already there, waiting in the open doorway. Judging by the vehicles out front, it looked like the other three were home.

"Get out," I said.

Gallagher didn't argue.

I took him inside and wordlessly pointed to one of the chairs at the dining table. With my brothers and Grace all staring at him, he sat. Sasquatch stood guard in front of him.

"Fiona's been kidnapped and I need your help." Saying those words—I need your help—released some of the weight threatening to crush me.

"Holy shit," Logan said. "Are you serious?"

"Have you called Jack?" Asher asked.

"Not yet. That asshole's her father, Shane Gallagher." I pointed to him and he shrank back slightly. "They took her to get to him, and he says no cops or they'll kill her."

Everyone stared at me in disbelief.

"I wish I was pulling a shitty prank on you guys right now, but I swear I'm not. I found her car partway to my place. I think they ran her off the road and took her."

"He's right," Gallagher said. "These guys want me. I have until three to respond to them."

"What do they want from you?" Asher asked.

"Probably to kill me."

"Fuck," Levi said. "What do we do?"

I fought back the sense of helplessness and desperation threatening to overtake me. "I don't know. If we call the cops, I'm afraid they'll kill her. If we give them what they want, namely him, they still might kill her. I can't fucking lose her. I can't."

"I'll be right back," Grace said. "I need to make a call."

"Grace—"

"Just... give me a minute." She whirled around and raced out the door.

"Do you know where they took her?" Levi asked.

"No," I said.

"If I agree to turn myself in to them, they'll give me a location to meet," Gallagher said. "Presumably that'll be where they're keeping her."

"Well, do it," Levi said.

"Not yet." I held up a hand. As much as every cell in my body cried out to know where she was, we needed a plan. "We have to think this through. As soon as he calls them, I'm sure there'll be a ticking clock."

"He's right," Asher said. "We need a plan."

Grace burst back in the house, her phone to her ear. "Thank you so much. Hang on and I'll give you to Evan." She held her phone out to me.

I held the phone up to my ear. "Hello?"

"Evan, it's Leo Miles. I'm on my way now. First off, don't panic. I can help."

I'd met Leo a few times. He was one of Grace's half-brothers. I didn't know him well, but he was retired military and one of those men who projected an effortless *I'm a badass* vibe.

"Doing my best."

"Good. Now give me the rundown. What do we know?"

I explained the situation, giving him the details I knew. When she'd left home this morning. Gavin confirmed when he'd last seen her. The discovery of her car, wrecked on the side of the road. And everything her dad had said—who had her and why.

"Okay," he said when I'd finished. "Gallagher has to respond by when?"

"Three."

"Good, that gives us a little time. I'm about fifteen minutes out, so I need all of you to sit tight until I get there. I know waiting is the last thing you want to do right now, but trust me. I'm driving as fast as I can, and as soon as I'm there, we'll talk next steps and make contact with the kidnappers. Understood?"

"Got it."

"Hang in there, man. We'll get her back."

The next fifteen minutes were the longest of my entire fucking life.

I paced around the house, too agitated to stand still, even for a minute. Asher and Levi casually took up positions in front of Gallagher, either to keep him from trying to bolt, or to keep me from losing my shit and wrecking his face.

Probably both.

Logan and Gav had enough presence of mind to keep their mouths shut. No jokes, no attempts to cut the tension.

We just waited.

Finally, Leo arrived. He had a thick beard that partially hid scarring on one side of his face, and his dark hair was pulled back. Tattoos extended down over the back of his hand on his scarred side. He gave Grace a quick hug, then brought his laptop to the table.

"First order of business, we need to locate Fiona," he said. "We need to know what we're dealing with so we can plan the extraction."

"If Gallagher makes contact, they should give him a location for an exchange," I said. "But I don't trust that they'll give her up."

"We trust nothing." Leo turned to Gallagher. "Text them back and ask for proof of life before you'll agree to meet."

Gallagher nodded and typed a message. Asher leaned over to watch, then met my eyes and nodded.

While we waited, Leo quietly asked Levi for the Wi-Fi password. I stared at the floor, my heart pounding.

A moment later, Gallagher held up his phone. "Got it."

Surging in, I ripped the phone out of his hand. The pieces of shit had her tied up on the ground. She had a bruise on the side of her head and her face looked so pale.

I fought down a flare of white-hot rage. Losing my temper wasn't going to help Fiona.

Leo took the phone. "I know this seems bad, but she doesn't look seriously injured. She's going to be okay."

"I know," I said with a nod. She was going to be okay. I was going to make sure of it. "So Gallagher agrees to meet?"

"Yes," Leo said. "We need the location."

Gallagher looked like he might be sick. He typed on his phone again while Asher watched.

Once again, we waited.

The text came in and Gallagher's forehead creased. "It's coordinates."

Leo took the phone and brought up a map on his laptop. "This isn't far from here, which doesn't surprise me. They probably followed you out here, and there are dozens of spots in the mountains used for drug running, human trafficking, that kind of thing. It's remote, and difficult for law enforcement to cover."

"That's—" Gallagher closed his mouth before finishing.

My eyes snapped to him. "What do you know?"

He started to answer, but stopped again.

I took a few steps closer, staring him down. "You said this Orman guy was into more than stealing cars. Stuff you didn't want to know about. Is that what you meant? Human trafficking?"

"Yeah." He shrank back from me. "Runaways, girls addicted to drugs. I don't know what he does with them. I didn't want to have anything to do with it. I didn't want to know."

I turned to Leo and he nodded once. He didn't have to say it out loud. We both knew. Orman wasn't going to kill Fiona, but he wasn't going to give her up, either. He was going to sell her.

Fuck that. Not my girl.

I went back around the table to look at the satellite image on Leo's laptop. "She's there?" I asked, pointing to the spot.

"Yeah."

"I know where that is. We used to ride dirt bikes out there. There's an old mine entrance nearby, just off that logging road. Let me see the picture." I took Gallagher's phone. This time, I looked at everything around Fiona. The photo was dim, but I could make out the rough stone walls and what might have been a timber supporting the ceiling. "This looks like it's inside the mine."

"Agreed. Let's see if we can find a map." Leo pulled out his phone and made a call. "Hi, baby. I'm sending you a location. It's close to an old mine. Can you help me find a map or rendering?" He glanced my direction. "My wife, Hannah."

I nodded.

In less than a minute, he had an old rendering of the mine on his screen.

"You're amazing. Kiss the kids for me. I'll be home soon." He put down his phone. "Okay, now we're talking."

"That must be the entrance near the logging road," I said, pointing. "There's another one down here."

Gavin looked over my shoulder. "I've been in there."

"Of course he has," Logan said.

"I'm serious. Some kids dared me to see if it went through to the other side. It does. Or it did ten years ago."

"How did it look inside?" I asked. "Do you remember any cave-ins or blocked-off passages?"

"No, I remember thinking the other kids were wussies for not going in. The entrances aren't even blocked off. It was fucking dark, but all clear."

"I only see two entrances on the rendering," Leo said. "If they still connect, that's good news for us. The location they gave Gallagher is closest to the north end. That's probably the side they're using."

"So we could go in the back and get her out," I said.

"Not without some kind of distraction," Leo said. "Something unexpected to draw them out on this side. We don't know how many guys they have, but I'd say three to five is a safe bet."

"Fire," I said.

"Wait, what?" Levi asked.

"Hear me out. It's not wildfire season yet, but it's been dry. You guys sneak over there and stage a brush fire near the mine entrance. Just a controlled burn. It's right off a logging road, you could even get an engine back there. Put it out before it spreads."

"This is brilliant," Logan said. "We don't even need to

start much of a fire. Just enough to get smoke blowing to explain a big ass fire engine roaring down that road. That'll be a distraction."

"Can you pull that off?" I asked.

Logan scoffed. "Of course we can."

"We can take the engine. We'll just leave Chief a note," Gavin said.

"A note?" Levi shook his head. "This could definitely get us all fired, but fuck it. I'm in."

"Okay." I took a breath. "I'll go in the back entrance and get Fiona out while you guys play with fire on the other side."

Leo glanced at me, raising his eyebrows.

"She's my girl," I said. "I'm going in to get her."

"I'll go with you," Asher said.

I nodded once.

"What do we do with him?" Logan asked, jerking his thumb at Gallagher.

"Grace and I will watch him," Leo said, a hint of danger in his tone. "I'll get law enforcement on standby, ready to move in once you have Fiona."

I nodded again and a potent surge of relief and gratitude flooded my chest. It was my girl in trouble, but my family was here, ready to risk themselves to help me save her.

What the fuck would I do without them?

"We all have a job to do," I said. "Let's move."

Hang in there, baby. I'm coming for you.

42

FIONA

*N*ow I really had to pee.

I'd been staring at the ceiling for what felt like forever. Struggling against my bonds was pointless. That got me nothing but a few amused glances from my guard. I hated feeling so helpless, but what more could I do?

Just wait. And hope.

A whisper of fresh air cut through the gravelly smell. It looked like we were in a wide passageway, although it was hard to be sure. One direction disappeared into darkness. There could have been another wall there, but the lantern light didn't reach that far. The other direction turned a corner not far from where they'd dumped me on the ground. Felix had gone that way. The occasional whiffs of outside air made me wonder if we weren't far from the entrance.

Where was Evan right now? Did he even know something was wrong? I'd stormed out and left. He probably assumed I was still mad.

I pictured him working on the Pontiac. Leaning over the engine or sanding the body, his back muscles rippling, his big hands making magic. Was he so focused on the car that he wasn't even thinking about me? Or was he out looking because he had realized I'd been gone too long?

My sense of time was skewed. It was hard to tell how long I'd been here. My guard—I was calling him Stoneface in my head because I didn't know his name—hadn't left once for a break. It seemed like eventually he'd have to eat or pee or something. But he just sat there, messing around on his phone, like this was the most boring job he'd ever had in his life.

I was trying not to take that personally. But couldn't he at least put in a little effort? Sure, I was lying on the ground with my wrists and ankles tied, but he didn't have to act like I was completely helpless.

"Do you get a signal out here?" I asked. My voice sounded odd in the hollow space.

His eyes flicked to mine, but he didn't answer.

I sat up. I'd been changing positions once in a while and as long as I didn't try to stand—which I wasn't sure I could manage anyway, given the tie around my ankles—Stoneface didn't say anything. Sitting wasn't comfortable either, but nothing was comfortable right now.

If I'd ever considered a little bondage with Evan, that was probably off the table at this point.

Assuming I ever got out of here.

I *was* going to assume that. I was getting out of here. Somehow.

"You must be playing a game. Maybe one of those puzzle games or that quest one. That one is so addictive."

He looked at me again. Still silent and expressionless.

"I'm just saying, you don't strike me as a social media guy. I doubt you're sitting there scrolling through Instagram. Although you never know, people are often surprising. Or maybe you're reading the news. You'd need a signal for that, but you might need a signal for a game, too."

"Shut up."

Rude.

Although what did I expect? The guy was armed, guarding a helpless tied-up girl in a cave. That didn't exactly scream *manners*.

A noise echoed further down the passage. Then silence again. Felix hadn't been back since he'd taken my picture. He'd obviously sent it to my dad. Apparently I was either collateral or bait. Maybe both. But I assumed he was still here somewhere. I hadn't seen any other people, but I'd heard footsteps a few times.

But that sound had been different. Stoneface seemed to think so too. He looked up from his phone, pausing like he was listening.

There it was again.

Did I smell something? I inhaled through my nose, trying to place it. It was different from the dusty gravel scent. Almost like smoke.

A second later, it was gone. I'd probably imagined it.

But I hadn't imagined the sound. Stoneface had heard it too.

Footsteps echoed from around the bend in the passage and Stoneface stood.

It was another guy with a gun. He wore a plain t-shirt and jeans and had a beanie on his head. I decided his name was Hatterson, because hat.

Stoneface and Hatterson. Not my most creative names, but I was in a crisis here.

Okay, this meant Felix had at least two henchmen.

I almost laughed at myself. What was I doing, taking inventory? One guard or ten, it didn't really matter.

That scent tickled my nose again. It did smell like smoke.

That wasn't good.

Stoneface walked a few feet further away and lowered his voice, but I could still hear him. "What the fuck is going on?"

"I don't know. Do you smell that?"

"Yeah. Where's Felix?"

"Out in the fucking car." Hatterson cast a glance down the passage, toward the direction he'd come from. "It's stronger this way. Maybe a brush fire outside?"

"Whatever, it doesn't matter. Gallagher should be here any minute."

"Doesn't matter? A fire means firefighters."

"Out here?"

"We're not far from a town. And someone could see the smoke from the highway."

"Is there a lot of smoke out there?"

"I don't fucking know. But maybe we need to up the timeline." Hatterson glanced at me.

A renewed jolt of fear shot through me. The acrid tinge of smoke in the air was unmistakable now, but a fire—wherever it was—wasn't exactly my biggest concern.

"Go ask Felix," Stoneface said.

"You go ask him."

I heard a faint rumbling sound, like the noise of faraway traffic.

Hatterson glanced back again. "Must be Gallagher."

A single blare of a siren echoed off the walls, the muffled whoop startling me.

"Cops?" Hatterson asked.

"Not unless they're stupid cops," Stoneface said. "Come on."

"What about her?"

Stoneface glanced at me and picked up his lantern. "She's not going anywhere."

The two men disappeared around the bend in the passage, plunging me into darkness.

This was not better.

The smell of smoke grew and faint noises I couldn't place seemed to bounce around me. I swallowed hard and bit the inside of my lip. It was so dark, I could barely see my hands in front of my face. Squeezing my eyes shut, I fought against the disorientation, willing my stomach to stay steady.

More noises. Was that coming from the other direction? I couldn't tell.

"Fiona."

My eyes flew open at the barely audible whisper behind me. Oh my god. It couldn't be.

Evan.

I whipped my head around, but before my brain had time to catch up, he was cutting through the bonds with a pocketknife. A bewildering mix of relief, elation, and heart-squeezing love exploded inside me, driving out the fear. With my ankles free, he sliced through the tie at my wrists, then cupped my face.

"I love you," he whispered. "I love you so much. Are you okay?"

I nodded and he surged in, quickly pressing his lips to mine.

Another voice. "Let's get her out of here."

Evan took my hands and helped me to my feet. Asher stood a couple feet away, holding a flashlight.

Asher? Was this even real?

Without a word, Evan scooped me into his arms, picking

me up off the ground. I held on around his neck, vaguely wondering if I was hallucinating. Because Evan Bailey couldn't be carrying me through a pitch-black stone passageway, following the beam of his brother's flashlight.

But the warmth of his body and the feel of his thick arms around me were very real.

Faint voices reverberated in the passage behind us. Evan carried me as if I weighed nothing. I had a million questions —starting with how on earth had he found me—but the answers could wait. For now, I just held on.

We followed the beam of Asher's flashlight through what seemed like a never-ending maze of tunnels. Asher stopped at a turn and he and Evan quietly conferred, checking a map on Asher's phone. My sense of direction wasn't great on a normal day and waking up down here— wherever this was—had left me totally disoriented. They agreed on a direction and we kept going.

A man's voice shouted somewhere behind us, and Evan's arms tightened around me. I had a feeling Stoneface had just realized I was gone.

Asher slowed, glancing over his shoulder.

"Keep going," Evan whispered.

Fast footsteps echoed, getting closer. He was going to catch up with us.

"He's armed," I whispered.

"Yeah," Evan said without stopping. "Can't go too fast or we'll get lost."

The footsteps grew louder. Stoneface was running. My heart beat so fast I thought it might burst.

"Wait," Evan said, and Asher turned. "Let me see the map."

Asher held out his phone. A second ticked by. Two. Three.

"That way." Evan gestured with a nod of his head. "I think there's a shaft leading down a level. Hopefully it still has a ladder."

Without hesitation, Asher followed Evan's lead. We rushed down the dark passageway until we came to an old wooden barrier in front of a wide hole. A ladder led down into the darkness.

Asher went first, then we heard his confirmation from below. "Go."

Evan set me down gently and I scrambled over the side. The rungs of the ladder were cold and hard. Firmly telling myself not to worry about what was down there—if there were rats or bugs, Asher had to have scared them away—I quickly made my way down.

Asher helped me off and Evan climbed down, jumping before he reached the bottom. He threw his arms around me and caged me against the wall while Asher doused the light.

I slipped my arms around his waist and rested my head on his chest. The darkness was consuming, but the sound of his heartbeat kept me calm. He held me against the rough wall as if to shield me from harm, putting himself between me and danger.

Oh my god, I loved him so much.

The sound of footsteps came from somewhere above us. Voices shouting. We held still and silent in the dark. I scarcely dared to breathe.

Finally, the shouting receded. Evan didn't move. The noises above grew fainter. Then silence.

Only then did Evan step back. Asher turned on his flashlight.

"Let's go," Evan said.

Asher went up the ladder first. I climbed up next and he

helped me at the top. Evan was right behind me. I was about to tell him I could walk—although I was barefoot—but he scooped me into his arms again.

He and Asher conferred with nothing but a few head nods and flicks of their eyes. Then we were on our way again.

The tunnels seemed endless but finally it felt like the ground sloped upward. That had to be a good sign. The passage widened and it grew lighter. We turned a corner and I squinted, seeing daylight.

Holding me tighter, Evan ran.

We burst out of an opening in the hill framed by thick timbers. I couldn't see anything but pine trees and dry brush, but Evan seemed to know where to go. He darted through the trees, debris crunching beneath his shoes.

His car came into view. I'd never been so excited to see a Camaro in my entire life.

"You drive," Evan said. He rushed to the passenger side and opened the door. Without letting me go, he ducked us both into the car, and I wound up in his lap, his arms still around me.

Asher was already in the driver's seat. Evan jammed a hand in his pocket and tossed him the keys. A few seconds later, the engine roared to life. Asher hit the gas and the wheels spit dirt behind us.

Evan held me against his chest, breathing hard as the car bumped along the rocky ground. Every muscle in his body was tense, his arms hot steel around me.

"We have her," Asher said. It sounded like he was on the phone. "We're clear."

Evan loosened his grip on me, but only enough to lay his palm across my cheek. His eyes searched my face, his dark brow furrowed. "Are you hurt?"

"Not really. Just bumped my head. I think I wrecked my car. Where are we? What happened? How did you—"

He silenced me with a hard kiss, then rested his forehead against mine. "I love you. I should have said it before. I love you so much."

"I love you, too."

"Fiona, I'm so sorry—"

It was my turn to silence him with my lips. "I'm sorry, too. It's over. We're fine."

The car jolted and we pulled out onto the road.

Evan's arms wrapped around me again and I settled against him. His chest rose and fell as he took a slow, deep breath. I didn't know how he'd found me, but he had. He'd saved my life.

Maybe all that love I'd sent out into the universe had actually worked.

I'd loved him before, but right now I loved him so much it burned inside me, hot and bright like the sun. I was banged up and bruised, my wrists and ankles chafed, and I had to pee so bad my bladder was probably going to have permanent damage. But I hardly felt a thing. Just the love I had for this man, and his love for me, answering right back.

43

EVAN

*F*iona sat on the couch in Gram's living room, wrapped in a dark blue afghan. Or more accurately, wrapped up in my arms on my lap with an afghan tucked beneath her chin. She was clinging to me like a baby koala, and I couldn't get enough of her.

I'd hardly stopped touching her since we got here. Hell, since I'd found her in the old mine. I'd let her go once out of necessity, so she could use the bathroom, but I'd kept her in my arms ever since.

Which was where she was going to stay.

Gram brought her a steaming cup of tea. "Here you are, Cricket. Are you sure I can't get you anything else?"

"No, I promise I'm fine."

Gram smiled and shifted the corner of the afghan to make sure Fiona's toes were covered. She went back to the kitchen and came back with her own mug of tea, then settled into an armchair.

Asher had driven us straight here. I didn't know how Gram had known what was happening, but none of our story surprised her. And she'd made fresh muffins this afternoon, as if she'd had a feeling we'd descend on her house after a bizarre crisis involving armed men in an old abandoned mine.

Grace arrived and flew into Asher's arms. I could hear him gently assuring her that everyone was fine. Sasquatch came in with her and immediately ran to sniff Fiona, checking to make sure she was okay.

"Hi buddy," she said, reaching out to pet him. "It's good to see you too."

"Where's Gallagher?" I asked.

Grace's eyes flicked to Fiona, her face full of sympathy. "There was a warrant out for his arrest, so Jack took him in."

"It's okay," Fiona said. "Unfortunately, that's what needed to happen."

"I'm sorry," Grace said. "But I'm so glad you're okay."

"Did Leo go home?" I asked.

"Yeah, he had to get back to his family."

"I don't know how to thank him," Fiona said. We'd given her the basics of how we'd found her, and how Grace's brother Leo had helped. "In fact, I don't know how to thank any of you."

I squeezed her, careful so she didn't spill her hot tea.

Asher put his arm around Grace and when he spoke, he met my eyes. "We're family. It's what we do."

Not for the first time today, I had to breathe through the tightness in my chest. But I didn't shy away from the emotions buffeting me. I felt them. I'd gone from gut-wrenching terror to overwhelming relief to heart-bursting love and gratitude. And it was worth the agony. She was worth it.

She was worth everything.

A vehicle pulled up outside and a few seconds later, the

chaos of my younger brothers crashed through the front door, all three of them talking at once.

"Fiona!"

"That was insane."

"So glad you're okay."

"Do I smell muffins?"

"Calm down," Gram said, her soothing voice carrying over the ruckus. "Everyone's fine now, and there's plenty for all of you."

"Thank god. I'm starving." Levi went straight for the kitchen.

"That was, hands down, the coolest thing we've ever done," Logan said.

Gavin's eyes were wild, glittering with excitement. "It so was. What a rush."

"What did you guys do?" Fiona asked.

"Evan and Ash needed a distraction, so we made a distraction," Logan said. "We got a fire going not far from the mine entrance. It wasn't very big, but we made it good and smoky."

"You're not telling it right," Gavin said. "First we stole a fire engine."

"Borrowed," Levi said from the other room.

"Fine, borrowed, although stole sounds more exciting," Gavin said. "We left Chief a note. I'm sure it's fine. Anyway, Levi drove us out there in the engine, then Logan and I went ahead on foot to start a big brush fire."

"Controlled burn," Levi called.

"Sure, controlled burn, whatever. So we got it going, and Gram, you'll be very proud of me: I had lots of ideas to make it bigger, but I was totally a grown-up and very responsible with my use of fire."

"He was, actually," Logan said.

Gram's lips twitched in a smile.

"Once the smoke looked convincing, Levi drove up and blared the siren once, just to get their attention."

"It was crazy. Guys with fu—" Logan stopped himself before he finished saying *fucking* in front of Gram. "Guys with guns came out. One of them started to run up the hill, like he was going to confront us or something, but another guy stopped him. So we just acted like we were there to put out a brush fire."

"But that's not even the best part," Gavin said. "We got the call from Leo that Fiona was safe and he said the FBI were on their way. But the bad guys obviously figured out Fiona was gone because they came out like they were going to pile in their SUV and get away. So we turned the hose on them."

"Are you serious?" I asked.

Gavin started laughing so hard he couldn't finish.

"Yeah, we actually did," Levi said, coming in with a half-eaten muffin in his hand. "We didn't hit anyone directly, just kind of herded them back to the mine entrance."

"So they didn't get away?" Fiona asked.

"Nope," Gavin said, obviously feeling very proud of himself. "We held them back until the FBI showed up."

"Well, you have had an exciting day," Gram said. "Good thing I made so many muffins."

Gavin let out a long breath. "Best day ever."

"Wait, how many of those have you eaten?" Logan asked Levi as he popped the last of a muffin in his mouth.

"Four," he said around his bite.

"That's it, brodentical, if you ate the last one, I'm destroying your face." He wound his arm around Levi's neck, trying to get him in a headlock, but Levi slipped out, twisting Logan's arm behind his back.

"Boys," Gram said. "Not inside."

They both stopped and said, "Sorry, Gram," in unison.

It was so weird when they did that.

Jack stopped by to give us an update. The FBI had Felix Orman and his goons in custody. They'd need to talk to Fiona, but it could wait until tomorrow. He apologized for having to take her dad in, but she assured him she understood.

Eventually, the muffins were gone, and everyone went home after saying their goodbyes. I held Gram a little longer than usual when I hugged her on my way out.

I took Fiona home. After feeding Sasquatch, we went straight to the bedroom, stripped off our clothes, and got into bed. It wasn't a sex thing. I just needed to touch her, have her body next to mine. I needed to feel her breathe.

She shifted so she could look up at me. "I need to tell you why I went to Luke's shop."

I brushed her hair back from her face. "I don't care why you were there. If you want to be friends with Luke, it's fine. You can go feed the squirrels together if you want."

"No, you don't understand," she said with a soft laugh. "I wasn't there just hanging out for no reason. Don't forget, I rejected him. It's not like he wants to be besties with me."

I tipped my head in acknowledgment. She had a point.

"I went to see Luke because he has literally the only compatible convertible carriage for the Pontiac in a five-hundred-mile radius. I swear, I called everyone I know and a whole bunch of people I didn't know. Nobody had one. Finally I found a guy who used to have one, but he told me he'd already sold it to Luke."

"Luke must have bought it thinking he'd get the Judge from Walt."

"Exactly. So I convinced Luke to sell it to you. And now I

just need to convince you to buy it from him and use it to finish the car, even though you've sworn you'll never do business with a Haven."

"How'd you convince him to sell it to me?"

"He needed a set of dials for a Mustang Boss restoration. I knew a guy who had them. And before you hear some crazy rumor about me running around town with Luke Haven, I did ride with him in his truck to go get it, but it was only so he'd agree to sell you the part you need."

Touching her face, I shook my head slowly. "Now I really feel like an asshole."

"You kinda should."

"Beautiful, I'm so sorry."

"It's okay. You also saved my life today. Although I would have forgiven you anyway."

I gazed into those hazel-green eyes that got me every time. "I don't know what I ever did to deserve you."

"Right back at you, Bailey." She nibbled her bottom lip. "I have another confession."

"How many new houseplants did you buy?"

"Zero," she said, laughing again. "But that's an excellent idea. Some plants would really brighten up the shop. No, that's not what I need to confess. And maybe I don't even need to tell you because it doesn't change anything, but I just think it would be wrong to keep this from you. You trust me and I know how special that is and I don't ever want to break that trust."

She was making me a little nervous, but I just nodded, waiting for her to continue.

"I called my mom this morning. God, was that really today? It seems like ages ago. Anyway, I was thinking, for just a minute, that maybe I should leave Tilikum for a little while and go to Iowa, like I'd planned."

I opened my mouth to tell her *no fucking way*, but she put a finger to my lips.

"I know, I know. Terrible idea. And I swear it wasn't because I was going to leave you. I promise. That's why I need to tell you, because I don't want it to come out later and you get the wrong idea. This morning, all I knew was that someone trashed your shop and the cops couldn't find my dad, and that could mean I was putting you in danger by being here. I thought maybe the right thing to do would be to go to Iowa until... I don't know, until they found my dad or until we could figure out a way to make sure we could be safely together. But..."

Her eyes shone with unshed tears and she glanced down.

"But what?" I asked gently.

"When I called her, she said no. They don't have room and it would have been too disruptive to her other kids. And it's fine, because I shouldn't have called her anyway. But, still."

"Oh my god, Fiona." I pulled her close and cradled her against my chest. After everything she'd been through, her own mother had rejected her. What the fuck was wrong with her parents? She was the most wonderful, incredible woman I'd ever known. How did they not see that? How did they not see her?

But that was the truth, wasn't it? They didn't see her. They never had.

I kissed her forehead. "I see you. I see how amazing you are. My family does too. And I love you. I'm sorry I didn't say it sooner, but I'm so fucking in love with you."

She pressed her face into my chest, muffling her voice. "I love you too."

I took a slow, deep breath. It didn't matter what happened, Fiona would always be mine.

44

FIONA

*T*he arena was packed. People wandered up and down the rows of cars on display, the light glinting off shiny paint and chrome. There was everything from muscle cars to Model T Fords to contemporary customs. A guy from Idaho was getting a lot of attention for his superhero-themed roadster, and there was a custom vintage fire engine that Evan's brothers would love.

But one of the biggest draws at today's show was the 1970 Pontiac GTO convertible. The Judge.

Evan had absolutely outdone himself. He'd gone for full authenticity, using the original blue paint with red pin striping and blue interior. Every detail was period-accurate and perfect.

It was a fucking badass car.

Luke was here too, with his '69 Mustang Boss. And, okay, it looked amazing. It was a super-hot car and he'd done a great job restoring it.

Whatever. It wasn't nearly as amazing as the Judge.

After Felix Orman's crappy goons had smashed up Evan's shop and damaged the car in an attempt to get to my dad by coming after me, he'd needed to work extra-long hours to finish it in time. I'd been there to help with anything I could, in the shop and otherwise. But he'd pulled it off.

No, he hadn't just pulled it off. He'd rocked it. It was the talk of the show.

I walked back with my iced coffee and found Evan standing casually next to the car while a horde of onlookers gaped at her. His arms were crossed, his stance relaxed, and anyone who didn't know him might think he was arrogantly aloof.

But I did know him. Behind that almost neutral expression was pride. He felt good about what he'd done and he was basking in the glory of his work.

He felt awesome today. I could see it in his eyes.

I was about to rejoin him—I'd just needed a little caffeine to get through the rest of the day—when a well-dressed man and woman approached the car. We'd seen them walking around earlier—the curators from America's Car Museum.

My eyes widened and I stopped in my tracks.

They did a slow circuit around the car, clearly appreciative—and how could they not be? The Judge was badass muscle-car perfection. Then they stopped to talk to Evan.

I was too far away, and the hum of noise around me too loud, so I couldn't hear what they said. But I could read the conversation in Evan's expression. They loved the car. In fact, with the way his eyes widened with disbelief, they might have more than loved it.

It was hard to hold back from running over there, but if I did, I'd probably just spew a bunch of verbal vomit about how great he was and how they had to choose his car for their museum.

Because they did have to. It was so perfect and he was so great and I could barely contain myself so I hoped they'd be done talking to him soon before I exploded on the spot.

Finally, he shook hands with each of them. His eyes met mine as they walked away and he didn't have to say a word. No movement of his lips or even a nod of his head. I knew.

He'd done it.

I ran for him, almost forgetting I was holding an iced coffee, and landed in his arms. He lifted me off my feet and spun me around in a circle.

"Oh my god, oh my god, oh my god," I said. "Tell me they're buying it. Tell me."

"They're buying it for the museum," he said, his voice muffled in my neck.

Squeezing him as tight as I could, I squealed with joy. "I knew they would. Oh my god, I knew it. I'm so proud of you."

He held me tight, sharing the moment with me. My body vibrated with excitement. I didn't know whether I wanted to laugh or cry or some crazy combination of the two.

All his hard work had paid off. Big time.

He loosened his grip and I slid down the front of his body until my feet touched the floor.

I bounced up onto my tiptoes. "I'm so happy I might puke."

He tucked my hair behind my ear—and honestly, was there anything swoonier than when he did that? "Don't puke."

"I'll try. This is just such a big deal and I'm having a hard time containing all my feelings right now."

The corners of his mouth twitched in a smile and I could

see that he was having a hard time containing all his feelings, too. He was just a lot quieter about it than I was.

He met my eyes and I stared into those mesmerizing whiskey browns. "Thank you. I couldn't have done this without you."

I grabbed his shirt and popped up on my toes to reach his mouth for a kiss. "Anytime."

His expression darkened and I had a feeling I knew why. Luke.

He approached with his hands in his pockets and gave Evan a short nod. "Bailey."

"Haven."

I briefly debated whether to step aside, in case this got ugly, or stay between them, in case this got ugly. But Luke's face softened.

"The Pontiac looks... amazing," Luke said, his brow tightening like it pained him to admit it. "You did right by her. Nothing but respect."

My eyes flicked to Evan, a spark of hope flaring. *Be nice to him, Evan. Or at least not mean.*

"Thanks," Evan said. "The Mustang turned out great. Well done."

"Thank you."

Evan stepped forward and offered his hand.

I bit my lip.

Luke took his hand out of his pocket and shook.

"Oh my god, you guys are so—"

Their gazes swung to me and I realized I needed to just... not.

"Never mind. Pretend I'm not here."

They finished their handshake without any sign that either of them was trying to out-alpha the other. I didn't have any illusions that they were going to become best friends, but not mortal enemies would be a big improvement.

I was so proud of them.

Luke stepped back and turned to me. "Can I talk to you for a second?"

I glanced at Evan. I didn't need his permission, but I didn't want to make him uncomfortable, either. Especially today. He kissed my forehead—an act of possession that was both sweet and respectful—and went back to his car.

"Sure, what's up?"

Luke pulled an envelope out of his back pocket. "I asked my great-aunt about John Haven, the guy in the racing photo. She didn't know anything, but she had this box of old stuff and told me I could take a look if I wanted. I dug through it and found this, along with a first-place auto racing plaque someone had kept."

He handed me the envelope.

"There were a couple of partial newspaper clippings about John winning a race. I guess it was a really big deal at the time because of the prize money. He won fifteen hundred dollars, which is the equivalent of something like thirty thousand today."

I pulled out a piece of paper. It was a copy of two old newspaper articles.

"The first one is about the race," Luke said. "The second one was attached to the first one."

The second headline read *Missing Auto Racing Champion Presumed Dead*.

"He went missing, too?"

"Yeah. Crazy, right? Apparently it was right after he won and there was some sketchy stuff about the prize money. They suspected he was killed in a robbery, since so many people knew he'd won all that money. But it doesn't sound like they found his body, although maybe they did later. It's hard to tell from these, and there weren't any other clippings in the box."

"This is amazing. Thank you so much. But, can I ask what made you decide to do this for me?"

He glanced away. "I kind of felt like I owed you."

"For what? I got you the dials for the Mustang, but that was in exchange for selling Evan the convertible carriage."

"Not for that." He rubbed the back of his neck. "You were right about Jill."

"Uh-oh."

"I don't know why I thought..." He sighed. "I saw her in town and we started talking, but I kept thinking about what you said. How she'd given Evan her number right in front of me and that had been a crappy thing to do. I blamed Evan for that whole thing—and it was mostly his fault—but I had to think about why she'd done that, you know?"

"Yeah, absolutely."

"So I was sitting there chatting with her and trying to decide whether to keep talking to her or move on when she started showing me house listings on her phone."

"Why?"

"For when we move in together."

"Did she actually say that?"

"Yep."

"Wow."

He shook his head. "I know. It was... a little much. We were just talking, we weren't even on a date together and she was ready to pick appliances."

"Wait until she starts texting you and asking why you've been ignoring her even though you've never gone out."

"Oh great."

I laughed. "Maybe she won't. Hopefully she'll find a guy who loves her brand of crazy."

"Yeah, I hope she does too. Anyway, after that I figured a goodwill gesture on my part wasn't a bad idea. Good karma and all that. I remembered you asking me about John Haven, so there you go."

"Thanks, Luke. I really appreciate it."

"No problem. I'll see you around." With a friendly chin tip, he walked away.

I tucked the paper back in the envelope. I couldn't wait to show this to Grace. Of course, her wedding was in a week, so maybe I'd wait until they got back from their honeymoon. She had enough going on.

My iced coffee had gotten very melty, but I took a drink anyway, then skipped back to Evan.

"What was that about?" he asked, then put up his hand. "Never mind. You don't have to tell me."

"He just did a little research for me," I said. "Tilikum history stuff."

He hooked an arm around my waist and drew me in close. "That was nice of him."

"Yeah, it really was. So could you possibly consider not hating him with all the burning fires of hell? Maybe tone it down to just mild antipathy?"

He laughed and kissed my forehead. "I think I can manage something like that."

"That's very big of you, Evan Bailey."

"We still need to prank them, though."

"What?"

The corner of his mouth hooked in a sly grin. "We haven't answered back for the goats at the Caboose. I have an idea, but I'm going to need your help."

I raised my eyebrows. "My first prank?"

"Gotta break the ice sometime. You're basically a Bailey, right?"

Smiling, I nibbled my bottom lip and nodded. Basically a Bailey. I really liked the sound of that.

In fact, maybe someday, we'd take out that little *basically* and I'd be an actual Bailey.

45

EVAN

"*I*'m so nervous," Fiona whispered, pulling the bill of her hat lower on her forehead. She had a nondescript cardboard box on her lap, addressed to the Timberbeast Tavern owner. It looked pretty legit.

I reached over to rub her thigh. "Don't be. You've got this. And you don't have to whisper, there's no one around."

She glanced out the window. We were sitting in my Camaro, parked down the street from the Timberbeast Tavern. It was a Friday and the place was starting to fill up. Luke's truck was parked outside and a few more cars pulled into the parking lot while we waited for my brothers to finish their part of tonight's prank.

So far, so good.

Fiona looked at the kennel secured in the back seat. "Do you think Peek and Boo are okay?"

The two shifty little squirrels were deceptively quiet. She'd easily coaxed them into the kennel with what she'd determined was their favorite treat—a mix of peanut butter, nuts, birdseed, and cookies. Fortunately, she hadn't trained them to open the kennel from the inside, although I'd feel better when they were no longer in my car, just in case they figured out the latch on their own.

You couldn't trust those little shits.

"They're fine," I said. "You spoiled them so much they don't even care that they're in a car."

"Yeah, you're probably right. Good boys, Peek and Boo. You're such good boys."

I shook my head. She was so fucking cute.

Logan ran up to the car, casting alarmed glances behind him. I rolled down my window.

"Are they coming?" I asked.

"Yeah." He looked over his shoulder again. "Are you sure you know what you're doing?"

"Positive."

"They won't hurt you," Fiona said.

Logan winced. "I'd rather not take that chance. This is the scariest fucking prank we've ever pulled."

"Don't be a baby." I spotted Gavin in the rear-view mirror, heading our way. Levi and Asher were coming from the other direction. Asher was getting married tomorrow, but he was still out here with us. "Okay, beautiful. Are you ready?"

Fiona took a deep breath. "I think so."

"Go get 'em."

"Be careful when you let them out," she said. "They might get confused."

"Don't worry." I leaned over and brushed her lips with a kiss. "I'll be careful with them."

She nodded, grabbed the box we'd made, and got out of the car.

Fiona had taken this prank extremely seriously—especially her role in it. And she'd been key to pulling it off. We needed someone to get in the tavern with a fake delivery.

Obviously none of us could do it. But Fiona wasn't as well known, and insisted she could disguise herself enough to look like a stranger.

I'd been skeptical, but she'd gone all out to make herself look convincing. Brown shirt and khaki shorts that at first glance looked a lot like a UPS driver. Her hat hid her face and she'd bought some non-prescription glasses, insisting that if glasses worked for Superman, they could work for her.

But she hadn't stopped there. She'd taken out her nose ring, since that was fairly recognizable, and dyed her hair. She looked hot as fuck as a blond, so I was not complaining.

My brothers caught up with us as she walked across the street and up the sidewalk toward the tavern, casually tossing nuts out on the sidewalk as she went.

"Bro, it's about to be squirrel-pocalypse," Gavin said. "I hope you're ready for what's coming."

"You guys did what Fiona said? You made the trails lead here?"

"Yeah. But you still haven't told us why we're luring every fucking squirrel in Tilikum over here."

I got out and took the kennel out of the back seat. Peek and Boo scampered around inside. Fiona was almost to the tavern door, and more squirrels started to arrive, following the trails of nuts my brothers had laid out all around town.

"Fiona's going to deliver the package, then her beady-eyed little friends here are going to do the rest."

"What's in the package?" Logan asked.

One corner of my mouth hooked in a grin. "Nuts, peanut butter, cookies. Squirrel crack, basically. And we rigged the box to explode when they open it, so it's going to send shit flying everywhere."

"How'd you do that?" Asher asked.

"She found a YouTube tutorial. The video was how to make a gift box that pops open and flings confetti. We just... modified it a little."

"Like a glitter bomb?" Logan asked.

"Yeah, except it's a nut bomb."

Gavin snickered. "Nut bomb."

Levi jumped out of the way as a squirrel ran by. "Jesus. But how are the squirrels going to get in? Is she going to hold the door open or something?"

I turned the kennel around so it was facing the trail of nuts that led to the building. "Nope. That's why we have them. Stand back."

My brothers took a few steps away and I opened the door.

Peek and Boo darted out of the kennel and circled around a bit, stopping to sniff the air. One of them noticed a few squirrels racing around the nuts Fiona had strewn and took the bait. The other followed.

"Come on, little shits," I said under my breath.

They went around to the side of the tavern, just like they were supposed to. We could just see them climb up the tree we'd baited with treats and follow the branch that led across to the roof.

"When did you set this all up?" Logan asked.

"Last night. Fiona taught them how to do an obstacle course at home, so we just used the same technique here. And there's a vent up there that I might have loosened so it would pop open if they pushed on it."

We watched the two squirrels Fiona had trained find the vent hole near the roof. They both disappeared inside. A few more squirrels went up the tree after them, like they were curious where their friends had gone.

"Holy shit," Gavin said.

Fiona came out of the tavern, minus the box. She glanced around, then held onto her hat and hurried over.

"Oh my god, my heart feels like it's going to burst," she said, her smile so bright it lit up the whole street. She took off her fake glasses.

"He took it?" I asked.

"He totally took it," she said. "But oh man, Luke was in there. So was Annika. But I don't think they recognized me."

Levi's gaze snapped to her, his eyes alarmed. I didn't have time to ask what his problem was. Fiona kept talking.

"I just kept my head down, but I thought any second, someone was going to yell my name or... I guess I don't know what they would have done. Not opened the box, that's for sure. Are Peek and Boo okay?"

"They're about to be the happiest little shits in town."

Logan winced again as more squirrels scampered around us. A few ran up the tree and even more scurried around on the tavern roof. "I'm so not comfortable with this."

"Now what happens?" Asher asked.

"Wait for it," I said. We ducked behind my car.

At first, all was quiet, except for the growing gang of squirrels running around the tavern. More of them found their way to the vent Peek and Boo had opened, their bushy gray tails disappearing inside.

More followed, until a steady stream of squirrels climbed the tree and crossed the branch to the tavern.

The muffled sound of a commotion suddenly rang out from inside the tavern. Loud bangs, like chairs toppling over, hitting the wood floor.

"I think the bartender just opened the box," Fiona said.

The front door flew open and customers raced out to the parking lot, squirrels darting around their feet. One of the little fuckers clung to someone's jeans. The guy stopped with a yell and kicked his leg until it let go.

As if they could sense the smorgasbord waiting inside, squirrels ran in through the open tavern door while the people rushing out narrowly missed stepping on them.

Pandemonium.

A steady stream of squirrels climbed the tree, crossed the branch, and went in the vent. More ran right up to the front door, dodging the feet of people trying to leave. Other squirrels ran out, carrying their treasure of nuts and cookies in their mouths and tiny clawed hands.

The Timberbeast Tavern had become Squirrel Central.

A squirrel ran out and darted in our direction, carrying something that wasn't a nut.

"Does he have a wallet?" Levi asked.

Another ran out with what looked like a half-eaten cheeseburger and disappeared down the street.

My brothers erupted with laughter, cracking up at the chaos that was the Havens' hangout. Their goat prank on the Caboose had been original, I had to give them that. But neither side had ever truly harnessed the power of the Tilikum squirrels.

It was fucking hilarious.

Fiona tried to stifle her giggles behind her hand. "Oh my word, this is crazy."

"Uh, guys?" Levi said. "Maybe we should get out of here."

The burly Timberbeast bartender appeared in the doorway, his face flushed bright red.

"Let's go," I said.

Asher, Logan, and Levi stuffed themselves in the back seat while Fiona and Gavin took the front. Abandoning the kennel—I'd come back for it later—I hopped in. A few seconds later, I was ripping us out of there, my arm slung over the bench seat, my girl at my side.

Careful not to hit any squirrels, I drove us out of town and headed for my place.

When we got there, everyone piled out. Fiona went in first and shrieked as soon as she opened the door. I flung an arm around her, twisting to pull her behind me.

But she was laughing.

Right in the middle of my living room stood life-sized cardboard cutouts of all my brothers, naked except for tightie-whitie underwear. With my face on the crotch.

As if that wasn't enough, there was one of me. Naked. They'd Photoshopped me holding a picture in front of my junk.

A picture of my brothers wearing underwear with my face.

How the fuck?

I stared at the ridiculousness in my living room while Fiona and my brothers erupted in hysterical laughter behind me, then shot an accusing glance at Sasquatch. "You let them do this?"

His tongue lolled out of his mouth. Traitor dog.

"Oh my god, those are even funnier in real life," Fiona said.

"How?" I asked.

Gavin clapped me on the back as he walked in. "Magicians don't reveal their secrets. Or, in our case, prank masters don't reveal their secrets."

Fiona slipped her hand in mine and squeezed. "I might have taken that picture of you."

I looked down at her—at those hazel-green eyes I loved so much—and laughed. I had to admit, it was well played.

"Oh!" Fiona exclaimed. "I need a pair of those Evan underwear. Did you guys order extras?"

"Of course we did," Logan said. "There's a box of them in the kitchen."

She bounced up on her tiptoes and clapped. "Yay!"

I just rolled my eyes.

Levi and Logan went to the fridge for beers, and for once I didn't bark at everyone to go home, or tell them I had too much work to do to hang out. It felt good to be included. We all grabbed celebratory beers, I gave my dog a treat—even though he hardly deserved it for letting them prank me in my own house—and settled on the couch with Fiona.

"Props to you for that one, brodown," Logan said. "That was a nicely executed, fine-tuned prank."

"Epic," Gavin said. "Fucking epic."

I held up my bottle. "Baileys."

Everyone lifted their bottles and a chorus of "Baileys" went up.

"Wouldn't have happened without Fiona," I said, squeezing her.

She'd ditched her hat and her newly blond hair spilled around her shoulders. "My heart's still beating so fast."

"Well done." Gavin lifted his beer. "To Fiona, the newest honorary Bailey."

We all toasted to that, clinking our bottles together.

I met Fiona's eyes. She smiled and I wondered if she knew what I was thinking.

I wondered if she knew that this prank wasn't even half of what I had planned. She wasn't going to be just an honorary Bailey much longer.

Not if I had anything to say about it.

46

FIONA

*C*ara had told me Grace and Asher were going to have the most beautiful wedding in the history of ever, and she'd been totally right.

It wasn't just the setting—her family's beautiful winery, surrounded by gardens, orchards, vineyards, and mountain peaks. It wasn't just the decor, although everything from the flowers to the twinkle lights were gorgeous. It wasn't even how stunning Grace looked in her dress or how dapper Asher was in his tux.

It was all of that and more.

And mostly, it was them.

There was hardly a dry eye in the garden when they said their vows. They'd been down such a hard road to get to this moment, and everyone, even me, knew how perfect they were for each other. We all knew what this meant.

I sobbed my way through the ceremony.

Evan stood up front with his brothers, looking unbelievably hot in his suit. God, he cleaned up good.

And even my grumpy broody man wasn't immune to the deep emotion of this day. He didn't covertly swipe a tear when he thought no one would see, like both Logan and Gavin did. But right at the moment when Asher said his vows, Evan looked at me. Our eyes locked and my heart sped up. His gaze softened, that intense brow furrow smoothing, his whiskey-brown eyes clear and pure. And he smiled.

It wasn't my wedding—wasn't my moment—but my heart nearly burst right there.

The reception started off with wine and hors d'oeuvres while guests mingled and the bride and groom took pictures. I finally met Grace's brother Leo, who'd helped Evan save me from Felix Orman. I hugged him, possibly with a little more enthusiasm than was necessary, but who could blame me? I'd been through a lot that day, and he'd helped save my life. Helped reunite me with Evan.

I updated him on my dad. He was facing multiple counts of grand theft auto, among other things. He'd face some prison time, but from what I understood, he was cooperating with the feds to put Felix Orman and his ring of thieves and human traffickers behind bars. So he'd probably get off easy.

Honestly, I didn't care anymore. I did care about him— he was still my dad—but I'd washed my hands of feeling responsible for him. He'd pay for his crimes one way or another. It wasn't my problem anymore.

As the reception went on into the night, people danced and laughed and ate and drank. Grace looked so happy I wanted to cry every time I looked at her. Cara pretty much did. She'd burst into tears so many times, she'd given up on fixing her makeup.

She still looked amazing, though. Cara always did.

It was close to midnight when Evan and I finally said goodbye. I left the winery on Evan's arm, floating on a cloud of joyful contentment. Being surrounded by the Baileys and the Miles family, with everyone so freaking happy, had left me drenched in bliss.

Laughing, I did a little twirl next to Evan's car. "That was the best night ever. Asher and Grace are so happy, and everyone there was so happy, and I'm just so happy for them."

His mouth hooked in a smile. "Me too."

We got in and Evan started the car.

"Did you have fun? I had so much fun."

"I did, actually. It was great."

I sighed. "And you thought you hated weddings. They're so romantic."

He didn't say anything else. Just glanced at me from the corner of his eye.

We drove home in the darkness, leaving the jubilant celebration behind. Evan glanced at me a few times, like he had something on his mind. I wondered what he was thinking. Maybe he was just happy for his brother.

The lights were on in the shop when we parked out front, which was weird because I thought we'd shut them off.

"Did we leave those on all day?" I asked.

Evan shrugged. "Not sure."

We got out of the car and went over to the shop door. Evan unlocked it, but before we could go inside, he took my hand. I met his eyes, but he didn't say anything. Just opened the door and led me in.

I took a few steps, then stopped, my eyes widening.

There were plants everywhere. Tall plants in large pots. Skinny plants, trailing vines, little plants with white flowers.

"What is all this?"

"Some of these will probably need to go live in the

house," he said. "But I figured you love plants, so... here's twenty. Do you like them?"

I took slow steps through the shop, trying to look at each one. "I love them so much."

"The pots all have chalkboard labels on them," he said, gesturing. "That way you can write their names on there if you want."

My eyes filled with tears and my throat felt so tight I wasn't sure I'd be able to speak. "This is the nicest thing anyone's ever done for me. When did you do all this? *How* did you do all this?"

He casually shrugged one shoulder. "I had help."

I rushed back to him and landed in his arms. "Why are you so amazing?"

He squeezed me tight. "I just love you. There's something else you haven't noticed though."

"What?"

"The car sitting in the middle of the shop that wasn't there before."

I blinked in surprise. There *was* a car sitting in the middle of the shop that hadn't been there before. It was covered with a canvas, and surrounded by my new plants.

"What is it? Our next restoration?"

"That's exactly what it is."

A zing of excitement pinged through me. "What is it? Who's it for? I didn't know we were getting something new already."

"I think maybe you should just look."

Nibbling my bottom lip, and with no idea what to expect, I drew the cover back. And couldn't believe my eyes.

"Oh my god. Evan. Is this what I think it is?"

"Sixty-five Plymouth Belvedere."

I stared at the stripped body. The interior looked rotten

and I didn't even know if there was an engine under the hood. But it was my car. My favorite. The funky boxy badass car I'd always loved.

"How did you even know about this?" I asked through tears.

"You told me. The first day of our road trip, you told me this was your favorite." He rubbed the back of his neck. "I've kind of been looking for one ever since. And I figured since your car was totaled, you need something new. We can work on this together."

Happy tears made hot trails down my cheeks. "I don't know what to do with myself. I love it so much. I love you so much. I can't stop shaking."

He gathered me in his arms and gently touched my face. His lips met mine and I laughed and cried and kissed him all at once. I was a big, soggy mess of feelings, but he held me together, like always.

"I love you so much," I said again. "Thank you."

"I'm glad you like it. But I have a confession."

He let go and I looked up at him. "What?"

"These were just to butter you up for what I really want to give you."

I had no idea what he could possibly give me that could be better than an entire family of beautiful houseplants and the car of my dreams, ready for us to restore together.

Until he lowered down onto one knee.

My breath caught in my throat.

"Fiona." His deep voice was so soft, his brow furrowed with intensity. "I love you more than anything. I want you to be mine, always. And I'll always be yours. Will you marry me?"

Oh.

My.

God.

Evan Bailey was down on his knee with a ring in his hand.

A ring for me.

"Yes, yes, yes, oh my god yes."

I struggled not to bounce while he slid the ring on my finger. Then he scooped me in his thick, strong arms and picked me up off my feet. I threw my arms around his neck and held on tight.

He was mine, and I was his.

My hero. My wolf. My love.

Forever.

EPILOGUE

"*S*kylar, we need to talk."

It wasn't just that phrase—naturally so loaded with meaning—that made my stomach twist into a knot of dread. It was Cullen's tone. Flat. Emotionless.

"Sounds serious," I said, trying to keep the mood light in case I was overreacting. Maybe we needed to talk about where to make dinner reservations, or a similarly innocuous subject.

Cullen stood in the kitchen of our apartment, all California-boy handsome with his ice-blue eyes, tan skin, and natural highlights in his thick, dark blond hair. Trade his button-down and slacks for a pair of board shorts and a muscle shirt, and he would have fit right in on a beach somewhere.

Which got me thinking... a California surfer boy discovers a body while he's on a deserted beach at sunrise—

"Skylar," Cullen snapped. "See? You're not even listening to me."

"I'm sorry, I just had an idea. What did you say?"

"It's over."

His words hit me like the jab of a needle straight into my chest, the shock of them rendering me briefly speechless. I stared at him while he took his phone out of his pocket and the corner of his mouth twitched in the hint of a smile.

"What did you say?"

He pocketed his phone, his eyes flicking up to meet mine. That almost-smile on his lips melted into pinched annoyance. "You're going to make me repeat myself again? Let me guess, you were brainstorming more book ideas that you're never going to write."

Ouch. Talk about hitting below the belt. "No. I just don't understand what you're saying right now."

"Why are you making this hard?"

"How am I making this hard? You throw the words *it's over* at me, completely out of nowhere, and I'm supposed to just carry on with my day?"

"Well, no, obviously not."

"Then what do you think I'm going to say? Of course I'm going to ask you what you mean."

"Fine," he said, like my asking for clarification was the most annoying request ever. "I'm not happy. I haven't been for a long time. So this is it. I'm done."

"Since when are you not happy?"

"I just said I haven't been for a long time."

I stared at him, bewildered. Cullen wasn't what you'd call a happy person—never had been. He was serious and stoic. Focused and responsible. Happy wasn't his vibe. But the idea that he'd been unhappy *with me* was such a foreign concept, I didn't know how to make sense of it.

There had been no warning. None at all. I'd thought he was fine.

I thought *we* were fine.

That wasn't even the half of it. I thought we might be forever.

The buzz of the refrigerator suddenly roared in my ears, like a thousand mosquitos flying around my head. I tried to hold still—tried not to twitch. He'd tell me I was being dramatic and unreasonable. *Calm down, Skylar, the fridge isn't loud.*

The vibration crawled up my spine. I couldn't stand still anymore. Not right here. Stopping myself from sticking my fingers in my ears, I wandered into the living room.

"This is just... really sudden," I said.

"That's not my fault."

"Excuse me?" I whirled on him. "You're breaking up with me and it's not your fault?"

He let out a heavy sigh. "No, it's not my fault that this is taking you by surprise. You should have seen this coming."

"How could I have seen this coming? We had sex *last night*. You didn't seem unhappy when you had your dick in me."

"Jesus, Skylar, don't be vulgar."

"Why didn't you ever say anything? Why didn't you tell me you weren't happy?"

"It's not like you've been fully invested in this relationship. You moved out for months."

"I moved in with my mom so I could take care of her after her surgery. What does that have to do with anything?"

"You said it would be a few weeks, and months later, you were still living there."

I gaped at him. "I moved back. And she's my *mom*, Cullen. She needed my help."

He shrugged, like her relationship to me wasn't a factor. "We grew apart a long time ago. You're just too busy living in fantasyland to realize it."

I swallowed hard. Was he right? I was distracted a lot. Had I been so lost in my own head that I'd missed the signs? Had I neglected him so much that he'd fallen out of love with me?

He pulled out his phone again and typed something.

"What are you doing?"

He finished, then slipped his phone back in his pocket. "Nothing."

"Will you stop having a conversation with someone else while you're throwing my life in the garbage?"

"Don't be so dramatic."

"I'm not being dramatic. Are you dumping me as a client too?"

"That's best for everyone involved."

I couldn't think clearly. Too many emotions whipped around inside me, like a tornado flinging debris across the landscape of my heart. Cullen Bell wasn't just my boyfriend of three years and the man I currently lived with. He was my literary agent. My link to the editors at the big publishing houses.

Including the publisher who'd dropped me last year.

And the others who might pick me up.

Not that I'd written anything new in months.

Oh my god.

"So that's it? You're done with me?"

He opened his mouth to answer, but his phone buzzed in his pocket and he pulled it out again.

A sick realization spread through me, like dark smoke filling a room. The back of my throat burned and the knot of dread in the pit of my stomach grew.

"Who is she?"

His blue eyes lifted, his expression devoid of any emotion. "Don't."

"Are you cheating on me?"

"Skylar, don't make this worse."

"Answer the question."

"I'm trying to make this easier on you. You don't need to go there."

"By acting like this is my fault?" I crossed my arms. "Who is she?"

He glanced away.

"If you're leaving me for another woman, the least you can do is tell me who she is so I—"

"Pepper Sinclair."

I clicked my mouth shut. Maybe he was right. I should have seen this coming.

Pepper Sinclair was perfect. A New York Times bestselling author of inspirational women's fiction. She was stunningly beautiful with flawless skin, perfect bone structure, a gorgeous smile, thick hair, and the type of boobs that most women had to pay a lot of money for.

Her social media following numbered in the millions, men and women hanging on her every word, clamoring for glimpses into her perfectly tailored, manicured, pristine life.

Everyone loved her.

Including, apparently, my boyfriend. Who was also her agent.

"Wait, Pepper's married."

"Not that it's any of your business, but she's getting a divorce."

Maybe not so perfect after all.

Not that it mattered. She was still stealing my boyfriend.

I looked away, my eyes stinging with tears. Cullen had taken her on as a client last year, after they'd met at a writer's conference in Denver. I'd been there, too, dutifully attending the meetings Cullen had set up with editors, trying to salvage my quickly spiraling career.

And I'd seen them together at the hotel bar.

They hadn't been touching—nothing overt. But the way he'd looked at her...

Weeks later, after mulling it over for way too long, I'd asked him about it. He'd gotten mad. Accused me of not trusting him.

"How long?" I heard myself ask.

"Does it matter?"

"Yes. How long?"

"Why are you making this harder on yourself?"

"Because I need to know the truth."

He let out an irritated breath. "Denver."

My lip trembled. I caught it between my teeth so I wouldn't cry. I was *not* letting him see me cry. He'd just tell me I was being overly sensitive anyway.

I took a slow breath through my nose. "You've been cheating on me with Pepper Sinclair since last year?"

"You're making it sound worse than it is. In Denver, we..."

He trailed off, looking away again. But there was no shame or regret in his posture or expression. He just wanted to finish this conversation so he could move on with his day.

"In Denver, you what?"

"Why are you—"

"I'm not making this hard, Cullen. That's on you. I didn't make you have an affair with a married woman who's also your client. You did that."

"Fine, you want to make me say it? In Denver, we didn't sleep together, but... other things transpired. Since then I've been seeing her when I go to New York. I didn't tell you because I didn't want you getting all depressed. Things were bad enough after your series got dropped. I figured I'd give you some time to at least get writing again. But that's obviously not going to happen, and I can't keep waiting around for you to decide you're over your writer's block."

It was hard to get any words out, my voice almost a whisper. "All that time?"

"What do you expect? You're always distracted, always thinking of some plot or another, but you haven't written anything in who knows how long. You spend all your time watching serial killer documentaries and looking up poisonous household chemicals or the best ways to hide a body. It's disturbing."

"I write suspense novels. It's research."

"It's like living with the creepy goth girl who sat in the back of class and threatened people with voodoo dolls, only wrapped in a beautiful package. You look so normal."

If I'd ever wondered what it would feel like to have my very existence completely rejected, apparently this was it.

"Look, you need to move out," he said. "Pepper's telling her husband today and she's bringing her stuff here after."

"You're moving her in?"

"Well, yeah, she's leaving her husband. She can't exactly stay there."

"You're leaving me. Why don't you move out?"

He looked at me like I'd just suggested he start eating meat again. "It's my apartment."

The refrigerator's buzz ceased, leaving behind an emptiness in the air. It was his apartment. He'd lived here first. In fact, everything in it was his. It had been fully furnished, the kitchen and bathrooms fully stocked, when I'd moved in. Almost nothing was mine.

I was simply a guest who'd been here for an extended sleepover.

A guest who'd overstayed her welcome.

Calmly, I turned and walked to the bedroom. Took my suitcase out of the closet and started packing.

So calm. Deadly calm.

The beginning to a domestic suspense novel flitted through my head. A jilted wife, forced to move out of the home she loved due to her husband's infidelity. Her husband is found dead the next morning. She's the prime suspect, and—

"What are you doing?"

I glanced over my shoulder at the man I'd once thought I might marry. My voice sounded strangely flat. "You just broke up with me, so I'm packing."

"You were staring at the wall."

Turning to face him, I crossed my arms. "You know what, Cullen? Fuck you. You were never trying to make this easier on me, or give me time to start writing again, or keep me from getting depressed. You wanted to avoid telling me that you're a cheating piece of shit. Because deep down, you know you were wrong. You know you betrayed me. And one of these days, you're going to wake up and realize it. You're going to realize what you lost. And when you do, I'll be long gone. So get out and let me pack."

He held up his hands in a gesture of surrender and backed away. "Fine."

I went back to folding my clothes and placing them neatly in my suitcase. They weren't all going to fit, and I didn't have another bag.

I decided to take Cullen's.

Because fuck him.

But when I pulled his suitcase out of the closet—it matched mine—I couldn't hold back the tears.

Strands of long hair stuck to my wet cheeks as sobs

bubbled up from my chest. I splayed my hand over my heart, suddenly understanding the term *heartbroken* with perfect clarity.

I'd thought I loved him. I'd thought he loved me.

Apparently I'd been wrong. Horribly wrong.

I needed to call my mom. I'd have to go to her place. I wasn't the sort of girl who had many friends; I was too shy. And my best friend Ginny didn't live nearby. Fortunately, I knew Mom wouldn't mind.

Except I scrolled past my frequently used contacts— which was all of three people, Mom, Cullen, and Ginny— and stopped at a different number.

Dad.

Norman Stanley. Fire Chief, Tilikum Fire Department.

I didn't know why I had the urge to call him. He wasn't the parent I normally went to in a crisis. In fact, I didn't even see my dad all that often.

But somehow the pieces of my cracked and bleeding heart yearned for the comfort of my father's voice.

If he'd even answer. He was probably on duty. It seemed like that was all he ever did—work.

Still, I decided to give it a try. I brought up his number and hit send.

He answered on the first ring. "Hey, Skylar."

A flood of renewed tears ran down my cheeks and I could barely croak out a single word.

"Daddy."

DEAR READER

Dear reader,

I sure do love me a grumpy hero.

Evan has a lot going on under his hood (see what I did there?) and I couldn't wait to dig in to his broodiness. I wasn't quite sure how readers would feel about him after his stunt with Jill in Fighting for Us. But that was just who Evan was at the time. Gruff, standoffish, kind of a jerk.

One of my favorite things about writing a grumpy hero is the potential for growth. The heart of any story is the character arc (or arcs) and an asshole hero gives me so much to play with, making for a very satisfying arc. There's just something about watching him start to crack and finally melt for his girl. I love it, every single time.

And man, did he melt for Fiona.

I love "the grumpy one is soft for the sunshine one" too, and I saw Fiona as being a little bit of a badass twist on the sunshiney heroine. She is sweet and optimistic, and doesn't get ruffled by Evan's broodiness. But she's also not afraid to get dirty underneath a car. She has a latent confidence in her abilities that finally gets to come out.

With Evan, she blooms, like one of her happy houseplants.

Needless to say, these two were so much fun to write.

As for what was on the counter? I know, I know, that was a lot of build up and then... she wasn't the heroine. Neither was Jill.

I won't even pretend I didn't know what I was doing there.

#sorrynotsorry

As for what comes next, it looks like Chief Stanley's daughter will be making an appearance. Which Bailey is destined to be her hero? You'll have to keep reading to find out. But trust me, it's going to be goooooooood.

Thanks for reading!

CK

ACKNOWLEDGMENTS

A deep and heartfelt thank you to everyone who helped make this book possible. My team is THE BEST.

Lori, I love, love, love what you did with this cover. It's perfection.

Golden, you're not only a badass photographer, but an awesome human. Thanks for being so great to work with! And for taking hot pictures of sexy men.

Thank you to Elayne for a fabulous editing job and to Erma for taking the time to help proofread. I have total error blindness when it comes to my own work. I shudder to think of what my manuscripts would look like without you.

A huge thank you to my team of admins and beta readers: Nikki, Alex, Jessica, Emily, Joyce, and Tammy. You're all the best!

A special thanks to Alex for sharing your man Evan with the world. I know it's not easy, but your sacrifice is appreciated by Bailey Brothers fans everywhere.

To my family for being the best ever. I love you endlessly.

And to the makers of the Calm meditation app and the

lovely people at the Hilton Homesuites. I don't think I would have finished this book without learning to calm my busy brain and for my last-minute writer's retreat for one. Thank you for doing what you do!

Last, but certainly not the least bit least, thank you to my readers. Your love and support has made this silly writer girl's dreams come true. I love sharing this world with you and I can't wait to continue this journey together.

ALSO BY CLAIRE KINGSLEY

For a full and up-to-date listing of Claire Kingsley books visit www.clairekingsleybooks.com

The Bailey Brothers

Steamy, small-town family series. Five unruly brothers. Epic pranks. A quirky, feuding town. Big HEAs.

Protecting You: Series Origin Story

Fighting For Us

Unraveling Him

More Bailey Brothers coming soon!

The Miles Family

Sexy, sweet, funny, and heartfelt family series. Messy family. Epic bromance. Super romantic.

Broken Miles

Forbidden Miles

Reckless Miles

Hidden Miles

Gaining Miles: A Miles Family Novella

Dirty Martini Running Club

Sexy, fun stand-alone romantic comedies with huge... hearts.

Everly Dalton's Dating Disasters

Free Faking Ms. Right prequel

Faking Ms. Right

A hot fake relationship romantic comedy

Love According to Science

A hot enemies-to-lovers romantic comedy

Bluewater Billionaires

Hot, stand-alone romantic comedies. Lady billionaire BFFs and the badass heroes who love them.

The Mogul and the Muscle

A billionaire and her bodyguard hot romantic comedy.

The Price of Scandal, Wild Open Hearts, and Crazy for Loving You

More Bluewater Billionaire shared-world stand-alone romantic comedies by Lucy Score, Kathryn Nolan, and Pippa Grant

Bootleg Springs

by Claire Kingsley and Lucy Score

Hot and hilarious small-town romcom series with a dash of mystery and suspense. Best read in order.

Whiskey Chaser

Sidecar Crush

Moonshine Kiss

Bourbon Bliss

Gin Fling

Highball Rush

Book Boyfriends

Hot, stand-alone romcoms that will make you laugh and make you swoon.

Book Boyfriend

Cocky Roommate

Hot Single Dad

Remembering Ivy

A unique contemporary romance with a hint of mystery.

His Heart

A poignant and emotionally intense story about grief, loss, and the transcendent power of love.

The Always Series

Smoking hot, dirty talking bad boys with some angsty intensity.

Always Have

Always Will

Always Ever After

ABOUT THE AUTHOR

Claire Kingsley is a Top 10 Amazon bestselling author of sexy, heartfelt contemporary romance and romantic comedies. She writes sassy, quirky heroines, swoony heroes who love their women hard, panty-melting sexytimes, romantic happily ever afters, and all the big feels.

She can't imagine life without coffee, her Kindle, and the sexy heroes who inhabit her imagination. She's living out her own happily ever after in the Pacific Northwest with her husband and three kids.

www.clairekingsleybooks.com